Pav THE Way

A NOVEL BY LISA LABON

Paving THE Way

A NOVEL BY LISA LABON

Published By Open Scroll Publications

Copyright © 2019 Lisa Labon
lisalabon.co.uk

Second Edition by:
Open Scroll Publications Ltd,
Kemp House, 160 City Road,
London, EC1V 2NX.
www.openscroll.co.uk

ISBN: 978-1-9999856-6-0

The names and identifying details of some individuals mentioned in this book have been changed to protect their privacy.

A CIP catalogue record for this book is available from the British library.

Edited by Diane Wilkie. Email: dee.wilkie7@hotmail.co.uk

Cover design and Typeset by Open Scroll Publications Ltd.

Printed in Great Britain.

Dedication

This book is dedicated to Dave Reader one of the loveliest people I have ever known. It was a pleasure knowing you my friend!

Acknowledgements

I would like to thank my two friends Lynsey and Sarah who have always encouraged me generally, but even more so through the publishing process. You cheered me on and were right beside me all the way! Thank you, beautiful ladies.

Thank you, Diane, for all the love and encouragement you have shown me over the past year. You have been a Godsend and a true giver of peace. I look forward to where the future of our friendship will take us!

I would also like to thank Jim, a fellow author himself. You always had time for me when things were not going the way I expected them to, and your encouragement kept me going. Twenty years ago, we each talked about writing a book. It seemed to be a dream way too big and far too distant for us to imagine coming true. Here we are however, and those dreams are progressively becoming reality.

Finally, I would like to thank everyone who has read and liked book one, 'In the blink of an eye.' Thank you for taking that risk! I hope it was a worthwhile investment!

Part One

CHAPTER
ONE

*C*losing his eyes, Panos pictured Danielle's face in his mind. The image of her was so clear, as she smiled at him; her big, emerald eyes sparkled, inducing a smile across his grief-stricken face. Taking a deep breath, he breathed in the memory of the woman that had stolen his heart, filling his lungs with every precious moment spent with her.

Time ran away from him as he reminisced about when he held her in his arms, and he felt a little comforted by the thoughts conjured up in his mind.

The last two weeks had been the best two weeks of his life, but now they had come to an end and he had to get back to the normality of his so-called life. A stubborn frustration rose from the pit of his stomach, as this harsh reality consumed him. He didn't want to return to a mundane world that didn't include Danielle. What he wanted more than anything in this world was to have her by his side for the rest of his days; to feel her next to him while he slept, to see her laugh when he was feeling down, and to make love to her. Oh, how he yearned to make love to her. These distressing feelings brought tears to his eyes, and it took all his mental strength to fight the urge to let them fall. For a split second it was as if she had been just a wonderful dream, as his mind played tricks on him, and he started to wonder if she was just a figment of his imagination!

"No, she was real," he said out loud, as if to convince his deceit ridden conscience.

"No, my Danielle was here," he said, his voice now just a whisper. He didn't want her to end up being just like the plane that had taken her away from him, to become a distant memory soon to fade away into the horizon of his past. The pain of his loss was so unbearable that he had to force himself, to come to terms with the way that it had to be and pull himself together. He felt so powerless over the situation and hated the feeling that dominated his willpower and overrode his control.

Putting his head in his hands, he had the urge to squeeze his temples, but resisted, when he was suddenly interrupted by the phone ringing in his pocket. Pulling it out of his pocket he looked at the screen. When he saw it was his brother, he felt both annoyed and relieved by the disturbance, which temporarily brought him out of his despair. He thought twice about answering it, but in the end just stared at it until it finally stopped ringing. He felt a pang of guilt for ignoring his brother's phone call, but he just didn't have the strength to talk, not even to Yannis. He soon convinced himself that Yannis would understand, when he eventually explained himself.

As he looked around the car park, he suddenly became aware of the silence around him. The car park was deserted, and a deep sense of abandonment engulfed him. He felt so lost and alone, a feeling he had never experienced before and somehow this began to scare him. Then he looked at his watch and realised he had been standing there for almost two hours. Taking a deep breath and purposely pushing the alien feelings away, feeling defeated, he walked to his car and turned on the engine. As soon as he did the familiar sound of a love song filled the car. The sudden sound of the woman singing took his breath away, as he remembered the many times; he had sung it to Danielle. She invaded his mind again, so much so that he had to turn the stereo off, because the memory of her lovely face induced such pain, it felt like he had been kicked in the stomach. Forcing down the tears that had violently erupted, with great effort he composed himself and began the short journey back up to the hotel. He couldn't help noticing all the young lovers walking hand in hand down the road. They interacted passionately with each other and a pang of jealousy overwhelmed him as he watched their smiling faces.

One couple in particular caught his eye when they stopped briefly as they were walking. The man stole a kiss from his partner, and then they carried on without a care in the world. His heart hurt as he remembered that it was only a short while ago, when he too was the other half of a couple. Now he had to face life alone, while everyone else around him seemed to have a common bond of love that tied them together. This only served to deepen his loneliness, making his heart so heavy that he felt like a broken man. He suddenly felt an overwhelming need to be with his family. He desperately needed the security of being with his loved ones. Surely, he was sure to find somewhere safe where he could come to terms with his great loss. So, he put his foot down on the accelerator and made a speedy getaway from the love-struck couples who, unbeknown to them, tormented his own existence.

Once again, his phone began ringing in his pocket, but this time he resisted the urge to ignore it and answered his brother, who was understandably worried about him. He reassured Yannis that he was alright, and that he would soon be home. When he hung up the phone, a smile escaped from his lips as he recalled the concern in his brother's voice. He knew then that it would take time, but with his family's support, he was going to be alright.

Arriving back at the hotel he closed his eyes for a minute trying to pull himself together. The sun was high in the sky and felt very warm against his face. He let its comforting rays sink into his skin as the warmth enveloped him. Then, as if by magic, a surge of strength rose up from deep inside him, enabling him to walk up the steps to face his life as a hotel manager again. Taking a deep breath, he put Danielle to the back of his mind, and then walked into the hotel.

Yannis was behind the reception desk and looked over to his brother. His face showed no emotion as he studied Panos's face for any sign of distress, and he was relieved when Panos smiled and nodded his head to reassure him. Panos continued past him and walked over to the bar where a man was standing eagerly waiting to be served.

"What can I get you sir?" he asked proudly, a wide smile dominating his face. On the outside it was if he hadn't a care in the world, but the pain that was still raw in his heart told another story. 'I will get over this,' he kept telling himself, as he poured the gentleman's drink.

Danielle looked out of the window of the plane, tears flowing down her cheeks. The pain she felt inside was too hard to contain, so she helplessly let the tears continue to fall. They were high up above the clouds, but the beautiful, clear blue view that surrounded her was no deterrent to how she felt. All she could think about was Panos and the love that they had shared, which had now been cruelly snatched out of her hands. Her heart felt like it was made of lead as she recaptured every moment spent with the man of her dreams, reliving every touch, every kiss, and every heart rendering memory of being safe in his arms. Regret pierced her heart as she chided herself for the sheer stupidity of letting him through the barrier that she had built up over the years to protect herself. Now here she was, her heart broken into pieces, and at a place she had vowed never to allow herself to be. Sighing heavily at her weakness, she clutched her stomach symbolic of the place where the root of her pain resided, provoking the tears to flow faster down her face.

Why did I let this happen? She thought. How could I have been so careless? She closed her eyes as a picture of Panos spontaneously came into her mind. She wanted to rid herself of the vision, but found that she couldn't, because she realised that she didn't want to lose the memory of his handsome face.

Mick sat next to her and his heart went out to his heartbroken friend. He had watched her stare out of the window and felt helpless at her sorrow. He tried his hardest to take her mind off Panos by telling a few jokes, but she was oblivious to his jibes. He wanted to tell her that it was all going to be alright, but these words seemed so powerless and empty, that he chose not to say them.

Turning to Matt for moral support, on the other side of him, was pointless. He had his eyes closed and was lost in his own thoughts. Thankfully the stewardess came down the aisle pushing the drinks trolley, which was a welcome distraction. Uneasiness flew through his body as he remembered the earlier promise he had made to himself. Fear consumed him at the prospect of never having a drink again, and the determination he had felt earlier suddenly vanished into thin air.

I will do this, he thought, trying to claim back his strength. Technically my holiday doesn't end until we are back in England, he thought finally convincing himself, his fears dispersing as quickly as they had appeared.

"Yes sir, what can I get you?" asked the pretty dark-haired stewardess as she smiled. He hadn't even been aware that he had his hand up, when he suddenly realised that she was speaking to him. He guessed that they had been in the air for about two hours, so he thought carefully about his answer.

"Oh, yes a drink. Could I have a large..." he hesitated and turned to Danielle who was still staring out of the window. "Sorry could you make that two large vodka and oranges please, one for my friend."

If she doesn't drink it, it will save me ordering another one later, he thought strategically.

The stewardess gave him his requested drinks and then carried on down the aisle, smiling professionally at her potential customers. He took a big sip of his drink and relished the peace that it enticed. Confidence soon made an entry as he imagined his new life of sobriety.

I can and will beat this, he thought self-assuredly. When I get home, it will be easier.

Matt's mind was racing with all kinds of thoughts, but his feelings for Danielle were his main concern. He tried desperately to wipe her out of his mind by thinking about being back at home, but she would sneak uncontrollably back into his thoughts. He could see how deeply upset she was and felt an irrepressible need to put his arms around her, just like he used to when she was hurting. He felt so confused because of the pain that she had caused him, but somehow that did not seem to matter now. As far as he was concerned, Panos was three thousand miles behind them, out of sight and out of her reach where he belonged. Tears stung the back of his eyes as he reluctantly remembered them being together. It induced a familiar pain that never failed to penetrate his heart. He opened his eyes and stole a glance at Danielle. He could see tears glistening on her cheek and found himself mesmerised by them as they rolled down her face and onto her arm.

Why couldn't she feel like that about me? He thought regretfully. Why couldn't she love me like she loved him? What did he have that I didn't? Closing his eyes and taking a deep breath, he was able to stop his own tears from escaping and prompt his thoughts to move quickly on to something else.

They spent the rest of the journey in silence. Although there was great excitement amongst all the other passengers, it was as if a dark cloud of sadness hung over the three friends.

At last the captain's voice filled the cabin as he informed them that they were now coming in to land. Danielle was brought out of her thoughts by his voice, as she mindlessly put on her seat belt. Wiping away her tears she consciously put Panos to the back of her mind. Suddenly, she felt an excitement stir up in her stomach at the thought of seeing her three children again. This encouraged a smile to form on her face, and her strength made a comeback as she pictured her babies in her mind.

I will get over this, she thought positively. I have to for their sake. She realised then that she felt better as her excitement had managed to overrule her sadness.

The plane brought them back into their world safely, and soon they were able to leave the aircraft. Matt was the first to get off, closely followed by Mick and Danielle. They left in single file, walking all the way through to the airport lounge. Here they found they were able to walk side by side. Danielle looked at Mick and smiled. No words were necessary as he put his arm around her and kissed her head. He felt so relieved to see her smiling again that he gently squeezed her side. For once he didn't feel the need to say something funny as the three friends went to get their suitcases.

They were waiting patiently for their luggage when Danielle walked up beside Matt. She felt awkward as she stood by his side, but she really wanted to say something to him. Her words swam around in her head, unable to reach her mouth, blocked by her guilt. Matt became aware that she was there. He looked at her and smiled half-heartedly, because he felt weary with it all.

"M-Matt..." she said shakily. "Matt I am so sorry. I honestly didn't mean to hurt you. The whole situation took me by surprise," she offered. Looking down at the ground, she was frightened to show the shame that her eyes portrayed, for ruining their friendship.

"Dan, it's ok babe," replied Matt, recognising the sincerity in her voice. "That is all in the past now, and I am sorry too. It's not all down to you sweetheart, and I really hope we can be friends again!" His words were genuine as he put his arm around her and gave her a big hug. The thought of never seeing that Greek man again reassured him that their friendship had a good chance of restoration, and this made him squeeze her tighter.

Mick looked over at the friend's embrace and smiled at the heart- warming reunion. He still felt slightly guilty about what had happened between Panos and Danielle, but he convinced himself that now they were back on English soil, everything would get back to how it used to be. He also hoped he and Panos could still be friends, and that they would keep in touch. They were, after all, like brothers, and this, he guessed, would not change.

He decided to catch up with his two friends, so quickened his step and began walking towards them, but as he got closer, his sandal got caught on the step and he went flying into the back of Matt's legs. Matt was taken by surprise as his legs buckled beneath him and was more than shocked when he noticed Mick sprawled out on the floor.

"Mick, what are you doing?" he asked not knowing whether to laugh or be concerned for his clumsy friend.

"These bloody Greek..." said Mick without thinking, then stopped himself just in time once he realised what he was about to say.

"These bloody English steps, they are everywhere," he burst out, laughing at his humiliation, causing Matt and Danielle to follow suit. All three laughed hysterically, causing everyone around them to stop and look at them, curious as to what was going on. Yet again they became the centre of attention, and Mick, being Mick, was the culprit behind the disturbance. Matt bent down to help his friend up off the floor, tears of joy streaming down his face.

"Thanks Matt, me 'ole mate. It's good to be home. Hello England, we are back!"

Danielle thought her sides were going to split as she watched Matt haphazardly pick Mick up off the floor, and tears were now streaming down her face. It was a relief that these were happy tears for a change. It was a good sign that she had successfully locked Panos away in a vacant box in her mind at least for now, and she was pleased she had managed to do so. Standing between her two closest friends, she almost felt content. They got their luggage and then prepared to take the final part of their journey home.

Matt helped Danielle with her suitcase, so she took the opportunity to phone her mother to let her know that she would be home shortly. She was overjoyed to hear a voice from home, especially her mum's precious voice. She was pleased to hear that everyone was at home eagerly awaiting her return, and excitement bubbled in her stomach. She could hardly wait to be with her family again.

It was also a weight off her mind that Matt seemed to be alright with her, and she felt honoured because he was willing to salvage what was left of their friendship. She looked over at him as he was shutting the boot of the taxi and smiled. He was so special to her, and she couldn't believe that she had nearly ruined the close bond that they shared. She knew that her feelings for him were platonic and was somehow relieved that he now knew it too. Nothing or no one could ever take that away.

"Come on Dan, time to get you home," said Matt enthusiastically, pulling open the back door of the taxi.

"I can't wait to see my babies," squeaked Danielle excitedly. "Thanks Matt, you are a true mate." She gave him a quick peck on the cheek and got into the car.

The atmosphere in the taxi was electric as Mick had everyone laughing at his silly ways. Panos was not mentioned at all but they did speak about Stuart and wondered whether he had been in the King's Head and if so, what he had said. Danielle felt guilt raise its ugly head as they went through the whole Stuart saga. She hoped he had found the help he needed, and that when they met again, he would be the same Stuart that had first come away with them. Feeling a positive conclusion would come of the Stuart situation, she focused her mind back on being reunited with her children again.

Panos came to the forefront of her mind many times, but she skilfully managed to push him out of her thoughts. The memory of him still provoked a terrible pain in her heart, so she did not want to put herself back in that place unnecessarily. She had now accepted that this great love story had come to an end, and when the time was right, she believed she would have the strength to think back to those wonderful times.

They had been on the road for a while and thankfully there had not been much traffic. Danielle's heart skipped a beat when she saw the familiar sight of the local Holiday Inn, a sure sign of coming onto home ground.

In a matter of minutes, I will be back under my own roof, she thought, realising just how homesick she felt. She couldn't wait to be in the comfort of her own home with her beloved children.

Pulling up outside her house, Matt got out first to help her with her suitcase. She only had time to get one leg out, when the front door of her house flew open, and a very excited Charlie came running out, followed closely by Marie. Charlie ran around the side of the car, and flung his arms around his mother, kissing her frantically on the cheek. She managed to pull herself out of the car with Charlie hanging around her neck like a baby monkey. She dropped her bag on the floor to free her arms and held her son so tightly that she was in danger of crushing his ribs.

"Mummy, mummy, I have missed you so much," Charlie confessed continuing to kiss her face.

"Have you got me a present?" he asked. Danielle burst out laughing.

"First things first, Charlie," she said, looking into her son's gleaming, brown eyes.

"I missed you too sweetheart," she continued, trying to prise his arms off her neck, without much success.

"And, yes I have got you a present." That seemed to do the trick as his grip finally loosened, and he dropped to the ground.

Then Marie came up to her, to have her turn. She had been patiently waiting at the curb side for her mother's attention, and flung her arms around her, squeezing her tight.

"Mum, I have missed you, and I am so glad that you are home…Wow mum, you are so brown," she said, taking a step back and looking her mother up and down. She suddenly remembered herself and flung her arms back around her mother again.

"Have you got me a present too?" she asked jokingly, and they both started laughing as her mother nodded her head.

"I wouldn't forget you, my beautiful girl." This time Danielle eyed her daughter up and down. "My beautiful grown-up girl, you have got to be two inches taller than when I left. That's amazing. I can't believe how much you have grown." Pride overwhelmed her as she held her daughter tight. She looked over to the doorway of her house where her mother, brother and sister in-law were standing at the threshold, smiling at the heartfelt embraces between Danielle and her children. Then Danielle became very confused when she realised that one person was missing.

"Where is Billy?" she asked. Tears began to sting the back of her eyes as she pulled away from Marie. Induced by his absence, her heart felt like it was going to stop, but then her brother Tony moved out of the way, clearing a space for Billy to appear.

"I am here mum! You didn't think that I would miss being here to meet you, did you?" he asked, a big grin on his face as he walked towards his mother. The cloud of confusion quickly lifted from Danielle's mind as she watched her son walk towards her, and a huge smile swept across her face.

"Billy, oh Billy, it is so good to see you," she said, putting her arms out to claim her first-born son.

"Look at you, you have grown too, and you are more handsome than ever." She fought back her tears as he walked into her outstretched arms and hugged her. It felt so good to have him in her arms again and as she kissed his cheeks, time seemed to stand still.

Matt placed her suitcase down next to her, and she was forced to let him go.

"Sorry Dan, but we've got to get going. The meter is ticking away here," Matt said, feeling bad that he had to interrupt the happy reunion. The journey had made him tired and he longed to be back at home. Billy picked up his mother's suitcase, as Danielle said goodbye to her dear friends, and walked into the house, followed by his brother and sister. Meanwhile, she watched the taxi disappear out of her road, then, taking a deep breath, walked into her house to be with her family.

CHAPTER

TWO

*P*anos spent the rest of the afternoon consumed in his work. The hotel was busy as usual, and he was grateful for the multitude of guests that took his focus off the turmoil that was churning around in his mind. He catered for their every need, displaying a professional mask with confidence that skilfully hid the truth behind his smile. He found himself so engrossed in his work that his charade took effect, and his thoughts of Danielle were kept nicely at bay.

His mother watched her son interact with the guests from a distance, and was taken by surprise at the strange, 'normal' manner in which he conducted himself. She had expected him to return from saying goodbye to Danielle heartbroken, but by the way he was acting, it was like she had never even been there. This unpredicted behaviour provoked a disturbing worry to her mind, and she had an overpowering sense that something was not right.

She knew her son well and was reminded of the way he had previously handled the devastation of when Sophia had left. The aftermath of that situation was too much for her to deal with, and the thought of history repeating itself made her go cold inside. She felt a desperate need to talk to him, but knew she had to choose her timing carefully. She decided to wait until she could get him on his own, then she would find out what was really going on in her son's heart. With her mind made up, she went back into the kitchen to help Anna prepare the evening meal for their hungry guests.

The afternoon and evening soon passed and welcomed in the night to gently take over, and Panos found he was alone in the bar. He did not want to go to bed and had tried his best to encourage the last of his guests to stay for a nightcap. His powers of persuasion failed him miserably as they regrettably declined, telling him that their beds awaited them after a busy day in the sun. As he watched them retreat to their rooms, the now familiar sense of loneliness consumed him. He could hear voices coming from the kitchen but felt a stubborn need to be on his own. The busy afternoon had kept his mind from wandering, but now he was alone, the thoughts of Danielle flooded uncontrollably back into his mind. The pain of his loss accompanied the memory of his love for her, and tears began to well up in his eyes. The thought of never seeing her again triggered off such a pain in his heart he thought that it was going to rupture in his chest. Suddenly he found himself walking towards the french doors, and his legs seemed to have a will of their own, taking him out onto the terrace. He stood still and quickly closed his eyes, frightened to face the view that awaited him. The full moon hung majestically in the sky. It was as if its magnetic power was forcing him to open his eyes to show off its splendour. Then, just as he had lost control of his legs, he lost the strength to keep his eyes closed, and they miraculously opened, leaving him confronted with the very thing that he was trying desperately to avoid. The vision of the moon took him straight back to the previous night when his precious Danielle was in his reach. He suddenly went weak at the knees as he imagined her being by his side, and he had to sit down. He put his head in his hands, fighting back the tears that the memory had induced, as a gut wrenching pain gripped hold of his body. All of the feelings he held for her rushed up to the surface of his heart like a torrent of rushing water, skilfully crashing down the wall of protection that he had managed to build around it. A deep yearning for his lost love grew rapidly through his body, armed to triumph over his sanity, and his tears began to flow. When the vision of her beautiful face stained his mind, his head felt like it was going to explode because the pain was so unbearable. He opened his eyes, unable to contain his tears, and looked back up into the night sky.

"Danielle, oh how I miss you. I love you, and wherever you are, I pray that you are safe," he said quietly into the moonlit heavens. He closed his eyes again, and then put his head in his hands as he began to sob.

Panos's mother walked through the restaurant into the lounge looking for her eldest son. She was confronted with the empty room, and wondered where he could possibly be, when she noticed the door leading to the terrace was open. She quickly made her way towards the door, hoping that was where she was sure to find him. When she walked out onto the terrace, she was overcome by a deep wave of sadness, as she witnessed her son's heart-breaking right before her eyes. All her motherly instincts came into play, and she walked over and put her comforting arms around him.

"It will be alright son," she said quietly, stroking his dark brown hair. "I am here, and I promise you that it will be alright." Panos couldn't find the strength to talk, so he just let himself be immersed in his mother's embrace.

His father stood quietly at the doorway and was once again confronted with Panos in his mother's loving arms. He knew that his son had deliberately avoided him all afternoon, and fully understood the reasoning behind him keeping out of his way. He loved his son dearly, and hated seeing him upset, but felt confident that after a few days he would have gotten over Danielle. He knew the strength that Panos had inherited from him would suffice and help to get him back into his normal routine, which encouraged his prediction.

He had watched his son's conduct with the guests earlier and felt proud that Panos hadn't let his situation get in the way of the work that was entrusted to him. A wave of compassion flowed through him as a picture of Elizabeth flashed through his mind. He was surprised that, even after all these years, he could still remember how beautiful she was, but he quickly blocked out the memory, forcing her back into the past where she belonged.

As he stared at his wife, he was reminded of when he had first met her, and a smile escape from his lips as his mind wandered back to that time. She was the most beautiful girl in their village, and had all the young men wanting her affections, but she chose to be with him. To his delight, all his family adored her. They welcomed her with open arms, and the proudest moment of his life was when she accepted his hand in marriage and became his wife. He was the envy of the village, which made him hold his head up high with pride. She proved to be the best wife and mother that a man could ever wish for. His smile widened, and his heart filled with love for her as he remembered their wedding day. He realised that he could never have imagined loving her more, but he did. These thoughts quickly brought him back into the present, and to the successful hotel that they had managed to build together. He was so grateful to his father for telling him the truth about Elizabeth, as his life could have turned out so differently, and this assured him that Panos's life would go on without Danielle. So, with these comforting thoughts in mind, he went back into the hotel and left the two of them alone together.

Danielle had her family hanging on to her every word, as she spoke excitedly about her experiences in Skiathos. She explained what had happened with Stuart, and all their mouths dropped open as she went through the details of his unprovoked behaviour.

"So, what happened to him in the end Dan?" asked Louise bewildered.

"I don't know, but hopefully I will find out when I go back to work tomorrow," replied Danielle solemnly. "I'm sure that he is ok though."

Then, she filled them in on her hilarious times with Mick and had them all laughing at his ludicrous ways.

"That sounds like the Mick we all know and love," said Tony completely amused. "He is such a funny man."

She touched only briefly on the subject of Panos, by telling them what a wonderful hotel he owned, and that they would absolutely fall in love with the place, just like she had. She deliberately failed to mention the fact that she had fallen in love with him too, as she couldn't risk bringing up the feelings that could so easily dominate her heart and re-open that painful wound again.

"So, what was he like Dan? Was he a handsome Greek Adonis? Did he like you? Was there any sign of romance between you?" asked Louise curiously, wanting to know all of the juicy gossip.

"Louise, trust you to ask that," Tony intervened, before Danielle could answer. "Danielle went on holiday to get away from a man, not to get involved with another one, especially not a Greek man! Honestly you girls are all the same. Romance indeed! That's the last thing she needed."

"Well you never know! You have a good-looking sister here, and any man would be crazy not to fall in love with her," Louise retorted defensively. She felt quite hurt by her husband's comment.

"Anyway, I only asked. There's no need to jump down my throat," she continued, folding her arms and pouting in disgust.

"Now, now, you two, there's no need for an argument," said Danielle laughing.

"And, in reply to your question Lou, yes, he was quite handsome, and no, there... there wasn't any romance," she lied. "He was just a lovely man who owned a lovely hotel." She felt herself cringe inside at being so deceitful because it couldn't have been further from the truth.

Maybe if I say it enough times, then I'll begin to believe it myself, she thought, wrestling with tremendous guilt. She abruptly changed the subject and began to give out the gifts that she had brought for them.

Christine watched her daughter as she distributed the presents and was so pleased to have her daughter back in one piece. While she was away, she couldn't help worrying about her being so far away in a foreign country. She spent so much of the time fighting horrible thoughts about all the terrible things that could happen to her abroad! Now that she was back home safe and sound, all her dark worries disappeared, and she breathed a sigh of relief. As she studied her beautifully tanned face, she had to admit that it did suit her. She couldn't help noticing that she seemed different somehow. She couldn't put her finger on what it was, but when Danielle mentioned Panos, she noticed that something changed in her eyes. It was if there was a flicker, a spark, which lit up. Even though she only mentioned him briefly, there was definitely a glimmer of something that told her there was more to it than she was letting on. She wondered if her daughter was really telling the truth, and if not, why not? Deciding to keep her suspicions to herself for the time being, she resolved to catch her on her own later and confront her.

Danielle spent the rest of the afternoon in awe of her children, as they filled her in with everything that had gone on in her absence. It was now her turn to hang on their every word. Listening intently to them, she was overcome by so much pride she felt her heart would burst.

Louise and Tony got up to leave, so Danielle followed them out to see them off. She thanked them for looking after Marie and Charlie and felt completely overwhelmed, still finding it hard to come to terms with their generosity and the kindness, love and support they had shown her.

She started dinner, and her mum offered to give her a hand. It was the first meal that she had cooked in two weeks and was relieved to find that it was so easy to make the quick transition back into motherhood. They called the children to sit at the table and ate their meal, as a comfortable silence descended. They all enjoyed being together again and relished this simple special moment and one another's company.

The peace and quiet won over Danielle's mind, so automatically her thoughts drifted to Panos, which made her lose her appetite. It had only been twenty four hours ago since she had been in his loving arms! Her heart ached with the very thought of him, and the love that they had shared. Indulging in this private hell even temporarily induced a violent eruption of pain in her heart. Within no time at all she felt so confused with the mixed feelings she felt. She went from being giddy with happiness to be back with her children, to an overwhelming loneliness threatening to devour everything she was. She had to fight back the tears that made her eyes sting.

I can't cope with this, she thought closing her eyes, desperately trying to stop the tears from escaping. I have to be strong, she told herself as she swallowed down the intense pain. When she opened her eyes, she was horrified to find her mother looking at her.

"Are you alright darling? You don't look so good. Has something happened?" she asked, concerned for her daughter.

Danielle looked into her mother's eyes, and Christine became aware of the pain that her daughter was feeling.

"Yes... yes, I'm OK mum. No... No, nothing has happened," she stammered answering feebly, hoping she sounded convincing. Thankfully the children seemed totally unaware that something was obviously wrong.

"Well I am not convinced, but I am here if you need to talk sweetheart. You know that, don't you?" answered her mum.

She simply nodded, and then had a sudden urge to tell her mum all about Panos, but quickly thought twice about it as Charlie looked at her.

"Mummy, I am so glad that you are home, I really missed you loads," he said, leaning over to her, giving her a big hug.

"Yes, I'm glad you are home too," both Billy and Marie said in unison, causing them all to laugh.

"It is good to be back with you guys too. You three are what my life is about," she said her words filled with emotion.

Christine thought that was a strange thing for her to say, but decided to keep her thoughts to herself, as she helped to clear up. The kids carried on into the lounge to watch TV.

"Mum, do you mind staying until the kids are in bed?" asked Danielle casually.

"Yes, of course I will. I can stay as long as you want me to," replied Christine resisting the urge to find out the reason why.

"Thanks mum," she said giving her mother a hug, before finishing off the tidying up.

Once the kids went to bed, the two women sat together

and watched TV, until Danielle got up to put the kettle on. She knew that time was getting on but didn't want to be on her own, so she figured that a cup of tea would prolong her mother's stay. As she walked out into the kitchen and filled the kettle, she caught a glimpse of the night sky out of the window. Suddenly, she had an uncontrollable need to open the back door so she could recapture her time with Panos. All of her power to keep him locked away vanished as she looked up to the stars, letting the picture of him come freely into her mind. Gazing up at the moon, which was way up in the distance, she smiled. It was so small compared to the way it looked in Skiathos, she found it hard to believe that it was the same moon. Then, she recalled every word that Panos had said the night before, and it filled her heart with a deep longing to be by his side again. Suddenly, her pent up tears began to fall, as the thought of never seeing the man of her dreams again dominated her mind.

"Panos, I miss you so much. I wish you were here," she whispered into the cool night air.

"I love you, and I hope that you are alright!" She fell down on the chair, utterly crushed and sobbed.

Christine took her eyes off the TV screen wondering what on earth was keeping Danielle, because she was taking her time with the tea.

"Danielle, what are you doing out there? I'm dying of thirst here," she shouted towards the kitchen, hoping to hurry Danielle along.

"Dan, Danielle are you ok?" she asked becoming very concerned when her daughter remained silent. She quickly got up to investigate and noticed the back door was wide open. Thinking it strange, she walked out into the garden, where she found her daughter slumped down on a chair, sobbing hysterically. Her maternal instincts impulsively took over, so she sat down next to her daughter and put her arms around her.

"Oh mum," was all that Danielle could say as she fell into her mother's comforting arms. Her mother cradled her close until she began to pour her heart out about Panos and the torture that was going on inside her.

"I knew something was wrong, a mother knows these things," she said when all of Danielle's anxieties had been released. She found tears running down her own cheeks too, instigated by her daughter's pain. She hated seeing her like this.

"It's going to be OK, my darling I am here for you, and I promise that everything will be alright," she said soothingly.

Matt walked into the hallway of his apartment, and was relieved to finally be home. Putting his suitcase down he picked up the pile of letters that was strewn across the floor. The journey had really taken its toll on him, and he was desperate for a nice hot bath. So, with the letters in his hand, he went into the bathroom and turned on the taps. As he fingered through the usual pile of bills and junk mail, relishing the thought of his long awaited soak, he came across a letter that stood out from the rest. The word "confidential" was written in bright red letters on the bottom, left hand side of the envelope, causing him to feel slightly on edge. It looked to him to be too official, so reluctantly opened it. His heart dropped as he became aware that it was from the solicitors, informing him of his wife's petition for divorce. The word divorce seemed to get bolder as he just stared at it, and felt that he had just been stabbed in the heart. "This is all I need," he said out loud, screwing the piece of paper up in his hand. Feeling a sudden urge to get out of there, he picked up the phone and began dialling.

Mick felt apprehensive as he put the keys into his front door, and couldn't help wondering what kind of homecoming he was going to get from Tracey. His heart raced as he tried his hardest to ignore his craving for a drink, so taking a deep breath he walked in.

"Hi Honey, I'm home," he shouted out sarcastically, but was quickly met by silence. He felt a wave of relief at the house being empty, but shouted out again, louder this time for good measure, just in case Tracey hadn't heard him. Thankfully his suspicions were confirmed when there was no reply, and he walked merrily into the kitchen.

His first reaction was to go to the fridge to see if there were any beers in there, but he remembered the promise he had made to himself earlier. So, he consciously stopped his compulsive thought pattern and put the kettle on instead. Getting a cup out of the cupboard, he congratulated himself, feeling very pleased with his choice. Then, he noticed a note propped up against the vase on the table. Recognising his wife's handwriting, he went over to pick it up see what she had to say. As he read her words, the craving for a beer that he had managed to keep at bay till now, quickly defeated his strength. She informed him that his time away had given her a lot of time to think, and that she had decided that she wanted him out of the house!

She couldn't take any more of the arguing, so she was giving him a whole week to get his things together and get out of the house and her life! She would be back from her parent's house then and expected him to be gone. Apparently, her decision was final and there was absolutely no way that their marriage could, or ever would, be restored.

"Since when do you make all of the decisions?" he shouted at the piece of paper in his hand.

"This is my house too!" He screwed up the note in complete disbelief of the sheer audacity of her telling him what to do. He was so enraged that he actually welcomed the urgent need he felt for a drink to calm him down! Going back over to the fridge he opened the door violently, looking for the answer to his annoyed state of mind. His heart skipped a beat when he saw that the fridge was empty of any alcohol. Frantically he began tearing through all the cupboards but was met by the same lack of liquor which took the irritation he felt to a whole new level.

"Since when has my house been an alcohol-free zone? She constantly moans about my drinking, and then springs this on me. Oh yes Tracey, good move. This will really help me!" he shouted sarcastically into the air, desperately hunting for his fix. The fury that he felt for his wife heightened, as his need for a drink grew. His rage was interrupted by his phone ringing, so quickly answered it, and to his relief, it was Matt. As he listened to his friend speaking, he was overcome with a feeling of delight, which instantly calmed him down.

"Ok Matt, that's a good idea. Your timing couldn't have been better, mate. I will see you in the pub in ten minutes."

All of Mick's willpower to overcome his problem suddenly buckled, so grabbing his keys he walked out of the house, slamming the door behind him.

CHAPTER
THREE

*T*hings got back to normal and fell into the usual routine in about a week. Danielle was back behind the bar at the King's Head, and soon the time spent with Panos became a faint memory. Mick's life of sobriety also became a thing of the past, when the thought of never having a drink again was put safely behind him. On further consideration, he decided that life would prove to be simply unbearable for him at home with Tracey, based on their irreconcilable differences. He figured the best thing would be to move in with his parents, until he was able to find a suitable place of his own. The thought of being under the same roof as her soon became completely unappealing, so he made sure that he wasn't there when she returned home.

"Besides, without her constant moaning, I can drink as much and as often as I please," he reasoned.

Matt tried his best to come to terms with his divorce but found that it was a struggle. So, when he got a phone call from his sister who lived in Yorkshire, inviting him up there to stay, he took great delight in accepting her offer to get away from it all. Work at the car yard was slow, so Mick agreed to give him some time off to sort himself out.

With Matt gone away, Mick spent most of his time in the pub. With the distinct lack of work, he had more time at his disposal, so he filled his day by chatting to Danielle as she worked. He found spending his evenings with his elderly parents rather boring, so he dragged out his day by meeting up with different people who took kindly to his generosity and to his loneliness. He missed being with Matt because it felt like a part of him was missing, and could hardly wait for his friend's return. He felt so lost without him.

There had been no sign of Stuart since his departure from Skiathos. All that happened was a complete mystery to Danielle and none of it made any sense to her at all. She was extremely worried for him, not knowing his whereabouts. She however held on to the hope that he would show up safe and sound sometime soon. With her work and the children keeping her busy, she found she was able to make herself forget about her wonderful time with Panos. Sharing her heartache with her mother helped her in combating her loss, and she soon convinced herself that he was now in the past, where he belonged. Her future did look bleak, but she knew that after time, she would accept her fate, and get into reality of what was in store for her as a mother and nothing else. She had successfully managed to rebuild the wall around her heart, and just concentrated on making her children happy, a sacrifice she was willing to make. Cracks would appear at times when Panos would unwillingly come into her mind, but she quickly disarmed the thoughts before she could lose herself in the memory of being in the arms of the man of her dreams. This would be the only time that she was grateful for her ex-husband and Brad, for equipping her with the strength to overcome the terrible pain that she felt inside, gratitude that she thought she would never be capable of feeling.

Panos on the other hand found it hard to forget Danielle. Most nights he lay awake remembering their time together. He just couldn't get used to being on his own, especially during the night. He longed for her to be by his side, and he could not get her out of his mind. He hated himself for being so weak and feeling this way, but the imprint that she had left on his life was too great for him to put aside and just ignore. The truth was that she meant the world to him, and the thought of her getting on with her life without him, ate him up inside. He found that he could cope with her absence during the day, as his bountiful workload was enough to occupy his mind. The problem was that as soon as he got into bed, memories of her ferociously attacked his thoughts, till he was instantly propelled back into a time when he was lost in her loving arms.

It was absolute torture watching couples together at the hotel, as he was constantly reminded of the love that he had to let go of. His father sensed the distance forming between the two of them. He tried in his own way to help and take his mind off Danielle, by reassuring him that he would meet a good Greek girl some day. That however made things worse, especially as Panos told him openly that it was the last thing on his mind. The thought of replacing the love of his life was too much for him to bear, and his father's insensitivity succeeded only in making his blood boil.

He still maintained his professionalism with the hotel guests, but became very short-tempered with his father, causing them to argue frequently. He found it hard to contain his anger when his father made his intentions known, and he totally rejected the idea that his father knew or understood was he was going through. During one such argument, he actually told him that he should mind his own business.

His father looked at him in disbelief, and it took everything he had not to retaliate. Instead he chose not to, because he remembered how his own father dealt with him in the days when he had been in love with Elizabeth. He felt so frustrated, because he had kept the secret about his long-lost love locked up inside for so many years. He wanted more than anything to tell his son that he really did know how he felt, but quickly resisted the temptation to reveal this undisclosed truth. He was convinced it would be more trouble than it was worth and only open up a can of worms. Instead, he just threw his arms up in the air, telling his son that he must soon get a grip, and concluded that his life would go on without Danielle.

Panos stood watching his father walk away and could have cried. He was sorry for the way he had spoken to him and regretted it but felt compelled by the turmoil he felt inside which simply could not be hidden. He had desperately tried to ignore the dull ache in his heart that had become a constant unwelcome companion. It dominated his heart, and the love he felt for Danielle was crippling him, and he could not deny it, or do anything about it. He felt stuck in limbo, unable to go back and change anything, but unable to move forward and just get on with life.

"Why can't I forget her?" He constantly asked himself.

"Please help me," he prayed. He suddenly had the uncontrollable urge to take his phone out of his pocket. He stared at the screen, went into his contacts list and pressed M. Michael's name and mobile number instantly appeared in bright green letters. He toyed with the idea of phoning him as he looked at his watch. It was four thirty Greek time.

Danielle will still be at work, and Michael might be with her, at this very moment, he reasoned. Staring at the screen, with his finger on the ring button, he felt an irresistible need to phone Michael. His fingertip hovered over the phone. He tried to take it away but found that he couldn't.

"But what if she isn't there?" he asked himself. Then I'll just ask Michael how he is, he quickly convinced himself. He was aware that he was shaking, and his heart was racing in his chest. With an apparent life of its own, his finger pressed down, and after a few moments, the phone the other end, began to ring.

Mick was sitting in the beer garden of the King's Head and it was one of the rare occasions that he was alone. He had his eyes closed and he basked in the English sunshine and daydreamed about being back by the pool in Skiathos. A smile escaped from his lips as he remembered his time there and wished that he had never had to leave that wonderful place. He thought about his friend Panos and wondered what he was doing.

Oh, what a life he's got! All those beautiful women to choose from...Yes, that would be the life for me, he thought enviably. His smile widened as he imagined being in his shoes, having all those gorgeous ladies at his beck and call, beer on tap, twenty-four hours a day, seven days a week.

Relishing the thought and immersing himself in the image, he was lost in his own little world until he was disturbed by Danielle when she put a pint of beer down on the table beside him.

"There you go Mick, this one is on me," she said pulling up a chair and sitting down.

"It's dead in there, so I decided to join you out here. Maggie is behind the bar, and she knows where to find me if we have a coach load of people turn up," said Danielle laughing.

She noticed Mick's mind seemed to be elsewhere.

"Penny for your thoughts Mick... Mick," she said shaking his leg for some kind of a response.

"W... what oh, Danielle, it's you. I was miles away then," replied Mick smiling at his daydream, noticing the fresh pint of beer on the table.

"Oh thanks, Dan, for the beer."

"So where were you then? Let me guess," she replied.

She thought it odd that, out of everything she had said, the only thing he picked up was her mention of the beer. She laughed at his obvious ways and waited patiently for his reply.

"I was in Skiathos lazing by the pool Dan. It seems a lifetime ago since we were there," he said picking up his beer and taking a big swig.

"We had a good time eh Dan?" he hesitated before divulging his next question.

"I was just thinking about Panos. Do you ever think about him Dan? I know that it must have been hard to coming away from him. One thing I do know is that he thought the absolute world of you. He definitely proved that."

This was the first time he had mentioned Panos since they had returned home. He'd sensed that she was feeling sensitive about the whole subject, so chose not to bring him up in conversation before. Now however the timing seemed right.

"Yes, we did have a good time, and no, Mick, I try not to think about him. It still hurts me, so I stop myself from remembering that time." She stopped herself talking about it, as thoughts of Panos tried to invade her mind again. She quickly stopped his face from appearing, by forbidding her imagination from going any further as she swallowed memories of him back down, proving to herself just how easily it could be done.

"It doesn't exactly help when I get reminded by a certain person," she said half-jokingly, giving Mick a serious look.

"Sorry Dan... What about those two Greek girls. That was a close call. I would have loved to have been a fly on the wall when you gave them what for," he said laughing; quickly changing the subject.

"Yes, Mick, that was a night to remember. You two ole fools did have a lucky escape," Danielle replied, closing her eyes and picturing that night, smiling to herself at the memory of their frightened faces.

"Blimey Dan, it doesn't bear thinking about what could have happened if you hadn't overheard them. Did I ever thank you? If not, thank you for that. You are a good girl Danielle, a true mate."

"Thanks, and yes, you did thank me.... about a hundred times," she said patting him on the knee.

"Now, that makes it one hundred and one."

There was a moment's silence, and Mick took another sip of his drink, enabling him to build up the courage to say his next statement.

"I think Panos really loved you," he said, looking her in the eye.

"I have never seen him like that before, even when he was engaged to..." Mick racked his brains for the name of Panos's ex-girlfriend. "Sheila... No, that's not it... Sandra... That doesn't sound right...oh, what was her name...?" He asked scratching his head.

"Sophia. Yes, that was it, Sophia. No, Dan, he didn't act like he did with you, when he was with her, even though he was going to marry her. No Dan, you definitely had an impact on him my girl."

"He never said anything to me about being engaged," she said mystified that he had failed to mention a fiancé.

"So, what happened, why didn't they get married?" she asked sitting up straight and looking into the pub. She was really hoping that they would not be disturbed; intrigued by where the conversation was going. Mick took her interest as a good sign to share what he knew.

He recited the story that Panos had shared with him. Her mouth dropped open at the thought of him being so deeply hurt by this woman.

"That must have been what his mother was talking about," she said when he had finished the story.

"She told me that he had been really hurt in the past. Oh, poor baby. What a way to find out you have been dumped. Poor, Panos." Suddenly, she was overwhelmed with compassion for him, making way for the feelings she had for him in her heart, to rise up from the deep places she had pushed them.

"I know that it took a long time for him to get over her, and he didn't honestly think that he could ever love again, but then you came along, Dan, and he realised that he could. No one was more surprised than he was. You, my dear, are the one responsible for that. He confided in me and told me so himself, honest!"

Looking at Mick Danielle had to do a double take, as she imagined Panos's mother standing in front of her saying the exact same thing. She shook her head in disbelief. Tears began to sting her eyes, and she took a deep breath, desperate to keep them at bay.

"B... but if he loved me so much, then... then why hasn't he tried to get in touch? He's got your number Mick; he could have phoned you. It's been over a week. Surely he would have phoned by now?" she asked. She could feel her heart weakening as her words came tumbling out. She tried so hard to stifle her tears that her throat started to hurt.

"Maybe he feels the same way you do Dan. Maybe like you, he feels he has got to be strong, and is doing his utmost to keep you out of his mind, just like you are, babe. I know how much you two were in love; I saw it with my own eyes. You cannot forget someone like that after a week. Who you trying to kid, Dan?" he asked gently.

The truth in his statement felt like a knife in her heart. She wanted to cry and wanted him to take back what he had said, all at the same time. Her heart felt like a volcano ready to erupt, as her dormant pain began to bubble and churn, waiting for an escape to blow.

"How do you know how I feel?" she asked defensively, raising her voice.

"How do you know what is going on inside of me? You haven't got a clue, Mick," she shouted, a single tear rolling down her cheek.

"Dan, I know I am just an old fool who drinks too much, but that doesn't mean that I'm an idiot, or that I am blind. I can tell by your eyes, babe. They give you away. They really are the windows to your soul, so whatever you say with your mouth, your eyes speak the truth," he said gently, deliberately ignoring her outburst.

"Like I said, I saw the two of you with my own eyes. You can't kid a kidder," he said emphatically.

Danielle could not believe what she was hearing. She would never have guessed, in a million years, that Mick could be so wise and knowing.

Am I so easy to read? she thought to herself, suddenly feeling weary. She hated to admit it, but he was right about everything and it really unnerved her. His wise words had stopped her dead in her tracks. She had no ammunition to fire back at him, even though she tried frantically to think of something to say to prove him wrong. Instead she found she was lost for words.

Mick's phone started ringing, interrupting the moment. Danielle was grateful for an escape, so she took the opportunity to run into the toilet to think about what Mick had said, as he had most definitely touched a nerve. To her relief the toilet was empty. She walked past the mirror and caught her reflection. She moved in closer focusing on her eyes, trying her hardest not look away. She hated looking at herself at the best of times and it was not easy to stay fixed on the image that stared back at her. Although feeling extremely uncomfortable, she managed to stay focused, long enough for the tears to begin to well up in her eyes.

"I do miss him, and Mick is right, you always give me away," she said to her reflection.

Her face twisted when she spoke to her reflection, instigated by the self-loathing that bore into her soul. Why did you let him into your heart? Why didn't you stop this from happening? You're a fool, and an idiot! She thought hesitating as she watched the tears roll down her face.

"Oh Panos, I miss you so much," she whispered. Closing her eyes, she sighed deeply as she gave her pain the freedom to escape from her heart.

Mick picked his phone off the table and impulsively looked at the screen, anxious to see who had interrupted his moment of wisdom. He felt slightly guilty for being so blunt with Danielle but was somehow relieved by the truth that he had relayed, which needed to come out. He hated that he had hurt Danielle's feelings, but in the grand scheme of things, felt it was important. What he said needed to be said, and was purely for her benefit, not for his own selfish need for glory.

He'd asked her many times if she was alright, and every time she had reassured him that she was fine. He could however see the pain that she was so frantically trying to hide, clearly portrayed in her eyes; the evidence of truth, manifested by the reality of what was really going on in her heart. He knew that look well, because he had seen it in his own wife's eyes many times, especially when they were arguing. He was quite confused by the compassion he felt for Danielle, compassion which had been lacking when it came to his wife. Then it suddenly dawned on him.

It is because Danielle doesn't go on about my drinking, he concluded, laughing to himself. He was reminded of his phone ringing, and the smile remained on his face, when he saw who was unexpectedly calling.

"Panos, me ole mate, I was just talking about you. How the devil are you my friend?"

"Michael, Michael, I am fine, thank you. How are you?"

Mick chuckled at Panos's answer and thought that his eyes most probably told the same story as Danielle's.

Fine indeed, he thought doubtfully. Ok Panos, if you say so!

"I am ok my friend, but miss being in the glorious Greek sunshine," he answered diplomatically, pleased that he had kept his notions to himself.

"No doubt it is as lovely as ever where you are, and talking of lovely, I am in the pub with Danielle," hesitating he waited for Panos to respond, and was relieved to have managed to get her into the conversation so quickly.

"You are with Danielle; can I speak to her please?"

There it is the response I was waiting for. Oh, Panos you are so predictable, thought Mick rather smugly.

"Well when I say I am with her, I mean she is inside working, and I am in the garden. Tell you what me ole mate, why don't I give you her number, and then you can phone her yourself. She'll be finished in about ten minutes and will be so pleased to hear from you!"

Mick felt his chest puff up with pride at the way his cunning plan was working like a dream. He felt very pleased with himself as he proceeded to give him her number.

"Right you are my friend, speak to you soon." He hung up just as Danielle walked back out into the garden with her bag in her hand.

"Are you ok Mick?" she asked putting her bag down on the table, noticing a big grin across his face. "You look like the cat that has got the cream."

Panos came off the phone in a complete daze. He had never had such a short conversation with Mick before, causing him to feel slightly suspicious.

What is going on in my English friend's mind? he thought looking at the piece of paper in his hand, an excitement stirring up in his stomach. I can't believe that I will be talking to her, he thought. I will hear my Danielle's voice.'Suddenly he was overcome by an overwhelming nervousness.

"But what if she doesn't want to talk to me? What if she has found someone else?" he asked out loud. Panicking, he felt nauseous at the thought of her being in another man's arms.

No don't be silly, that is crazy, he reassured himself.

That is just crazy. Looking at his watch he was disappointed to see that only five minutes had passed. His palms felt sweaty, and his heart was beating so hard in his chest that he thought that it was going to jump out and end up on the floor.

Calm down Panos, you don't want to give yourself a heart attack!

Dreading another panic attack, he suddenly realised that a guest could walk in at any minute! He didn't want to be interrupted when he was talking to his Danielle. This was far too important to mess up now! He informed his brother that he needed to go to the toilet, and that he would be five minutes and quickly made his way out from the bar.

There, no one can disturb me here, he thought pleased with his tactical manoeuvre. Pulling out his phone and the precious little piece of paper, with her number on it he began dialling.

Danielle sat down next to Mick puzzled by the beaming look on his face. There was a boyish glint in his eye that made her wonder what he was up to.

"Well, are you going to let me in on the reason behind your cheesy grin?" she asked half smiling to herself. He didn't answer but just looked at her. Her phone distracted her when it started to ring, and he took great pleasure in seeing her expression drastically change, from a flicker of confusion to sheer joy as she held the phone in her hand.

"Don't you think that you had better answer that Dan?" He encouraged.

She just nodded, warily answering her phone.

"Hello," was all that she could manage, completely taken aback by her unexpected caller.

"Danielle, Danielle is that you?" asked Panos enthusiastically.

"Yes... yes Panos, it is me. How did you get my number?" She looked over at Mick. Before Panos could say anything, the reason behind Mick's cheesy grin became apparent to her, and she immediately knew the answer to her question.

"Michael gave it to me," Panos answered dubiously. "That is OK, isn't it?" he asked afraid that he had done the wrong thing by phoning her.

"Yes...yes of course it is OK. I... I just didn't think that I would ever hear from you again. It is so good to hear from you," she admitted finding it hard to disguise the excitement in her voice.

The sound of his voice made her tingle inside, causing goose bumps to appear all over her body, and she was once again mesmerised by his Greek accent. She could feel her emotions stirring within her, and tried desperately to keep them under control. Suddenly she became aware of a battle brewing, where her brain was telling her one thing, completely contradicting what was going on in her heart. So, she decided to go with her mind, which seemed to feed her strength, and ignored the feelings that were trying to override her willpower. Panos asked her how she was. She answered him calmly, feeling confident that she was now in control of her conflict of emotions.

"So, how are you?" he asked.

She answered him calmly, feeling confident that she was now in control of her conflict of emotions.

"Danielle I am sorry, but I have to go," he said regrettably becoming aware of the time.

"Can... Can I phone you later. I will have more time to talk then. I really want to speak to you."

"Yes, I would like that," she answered shyly. "I would like that very much."

"OK, I will speak to you then. Goodbye... and... Danielle..." he hesitated, holding on tightly to his next statement, afraid to let the words pass from his lips. "I miss you." There, he had said it.

There is no going back now, he thought, relieved that he had found the courage to say how he felt.

"Goodbye Panos... and I...I miss you too," she replied, her heart masterfully overruling her mind.

The phone went dead, and she was left holding the phone, overwhelmed by what had just happened. There were a few moments silence before she finally put the phone down on the table. She looked at Mick who was just staring at her, the big grin still on his face.

"Now who looks like the cat that has got the cream?" asked Mick slyly. "Well Dan, what did he say?"

She realised that she wore the same cheesy grin as Mick and burst out laughing.

"He said that he is going to phone me later. I don't believe it," she shrieked. "And... and he said that he missed me. Oh Mick, he sounded so lovely, and I miss him too."

She stopped and stared into Mick's eyes, a serious look washing over her face.

"Looks like you were right mate, and I am sorry that I shouted at you."

"That's OK babe. I know that the truth hurts sometimes, and it is hard to hear, but it was worth it just to see the look on your face now. You are simply glowing my girl, a look that suits you much better," he replied, recognising something completely different in her voice.

"Now that's enough wise talk for one day, it's giving me a headache, and it is getting in the way of some serious drinking," he said, looking at the near empty pint in his hand. "Best I get myself another one. Do you want a drink Dan?"

She looked at her watch, and realised that she had to get home, so regretfully declined, the big smile returning to her face. Getting up, she kissed him on the cheek, thanked him for being a good friend and made her way home.

Mick watched her walk away, feeling pleased with himself for the part he'd played in getting them to talk to each other again. He wondered what the future held for them, but he couldn't help feeling somewhat thrilled for the now happy couple. Part of his decision to help, came from knowing that life is just way too short to waste on regretting what could have been. He wanted so much more for them than that! He was the number one record holder of missed chances in that department and wore the t-shirt to prove it. This bitter reality made him look back over his life, at all the mistakes and wrong choices that he had made.

As he reminisced back to those times, an attack of guilt pricked his conscience. He suddenly realised that alcohol was the common denominator responsible for his failings, and this unwanted revelation sent shivers down his spine.

My life was running smoothly until you came along, he thought, looking at the drop of beer left in the bottom of his glass. Racking his brains, he tried to place the time when his dependency on alcohol had taken a serious hold of him, but his mind drew a blank.

Oh well, at least you don't moan at me all the time, and I do get more pleasure out of you, he quickly reasoned with himself, drinking down the last mouthful of beer. He got up and went back into the pub to get another, quickly putting his melancholy thoughts behind him.

Panos could have cried with joy after speaking to his love. The huge cloud of sadness that had hovered over him was now gone, and all that he could think about was the conversation he was due to have with Danielle later. Walking back into the bar there was a spring in his step, because he was relieved that the terrible burden he'd been carrying, had now been lifted off his heart. Yannis watched him walk back in and could not help but notice his brother's quick change of mood. It was as though he was a different man from the one that had left just ten minutes before. He wondered what could have happened in the short space of time that Panos was gone.

He must have spoken to Danielle, he thought, as he remembered Panos being on the phone minutes before he had left to go to the toilet. He observed his brother as he worked behind the bar, only to be convinced of his suspicions when he started to sing.

He hadn't seen him act this way since Danielle had been there, and this unexpected behaviour made him smile. He was aware that from the day that she'd gone back home, Panos's attitude had drastically changed, and although it hadn't interfered with his running of the hotel, it troubled him greatly as his brother. It was as if the light had gone out of Panos' smile and this made his heart go out to his brother's plight. He had on many occasions, wanted to reassure him that things would get better in time, but the look on Panos's face, and his erratic behaviour towards their father, convinced him to stay out of his way.

He did confide in his mother, telling her of his concerns, but she persuaded him not to worry, telling him that time was a great healer. She had encouraged him to give Panos the space he needed to get over his loss. Now here he was, witnessing his brother's obvious change of heart, and he felt an irrepressible need to go over and talk to his now happy sibling.

The bar was empty of guests, who were getting ready for the evening ahead of them. So, he took this opportunity to confront Panos with his suspicions, wanting to confirm the reason behind his smile.

"Panos, you are in a good mood, has something happened?" he challenged his brother, optimistically. Panos was wiping down the bar when Yannis approached him and was somewhat taken aback by the question.

Is it that obvious? he thought to himself. He stopped what he was doing and looked directly into Yannis's curious eyes.

"Why yes, my nosey brother, something has come about," he answered cheerfully.

"Something has made me a very, very happy man." He carried on wiping down the bar, not wanting to give too much away.

"Oh, is that so? I noticed that you have started to sing again. I thought that there was a dying cat behind the bar, then I realised that it was you who was responsible for that horrendous sound," teased Yannis trying not to laugh.

"Oh brother, you can't hide your jealousy, my friend, just because I was blessed with the voice and the looks. Tut, tut, your envy doesn't become you Yannis." They both laughed simultaneously. Yannis was grateful for the banter that had been revived between them and was relieved to have the old Panos back again.

"So, I'm guessing that you've spoken to Danielle. That has got to be the only explanation to your quick change of mood, considering you have been like a bear with a sore head all week," asked Yannis cheekily.

Panos stopped again and looked back at Yannis as a smile escaped from his lips, provoked by the bluntness in which his brother had spoken.

"Yes Yannis, I have spoken to Danielle. Ten out of ten for observation my friend. You are in the wrong profession you know; you should have been a detective," replied Panos sarcastically, laughing out loud.

"And you, my brother, should have been a comedian," retaliated Yannis, also laughing.

A few moments of silence stole the moment and then Panos put his arm around Yannis and hugged him.

"Was I that bad?" asked Panos, his tone softening.

"I'm sorry about that, but the pain that I felt inside was unbearable. I miss her so much. But, now that I have heard her voice, my heartache has miraculously disappeared."

Yannis could detect the sincerity in his brother's voice, and quickly realised just how much his brother had missed

Danielle. He smiled confidently at the openness that Panos shared concerning his feelings., And he felt honoured to be entrusted with the truth behind the way that his brother felt.

"So, what's going to happen now, Panos? Will Danielle be coming back?"

"To tell you the truth, I haven't thought that far ahead. I am just so glad to have spoken to her. Who knows my dear brother?"

Panos took his arm away from Yannis's shoulder and looked up.

"If that's what is meant to be, then He knows?" he replied quietly, pointing up into the air. They both looked around as their father walked out from the restaurant. Instantly they were reminded of their heritage and the legacy that could hinder the plan of her return.

"It's not Him you have to worry about," whispered Yannis.

"Its Papa's old-fashioned ways that are the problem, but I'm sure that he will understand when he sees you so happy again," said Yannis patting his brother on the back.

"Even he was fed up with your constant bad mood. So, who knows, maybe your grumpiness has given him a change of heart?" he said hopefully.

Panos watched his father walk through the lounge and felt a heaviness creep into his heart. He thought that the likelihood of him accepting Danielle was low, and at the same time, he really didn't want to disappoint his father. But, as the love that he felt for Danielle was greater than his need to stay confined within his culture, it caused strength to evolve from deep within him.

"I will deal with Papa, when and if I need to. But, like I said Yannis, I have not thought that far ahead, so I will see what happens. For all I know, she might not want to come back; after all, she does have a life of her own back in England," he concluded trying not to get his hopes up too much.

Suddenly his strength evaporated when he remembered her children, and the fact that she was a mother. He had convinced himself that there could be a small possibility that his father could be persuaded concerning her, but taking on another man's children, well that was quite another matter. Even he knew that would never be accepted.

"Well, it would be nice to see her again, Panos, if only for one more time. I know that she makes you happy, and that makes me happy. I also know that she will never be your wife," admitted Yannis, when he too was reminded of her children. "But you have to grab every chance of happiness, even if it is only temporary. Who knows, this could be the beginning of a great friendship: she is beautiful, and I know what I would do."

Panos looked at his brother and smiled. What he said was food for thought, and he had to admit that he did have a point.

"Could I cope with letting her go again," he asked himself. "Of-course I could, I am my father's son and I can handle anything!"

The bar suddenly became overrun by thirsty guests, so with these confident thoughts in mind, he went about his business, only this time, the smile displayed across his face was genuine.

CHAPTER

FOUR

As Danielle drove home her thoughts were on her conversation with Panos. She couldn't believe that he had actually phoned her! As she turned on the radio, Tom Jones's Sex Bomb filled the air, taking her straight back to the night of her birthday in the Borzoi club. She smiled at the memory, allowing herself to be catapulted back to that awesome night. The memory of being with him at the beach, and the way he'd held her in his arms was one she cherished. Remembering how easy she could have got lost in his desire to make love to her, she was overcome with pride as she recalled how hard it had been not to let him, and she was thankful for the self-respect she'd had for herself that had been installed in her at an early age.

She was overcome by a deep sense of admiration for Panos because he had respected and valued her wishes, rather than pressuring her into something that she did not want to do. Instead he had been the perfect gentleman, choosing just to hold her in his arms, and happy to do just that. Showing her such respect just made her fall deeper in love with him.

That was our first night together, she thought as she imagined being close to him, in her mind's eye. She sighed deeply at the image conjured up, especially when a deep longing to be back by his side almost overwhelmed her. It seemed so long ago; the beginning of a love affair that only dreams were made of where she had been thrown into a fantasy, worlds apart from the reality of her own life.

The more she thought about it, the more doubt entered, trying its best to convince her that it was all in her head, and that her wonderful time with Panos was just a figment of her imagination.

"No, he was real," she said out loud, trying to claim back her sanity. "That did actually happen to me!"

Suddenly, she found herself outside her house. She had been so lost in her thoughts that she couldn't remember driving home. This lapse of time shook her, and she blamed her lack of concentration on Panos. It took her a few minutes to re-establish her bearings. She had taken the keys out of the ignition and got her bag off the floor, when she noticed her phone on the front seat. She stared at it for a few moments before picking it up and then went into the call log so she could retrieve Panos's phone number.

"See he is real, I didn't imagine him," she said out loud, looking at the number displayed on the screen, trying to convince her mind that had tried to deceive her and tell her otherwise. She laughed at the stupidity of her talking to herself, put her phone back in her bag and went into the house.

Christine had picked Charlie up from school and they were already there when Danielle came through the door.

As she walked into the front room, Charlie seemed to appear out of nowhere. He lunged himself at her, planting a big kiss on her cheek. Danielle was thrown by the over excited Charlie, who was now hanging from her neck, but as soon as she realised it was him, she retaliated by planting a big kiss on his lips. She proceeded to swing him around, and his shrieks of laughter could be heard in the kitchen where Christine was making a cup of tea. She looked through to the lounge, and saw her daughter, pin Charlie down to the ground, and was tickling his sides. She smiled at the comical sight relieved to see that Danielle had come home in a good mood.

The past week had been quite an ordeal for her as she had watched her daughter piece back together what was left of her fragmented heart. She could see that she was trying to be strong for the sake of her children, but the lifeless look in her eyes told another story. Neither of them had mentioned Panos since the night that she had poured her heart out to her. She felt sensitive to her plight, so chose not to speak about him until Danielle decided otherwise. She had caught her looking into space many times, and always asked her if she was alright. She also reassured her that she was there for her if she needed to talk. Danielle usually put on her stubborn head though, telling her not to be ridiculous as she continually claimed that she was 'fine', absolutely 'fine!' Christine felt the best way to handle it was to choose to ignore the attitude she heard in her daughter's voice. She convinced herself that after a couple of weeks Danielle would soon be back to being, her usual happy-go-lucky self.

"Hello Mother, thanks for getting Charlie for me, you're an angel," said Danielle picking up her cup from the side and looking at her mum and smiling.

"So how was your day?" she continued, taking a sip of her tea.

"You're welcome sweetheart, and yes I am. My day has been good, thank you," replied Christine, noticing that the spark had returned to Danielle's eyes.

"And... And how was your day? You seem to be in a good mood! Is there anything that I should know about?" she asked suspiciously. Danielle stared at her mother, with a big grin across her face. She had tried her hardest to keep it at bay, but the joy that she felt in her heart made this an impossible task to carry out.

"There might be," Danielle said sheepishly, taking another sip of her tea. "Panos rang me," she blurted out, unable to contain her excitement any longer.

"He did?" asked Christine, concerned and confused, as she wondered whether that was a good or a bad thing.

"Yes, this afternoon, just after I finished work. He took me by surprise, mum. I didn't think that he cared, but he does, and he is phoning me again later. I am so excited. He told me that he missed me. Mum, I have never felt this way about anyone before in my life, he is so gorgeous." She put her hands up to her chest, closed her eyes and spun around like a wooden top.

"I am so happy, I could cry," she said when she finally stopped.

Christine looked at her daughter, who had become a completely different girl in a matter of hours. She felt like her head was spinning similarly to the way Danielle had spun only moments before.

"Slow down Dan, you are making me dizzy," she said, with a thoughtful look in her eyes and a half-hearted smile.

"I don't mean to rain on your parade, but the thought of you being hurt again makes me feel so anxious. I care about you, and I don't want you to get hurt."

Danielle turned to her mother and laughed.

"Oh mum, I love you so much, and I know that you worry about me, but he is not like that, I promise. He is the kindest, gentlest, most loving man in the world, and believe me, I know, because he had to prove that to me, and he passed the test with flying colours... Oh mum, he is so wonderful."

She led her mum into the front room to sit down and proceeded to take her through every wonderful detail of the time she had spent with Panos. Christine listened to her daughter's amazing story and had to admit he did sound adorable. She liked the look on Danielle's face when she reminisced about being with him. Her lovely tanned skin radiated a silky glow when she spoke, and at the very mention of his name, her eyes sparkled like precious jewels, winning Christine round into becoming very fond of this Greek man whom she had never met.

When Danielle got to the part when he had taken her shopping, she stopped in mid flow and went running up the stairs. Charlie had entered the room halfway through the conversation and was confused about what he'd heard and what was going on as his mother disappeared upstairs. He hadn't seen her this happy in a long time and wondered what this Panos had to do with it. He looked to his Nan and shrugged his shoulders, causing her to laugh out loud.

"That's love for you sweetheart," she said to him still laughing, infectiously. She'd been touched by Danielle's tale of romance.

"It does funny things to you. Don't worry, no doubt you will experience it too one day."

Charlie just looked at her, a serious look staining his face.

I don't think so, I don't even like girls, he thought to himself utterly disgusted.

Danielle ran back into the room holding a small box in her hand and proceeded to take out the content. As she put it on her finger, Christine realised it was in fact a ring. Danielle proudly showed off the impressive diamond, holding up her hand for all to see.

"Danielle, that's so beautiful," she gasped, taking her hand.

"It must be worth a fortune. Has he got a father?" she asked laughing at her own joke, mesmerised by its splendour.

"Yes, he has but Panos is nothing like him, and sorry, he has a mother too, who is such a lovely lady. Anyway, enough about him, where was I?" she asked as she continued to tell her story, stopping only briefly to catch her breath, her mum hanging on her every word.

She took her through every memorable moment spent with him. By the way that she described this honourable gentleman, Christine found it hard to believe that such a man existed. All the men that she had been involved with in the past had turned out to be rotten to the core, and she felt that it made a nice change that Danielle had actually met a nice guy.

As the events of the holiday begun to unfold, Christine's mind that had been closed for so many years, regarding the opposite sex began to open. She was relieved to find that Panos had treated her daughter well, and this revelation was starting to restore her faith in men. She too had nursed a broken heart because of Danielle's father, who had left her for another woman after twenty-three years of marriage. Danielle and Tony were grown-up when he dropped the bombshell, but she still found it a struggle getting used to being on her own.

Although it had taken a few years for her to come to terms with her marriage break up, she was now content with her life, but the trail of mistrust that still followed her was a constant reminder of how easily things can change for the worse. It had broken her heart to see her daughter's life going the same way as hers, but now Panos seemed to be leading her into a new and better direction, bringing hope into her otherwise hopeless world. Her smile widened at her daughter's obvious state of heart. She had thought the day would never come when she would see her so happy, but now here she was, that day had finally arrived, and her daughter's gleaming face said it all.

"So, that is what happened to me, and how such a wonderful man entered my life," concluded Danielle, when she had finished her tale of love.

Christine looked at her; sensing the truth behind Danielle's words, and smiled.

"Well Danielle, he does sounds like a wonderful man. I hope that I will get to meet him one day," she said sincerely.

"Does that mean that we will be moving to Greece then mum?" asked Charlie innocently, getting up on to his mum's lap. "I don't want to leave my friends," he continued.

Danielle combed her fingers through his hair and kissed him on the cheek.

"No sweetheart, we will not be moving anywhere. This is where our home is," she replied reassuringly.

"But what if he invites you back over there? It wouldn't surprise me if he did Dan," said Christine.

"What are you two like? I haven't even had a proper conversation with him yet. I have to keep my feet firmly on the ground." The conversation was brought to an abrupt end when Billy and Marie walked in from school.

Billy said hello and walked straight into the kitchen to get a drink, whilst Marie went over to her mum and gave her a kiss on the cheek. Danielle responded by hugging her daughter, and as she pulled away, Marie noticed the diamond ring on her finger.

"Wow mum, where did you get that from? You weren't wearing it earlier, it's beautiful," she said taking her mother's hand and fondling the giant solitaire.

"It's from a friend..." Danielle began to explain.

Christine quickly intervened. "Your mother has got an admirer, Marie, but not a secret one, because she definitely knows who he is," said Christine. "Your mummy's in love. Your mummy's in love," she chanted, unable to resist the urge to tease her daughter.

"Yes, his name is Pasmos, and she met him on holiday." Charlie piped up. "My mummy's in love. My mummy's in love."

"Mum!" said Danielle putting her hands on her hips.

"And you Charlie. Both of you behave yourselves. And his name is Panos."

Marie looked at her Nan, then turned to her brother and wondered what on earth was happening.

"Is someone going to tell me what's going on here...? Mum?" she said, feeling quite hurt by their secrecy.

"So mother, are you going to tell her, or are you going to let me get a word in and allow me to tell her myself?" asked Danielle, glaring at her mum and trying not to laugh, all at the same time.

"No Danielle, you tell her, it is your story and you tell it so well," replied Christine sarcastically, unable to contain her laughter.

Danielle sat down next to Marie and told her the story behind the new addition to her jewellery collection. Marie sat quietly listening to her mother's enchanting account of her time in Skiathos, completely captivated by the rendition of love that was responsible for the twinkle in her eyes. Billy walked in halfway through the chronicle of Panos, rolled his eyes and waited impatiently for her to finish. As Danielle talked them through the last instalment of her story about leaving Panos at the airport, she realised that Marie and her mother both had tears in their eyes, because of the very sad ending to the story.

"Aw mum, that's so sweet. You have to see him again," said Marie, wiping the tears from her eyes.

"That explains why you've been so grumpy," said Billy bluntly, suddenly becoming aware that three sets of eyes were boring into him. "I was only saying. She's been miserable since she came back," he continued defensively.

Marie just glared at her brother, resisting the urge to slap him.

"Well she has," he said to his irate sister, sticking out his tongue.

"After that holiday, and having to come back to you, I am not surprised that she was sad, I would be too," retaliated Marie as she stuck her tongue back out at him.

Danielle chose to ignore the sibling rivalry and began to laugh, trying to defuse the argument that was brewing between her two children.

"Kids I'm sorry that I acted that way, but yes, you are right Marie, I was very sad. But, now that I've spoken to him, my mood will be a lot happier, I promise."

She got up and walked over to Billy, whose face was like thunder, and began to tickle him.

"OK, Billy boy?" she said trying to induce a smile from him, but to no avail.

"I said, OK, Billy boy?" she repeated, tickling him harder. It seemed to work as a smile began to creep across his face.

"OK, OK," he said, now laughing. "Just stop tickling me."

"Right, all of this talk has made me hungry. Who's up for some fish and chips?" asked Danielle reaching for her purse.

"Are you staying for dinner mum?" she asked.

Christine nodded her head as she watched all her grandchildren excitedly say yes at the same time, putting their hands up in the air and clapping. A deep sense of pride rose up out of her heart when she witnessed this act. Until now, she hadn't realised just how much she loved her daughter and grand children.

"I would love to stay for tea, Dan, and this is my treat!" Suddenly, she was bombarded by the ecstatically happy threesome, as they all clambered over each other to cuddle her, nearly knocking her off her feet.

"Be careful you lot; you nearly had me over," she said, trying to cuddle them all together. "So, what is everyone having?"

Panos spent the rest of the afternoon watching the clock. The hotel was inundated with people wanting his attention, which filled his time nicely until he was due to speak to Danielle again. His spirits were high, and this was evident by the jovial way that he interacted with the guests. The smile that was permanently displayed across his face was a constant reminder of the joy that he felt inside, a joy he found he could not hide. As he had everyone laughing at his silly jokes, his heart rippled with laughter that escaped through his smile.

Many of the guests were taken aback by Panos's obvious change of mood. They were quite intrigued and asked Yannis what was the reason behind his brother's sudden spurt of happiness. He smiled at their observations and reassured them that Panos had a very good reason for the way he was acting. He did not want to give too much away, because he felt that it wasn't his place to reveal the whole truth behind Panos's unpredicted behaviour, so he sent the enquiring guests away empty handed.

His brother's outlandish frame of mind not only caused the guests to become suspicious, but also Anna when she was confronted by her overzealous future brother in law as she walked into the bar. She was stopped in her tracks when she came face to face with the Panos that she had grown to adore over her time spent at the hotel, and was pleased that he had at last returned. The past week had been a long seven days as she witnessed Panos's dejected demise. She had watched him go from a happy, carefree person, full of life, to a shallow, lifeless robot. She could not fault his professionalism towards the guests, but the twinkle in his gorgeous brown eyes had disappeared, exposing a cold empty man that she did not recognise. It broke her heart to see this unhealthy transformation take place before her eyes, and she held on to the hope that he would find the strength to pull himself back from the brink of his despair. She had convinced herself that, after a few weeks, he would have put back the pieces of his life without Danielle, but here she was, just a week down the road, witnessing a Panos who was now fully intact. This unforeseen behaviour caused her to feel delighted for his happier disposition, but also confused by the swiftness of his altered state of mind. She was relieved to finally have the Panos she loved in her sight again, but she could not help wondering what was behind his sudden change of character. So, armed with her curiosities, she walked over to Yannis hoping he could supply the answer to her inquisitiveness regarding her transformed brother in law. Yannis was at the reception desk when she approached him. He was talking on the telephone, so Anna waited patiently for him to finish his conversation before getting his undivided attention. A few minutes later, he put the receiver down and turned to his fiancé.

"Hello, Anna is everything alright?" he asked suspiciously, concerned by the questioning look in her eyes.

"Well, that's what I was going to ask you, Yannis. What's happened to make Panos so happy? He is a completely different man from twenty-four hours ago, and I was wondering if you knew the reason behind his obvious change of heart."

"N... no Anna, nothing has happened, he's just in a good mood, that's all," he replied flippantly.

Anna wasn't convinced by his statement and would not be deterred. She looked deep into his eyes searching for any sign of the truth that he was obviously keeping from her. Suddenly she saw it, a glimmer of a smile flashed through his eyes, instantly giving away a secret that he was trying desperately to hide.

"Yannis what's going on? If I'm to be a part of this family, then there can't be any secrets. We can't build our marriage on that," she said, feeling quite hurt by his blasé attitude.

He kept his eyes fixed on her. It even crossed his mind to tell her to mind her own business and that Panos was not her concern, but he couldn't bring himself to say those harsh words. Fortunately, he'd inherited more of his mother's traits than his father's and was grateful to have been blessed with her more gentle personality, unlike his brother, who was more like their father.

On many occasions throughout his life Yannis had

envied Panos's strength and boldness. He looked up to his older brother and admired the respect that he received from both the locals and the guests. Nevertheless, it was hard living in his shadow, always having to be the polite one whose opinion never seemed to count. At times he felt so over shadowed, that he was in danger of becoming invisible. He was often reminded of his place in the family, and so the harsh reality eventually had to set in. The role he had to play as the younger brother had been engrained in him from an early age. He loved his family dearly and knew that this was the way that it had to be. He soon learned to settle for being second best.

As he stared at Anna, his heart softened, and he was overwhelmed by the deep sense of gratitude that rose up from the pit of his stomach. He was so thankful that she was a part of his life. Whatever his father expected of him, with her by his side he could take on the world. He was comforted by the knowledge that he was the number one man in her life, and marvelled at being at the top of her hierarchy, even if it was behind closed doors. This part-time authority was sufficient for him, because he was the one who possessed Anna and her wonderful ways, and neither his brother nor his father could ever override that. He smiled at his possessive thoughts and then impulsively kissed her on the cheek.

"Oh, my dear Anna, nothing gets past you," he laughed, staying close to her.

"Yes, you are absolutely right, we cannot have any secrets. If you must know, Panos has spoken to Danielle and he will be speaking to her again later," he replied, looking deep into her eyes, the smile remaining on his face.

"Well, that's good news, isn't it?" she asked, relieved by the information relayed to her, and at last being able to make sense of what was behind Panos's happier attitude.

"Yes Anna, it is good news. At least now we can expect to see a cheerier Panos. I was beginning to wonder if he would ever return. He has been in a foul mood all week. But since his phone call to Danielle, he has made a very welcome comeback," he concluded laughing.

He looked over to his brother who was arm wrestling with one of the guests. Anna followed his gaze and nodded as she witnessed Panos pushing the guest's arm down on to the table whilst laughing at the top of his voice. This act of strength and the level of joy that followed it, also made her laugh, and she was pleased to know that Danielle was responsible for this turnaround of mood.

"So, does this mean that Danielle will be coming back, Yannis?" she asked him, her eyes still on Panos.

"I don't know, but it wouldn't surprise me. We'll have to wait and see."

They were interrupted by the phone ringing; Yannis tore his eyes off his brother and answered it. Anna, remembering that she had work to do, quickly left to help her future mother-in-law in the kitchen. She felt pleased for Panos, as she'd taken a surprising liking to Danielle, who she knew had brought out the better side of his nature. She had not shared her thoughts with anyone before, but she really felt that they made a lovely couple, and the the thought that Danielle could be coming back made her smile widen. She looked forward to the next instalment of this great love affair, hoping that it would happen sooner rather than later. With these exciting thoughts in mind, she walked into the kitchen to carry out the rest of her work.

To Danielle's relief, the evening came quite quickly. She had busied herself hoping to persuade time to pass as she expectantly waited for Panos to call. Her stomach bubbled with excitement and the butterflies returned every time she imagined hearing his voice again. She kept looking at her phone every two minutes, and this impulsive behaviour was beginning to get on her nerves. Every time her phone did ring, her heart jumped into her throat, and then she was consumed by disappointment when it was not Panos.

Of all the nights to be popular, she thought impatiently to herself, as she hurried her callers off the phone.

At one point a very drunk Mick phoned her, telling her that he was really missing his wife. Her heart went out to him, but she couldn't help feeling quite annoyed by his repeated statements of loneliness. She tried desperately to console him by telling him to be strong, but her advice went right over his head and was ignored. The drunkenness was evident in his voice. He did however finally listen to her, agreeing that he needed to sleep it off and then things wouldn't seem so bad in the morning. His cries of desperation were heartfelt to her, so she reassured him that she would speak to him the following day. This seemed to calm him down, and he eventually hung up the phone.

The children were all in bed and her mother had gone home and finally Danielle was relieved to be on her own. Listening to Mick's rather slurred words had brought the reality of his problem to the forefront of her mind, and she couldn't help feeling remorseful for his sorry frame of mind.

She knew that his dilemma was a cause for concern, so she consciously made the decision to assist him in finding the help he needed to be able to combat his problem. She loved him dearly and was comforted by the role she was hoping to play, as his friend, to help him overcome this terrible time of his life.

She looked at her watch for the hundredth time, her thoughts going to Panos. It was coming up to ten o'clock and a sudden gut wrenching feeling swum over her, and she convinced herself that he wasn't going to phone her now, not at this time. Her heart sunk to her stomach, and just as doubt was about to take over her mind, her phone began ringing. To her sheer relief, it was Panos, and her sunken heart shot up into her throat as her excitement successfully rubbed out any trace of doubt, instigating a smile to form on her face.

"Hello Danielle, I'm so sorry that it is late, but I wanted to be alone when I phoned you, and the last of the guests have only just gone off to bed," he said apologising before she could say anything.

"How are you, beautiful lady?" His words and the gentle way in which he spoke to her sent shivers down her spine and reminded her of the love that she felt for him, and her

sadness at having to to leave it behind.

"Hello Panos, I am fine, thank you. How are you?"

"Ah Danielle, Danielle, I am happy now that I've heard your voice..." he hesitated, his mind full of what he wanted to say, but he didn't know where to begin.

An awkward silence fell between them, and Danielle was reminded of their first meeting on the stairs of the hotel, at the very beginning of their romance.

"I have so much to say to you, but I don't know where to start," he laughed nervously, reminded of the memory that seemed so long ago.

"It's funny that when I was with you, I was lost for words, and now you have the same effect on me, even over the phone!"

He laughed again, desperately trying to defuse the silent atmosphere. Danielle also laughed as she pictured him taking her hand on the stairs and gently kissing it. She closed her eyes and could almost feel his soft lips on her skin. Taking a deep breath, she enjoyed the image she had conjured up in her mind.

"I meant it when I said that I missed you, because it is the truth. I don't know how I've managed to get through this past week, without you. I've been so miserable," admitted Panos. He resisted the polite need for small talk choosing instead to get straight to the point. "Have you missed me too?" he asked almost holding his breath as he waited impatiently for the answer. Once again there was silence. Although her mind was racing with what she wanted to say, her words got stuck in her throat and she just nodded.

"Danielle, Danielle can you hear me OK?" he asked anxiously, fearing that the connection had somehow been broken.

"Yes," she squeaked, finding the strength to clear her throat.

"Yes Panos, I can hear you..." She hesitated, frightened of letting the next sentence out of her mouth, but gave in, against her better judgement. "Yes, I've missed you too, and yes, I've also been very unhappy!" There she had said it, and she could not take it back.

A big smile swept across Panos's face. He felt his anxiety deflate as she said the words he had been waiting to hear.

"That is good. I mean you missing me is good. I didn't mean that it is good that you've being unhappy." They laughed simultaneously, the laughter breaking through the thick atmosphere like a knife.

"Ah, my Danielle, I did not think that I would ever speak to you again. I tried my hardest to forget you, but I couldn't. When I phoned Michael, I was secretly hoping that you were with him. I'm so glad that he gave me your number. Speaking of Michael, he phoned me tonight and he was very upset, and wants to come back to Greece."

"I spoke to him too, but he didn't mention talking to you, and he didn't say anything about going back," she replied, feeling confused that Mick hadn't said anything to her about going back to Skiathos.

"Well, he wants to come back in a couple of weeks, and I... I was hoping that you would come back with him. Will you come with him? Please Danielle, say yes my darling." As he waited rather impatiently for her reply, he could not hide the excitement in his voice.

"But Panos I... I can't. I..."

"Please Danielle, if money is the problem then I will pay for your flight, and it won't cost you anything to stay here because you will stay with me," he said interrupting her, deliberately stopping her from using any excuse for not going.

"Please say yes. I want to see you, hold you in my arms. Feel you next to me. Kiss you."

Taken aback and totally unprepared for his request, her head began to spin. She had to admit and couldn't deny that she wanted the same thing he did, but her reasons for not being able to go back, outweighed the reasons, for her to just drop everything and return to Greece because there were things she simply could not ignore.

"But Panos, I have my children to think about...This, I was not expecting...You have taken me totally by surprise... I can't just leave them again."

"I'm sure that you can sort something out. I'm sorry if I am being selfish, but I want you all to myself! It would only be for a week... Please Danielle, don't say no straight away. Just think about it, please."

She nodded as the desperation in his voice weakened her logical thinking.

"OK Panos, I'll think about it, but I can't promise anything. You have to understand that my children come first. If they are not happy with it, then it is a no, OK." As she spoke, his heart filled with compassion. He was reminded of her love for her children, and this he remembered was why he loved her so much.

"OK my beautiful lady, I will leave it in your hands." Relenting, he felt confident that, in a couple of weeks, the woman of his dreams would be back by his side. They spoke for a few more minutes and he reassured her that he would phone her again the following day. When he finally did say good night, the excitement was evident in his voice, as he thanked her again for coming into his life. He confessed his true feelings for her and spent time pleading with her to believe that he really did love her. Just as she shyly told him that she loved him too, the phone went dead, and she was left staring at the screen. She imagined being back in his loving arms, and all her emotions for him made a welcome return. The possibility of being back on the Island, and back in the Oasis hotel, provoked a huge smile to appear across her face.

"Could this really happen?" she asked herself. She suddenly remembered what her mum and daughter had said when she had shared her story earlier. They had both been very keen on her seeing Panos again. Thinking about it made her smile widen, and her heart palpitated at the possibility of this actually happening, and perhaps being on the horizon. She couldn't wait to tell them of Panos's intentions, but consciously told herself to keep her feet firmly on the ground just in case it was not meant to be. She also remembered that she needed to have her son's blessings too, because their feelings also needed to be taken into consideration.

The reality of home life quickly brought her back down to earth, but she couldn't help secretly hoping things went in her favour, and that she would find herself back in Skiathos in a couple of weeks time. Comforted by these thoughts, she took herself off to bed, trying her hardest not to allow wishful thinking to get the better of her.

Panos had been in his room when he had phoned Danielle. He was sitting on the end of his bed, and the sound of her voice shaped his heart into believing that the probability of her being in his sight again was very high. This pre-ordained outlook brought a lump to his throat.

The thought of her lying next to him became overwhelming, bringing a tear of joy into his eye. He couldn't believe that only twelve hours earlier, she was just a lovely memory, and time spent with her a thing of the past. But now here he was, facing a future with his Danielle in his grasp, and he couldn't have felt happier.

The rather distressing call he had received from Michael had taken him by surprise, and he became frustrated by the upset that Michael had relayed. He felt helpless regarding Michael's situation, but consoled that he wanted to come back to the hotel, in an attempt to put together the pieces of his broken life. It hadn't even occurred to Mick to have Danielle accompany him, but to Panos, it made perfect sense. So, when they had spoken earlier and he suggested it to him and Michael agreed, Panos's plan for their return began to unravel. He realised that he could kill two birds with one stone. He would have the woman of his dreams back by his side, and at the same time help his good friend restore his somewhat miserable life.

He took hold of one of his pillows and held it tight as he imagined the prospect of the two people he loved dearly back at his hotel. He laughed out loud and squeezed the pillow tighter as the reality of this actually happening became imminent. He was however brought down to earth with a bump, when a picture of his father's stern face invaded his mind. He knew that his father would not be pleased with Danielle's return but felt comforted, when he remembered the positive opinion his brother had shared with him earlier.

"You have to grab every chance of happiness, even if it is temporary," Yannis had said.

"This could be the beginning of a good friendship. She is beautiful, and I know what I would do."

His brother's words echoed in his mind, birthing a strength that would enable him to deal with his father's predicted fury.

It's my life, and I'll do what I like with it, thought Panos defiantly, as he held on to the boldness that had been reborn. It's only for one week after all, so my father will have to deal with it, his train of thought continued flowing profusely, adding to the conception in his rebellious mind. The smile soon returned to his face, brought on by this wave of confidence. It never even crossed his mind that she wouldn't be coming back. Instead he revelled in the fact that she would soon be back by his side again.

He decided to take a shower. As the cool water rained down on him, he felt a song rise up from his heart and he started to sing. All his joy and happiness were in the lyrics of the song. His heartfelt words flew through the air like tiny air bubbles of life, brightening everything that they touched, bringing the colour back into his murky world. At last, he had regained his reason for living, and he allowed the happiness he felt, to take control over this new lease of life.

CHAPTER
FIVE

*M*ick woke up to the sun beaming on his face through the window. He opened his eyes and had to shut them again quickly, as its powerful rays made them smart. It was as if his eyes were being prodded by hundreds of tiny needles, causing them to water uncontrollably. His head was banging, and his insides were shaking. His first thought was about how he was going to bring his desperate body back into the land of the living. He couldn't ignore the usual craving for a drink to stabilise his delicate frame of mind, so with his eyes still closed, he felt around for his jacket in the hope of finding the only thing that would sustain his need.

To his relief he found half a litre bottle of vodka in one of his pockets. Without any hesitation he lifted the bottle to his mouth and proceeded to drink the contents down in one go. He could feel the flow of liquid instantly calming his nerves and leading him to continue to believe in the deception of this cure. He lay there for a few minutes welcoming the calmness that the vodka had provoked, until all the earlier shakiness had subsided. Finally, he found the courage to open his eyes again, and was overcome by the relief that they had stopped watering.

His mind went back to the previous night, as he tried desperately to retrace his movements. He remembered being with Danielle in the King's Head, talking to Panos and then going on to another pub a little while later, but then his mind went blank. At first, he racked his brains trying to fill in the missing gaps of his evening, but soon gave up because it was beginning to make his head hurt again. Instead, he wound his mind back to the vividness of his conversation with Panos, keeping it there, comforted by the memory. A smile swept across his face when he remembered the part he had played, in getting Panos and Danielle to talk to each other again, causing his heart to puff up with pride.

"See, I'm not such bad a bloke", he said as if to convince his hungover self.

Looking around the room he felt disorientated by his whereabouts, until he realised that he was in the spare bedroom of his parent's house. His feelings of loneliness from the night before began to re-surface as he came face to face with the prospect of having to spend his life alone. As a deep desperation won over his mind, this unwanted revelation triggered off his need for another drink, again telling him that this was the answer to his despair.

Leaning down he picked his phone up off the floor to check the time and noticed that he had a missed call from Matt. Going into his call log, he wanted to see if there were any clues to who he'd spoken to, when he came across Panos's number. The fogginess of his mind started to clear as he recalled the conversation with Panos late the previous night, jogging his memory about wanting to go back to the Skiathos. With the thought of escaping from his problems, his plan of returning suddenly made sense to him, and even became appealing to him.

He remembered Panos mentioning that Danielle should also accompany him, and this added to the reasons why he felt he should depart from his life in England. He made a mental note to speak to her about it, but first he wanted to return the missed call from Matt, as it could have been important. He missed having his right-hand man around and hoped that Matt had some good news about when he was coming home. His feelings of hope made a welcoming come back, weakening his need for a beer. Strengthened by his positive thoughts, he began dialling.

Matt was at a cafe eating breakfast with his brother-in-law when he received the call from Mick. His mind was in turmoil and he was in desperate need to talk to his best friend. He was relieved that Mick had finally phoned him. He had a very important decision to make, that could change the direction of his life, but he wanted to put it to Mick first before he made up his mind. It was good to hear a voice from home, and it caused a smile to sweep across his face, replacing the worried expression that he had worn over the past few days.

"So, Mick how are things down your end?" asked Matt casually, in an attempt to hide the discomfort of his divided mind.

"Things are good down here me ole mate, I've managed to catch up on a few old friends while you've been gone, so it's going well," he lied, trying to disguise the fact that he missed his company, and that he had never felt so alone.

"Well that's good. It's nice to hear that life is going on without me… So, how's work?"

This is the moment of truth, he thought, waiting for the right answer to confirm his reasons for going home.

"To be honest Matt, work is really bad. I have hardly done anything since you left. The work has been really scarce since that new garage opened up down the road," continued Mick only giving half the truth this time.

He was right in saying that work was bad, but the truth was that it was due to his lack of commitment to the job, and him spending most of his time in the pub. In reality it had little to do with the new garage that had just opened. He cringed at his deceitful statement, but soon dismissed it, as he couldn't own up to the real reason why his business was going down the drain.

"So, when are you coming home mate?" he asked optimistically in the hope that things would get back to normal, and pick up, whenever he did.

"Well that was what I wanted to talk to you about Mick," replied Matt hesitantly feeling quite anxious.

"Pete, my brother-in-law, has offered me a job up here, and I am in two minds about whether to accept his offer or not. And, to tell you the truth mate, I haven't got anything to come back for, and seeing that the work there is not good, it does seem like the right thing to do, but I just didn't know for sure. Speaking to you has kind of confirmed it for me," he admitted.

Silence fell between the two friends as Mick contemplated his life without Matt permanently. He felt quite hurt by his comment about not having anything to come back for, and suddenly realised then that their friendship didn't mean as much to Matt as it did him. He wanted to tell Matt of his feelings, but chose, to keep them to himself out of sheer stubbornness.

"I'm sorry to hear that Matt, but you've got to do what you've got to do," replied Mick hiding the disappointment in his voice.

An awkward silence fell again as Matt felt consumed with disappointment that Mick hadn't tried to talk him out of staying in Yorkshire but had instead accepted it so well. His apparent lack of concern hurt Matt immensely but helped him make his final decision, in taking up the offer of a new life away from Mick.

"So, how's Danielle? Have you seen much of her?" asked Matt, breaking through the silence.

"Danielle is good, and yes, I saw her yesterday, funny enough..." He hesitated, wondering if he should share their plans of going back to Greece. He took the plunge in the hope of projecting his hurt back onto Matt. "We are going back to Skiathos," he said smugly. "Panos has invited us back over there. She can't wait to go, and neither can I. We will be going in a few weeks."

"Oh...so...so she has spoken to him then? Well thanks Mick, I now know what to do. Speaking to you has made up my mind for me," he continued, feeling relieved to have finally had the confirmation that he needed for his decision.

Not only does Mick not care about what I do, but Danielle's put the boot in too, he thought. The thought of seeing her all happy about that man, ate him up inside, but he was comforted by the fact that those visions would soon cease as he would be two hundred miles away, and not have it continually rubbed in his face!

"OK then Mick, I'm going to go now. Take care and keep in touch."

"Yeah I will, you too mate, and good luck with your new life," said Mick finding it hard to disguise the sarcasm out of his voice. With that the phone line went dead, and Mick was left staring at the empty screen. His mind raced and he couldn't believe that he wouldn't see Matt again. This unforeseen situation fed his need for a drink, causing him to look at his watch. To his relief it was half past nine, and it was only half an hour before the King's Head would be open. He soon convinced himself that he could wait thirty minutes until his next fix, telling himself that a shower and shave would make the time pass quickly. The conversation with Matt increased his determination to leave England, and he couldn't wait to plan his escape with Danielle. With these comforting thoughts in mind, he got out of bed and jumped into the shower, because today was the day for new beginnings, for him too.

Danielle arrived at work and busied herself with getting the bar ready for opening time. Her mind was filled with excitement at the prospect of being with Panos again, and she couldn't wait until that evening when she would share her plans with her family. She had spoken to her mother that morning, explaining that she needed to see her later to ask her something. She didn't divulge any more information and was relieved that her mum had agreed without asking any more questions. She felt strangely confident regarding the outcome of her discussion later, but she still held on to the fact that realistically, things might not go as she had planned, because her family might not want her to go back to Skiathos. Her wishful thinking was restricted by this reality, so she decided not to get her hopes up, making a way for her to deal with disappointment incase it came. She put the last of the ash trays out on the tables and looked at the clock.

It was now ten o'clock, and Danielle looked around the bar, confident that it was now ready for opening. She walked over to the front door and opened it. It was unusual for there not to be anyone waiting, and she was somewhat confused by the lack of customers as she opened the door. This slight change of routine threw her because there was always someone for her to talk to, and now she was at a loss as to what to do. Hoping a customer would soon show up, she cleaned down the bar again, taking her mind off the boredom that came with having an empty bar. Pouring herself a coffee, she got out her paper. Just then the door opened and Jimmy a regular came in with a rather worried look on his face. He ordered his usual pint of bitter, and Danielle could not help but pick up on the distress in his voice.

"Here you go Jimmy," she said, placing his drink down in front of him. "Is everything alright?" she asked, as he gave her the money, taking a big gulp of his drink.

"Thanks Dan, and no, everything is not all right and neither am I to be honest sweetheart. I've just got back from the hospital, and they've said that I've got a brain tumour.

Apparently, I have to have an operation," he replied, taking another gulp of his pint.

Danielle's mouth dropped open and she was lost for words. She had always found time to talk to Jimmy, as he always made her laugh.

He was a typical cockney bloke, who was rough around the edges, but she was always intrigued by the tales of mischief that he shared. He had found love in the later years of his life, and was the father of two young girls, aged five and seven. The thought of them losing their father at such a young age made her want to cry.

"But, the chances of me surviving the op are quite high, so that's something to hang on to," he continued positively. "Oh Dan, did I tell you about the time that I worked on the docks..." he continued, completely changing the subject. She listened to his comical tale and was reduced to tears of laughter when it came to an end. By the time he had finished his story a few more customers had come into the bar, and he had them all laughing, instantly changing the atmosphere for the better.

Mick came hurtling in, causing everyone to turn their attention on him.

"I don't believe it; I nearly got knocked over by some idiot on a bike. He came out of nowhere when I was crossing the road, and he could have really hurt me. I think that someone is out to get me! ... Can I have a pint of the usual please, Dan?" he asked putting his fingers through his greying hair.

Danielle quickly obliged and laughed at the sight of her disheveled friend. His hair was all over the place, and his tanned face had gone as white as a sheet, causing her to be concerned for what had happened to him. But, when the truth behind his untidy look became apparent, all her worries disappeared, because this sort of thing seemed to happen wherever Mick went.

As she gave him his beer, he broke the news to her about Matt not coming back. She was stopped in her tracks as she listened to Mick's explanation as to why Matt was not coming home. She felt hurt that she had to hear it third hand, and that Matt didn't even have the decency to tell her himself!

"So that's it Dan, no more Matt, no more friendship. At least we have Skiathos to look forward to aye Dan?"

She looked at him and could detect a twinkle in his bloodshot eyes. He smiled at her which she found infectious and smiled back. She couldn't help wondering if his blasé attitude towards Matt was genuine. Her eyes fixed on his, searching for any sign of disappointment, but she was met by a look of excitement and nothing else.

Well you hide it well, she thought, not quite convinced of his statement of closure. She couldn't help thinking about the conversation that had taken place between them the previous night, when she was confronted with a heartbroken man overwrought with despair at the breakup of his marriage. She found it hard to believe that she was looking at the same man.

"Dan why are you staring at me like that?" he said concerned by the suspicious look in her eye. "You're beginning to scare me. I never trust a woman that stares at me, because they are usually plotting to do something horrible to me," he said, distracting her from her thoughts. She laughed at his comment. He took a long swig of his drink, and she soon realised that he was being deadly serious.

"Don't exaggerate Mick! Anyway, I was just thinking about Skiathos, and wondering whether or not I will be going back there," she lied, secretly congratulating herself on her swiftness in getting back on to the subject of Skiathos.

"Well, I do hope so, Dan, but I am going whatever happens."

She laughed again at his flippancy and explained about Panos's generous offer to pay for her airfare. She also told him of her intentions of putting the idea of the trip to her family, with the hope that they would all agree that she could go.

"Good luck with that, Dan, I am sure that it will be OK. Now, where is Jimmy, I need to talk to him about some work." With that, he grabbed his drink and walked over to the table where Jimmy was sitting reading the paper.

Her working day soon passed, and she was relieved when it was finally time to go home. Like any other day, when it was home time for her, all the regulars were their usual drunk selves. The thing that bothered her about this was their repeated chat up lines, because they got louder and bolder as the day went on. She had heard it all before and was always relieved to leave them behind, her as she walked out of the door.

As she left, she reassured Mick that she would phone him as soon as she knew if she was going away, but he seemed more interested in his conversation with Maggie, the busty barmaid, who'd taken over from her. She laughed at the way he blatantly stared at her chest while he spoke, not even able to take his eyes off it, even when she said goodbye.

Danielle picked Charlie up from school and then went home. She could feel a bubble in her heart and thanked her lucky stars that Panos had made her feel this way. Charlie was his usual talkative self and shared with his mother every every detail of his lunchtime football match, the excitement evident in his voice. He took her through every move that led to him scoring a goal. She felt so honoured to have him as a son that her bubbling heart could have burst with pride.

When they got home, Charlie went out into the garden to play, whilst she prepared the dinner. She was halfway through peeling the potato's when there was a knock at the door, and she was pleased to see that it was her mother. Christine came in carrying her usual bag of goodies and placed it down on the table.

"So, Dan what did you want to ask me?" she asked smiling as she looked at her daughter, smiling.

"Mum, I'm sorry, but you'll have to wait until Billy and Marie are here, then I will put you out of your misery," she replied, carrying on peeling the potatoes.

"He's asked you to go back, hasn't he? Panos, I mean," she asked, her eyes still fixed on Danielle. "I am right, aren't I Dan?"

Danielle carried on ignoring her mother's inquisitiveness, but a smile escaped from her lips, confirming Christine's suspicions.

"I knew it, Danielle; didn't I say that he would want you to go back? Oh darling, this is so exciting, I hope that you told him yes."

"Mum, I cannot presume that you would have my children, plus they have to be happy with it too," replied Danielle, wiping her hands.

She hesitated. "So, does that mean that you don't mind looking after the kids, I mean if I do decide to go back?"

"No, Sweetheart," replied Christine taking her daughter's hands.

"I've never seen you look so happy! Anyway, I knew that it would happen, so I'm prepared, and I thought that I could look after them here." Danielle burst out laughing at her mother's presumptuous thinking and concluded that her mum was more excited than she was.

Charlie came in from the garden and was happy to see his Nan and lunged himself at her, in order to plant a big kiss on her cheek. Before she could say anything to her over excited grandson, Danielle quickly put her finger up to her mouth shaking her head and forbidding her to say anything. Christine understood her daughter's sign of secrecy, so just inquired about his day. Danielle listened intently to Charlie's recital of his football match and laughed because it was even more dramatic than the version, he had told her earlier. The same familiar wave of pride swept over her, as Charlie had his Nan hanging on his every word. When he got to the part where he scored a goal, he staged the same manoeuvre, almost kicking her in the shin. Their laughter rippled through the air, and Christine was thankful that he had remembered to take his football boots off.

After his repeated performance, Danielle told him to get changed out of his school uniform. A still excited Charlie pulled his t-shirt over his face and proceeded to run up the stairs. Christine chose this opportunity to put the kettle on but couldn't help herself from gloating about her earlier prediction.

"I knew that he would ask you back," she repeated. "I knew it Danielle, a mother knows these things."

"OK mother, yes, you were right, but I have to see what Billy and Marie think, so don't go jumping the gun," replied Danielle looking sternly at her mother.

"Oh, Dan, they'll be fine. I'm sure that they would love to spend time with their Nan. They know that I'll spoil them rotten."

"That could be true mother, but I still have to ask them first."

They heard the key go in the front door as Marie walked into the house.

"Where is your brother Marie?" asked Danielle, confused that she had come in alone.

"Oh, hello to you too mum," replied Marie sarcastically laughing. "Billy is walking up the road with one of his friends. He is so slow, and they were talking about boring football, so I left them to it," she continued, putting her hand up to her mouth and faking a yawn. "What's for dinner; I am starving?" she continued into the kitchen and started rummaging through the cupboards, looking for a fix for her hunger.

"Don't eat too much because dinner will be ready in half an hour," replied Danielle shouted out into the kitchen. "And don't go off anywhere because I need to speak to you."

"What have I done wrong now? Whatever it is, it wasn't me it was Billy," replied Marie walking into the front room eating a sausage roll.

"What have I done? I wasn't even here…Mum tell Marie, will you? She's poking her tongue out at me," complained Billy as he walked through the door giving his sister an irate look.

"And you've got the nerve to put that back into your mouth, err you're disgusting," he continued, pulling a funny face at his sister.

"Stop it you two, no one has done anything wrong, I just need to put something to all three of you," replied Danielle, gesturing them over to the settee with her hands. She proceeded to call Charlie down, telling him to hurry up and get downstairs.

"Mum, this must be serious if it involves Charlie, because he can't make his mind up about what colour cup to use," said Marie, laughing out loud, causing Billy to agree with her and laugh too. Danielle chose to ignore her daughter's sarcastic comment and waited patiently for Charlie to come back down.

Five minutes later Charlie made an entrance wearing a bright green top mismatched with a pair of orange and yellow shorts. Danielle tutted at her son's uncoordinated attire and desperately tried to ignore the need to make him go back upstairs to change again. She gestured to him to sit down next to his brother. Pleased to have their undivided attention she chose her words carefully.

"Right, where shall I begin?" she started, trying to find the right words to say.

"Well, you all know about Panos…well… well, he phoned me last night… and he… he…"

"He's asked you to go back, hasn't he Mum? I knew he would," Marie said excitedly, stopping her mother in mid-sentence.

"Well yes, actually he did, and I was just..."

"I knew it! What did I say? Oh Mum, I hope you said yes!" She said interrupting, a big smile, staining her face.

"Does this mean that I'll be staying with you again Nan?" Billy then piped up, excited at the prospect of being with his Nan again.

"Well yes, and no, because your Nan will be staying..." replied Danielle trying to get a word in.

"That's good, because I liked staying at your house; we can watch DVD's again, and I can stay up late," continued Billy ignoring his mother.

"But... but will you be coming back, Mummy? I don't want you to live with Pasmos, and you can't even speak Greek," intervened Charlie looking very confused and not feeling as enthusiastic as the others.

"Don't be silly Charlie, of course she'll be coming back," replied Marie trying to reassure her younger brother when she noticed the concerned look on his face.

"Maybe Panos will come back with you," she continued refixing her gaze on to her mother.

"No Marie, he won't be coming back with me and no Charlie, I'm not staying there, I'll definitely be coming home; it's just for a week and your Nan will stay ..."

"What new films you got Nan? I can borrow the new James Bond film from my friend, I'm sure he won't mind. Can I sleep on the settee? Oh, please Nan..." said Billy looking at his Nan for her approval.

"Will you all be quiet and let me speak please!" interrupted Danielle needing to raise her voice and wait until the room went quiet. "Thank you, now, I can hear myself think..." she continued. "Now, Panos has asked me to go back in a couple of weeks, but only for one week this time. I wanted to ask you all if that was OK, and judging by your excitement, I'm guessing that the answer to that is yes? Your Nan has kindly suggested that she stays here to look after you, which I am happy to let her do. So, is everyone happy with this arrangement? Charlie are you OK with me going away again?" she asked turning her attention to her youngest son who was looking a bit lost.

"Charlie, sweetheart, is that OK? If not, I won't go."

"Charlie, it'll be alright," both Billy and Marie said together still trying to reassure him.

"Nanny will look after you and so will I," continued Marie. "Mummy must go back, Charlie; she loves Panos, and he makes her happy. You want Mummy to be happy, don't you?"

Charlie nodded at his sister's statement and then looked at his mother.

"I do want you to be happy, and... And, you will come back, won't you?" Danielle nodded, completely compelled by his sensitivity.

"You promise?" he asked looking deep into her eyes, as he still wasn't sure.

"I promise, darling, I promise."

"OK then, can I go out to play in the garden?" he asked causing Danielle to laugh. "Yes Charlie, you can go out to play." With that, Charlie got off the settee and ran out into the garden.

Danielle breathed in a deep sigh of relief and was somewhat surprised at how it had all turned out. She sent her two remaining children upstairs to get on with their homework until dinner was ready.

"Well, that was easier than I thought it would be," noted Danielle as she turned to her mother, who was grinning from ear to ear.

"I knew that it would be... Oh Sweetheart, I am so excited for you. Just think in a few weeks time, you will be back in the arms of the man of your dreams," replied Christine hugging her daughter.

"Oh Mum, you are so mushy, what are you like?"

Now that everything was all agreed and approved of by her family, Danielle allowed her mind to wander. She had to admit that she couldn't wait to see Panos again. She was relieved to know that her children were all for her return to Skiathos but couldn't help feeling a little bit sad that they didn't need much persuading.

In fact, they didn't need persuading at all, she thought feeling slightly disappointed.

The excitement however of actually returning to the island over ruled her sadness, as she imagined being back in Panos's loving arms again.

"Oh Mum, I can't believe that I am going back," she shrieked, unable to contain her excitement any longer. "I can't believe that I'll be seeing him again. Thank you for being the best mum in the world and making it possible for me to go." She grabbed her mum by the arm, pulled her close to her and began kissing her numerous times on the cheek.

"That's OK my darling, it is my pleasure. It is just so good to see you this happy, and I would do anything for that to happen." Danielle stopped in mid kiss, overcome by an amazing love for her mother. This overpowering feeling brought tears to her eyes, and she couldn't have wished for a better mum.

"Now Dan you had better let Mick know what's happening," suggested Christine becoming aware of her daughter's watery eyes, as she tried desperately to hold back her own tears.

"Yes, but I have to wait until I've spoken to Panos first. You never know, he might have changed his mind," laughed Danielle half-heartedly.

"I doubt that very much," replied Christine enthusiastically. "I doubt that very much," she repeated, emphasising the last two words.

The sun shone through the open window, and gently brushed against Panos's cheeks, transporting him out of his restful sleep. His first thoughts were of Danielle, instantly bringing a smile to his face. He suddenly realised that it was the first full night's sleep that he had managed to have, in a long time. He was so grateful for the calmness that he felt inside, and he knew that Danielle was responsible for his new frame of mind. He couldn't wait to hear the outcome of her decision, regarding whether or not she would be returning to the island.

He went about his normal routine, filling his day with the usual demands that came with running a popular hotel. His newly revived inspiration for life helped him deal with his workload, lifting the anxieties that went with his position as manager. His hopeful thoughts of Danielle's return eased this burden immensely, willing the smile to stay upon his face.

His father had also noticed his son's cheerier mood and was somewhat confused by the happy Panos that had resurfaced. Remembering how his son was when Danielle was around, his apprehensive mind became suspicious, but he soon dismissed these notions as being silly, and instead convinced himself that Panos had finally gotten over his English lady. With this in mind he straightened his back and held his head up high as he walked across the lounge towards the restaurant. On route, he greeted his two sons, who were at the bar, with a smile.

I feel that today is going to be a good day, he thought proudly, when he was met by giggling coming from the kitchen.

He stopped in mid flow when he thought that he heard Danielle's name being mentioned. Instantly his heart began to race with anger and his stomach churned as he strained his ears to hear his wife's conversation with Anna. Then he heard it again, confirming his earlier fears, and he shook his head in disbelief.

"I hope that Danielle does come back, it would be so good to see her again," his future daughter in law said in excitement.

"Yes Anna, she is so good for Panos, and it is lovely to see him happy again since he has spoken to her," replied his wife enthusiastically.

He couldn't believe what he was hearing and had no idea that Panos had even had a conversation with Danielle. Suddenly the penny dropped and Panos's sudden change of mood made sense to him, sending him into a furious rage. He had convinced himself that this English lady was now a thing of the past, where he had left Elizabeth, and he had even been thankful that the lid of that box was well and truly shut. But, now the very mention of Danielle and what his son felt for her brought back to the surface his own buried feelings. The memory of Elizabeth's face furiously entered into his mind, and he was thrown into uncontrollable confusion. His very being was torn in two, his mind was telling him one thing and his heart was telling him another. He couldn't afford to let his heart get the better of him, so he went with his mind, allowing its logic to take over. This seemed to work, as it configured his disarrayed heart into believing the consequences of Danielle's return. I cannot let this happen, he thought to himself. I have to do something now! So, with that, he turned around and marched back out into the lounge.

"Panos I need to speak to you in my office," he said sternly, ignoring the smile on Panos's face. "Now!" he bellowed across the room, causing both Panos and Yannis to jump at the tone of his voice.

The smile quickly fell from Panos's face, and he looked at his brother, confused. Yannis looked back at him and shrugged his shoulders, unaware of the motive behind their father's sudden change of mood. Without saying a word; Panos followed his father's command and reluctantly followed him up to the office. His insides began to shake, for the harshness of his father's words provoked a wave of nervousness to come over him, but he continued to tell himself to just stay calm. He walked into the room and shut the door behind him. His father walked over to the window and looked out over the pool.

"So, son I hear that we are going to get another visit from Dan... Dan..." stated his father, finding it hard to get her name out of his mouth! "From that English woman," He continued, his eyes staying fixed on the guests around the pool.

"You mean Danielle, Papa, her name is Danielle, and yes...yes, she most likely will be coming back," replied Panos looking down to the ground.

"I thought that it was all over between you two," accused his father. "You know my feelings towards her and that I do not agree with you being together, so why have you gone out of your way to defy me?" he asked, turning around to face his son. "Panos look at me when I am talking to you," he demanded.

Panos did as he was told and looked up into his father's eyes, and he was shocked to see them so full of anger.

"But Papa, I love her, and I..." he stammered.

"Love!" his father huffed. "How can it be love? You've only known her for five minutes. You don't know the meaning of the word... Love indeed, you fool," he laughed mockingly. "Panos, I've never stopped you from doing anything before, but... but if you do not stop her from coming back then I will forbid it. Do you understand?"

Panos stood still, frozen by his father's unfair statement. He felt like a child again until this unwanted feeling gave way for strength to rise up and take him over, instantly feeding his courage to speak out.

"Papa, please listen to me. I know that I've not known her for long, but I have tried to forget her, but can't ignore my feelings. I don't want to fall out with you over this. I speak the truth however when I say that I'm not a child that needs to be controlled. Rather, I'm a man who knows his own heart, and you've always told us to be honest."

Panos searched his father's face for any sign of understanding and surrender, but instead was met by a coldness that sent shivers down his spine.

"I do not care for your empty words. That's all they are, because they mean nothing to me. She'll hurt you. English women are not soft-hearted like Greek women. They are shallow, and superficial and only out to get what they want; I know this for a fact, son. Believe me when I say that she will hurt you," his father replied, banging his fists down on the desk in frustration.

Panos was taken aback by this outburst, but decided he was not going to be intimidated, not even by his father.

"How do you know that?" he shouted back. "And, how do you know how I feel? You talk like you have been in love with an English woman yourself," stated Panos sarcastically.

"That's because I have!" his father blurted out before he could control his words, instantly regretting this truthful admission from his past.

Panos's mouth dropped open and he was lost for words, as he stared at this man that he thought he knew.

"But how... and when? Does mother know?" he asked urgently, as his mind suddenly went into overdrive. He put two and two together and concluded that his father must have had an affair.

"No, she does not, and she must never know about this conversation, because it happened before I met her!"

His voice quietened down, and his heart softened as he decided to confide in his son about his time with Elizabeth. Panos listened intently to his father's story of love and was shocked to find that he was more like his father than he realised. He was surprised at the honesty that was shared, and he couldn't help letting his heart go out to his father as he began to appreciate the truth behind his father's reasoning concerning Danielle.

"So, you see Panos, I do know, and I'm grateful for the part your Grandfather played in my situation. Now do you understand my concern?"

Panos just nodded, trying desperately to identify with what had been said. He couldn't help wondering if his father was right in his description of English ladies. Almost immediately a picture of Danielle came into his mind. He was reminded of how she was with him and found the picture his father had painted, hard to believe.

"But Papa, Danielle is not like that, and anyway, I know that she will never be my wife, and that this is the inevitable outcome. I just love being with her." Panos hesitated, looking honestly into his father's eyes. "She makes me happy, and I haven't felt that way since Sophia. You have nothing to worry about though because, one day I will marry a good Greek girl, just like mother, I promise." He took hold of his father's hand. "Please be happy for me and give me your blessing; it would mean so much to me."

His father thought long and hard about his answer. Finally, his heart relented, and he couldn't help feeling empathy towards his son and how he felt about Danielle. He was also comforted by the fact that one day he would have a Greek girl to call his daughter-in-law, and this idea softened his heart more.

"OK Panos, you have my blessing, but this conversation must stay between these four walls, OK?" He couldn't have stated this more, but he also couldn't help feeling somewhat relieved to have shared the secret that had been a huge burden on his heart for so many years.

"Thank you. You are a wonderful father, and I love you very much," said Panos relieved. He pulled his father towards him and embraced him.

"Now, that's enough of that, son, haven't you got work to do?" he asked pulling away, his cheeks going scarlet red, because of this show of affection.

Panos nodded and then left the office to get back to the bar. He couldn't help thinking about the story that he'd just heard, and he couldn't believe that his father had kept Elizabeth a secret for all these years. The way that he'd been treated by Elizabeth had made him try to convince him to believe that Danielle was exactly the same. But he quickly disarmed the deception of this lie, by reminding himself that she was totally different from Elizabeth. In fact she was like no one that he had ever met before!

Looking at his watch, he hoped his timing was right and that all the guests were out visiting the town. His prediction was confirmed when he was met with an empty bar, and he decided to take the opportunity to phone Danielle. Going behind the bar, he stopped when he looked over to his brother who was washing up the glasses. Yannis noticed his brother walk back in and returned his glance, concerned for the meeting that he he'd just had with their father.

"Is everything OK, Panos?" he asked, stopping in mid-flow, waiting anxiously for a reply.

"Yes, my good brother, everything is hunky dory," he replied in posh English accent.

"Now, I am going to phone Danielle, so no interruptions please," he laughed sarcastically, reaching for his phone.

Danielle and her mum were clearing up after dinner when the call came from Panos. It was a lot earlier than she had expected and her phone was left unattended on the coffee table in the front room.

"Will someone please get that?" shouted Danielle from the kitchen, oblivious to who the caller was. Billy's eyes stayed glued to the TV, so Marie, feeling quite agitated by her brother's ignorance, got up to answer it.

"Hello," she said sternly, not recognising the unusual number that was displayed on the screen. "What do you want?"

Suddenly a smile swept across her face, and her eyes lit up when she heard the unfamiliar, accented voice, that quickly revealed the identity of the person on the other end of the line.

"Oh, could you just hold on please and I will get her?" she replied politely, putting the phone down to her chest.

Danielle walked into the room, noticed that her daughter was waving her free hand around in the air and was rather puzzled by this strange display of behaviour.

"It's Panos," mouthed Marie, the phone still held close to her chest.

"Who?" asked Danielle, still perplexed as she had been unable to make out what her daughter had said.

"Mum, it's Panos," she replied a little louder this time pointing at the phone.

"Well give it to me then, Marie," said Danielle wiping her hands, reaching for the receiver.

"Hello Panos, I wasn't expecting you to call so early." The excitement in her voice was evident, and the twinkle in her eyes made a comeback as she ushered Marie to sit down next to Billy. Marie did as her mother instructed, but her eyes stayed fixed on her as she spoke. Billy also watched their mother, as the mention of Panos's name had been a good enough reason to steal his attention away from the TV.

"Hello Danielle, I couldn't wait to speak to you, and all of the guests are away from the bar. So my beautiful lady, am I right in presuming that you will be coming back to my hotel?" he asked, holding his breath.

"I've spoken to my family, and... And they all agree that I should go back, so...so yes, I will be back at your hotel."

"That's wonderful, just wonderful," said Panos breathing in a deep sigh of relief. "Don't worry about anything because I'll sort out everything with Michael. I can't believe that I will be seeing you again."

His heart fluttered as he imagined her back by his side. A self-assured, glow radiated from his face as he spoke. On this occasion the conversation was short. It ended with Panos confirming his intention to take care of the arrangements, explaining he would phone Mick as soon as he had finished talking to her. Once they had said their goodbyes, Danielle was confronted by six pairs of beady eyes staring at her. Silent anticipation took the opportunity to steal the moment, as they waited patiently for her to break the silence and say something. She kept them hanging a little longer, and then blurted out,

"Well it looks like I am going back to the Oasis Hotel," she finally announced, a big smile spreading across her face.

"That's great," they all answered in chorus, as she opened her arms to claim her family.

"I am actually going to be with him again," she shrieked. "I am so excited." They danced around the room singing 'Holiday' at the top of their voices.

Panos became a man on a mission, and called Mick, immediately afterwards and was delighted to find him still quite sober. He explained his plans for their return to Mick, who was only too happy to book the flights at his end. Panos reassured him that he would repay him for Danielle's airfare, and thankfully Mick was content with this arrangement.

The following morning, on his way down to the pub, he stopped off at the travel agents and booked two tickets to Skiathos for ten days time. He relished the thought of being out of the country again; hardening his heart into convincing himself that he had managed to get one over on his estranged wife, yet again. These strengthening thoughts lessened his need for a beer, because the stress of his life was lifted for the time being, making him believe that he now had it under control again.

Confidently strolling into the King's Head instigated by these new positive thoughts and feelings, he informed Danielle that their holiday was now all booked. He took great pleasure in seeing the sheer look of delight on her face when he handed her the tickets! She was overwhelmed by the proof of their return, placed in her hands.

"So, Dan in ten days time I shall be back by the pool and you will be back in Panos's arms. It doesn't get any better than that! Hello Skiathos, we're coming back."

CHAPTER
SIX

*T*he day of their departure finally arrived, and Danielle busied herself with last minute preparations that she needed to make before leaving her children again. Their flight wasn't until lunchtime, so with her mind distracted by these finalities, her excitement was kept adequately under control. She had said her goodbyes that morning, when she saw Billy and Marie off to school, but she couldn't help feeling apprehensive about leaving them. Marie, however, soon took on the parental role, encouraging Danielle that they would be fine, and that she should just worry about having a great time with Panos.

Billy backed up his sister's words of reassurance, and Danielle was slightly hurt by their laid-back attitude. She suddenly realised how grown up they were, and this harsh reality took her by surprise. It seemed their dependency on her seemed to lessen with every passing day. She got some comfort by reminding herself that this was a good thing, because she had managed to pass on the great attribute of independence that was installed in her by her own mother. She was overwhelmed by the familiar sense of pride that confirmed her role of being a good parent, which quickly extinguished the doubts that had invaded her mind.

Her next task had been getting Charlie off to school. This proved to be a bit more difficult, as he struggled to let go of his mother's hand. She did her very best to reassure him that he would have a great time with his Nan, and that she would be home before he knew it. She continued declaring her love for him, hoping he would trust her words, but his grip tightened. A lump rose up in her throat when she noticed tears in his eyes, and she could have so easily cancelled her trip at that point. She made a final attempt to sway her son into believing that she would return home, by saying that she would bring a big present back with her for him, even bigger than before. This shot at bribery finally did the trick, and eventually he let go of her hand and ran off to be with his friend. Danielle couldn't help but laugh at the swiftness of her son's sudden change of mind, but she was relieved to know that she could put the smile back on her face again.

Mick's day started in the usual way, with an overwhelming desire for a drink that was hard to ignore. His first thoughts were typical of his daily routine, and now he had accepted that a shot or two of vodka was the only way to kick start his body back to life. He stayed in his bed for a few minutes, welcoming the return of his sanity, and was relieved to find that his mind was finally breaking through the thick fog that clouded it.

With his newly revived body and mind, he focused his thoughts into what he needed to do to get ready for his escape. He had booked the taxi for half nine and had informed Danielle that he would pick her up on the way. He was relieved to find that he had an hour to spare, so chose to use this time carefully to prepare for his departure. Suddenly, an overpowering sense of excitement enveloped him, and he pulled himself out of bed and got into the shower. A smile formed across his face as he imagined being back in the Greek sunshine, and this made him hurry to get ready. Thankfully the taxi arrived on time, and he was relieved that he was all packed when he heard the welcoming sound of the car horn tooting outside. Saying goodbye to his parents he got into the car to make the journey to collect Danielle.

Danielle waited patiently for the taxi to arrive and felt the usual flutter of butterflies in her stomach when it pulled up outside. She placed a small note on the table with a list of instructions for her mother, double checked that all the windows and doors were locked, picked up her suitcase and walked out to the car. Mick got out to help her with her bags, and she was pleased to find him smiling from ear to ear.

"Well Dan, this is it babe. The time has finally arrived, and I'm so glad that we're getting out of here," he said excitedly.

She just nodded and smiled when she imagined seeing Panos again. Finding it hard to believe she was actually going back, she wondered what the week ahead had in store for her. Overcome by a deep sense of nervousness; the thought of stepping back into his life again plagued her with doubts.

What if I am making a huge mistake? She thought as a picture of Charlie's sad face invaded her mind. What if mum can't cope without me? As these thoughts ran through her mind, she felt the vibration of the phone in her bag. She was pleased to see that it was a text message from her mum, telling her not to worry and reassuring her that everything was going to be OK. She reminded her that she must have a good time and that she loved her very much. Her mum's uncanny timing quashed her doubts, causing the nervousness to fade, and her smile reappeared.

When they arrived at the airport, Danielle breathed in the busy atmosphere as Mick paid the driver. The infectious excitement of other holidaymakers filled the air, which helped confirm to her that she was doing the right thing by going back to Skiathos. Before long, she too felt excited, and her mind became free enough to relax and start to enjoy herself.

The two friends chatted while they waited to board the plane, touching on the subject of Matt and Stuart, reminiscing back to when all four of them were there not so long ago. It did feel strange that Matt was no longer around, but they both agreed that they would still have a good time without him. Instead, they raised their glasses to their absent friend, wishing him luck in his new life, and then quickly changed the subject. The time soon came for them to make their way over to the boarding lounge, where they were ushered onto the plane.

Panos's heart beat with a rhythm of pure joy, because this day was finally bringing his Danielle back to him. He had set his mind on her arrival and on all the things that they would do together, filling him with anticipation. He took great delight in getting his room ready for her, and was grateful for his mother's contribution of flowers, bringing the finishing touches of decoration to brighten the place up. He smiled at her willingness to help, and realised that she was just as excited to see her as he was. This unprovoked display of kindness didn't surprise him, because his mum had told him plainly of her feelings towards Danielle, explaining in great detail her liking for this English lady. Her generosity and loving words reinforced his belief that she was the best mother a man could ever wish for.

The morning brought about its usual duties, prompting the time to fly by until it was time to go down to the airport to pick up his favoured guests. He took it upon himself to meet them personally, choosing to do so in his father's Mercedes, and seeing that there were the only two guests to arrive, this was an easy task to organise. With the room and car ready, all Panos could do now was wait until four o'clock when the plane was due to land. He had informed all the hotel guests, of his coming visitors, explaining that they were very good friends from England. He couldn't hide the fact that Danielle was an extra special guest, because his whole face lit up at the very mention of her name. The hint of vulnerability that escaped through his sparkling eyes left an opening for him to be teased by some of the guests, but it was too late for him to defend himself, because even he knew that his feelings couldn't be disguised. Instead, he played the game as the banter flew across the bar, secretly knowing that he had one up on them, and he couldn't wait to see their faces when they saw his beautiful Danielle.

The flight was a good one, and Danielle's heart missed a beat when the Captain informed them that they were now flying over Skiathos. As the Island was so small, they had to circle it a couple of times before landing and both Mick and Danielle were relieved that the weather was very good. There was not a cloud in the sky, so the view of the island was not restricted like it had been on their previous trip. Looking out of the window, the butterflies in her stomach trebled when she was confronted with the beautiful sight that awaited her. She was immediately captivated by its vision of beauty, and the feeling of awe it inspired took her breath away.

Mick watched her as she stared out of the window and felt proud to have her as a friend. Her stunning good looks had caught the attention of every man on the plane; and every woman who couldn't help noticing their partner's dumbstruck glare. Mick found it amusing that Danielle was oblivious to all the attention she courted and the stir that she was causing. This air of vulnerability that she radiated reminded him why it had been so easy for Panos to fall in love with her, and this made his smile widen. He wondered if he would ever meet such a great lady, one that he too could fall in love with.

I doubt that very much, he thought, drinking down the last drop of his drink. No one's going to want a drunken, old fool like me. He was quickly brought out of his thoughts when the deafening sound of the brakes shook the plane. Twenty minutes later the two friends were walking through the Greek airport in search of their luggage.

Looking at his watch, Panos noticed it was time to go down to the airport at last. Ignoring the childish jibes coming from the guests as he passed the pool laughing, he put his hand up and waved dismissively at them. It surprised him that he felt nervous, but the thought of seeing his lovely lady helped him keep his nerves under control. He ran through the lounge where Yannis was standing talking to a guest and informed him where he was going. Yannis laughed at his brother's eagerness to get out of the hotel and was elated for him knowing the reason behind this enthusiastic departure.

Panos jumped into the newly polished Mercedes and began the short drive down to the airport. For the first time since Danielle had gone home, he let the sound of a love song fill the car, freeing his mind to remember how amazing it felt to have her by his side. The captivating memory of her, stole his heart which palpitated at the thought that, in a short while, the memory of her was to become reality. Singing as he drove down the winding road, the words of the song were so relevant that it was as if he had written it himself! They just confirmed his feelings for her, and he could have cried for joy.

Turning into the high street, he became agitated by all the people that were being so inconsiderate by idly walking across the road, and in the way. Their casual attitude annoyed him because he was conscious of the time, so he honked his horn in the hope of hurrying them along. The sudden blast that was sounded, and the stern look on his face, seemed to do the trick, and the rather irate tourists got out of his way. He finally arrived at the airport, found a place to park and made his way over to the entrance.

The place was teeming with holiday makers, and Panos strained his eyes to see if there was any sign of his friends. He found it hard to distinguish them from the huge number of people that crowded his view, so waited patiently by the main doors. Ten minutes passed, but he never let his eyes stray from the oncoming array of visitors in the hope of recognising a familiar face. His heartbeat quickened as he began to panic at the thought of Danielle changing her mind at the last minute. He tried desperately to convince himself that he was just being silly, but as the time went by, this dreadful realisation soon trained his mind into believing his conclusion. Disappointment consumed him as the crowd began to filter out, and with still no sign of Danielle, he turned around and headed out of the door.

Danielle and Mick waited patiently for their luggage. They had been standing next to the conveyer belt for what seemed like forever, when Danielle's suitcase finally came through. Hers was the last to come off the plane, and Mick's face dropped to the floor because for some strange reason his was nowhere to be seen. The thought of having to wear the same clothes for a week flashed through his mind, and this was beginning to annoy him. Danielle detected the fury in his eyes and did her best to calm him down. However, he ignored her words as she tried to pacify him and walked over to a Customs Officer who was standing by the exit.

"Oi, you!" said Mick angrily, tapping the man on his shoulder. The officer looked around startled, and instinctively pointed his rifle at Mick's head.

"Easy Bert, there's no need for that; I'm English you know," said Mick, looking down the barrel, shaking, and putting his hands up in the air. The man just looked at him and made no attempt to take the gun away.

"I only wanted to ask you if you had any idea where my suitcase was. I seem to have lost it," explained Mick calmly. "It didn't come off the plane."

The Officer shouted something in Greek to his colleague, who came over to assist.

"What's the problem here?" asked the second man sternly. "And, why are you harassing my officer?"

Mick felt slightly put out by this man's question but was relieved to find that at least he spoke English. He began to explain his dilemma to him, hoping he could help find his lost luggage. When he finished, the man, without saying a word, turned around and walked away. Mick feeling very frustrated, looked at Danielle and threw his hands up in the air in disbelief.

Ten minutes later the man returned and explained that, for some reason, his luggage wasn't put on the plane. He apologised for the misunderstanding and took a contact number, so that when it came in, they would let him know so that he could collect it. Mick was about to give him a piece of his mind but thought twice about it when he noticed that the first man was still there holding the gun. Instead, he just nodded his head and kept his frustrated feelings to himself.

Danielle was still standing by the conveyer belt, watching from a distance as the men walked away. She couldn't believe they hadn't even been on the island for an hour and Mick had managed to catch everyone's eye by having a gun pointed at his head! She could see the disgust on the faces of onlookers and laughed that he had managed to become the centre of attention, yet again. Finally, she walked over to him to find out what was happening concerning his suitcase.

"Did you see that, Dan?" he asked. "He pointed that thing right at my head and could have really hurt me," he complained loudly.

Taking his arm, she escorted him to the main entrance, ignoring his exaggerated statement.

"Bloody Greeks, who do they think they are?" he continued, lowering his voice as they walked past the customs officer who earlier held the gun.

Danielle picked up the pace when she realised the time, feeling anxious that they had missed Panos. When they came to the main part of the airport, ignoring Mick's repeated story of his near-death experience, she scanned the room for Panos in desperation. Sheer horror consumed her when he was nowhere to be seen, and her blood ran cold at the disappointment she felt for him having to go off without them.

"Now look what you have done, Mick, Panos has gone," she blurted out accusingly, finding it hard to disguise the fury in her voice.

"Now hold on, Dan, it wasn't my fault that they lost my case," he replied, feeling hurt by the misplaced blame that she had put on his shoulders.

"I was only standing up for my rights, Dan. Anyway, Panos could still be here," he said scanning the room for his Greek friend.

He looked over to the entrance, stopped and strained his

eyes on the back of a man who was walking out of the doors.

"There he is... Panos!" he shouted out, pointing to the entrance as he quickly recognised this man to be his Greek friend.

"Hey, Panos, wait up mate. We're here!"

Danielle looked in the direction where Mick was indicating with his finger, and her heart stopped when she realised that Mick was right. It was Panos after all. She stopped and suddenly it felt like everything was going in slow-motion, as Panos turned around, a huge smile sweeping across his handsome face. As he came closer, his recognition sparked off a twinkle in his eyes, which instantly reminded her why she had fallen in love with him. All the love she felt for him jerked her heart back into life, and it began to beat faster in her chest, permitting time to return back to its usual speed.

"Hello, my friend, sorry we're late, but there was a bit of a mix up with my luggage," explained Mick, putting his hand out to greet him. Panos, without saying a word, quickly shook Mick's hand. His eyes, though, remained firmly on Danielle. His inability to talk was evident as he stared into her big emerald eyes. All that he could do was smile. She smiled back at him, and his heart melted as her eyes shone like precious jewels, hypnotising him into an unavoidable trance. Without thinking, he took her hand and held it tight. His touch sent a surge of electricity up her arm, causing goose bumps to erupt all over her skin. He sighed deeply at the picture of loveliness before him. It was as if she had never left.

As silence reigned, Danielle thought that her heart was going to burst. All the emotions that she had put neatly away gushed up to the surface, pushing back the boundaries that were safeguarding them. Once again, time stood still as their eyes were locked together; it was as if they were the only two people in the room. The moment was interrupted when Mick cleared his throat in the attempt to disturb the couple, quickly reminding them that he was there. The rough, gruffly noise that came from Mick brought Panos out of his daze, and he pulled Danielle towards him and hugged her. To have her in his arms again felt so good, restoring all the hidden emotions that he had tried desperately to ignore. He kissed her mouth, holding her so tight that he almost suffocated her. She let herself be submerged into his caress, making way for the feelings that had once tormented her to escape through her lips.

"Sorry to interrupt you two lovebirds, but I would like to get to the hotel today, please," said Mick sarcastically rolling his eyes. "It's bad enough that I have to wait until tomorrow for my suitcase, and I don't want to have to wait until then to get into my room."

Panos looked at Mick, puzzled by his statement.

"Mick's right, but don't worry, Panos, no doubt he'll tell you all about it on the way up to the hotel," replied Danielle quickly, noticing the bewildered look on his face.

Panos laughed half-heartedly and reluctantly let go of her. Picking up her suitcase with one hand, he put his free arm around her waist and walked them to the car. It was easy to spot Panos's black Mercedes, because it was the last one left in the car park.

Danielle was surprised to feel that the sun was even hotter than before. The air conditioning in the airport had cleverly disguised the strengthened heat; it was as if she had walked straight into an oven, it was so hot. She was however not deterred by this climatic change especially as she realised that her tan would be topped up faster than she had imagined. Panos put her suitcase in the boot, and then they all got into the car and headed off to the hotel.

Mick took this time to explain the reason behind his non-existent luggage, fabricating the account slightly by stretching the truth about the man with the gun. This extended story was told with so much conviction that if Danielle hadn't witnessed the actual, true event herself, she would have made Panos turn the car around and gone back to the airport to complain. Danielle turned to Panos and realised by the distraught look on his face, that he had obviously been taken in by Mick's tale of impending death.

"Mick, you don't half exaggerate," said Danielle laughing. "You're a great storyteller; I give you that, but you're not doing much for the reputation of Greek security. You would get them all shot, if you had your way," she continued, not being able to hide the cynicism in her voice. Mick chose to ignore her sarcastic comment and carried on with his tale of maltreatment.

Shutting her mind off to what Mick was saying she looked out the window. They were heading up the hillside and the view of the beautiful blue sea, soothed and calmed her soul. She focused on the vision around her, and the variation of quaint buildings scattered around the island fascinated her. It was so picturesque, stirring her imagination into believing she was captured in a world that only postcards were made of. Sighing deeply, she closed her eyes, allowing her mind to bask in the reality that she was actually back on this wonderful island.

She was brought out of her thoughts when she felt the gentle touch of Panos's hand on her leg. Opening her eyes again she looked at him and her heart leapt with excitement at finally having the man of her dreams in her reach again. She was so looking forward to having him all to herself again. Her hand automatically went down to meet his, and Panos, with his eyes fixed on the road, squeezed it tight. The same thoughts were going around in his head, and he couldn't wait to finally be alone with his Danielle. He had waited so long for the moment of her return, and he found it hard to believe that she was now actually there with him. He squeezed her leg tighter to confirm to himself that she really was a reality and not just a figment of his imagination. The feel of her soft skin on his fingertips generated a desire to be alone with her. His heart beat with anticipation, and he craved the moment when they were alone, and she lay in his arms. The certainty of this outcome sent shivers down his spine, stirring up a whirlpool of emotions that had lain dormant in his heart. Her eyes were still fixed on his handsome face and they were like magnets, enticing him into looking at her. As he did so, he was overwhelmed by their beauty and found it hard to concentrate on his driving. He smiled at her, but had to stay focused on the road, because he could so easily have been seduced by her gorgeous stare.

Once again she was in awe of this Greek man. Her idea of true love had materialised beside her, inspiring a yearning from deep within. The smile that stained her face grew wider as they reached the top of the hill, and the familiar sight of the Oasis hotel became apparent in the distance. As they followed the tiny road up to their destination, her stomach turned over with excitement as they neared the magnificent building. The whiter than white structure presented itself so boldly, showing off the flawlessness of its stature. She hadn't previously taken much notice of just how perfect this place was, but now she felt proud to be a part of the man that owned it. They pulled into the driveway and Panos stopped the car at the bottom of the entrance steps. Instructing her to stay seated, he jumped out of the car, ran all the way round to her side, and then opened the door for her. Sheer benevolence flowed through her, brought on by this act of chivalry, and she happily took hold of his hand.

"Start as we mean to go on," he said winking at her. A dazzling smile dominated his face. "Welcome back!"

She stepped graciously out of the car, feeling like royalty, and for a split second, it was as if she was an heir to this wonderful place. She secretly laughed to herself at her imaginative train of thought, but quickly dismissed the fantasy that her mind had created. Mick got her suitcase out of the boot, and then the three friends walked up the steps to the hotel.

CHAPTER
SEVEN

A tall, dark-haired woman stepped off the plane and made her way down the makeshift stairs on to the tarmac. The sound of her stiletto shoes vibrated through the metal steps, and she was careful not to get her three-inch heels caught between the gaps. Tiny droplets of perspiration began to form on her forehead, and she wasn't sure whether it was due to her nervousness or the intensity of the heat that hit her as she came out from the aircraft. Her dark brown eyes narrowed as she looked around and she couldn't believe that she had finally found the courage to come to Skiathos. Confronted with this reality, mixed feelings flowed through her, but there was no going back now.

Her life had recently taken an unexpected turn and even though it was a hard decision to make, she was sure that Skiathos held the answers to the many questions that were swimming around in her head. The domineering thoughts of finding closure, gave her the strength to carry on with her mission. So, putting on her sunglasses, she continued on into the airport. A sense of expectancy bubbled in her stomach as she waited patiently for her luggage and she couldn't help wondering what the outcome of her trip would be. Tiredness soon crept over her and her feet were throbbing and the only thing that kept her focused was the thought of getting in a nice cool shower when she finally reached her hotel.

She breathed in a deep sigh as her eyes wandered around the large room, when they suddenly focused on a rather angry looking man. Her first thoughts were that he was on his own, and she instinctively felt the need to go and help him. But when an attractive lady came up to him and put her arm around his shoulder, it became evident that he wasn't alone after all. She watched the couple and could see that the woman was trying to console him, but by the irate look on his face, she wasn't having much luck. The mystery woman became distracted when the familiar sight of her bright pink suitcase came along the conveyor belt, and she bent over to pick it up. The couple was soon forgotten as she made her way through the lounge and started heading for the main entrance. As she came to the large glass doors, she reached for the handbag that was usually hung over her shoulder and was overcome with sheer terror when she realised that it wasn't there. Panic stricken, she desperately tried to think back to where she could have left it. She remembered having it while waiting for her suitcase, because she'd put her passport in the tiny compartment in the side. So, she turned around and walked back to the baggage lounge.

"Please be there, please be there," she said under her breath repeatedly, crossing her fingers.

Scanning the room, she was relieved to see her black patent handbag on one of the chairs. She thought this was rather strange because she had been nowhere near the chair but guessed that some kind person had picked it up and put it there in clear view to be found. She hurried over to claim it, furiously looked through the many pockets, and was pleased to find that everything was still there. She held her bag to her chest like a long-lost child and closed her eyes. Her heart was racing because she had feared the worst as it was not just her purse that was of great value to her. She took in deep breaths to overcome her panicked state, and by the fifth breath, her heart was back to its usual rate. Delighted by the outcome of this near disaster, she opened her eyes and took another look in her bag.

As she rummaged through the contents, she discovered the brown envelope. The familiar handwriting on the front caused her heart to miss a beat, quickly reminding her of why she was here. 'Only to be opened after my death,' were the words written in bold, black writing. Tears stung the back of her eyes as she re-read the heart rendering statement, and it took all her mental strength to keep them under control. Swallowing down the pain that had tried to reduce her to tears, she placed the envelope back in to her bag and walked back towards the main entrance.

With her head held high and her pain safely put away, she elegantly walked past the irate man from earlier. Strangely, he was now standing with a gun pointed to his head. He looked like a frightened rabbit, and from what she could make out, he was trying desperately to plead with the customs officer. His pleas for justice were obviously being ignored, because the officer was just looking at him with a very stern look on his face.

That man looks in need of a good lawyer, she thought to herself, smiling. It's a shame that I'm off-duty, her train of thought continued, as she walked out of the door conscious that she should not get involved.

With her prize possession back in her hands again, the tall, dark-haired woman stepped out of the airport. The flow of holiday makers was now just a trickle, which made it easier for her to find an available taxi. The heat from the sun was still very hot, and it didn't help that she was dressed in black. Her tight blouse attracted the intense temperature, causing it to stick to her skin, and the thought of that long-awaited shower was becoming more appealing by the minute. With her luggage in the boot of the taxi, she was driven to her hotel.

She had planned her quest with precise intricacy and had specifically chosen a hotel that was in the middle of the town. She felt that it was important for her base to be surrounded by the hustle and bustle of holiday life, where it would be easy to blend in with the other tourists on the island. If for any reason her plan was to backfire, she knew that she would be able to get lost in the crowd, and this was a comfort to her.

In next to no time, she was in the elevator of her hotel. Slowly, it went up to the seventh floor, and then stopped and the doors opened. Armed with her key in one hand and her luggage in the other, she walked along the corridor in search of her room. She was grateful for the air-conditioning, but still felt sweaty and uncomfortable from her journey. Her feet were now swollen, and she could not wait to take off the shoes, which were now causing her to limp. She found her room, opened the door and walked inside. Without hesitating, she flung off the shoes and gasped with relief when the cool air that circulated the room touched her throbbing skin. Putting her bags down, she looked around the room, and its quaintness took her breath away. Everything was neatly in its place. As she admired her accommodation, for a split second she forgot why she was there. The sun's rays that shone through the window lit up the room, radiating a warm glow that enhanced her surroundings. Suddenly, she had to remind herself of her mission, quickly bringing her back to her senses.

I'm not here on a holiday, she thought. I've got a job to do. She grabbed her handbag from the floor and went and sat down on the bed. There, she unclasped the bag and pulled out the brown envelope.

This is why I'm here, she thought, staring at the familiar handwriting on the front. This is why I have come all of this way.

Tears stung her eyes as bitter memories penetrated her heart, and she was taken back to only four months ago when her life had changed forever. She thought back to that day at her grandmother's house, and her tears began to flow. Back then, she knew who she was. Back then, she had direction, but the envelope in her hand, had changed all of that, revealing the lie that her life had been built on. Now, all of that had been cruelly taken away. A ball of resentment evolved in the pit of her stomach, bringing with it a deep sense of grief that made her feel sick. Still finding the truth hard to believe, she took a deep breath and put the envelope back into her bag.

I must be strong, she thought to herself, doing up the clasp

I cannot let my emotions get the better of me!

Wiping away her tears, she gathered her thoughts together and went over to get her suitcase. Her stomach rumbled and she looked at the time. She had no desire to eat anything, but she needed to keep her strength up. After her long-awaited shower, she decided to take a walk through the town in search of a good restaurant. On many nights, whilst away on business trips, she'd dined alone, and this would be no different, she thought. To her, this was all that it was, purely business.

Back at the Oasis Hotel, Panos and Danielle walked hand-in-hand up to Panos's room. They had left Mick down at the bar, busy telling Yannis about his life-threatening experience at the airport. Panos was relieved to have his beautiful Danielle back by his side again and this was evidenced by the smile that was now a permanent fixture on his face. The conversation flowed between them, and it was as if they had never been apart. Walking up the stairs, Danielle was in awe of her surroundings, and couldn't have been any happier. She was back with the man of her dreams and could have cried with joy. When they reached his room, she was overcome with nervousness as he opened the door. When he walked her over the threshold, her heart began to beat faster, and once again she was confronted by a welcoming bouquet of flowers. She stood still as he shut the door behind them. Her mind was instantly taken back to her previous visit and her last night spent in this room, and all the feelings of that special time came flooding back.

No words were spoken as Panos took her into his arms and kissed her. He sighed deeply at her response, and all his anxieties of never seeing his Danielle again deflated in their embrace. Time stood still, and they were overcome by a deep desire that they had tried to deny for the past few weeks. The love that had been cleverly disguised was ignited again, bringing with it a passion that was too hard to contain. Panos instinctively led her over to the bed and laid her down. He kissed her again, but then he had to pull away. He looked deep into her eyes and was once again mesmerised by their beauty. He was afraid to carry on, so just concentrated on calming down his quickened heart rate.

"You are so beautiful," he said, claiming back his breath. "I have missed you so much." They lay there, captured in each other's stare, and he smiled.

"I have missed you too, Panos. It is hard to explain just how much," replied Danielle locked into his soft brown eyes. He nodded aware of what she meant and kissed her again, pulling her closer and kissing every part of her face. He found it hard to believe that she was there and breathed in his special lady.

"I love you," he said, completely captivated by her. "Thank you for coming back to me."

Mouthing, "I love you," back she felt relieved to be able to say those words to him again. As he paused momentarily to confirm her consent, she nodded for him to carry on, and they made love. The promise he had made to his father quickly slipping from his mind.

Mick found himself alone at the bar as Yannis had been distracted by one of the guests, and this left him alone with his thoughts. His mind went straight to his estranged wife, and he couldn't help wondering what she was doing. He pictured her distraught face when she found out where he was, and he felt himself puff up with pride.

Now, who's got the upper hand? He thought. Now, who's in control?

He picked up his beer and took a big swig of it and relished the thought and freedom of being able to do whatever he liked and breathed in this wonderful feeling. Looking around the room he smiled.

I don't need Tracey, he thought to himself as he noticed a young lady sitting on her own. Oh, it's so good to be back.

Three quarters of an hour later, Panos and Danielle walked down to the bar. Mick was now talking to a group of people and he was happy to entertain them with his funny ways. He had plucked up the courage to talk to the young lady but was met by an unforeseen obstacle when she revealed to him that she was married. Her husband had gone back up to their room to get something. Mick was so disappointed when she explained this, but this didn't deter him from his happy frame of mind though, and he bought her a drink anyway. He still managed to get in his story of maltreatment at the airport before her husband reappeared and left her also feeling quite angry with the Greek security system. He wandered back over to the bar where a group of male guests had gathered. They welcomed him as he stood beside them, and he took this opportunity to share his story, relieved to have gotten their attention; and that's how he spent the rest of the time, while he waited for Danielle.

Panos kissed Danielle and walked behind the bar. As guests witnessed this act of love, the room went quiet. Panos watched the stunned looks on men's faces as they looked at Danielle, and pride oozed out of him. One man in particular caught his attention, as his mouth dropped open when he saw her. This made Panos laugh.

"You look like you've never seen a beautiful lady before," he teased as he aimed his statement at the gawping man. The man's face went bright red, so to hide his embarrassment, he just laughed along.

"This is Danielle, the lady I told you about from England," he continued. "And, I see that you have met my good friend, Michael… They are friends." Panos took hold of Danielle's hand and kissed it. "They will be staying awhile," he explained.

Danielle's face turned a deep scarlet, as all the guests at the bar said hello to her, each one welcoming her back to the hotel. She was overwhelmed by the response to her arrival and reminded of the way that people reacted to her whenever she was with Panos. She was overwrought with pride. Turning to Panos, she smiled. The expression on his face said it all, and she couldn't help feeling special in the presence of this man.

"Panos, my friend, drinks all round," said Mick interrupting their eye contact. "Just put it on my tab." Panos obliged and busied himself with the many orders that flew across the bar. Conversations flowed freely again, and the room was filled with laughter. Mick was the instigator of the joy that lit up the hotel, and Panos was delighted to have his two favourite people back in his life again.

Panos's mother walked out of the restaurant, and her face lit up when she saw Danielle at the bar. Instinctively she looked at her son and felt so happy to see him once again full of the joys of spring. She smiled at her son's fortune of having her back by his side and went over to greet her. Danielle turned around and her heart skipped a beat when she saw Panos's mother walking towards her.

"Danielle... Ah, Danielle, it is so good to see you again. Welcome back," she said, putting her arms out to embrace her.

"H-hello... It is so lovely to be back," replied Danielle putting her arms out in response to her kind gesture. Panos's smile widened as the two women embraced, but then he noticed his father standing at the entrance of the restaurant. He felt the smile slip from his face as his father looked at him, but it was soon restored when his father smiled. Panos was relieved to see kindness generated through his father's expression and felt honoured to have such an understanding father, and a secret they now shared. He turned his attention back to Danielle, as his father continued to walk over to the reception area.

Danielle felt at ease as she spoke to this adorable Greek lady. All her worries soon disappeared, and she felt right at home. The warmth of his mother's voice, and the kindness that was displayed on her face, reassured her that she'd made the right decision in coming back to this beautiful place.

She was soon greeted by Anna who also entered the bar and went straight over to say hello. The three women talked like long lost friends for almost half an hour, and she relished the friendliness of her Greek hosts. Panos was busy accommodating his thirsty guests, but he still managed to keep her in his sight. His heart was ready to burst as he watched her interact with his family. He couldn't have wished for a better start to the week he was to spend with the love of his life.

The town was an array of happy holiday makers, all taken in by this beautiful island. The dark-haired mystery lady walked through the bustling high Street and couldn't help being inspired by this wonderful place. As she mingled amongst the many people, she spotted a busy Taverna across the road. Now dressed in shorts and a vest top, she wandered in to get something to eat. She was met by a gorgeous Greek waiter who showed her to her table. After taking her drink order, he left her to look through the menu. She still felt sick to the stomach, so she decided to have something light. The waiter soon returned with her beverage, and she disclosed to him her wish for a Greek salad. He wrote down her order and then walked away. Her eyes searched the room and to her surprise, she started to feel extremely homesick.

Although she wasn't married, she missed her life back in England. She had many friends who occupied her spare time, and she longed to see a friendly face. Marriage was the last thing on her mind, because she was more than content with her work. She was a well-established lawyer, one of the top in her field, and this was more than a full time job for her. There was a special man in her life, but she had kept him at arm's length. He had been persistent in his pursuit of her, but she didn't want to get too involved. When the huge blow came that shook her very foundations, the last thing she needed was the bother of a long-term relationship. Instead she chose to focus on sorting out what was left of her crippled life. She sighed heavily and could have cried when she thought about the mess that it had now become. Her mind wandered back to that dark day and a tear escaped down her face.

Why did this have to happen to me? She thought, wiping away the solitary tear. Her food was placed down in front of her, and she took a deep breath to claim back her strength and began to eat.

An hour later, the mystery woman was walking back to her hotel. Darkness had crept over the island, and the selection of coloured lights coming from the many bars and restaurants stole her view. As she witnessed the happy people enjoying the welcoming atmosphere, she secretly wished that she was there on holiday, but once again was reminded of why she was there. The deep sense of sadness that had made itself a home in her heart did not deter her from her mission, when she found herself outside of her hotel.

Five minutes later, she was shutting the room door behind her. She turned on the light and lay down on the bed. Her mind was racing; she just didn't know where to begin. The events of the past few months had put her mind in complete turmoil, and she had never felt so confused. Leaning over the side of the bed, she picked up her handbag, reached in and pulled out the brown envelope again. Her hands were shaking slightly as she opened it, her heart beating quickly in her chest. Sitting up she took out a wad of papers and placed them on the bed. As her thumping heart echoed through her head, she stared at the letters and documents that were in front of her. She picked up one of the documents and carefully unfolded it. 'Death certificate,' was written in black bold letters at the top. Tears began to sting her eyes when she recognised her mother's name just below it: Elizabeth Mary Stiller. Her eyes went down to the cause of death and her tears began to flow.

'Cause of death: heart attack.' It was there in black and white, but the letters on the bed led her to believe another verdict was really behind her mother's death.

"It wasn't a heart attack," she said out loud. "It should say that she died from a broken heart," her voice now just a whisper.

As she folded up the death certificate and placed it back down on the bed, the tears flowed profusely down her face. She picked up one of the letters and began to read it. It was from her mother, apologising for missing her birthday. It was one of many that her mother had missed, and the pain that she had felt all those years ago as a child, was still just as real and intense. The reality dawned on her that her mother had never been there for her special day, and this was evident by the pile of letters that her grandmother had given her. She had only brought a few of them with her, because there were so many, and the memory of longing for her mother throughout her childhood replayed through her mind. She put down the letter with the death certificate and picked up the remainder of the bunch of letters that were neatly tied together.

She had never known her real father, but the letters in her hand had revealed the truth, and his identity was there in black and white. She rewound her mind to the day that her grandmother sat her down and gave her the letters she now held in her hand. Her heart felt heavy with pain, energising the tears to flow more rapidly. Putting the bundle of letters down she searched for another document that was in the envelope. Finding what she was looking for she unfolded the piece of paper and read what was written on it:

Helen Mary Stiller.

Mother: Elizabeth Mary Stiller.

Father: unknown.

Helen remembered, vividly, the conversation that she'd had with her mother regarding her father. It was on one of the rare occasions that she had paid her a visit, and the memory of that day was as clear as if it had been yesterday. She must have been about four or five years old when out of the blue, she asked the question. Her mother put her on her knee and explained that her father was dead. She remembered that her mother's breath smelt funny, but being so young, she thought no more of it. Her mother told her that he had died in a car accident when she was pregnant with her. Then she told her to go and play in the garden while she spoke to her grandmother. As she played on her bike in the garden, she could clearly hear the raised voices of the two women. This wasn't unusual because they always seemed to end up arguing whenever her mother came to visit.

Helen spent her childhood living with her grandparents. She grew up with stability in her life because they spoiled her rotten. She was the apple of her grandparent's eye, and they took great joy in lavishing her with the love that their mother had failed to show her. It wasn't until she was in her teens that they sat her down and explained the reasons behind her mother's absence, and she quickly came to understand her mother's irrational behaviour.

They explained how her mother battled with drugs and alcohol. Apparently, there had been a time when she once had a bright future ahead of her, but for reasons they didn't want to get into, she had ruined her chances of success by abusing her body with these substances.

Helen put two and two together and guessed that the problems her mum had developed must have been because of her father's death and she couldn't help but feel sorry about her mother's state of mind. She always held on to the hope that someday her mother would get well, and she believed this from the bottom of her heart. This false hope fed her will to succeed in her own life, so that one day she could get her mum the help that she needed to conquer her addictions. Unfortunately, that day never came. Instead her life took a turn for the worse as she was committed to a mental facility because of the drug abuse, and that was where she remained until her death, only four months previously.

On the night of Elizabeth's funeral, her grandmother took her upstairs and gave her the envelope.

"Please understand that I did it for your own good," she said, handing it to her, tears evident in her eyes. Helen looked at the distraught old lady, confused. Then her grandmother left her alone. Helen looked at the envelope and read what was on the front. 'Only to be opened after my death.'

She recognised her mother's handwriting and began to open it, curious to know what she would find inside. In complete bewilderment, she pulled out a bundle of letters. She sat on the bed and untied the red ribbon that was keeping them all together. At first, she was confused because they were love letters, but she soon realised that they were all written by her mother to a man whom she had never even heard of. They were dated the year before she was born and her life was suddenly thrown into turmoil when she began to read the last one telling this man that she was pregnant. Her mother had clearly stated that he was the father, and that he didn't have to worry because she was going to have a termination. Her heart dropped as she scanned through the other letters, and tears filled her eyes when she read the sentences overflowing with love for this man. As she continued to read, she realised that this man was Greek, and the bottom fell out of her life.

Oh my God, I am half Greek, she thought. Suddenly, it all made sense to her, her mother's addiction and as well as her lack of zeal for life. From what she read and could gather, her mother was madly in love with this man.

"Oh Mum. Why didn't you tell me? Why didn't anyone tell me?" she asked out loud. As she had no answers, she lay down on the bed and sobbed.

A while later her grandmother returned to talk to her. Seeing her granddaughter's anguish, she went and sat down next to her, and did all she could to reassure her.

"It's going to be alright Helen, I promise," was all she could say, as she put her arm around her.

"Why didn't you tell me, Nan? Why did I have to find out like this?"

Taking a deep breath, her grandmother tried to explain.

"Helen, it wasn't that easy. Your mother asked us not to tell you, and we gave our word that we wouldn't… It was so hard for us to decide what to do for the best. Please believe me. She was after all, your mother. How could we break our word to her? We had made her a promise. There were so many times that I wanted to say something to you, especially when she came up with the story of your father's 'so called death.' It broke my heart to hear her tell you that. That's why we always ended up arguing, because we thought that you had the right to know the truth. Your mother however wouldn't have it... I'm so sorry. I feel so guilty."

Helen looked up and stared at her grandmother. The tears were now streaming down her cheeks, and she felt immense compassion for her Nan, knowing it must have been very difficult for her over the years, as she tried to do the best for everyone involved.

"Oh Nan, it isn't your fault. You only did what you thought was right. I'm not angry with you," she sighed. "I'm just in complete shock. I would never have guessed that something like this was going to happen...Please, don't cry."

The distraught expression on her grandmother's face broke Helen's heart. She was, after all, the one who had put her life on hold to look after her. She was the one who was always there for her when she needed help. She felt sorry for this frail old lady who had just buried her daughter; whose life must have fallen apart when she realised that her daughter was an addict. As she squeezed her Nan in a loving hug, her heart went out to this amazing woman.

"So, who is he? And, why are there no letters from him?" asked Helen, wiping the tears off her face.

"He was a man she met whilst on a business trip in Greece," answered her Nan, feeling somewhat relieved to finally be able to reveal the truth.

"I had never seen her so happy! When she came back home, she couldn't stop talking about him. He was the manager of a hotel there, and they were madly in love. She went back and they they planned to get married. I was dubious about the whole thing at first, but I couldn't deny she was so happy. Besides, there was no way that I or your grandfather could change her mind. Anyway, I was just coming around to the idea when she appeared on our doorstep one day. She was crying so much that I couldn't understand what she was saying!" She hesitated and got a tissue out of her pocket and took a deep breath before carrying on.

"When your mother finally calmed down, she explained to us why she had come home. Apparently, the father of the man she loved hated her, and had said some dreadful things. She didn't go into much detail, but by the way that she was crying, he must have said something terrible that was enough to persuade her to break it off and leave him."

Helen could feel anger bubbling up inside her as she listened, to what happened to her mother.

"She loved him so much, Helen, and it broke my heart to see her in so much pain." She began to sob with the memory.

"Oh Helen, she came back a different girl. From then on, she started to drink heavily. It seemed the only way she could forget him. Then, things got complicated when she found out that she was pregnant. It seemed to make it worse. She was six months into her pregnancy and by then it was too late to have a termination. She poured her heart out in those letters with the intention of sending them, but she never did. She made me promise never to tell you.

The only time that she said I was allowed to tell you, was if she died," she said. "Oh Helen, it was such a mess. She never got over him, she loved him so much."

Helen held her Nan in her arms, letting the tears trickle down her cheeks.

"When you were born, she couldn't cope, and she literally fell apart. You were a constant reminder of the love that she cherished but had to leave behind! That is when your grandfather and I stepped in. She wanted to get you adopted, but we wouldn't let that happen, so you came and lived with us instead. The whole situation broke that poor girl's heart!"

Helen couldn't believe what she was hearing. It was as if she was in the middle of a nightmare and she wanted desperately to wake up.

"Nan are you telling me that there never was any accident, but that in fact my father is still alive?" asked Helen incredulous as she tried to keep herself calm.

"As far as I know he is. I never got in touch with him. I was tempted, but I didn't want to upset your mother. I just hoped every day that she would get over him, but she never did. Her heart was broken, and she just went from bad to worse," admitted her grandmother sobbing even harder. Helen just held her in her arms completely lost for words. The two of them sat there, tears flowing freely, each with their own thoughts for what seemed like an eternity.

"Well, I must get in touch with him. He can't get away with this. He has to know that I exist," said Helen finally, a strength rising up from deep within her. "Is this his address?" she asked pointing to the front of one of the letters.

Her grandmother nodded her head.

"But that was a long time ago. He's probably moved on from there. He's most likely got a family of his own by now."

"I don't care if he has. He must be told. If he's moved, I know people that can find out where he is. I know people in very high places," she replied determinedly.

Her grandmother looked at her with concern in her eyes.

"Don't worry, Nan, it will be ok. I only want to talk to him," she said reassuringly her voice softening, and she forced a smile on her face.

"You know Helen; you're very much like her. When she had her mind set, she couldn't be moved. You look like her as well. She was also very pretty, but the drink and the drugs..." She found it hard to finish her sentence because the pain was too great.

"I know, Nan. You don't have to explain... You've had a tough day. Come on. Let's go downstairs and have a nice cup of tea. Grandad will be wondering where we are," she concluded.

She didn't want to upset her anymore. She'd had enough heartache for one day. The tone of her voice was very soothing, but the anger that she felt inside told another story.

The next day Helen phoned a good friend of hers who was in the police force. She explained her situation, and was pleased to be told that, although it could take a couple of weeks, he was sure that he could find out where this man lived. She suddenly felt extremely glad to be in the profession that she was in.

I knew that it would come in handy one day, she thought. I have waited thirty odd years, so what are a couple more weeks?

Two months later, she received the phone call that she'd been waiting for. She had thrown herself into work, which hadn't been hard because her workload had been quite heavy. When the call came, her heart stopped. She quickly composed herself and wrote down all the information that was relayed to her. She found out that her father had moved to the Greek Island of Skiathos and that he owned a hotel there called the Oasis Hotel. She didn't ask any questions but thanked the caller, and said she owed him one.

When she came off the phone, she just stared at the piece of paper on her desk. She couldn't believe that there, in front of her, was the address of where her father lived.

"My father," she said out loud. It seemed so strange to say those words, but they just rolled off her tongue. "My father," she repeated. "My father... My father... My father..."

She stopped and got out her diary. Her days were packed solid with clients, causing her heart to drop. She skipped through the pages until she came to a blank week. She suddenly remembered that she'd booked a week off to go to the lakes with her friend. It wasn't for another two months, but she felt confident that her friend would understand her cancelling their trip, when she explained her reasons. Turning on her laptop she punched in, flights to Skiathos, and looked through the many flights that were available for that week. Realising the time, and that she had a client due to arrive in the next ten minutes, she decided she wanted to have booked her flight by then. Her heart raced in her chest, when she found the right flight and booked it. She didn't want to give herself the time to think about it, and perhaps change her mind. With two minutes to spare, the deed was done. In two months' time she would be going to Skiathos, to confront her long lost father. The next step was to book the hotel, but there was a knock on her office door, time had run out. She needed to think carefully about where she was to stay, so she decided to be patient and take her time to do it right.

Perfect, she thought, feeling very pleased with herself. At least I've booked my flight and got the ball rolling.

"Hello, Mr Perkins, it is so good to see you again. Please do come in."

Now here she was two months later, sitting in a hotel in the middle of Skiathos. The thought of seeing her father sent shivers down her spine, and she felt very apprehensive about the day when she would be standing in front of him.

She folded up her birth certificate, along with the letters and the death certificate, put them back into the envelope. Putting them back into her bag, she pulled out a map of the island. Tracing her finger along the page, it stopped when it got to the area where she guessed the hotel was situated. It was only a short drive from the town centre, so she decided to hire a car in the morning, just to take a look. Suddenly she realised that she felt very tired. Not only was she physically worn out, emotionally she was shattered. She looked at the time. The first day of her mission was nearly over and she needed to get a good night's sleep to face the day ahead of her. Her confused mind had managed to stabilise itself and she felt confident that the first part of her plan was now in place. Five minutes later, she was tucked up in bed. Even though she still had all her curiosities on her mind, she drifted off to sleep.

CHAPTER
EIGHT

*M*ick woke up with a jolt. His mind was overcome with terror as he dreamt about being at his own funeral! It took him a few moments to realise that it was just a dream, kick starting his need of a drink to calm his frightened state of mind. His next thought was to feed his craving, so he automatically reached down in search of his jacket. He found the bottle of vodka that he knew was there and gulped down the welcoming liquid. His quickened heart rate had just returned to normal, when it suddenly dawned on him where he was. A smile slowly formed across his face, and he was relieved to finally feel secure in his surroundings.

"Stupid dream," he whispered. I wouldn't be a guest at my own funeral...How ridiculous is that? Besides, I'm not going anywhere. I've got many years left in me yet, he thought as he dragged himself out of bed and got into the shower.

Panos walked down the stairs and made his way towards the bar. He had a spring in his step and was singing at the top of his voice. Danielle was still in his room getting ready, and he couldn't wait for her to be in his sight again. He filled his time by looking after the guests, keeping a close eye on the door leading up to the rooms. He was elated to have Danielle back in his life and went about his business without a care in the world. The phone rang constantly, and he was getting rather agitated by the many calls that brought him away from the bar. He was however perfectly professional and a smile swept across his face when he answered the phone for the twentieth time. It was an official from the airport informing him that they were now in possession of Mick's missing luggage. He thanked the customs officer and promised to let the owner of the suitcase know that he could go down to collect it.

That will please Michael, he thought, replacing the receiver. This is a good start to the day.

Yannis came into the lounge and walked over to the reception to give him a hand. Panos was relieved that he could now focus his attention back on to the guests who had gathered at the bar.

A little later Danielle walked into the room and Panos's heart skipped a beat when she came over to him. Once again, he was distracted from his work when she kissed him. All his feelings for her sailed through him, and he was instantly reminded of why he had fallen in love with this beautiful woman. All the guests said good morning to her before going out to the minibus that would be taking them into town.

Mick also appeared, and Panos took great pleasure in giving him the good news concerning his suitcase.

"Thank goodness for that," said Mick happily. "I was beginning to get worried, because it took five of those little bottles of shower gel that you supply, to wash this gorgeous body. I had visions of you having to order a coach load to get me through the week!" he remarked jovially.

Panos laughed as he poured out a beer for Mick.

"Blimey, that's what I call service my friend, I didn't even have to ask," he remarked looking very impressed. Panos patted him on the back.

"I know you too well, my friend. Just call me Doctor Panos," he replied, watching Mick take a big swig of his drink.

"I'm going to drink this and then take the bus into town. I'm going to give those people a piece of my mind for the way they've treated me. What are you doing, Dan?" he asked. Danielle looked at her watch and then at Panos, searching his face. His expression showed no sign of distress, in fact she was pleased to see that he was still smiling.

"You go, Danielle," he said kissing her cheek. "I have a lot of things to occupy me while you're gone. Besides Michael might need you. I wouldn't want them to threaten his life again," he said winking at her.

Mick ignored the sarcasm in Panos's voice and focused on finishing his drink.

"Yes, you've got a point, Panos; it is best that I go with him," she replied laughing.

"We won't be long," she promised kissing him goodbye. He wiped down the bar and began to wait patiently for her return.

Helen stood outside the entrance of her hotel. She looked up and down the road, the map of the island held tightly in her hand. She'd stapled the directions to the hotel and the map together, to make sure she didn't lose either. The hustle and bustle from the night before had cleared, and the quietness of the place made it possible for her to concentrate on what she was doing.

The hotel manager had given her directions to the car hire showroom, so she started to walk towards the High Street. Her night had been a disturbed one, because she spent most of it tossing and turning. She found it so hard to switch off from her worries, so she only managed to get a couple of hours sleep. Adrenaline flowed through her veins, keeping her tiredness safely at bay, and she was pleased to find that her restless night hadn't had much of an effect on her. She did, however, feel slightly light-headed, and blamed this on the fact that she'd skipped breakfast.

I'll grab something to eat on the way to the hire shop, she thought, feeling nauseous at the thought of food.

"I have to eat something," she said to herself as she came to a quaint Taverna and decided to go in there to sustain her weakened body. She nervously waited for her sandwich as she studied the map, finding the tiny road that led to where the hotel. This was undoubtedly one of the biggest things she had ever had to deal with in her life, and she had never felt so alone.

Mick held his suitcase and had never been so relieved to see his Armani case again. They were met by a very apologetic airport official and Mick couldn't help feeling very smug listening to the man's repeated apologies and admissions of embarrassment about what had happened when they first arrived.

"That's OK, mate," said Mick shaking the man's hand. "He was only doing his job. No harm done," he said.

Danielle tutted and rolled her eyes, in complete disbelief at his change of tune.

"You never cease to amaze me, Mick! You make it up as you go along," she said. "You certainly gave him a piece of your mind," she laughed, impressed at his sudden change of attitude.

The two friends headed back towards the town. As they walked through the High Street, Mick's heart stopped when they walked past the bar where he had met Demi. As he hurried Danielle past the small building, he had an overpowering need for a beer. He managed to persuade Danielle to stop for a quick drink and pulled her into a quaint Taverna nearby.

Helen was drinking her cup of coffee when she noticed two people walk in. Although her mind filled with confusion, she thought that she recognised the couple. She set her mind on placing their faces, when it dawned on her that she'd seen them at the airport.

That's the man with the gun to his head, she thought smiling at the memory. Her smile turned into a laugh when the man tripped up and fell to the ground right next to her table.

"Bloody Greek steps, they will be the death of me," Mick said angrily.

Looking up, he realised that there was an attractive lady looking down at him, causing his cheeks to go bright red.

Danielle laughed hysterically and tried to pick up her clumsy friend.

"Mick, what are you like, you nearly had this lady's table over," she said, not having any luck in getting him up. "You've got to be more careful," she chided.

Mick's embarrassment temporarily halted his ability to speak and all that he could do was smile at the lovely lady.

"Are you alright?" asked Helen.

Nodding his head he put his arm on her table to pull himself up. The weight of his body was unfortunately too much for the small table and he ended up a heap on the floor, bringing the table down with him. Helen's cup of coffee went flying and the hot liquid landed on Mick's carefully groomed hair. Two waiters came running over and the whole restaurant was looking at the sorry state that was Mick.

Danielle was at a loss as to what to do as she witnessed the two waiters trying to pick up her friend, tears streaming down her face. She watched helplessly as the men finally got him up and tried desperately to tidy up the mess that Mick had made. When the table was put back in its place, Mick managed to sit down on a chair that was put beside it.

"I'm so sorry," he said to Helen, combing his fingers through his sticky hair. "They should ban those stupid little things," he continued.

Helen looked at this dishevelled man and couldn't help feeling sorry for him. Then a strong smell of alcohol hit her, and she suddenly realised the real reason behind his unfortunate mishap.

"Let me get you another coffee; It's the least I can do for you," said Mick. "Dan, could you get the drinks please, babe? My legs seem to have turned to jelly." Danielle nodded and walked over to the bar.

You've managed to do it again Mick, she thought to herself smiling. I just don't know how you do it.

She ordered the drinks, and went and sat down next to Mick, who was busy complaining about the Greek building laws.

"Hello, my name is Danielle," she said introducing herself. "You'll have to excuse my friend; he is very clumsy. Your coffee will be over in a minute."

"Thank you, Danielle. Honestly there was no need," replied Helen smiling. "Those steps are very dangerous...I am Helen by the way," she said shaking Danielle's hand.

The waiter placed the drinks on the table. Helen wasn't surprised when Mick ordered a glass of beer and she shuddered as he began to drink it down.

"So, are you two here on holiday?" asked Helen forcing her eyes away from Mick's gluttonous behaviour.

"Yes, we're here for a week. It is such a beautiful island. I absolutely adore this place," replied Danielle. "Are you here on holiday too?"

Helen thought carefully about her answer because she didn't want to give too much away.

"Err... Yes, I have come here to get away from the rat race for a few days. I'm not sure how long I'll be staying. It is nice to have some peace and quiet for a change," she said and continued telling them about her work and just how demanding it could be.

"Blimey, I could have done with you yesterday," said Mick when she'd finished. "I had a really bad experience at the airport. I thought that I was going to get shot."

Oh, please don't go on about that again, thought Danielle bored of the story now. Mick was just about to explain the grimy details, when she stole Helen's attention.

"So, where are you staying Helen?" she asked quickly changing the subject, and giving him a disapproving look, which made him choose not to pursue the account of his life-threatening experience. Feeling quite hurt, he let Helen answer.

He really liked the look of her and was impressed to know that she was very high class.

Maybe I should set my standards a bit higher, he thought looking into her gorgeous brown eyes. Tracey would never believe that I could pull a lawyer. She'll be gutted!

"I'm staying in a hotel just around the corner. It's quite lovely. I've never been here before, and I'm quite taken by the place. I'm sure that I will be back again." She cringed when the reality of why she was here invaded her mind.

"So where are you two staying?" she asked quickly diverting her thinking from going down that road.

"The Oasis Hotel," answered Mick enthusiastically. "My mate Panos owns it. Well, his family does. He's a great bloke, isn't he Dan? They're a couple."

Danielle nodded, and Helen couldn't help seeing a twinkle in her eyes.

"Yes, he is a great guy, which reminds me, we should be getting back. He will be wondering where we are," replied Danielle, looking at Mick.

"It was nice to meet you Helen, and I hope that you have a wonderful holiday." She got up and shook Helen's hand again.

"OK Dan, you're the boss. If you're ever passing, Helen, come in and say hello. I'm sure that Panos won't mind," said Mick standing up. "Oh, again, I'm so sorry about earlier. At least I got to wear the coffee, and it didn't go over you!"

Helen shook his hand and watched the two friends leave.

I might just do that, she thought, intrigued by Mick's invitation. That would be a good way to get into the hotel. She couldn't believe her fortune. Of all the people to meet on this island and they just happen to be staying in the same hotel that's owned by my father, she thought to herself smiling. How bizarre is that?

She finished her coffee when she suddenly noticed that the map was no longer on the table. She searched the floor beneath her, but it was nowhere to be seen. She frantically looked through her bag hoping she would put it there for safekeeping, but she still couldn't find it.

"Oh, what have I done with it?" she whispered putting her head in her hands, her stomach in knots. Having another quick look around to her relief, she spotted it under the adjacent table. The directions were still attached, and she was pleased to see that all the sheets of paper, she needed were all there. That was her cue to gather her things together, put them safely in her bag and leave the Taverna. With the way the day had turned out, she felt a whole lot better. She felt energised and ready to carry on with her plan. She wandered up the road, her thoughts consumed with the idea of having a half-brother, and her stomach churned.

At least your father knows you, she thought, feeling nauseated by this fact. At least he has been there for you. Suddenly, she was filled with regret as she realised the impact that she was going to have on this family. Part of her wanted to turn back, get her belongings and run as far away from this island as possible. Tears stung her eyes and she could feel all her strength evaporate, but she knew that she had to be strong.

No, I haven't come all this way for nothing, she thought, taking a deep breath. They'll have to deal with it, just like I have had to, she concluded. She stopped outside the car hire showroom and taking a deep breath, she walked in.

Danielle and Mick got back to the hotel and Panos was working behind the bar. His heart somersaulted when his eyes fell on his Danielle, as he felt so relieved to see her again. They had only been gone a short while, but he couldn't stop his mind from imagining all kind of things and being tortured by thoughts of what she was doing. Every minute felt like an eternity, and he longed for her to be back by his side. He was just about to go down to the pool bar when she retuned, and all his anxieties disappeared.

"Ah, my Danielle, you are back," he said, kissing her cheek.

She responded to his welcoming gesture, pleased to finally be back at the hotel. She didn't think she was going to miss him so much, but being without him, even for a little while was unbearable. She promised herself she would never allow it to happen again! From that moment on, she decided to spend every minute she could with him.

Panos told her his plans for the day, and she was overcome with joy. The thought of soaking up the glorious sunshine whilst having the man of her dreams in her sight fed her elated heart and she smiled.

He poured Mick a drink before he left the bar and enquired about their trip down to the airport. Mick explained, while Danielle took the opportunity to go up to the room to get changed. Panos put his hand up to stop Mick's conversation and walked around the bar.

Taking hold of Danielle's hand, he pulled her towards him·

"Danielle, I have to say this," he whispered into her ear. "Being without you was intolerable. I thought that I would be able to cope with it, but I can't. We've only got a few days and I want to spend every precious moment with you. I'm sorry, but that's how I feel." He stared into her eyes, unable to look away, all the love he felt for her evident in his expression.

"That's funny because I felt the same way. I couldn't wait to see you again. So, it's a deal, we will be together!" she said emphatically. "But first, I do need to go upstairs to get changed," she laughed, feeling glad that he felt the same way that she did.

"OK my darling, but hurry up," he said, his voice now back to its normal tone.

"Sorry Mick, you were saying?" he asked.

Mick continued relating his story, but Panos's eyes remained on Danielle until she disappeared up the stairs.

Mick took his drink and followed Panos down to the poolside. He was just telling him about the stunning lawyer that he had met, when a sharp pain went through his chest. The agonising pain took his breath away, causing him to feel quite scared. Suddenly the memory of his nightmare flashed through his mind, sending a cold chill down his spine. His body shivered at the thought and he was literally stopped in his tracks. Panos noticed that Mick had stopped talking halfway through his sentence and turned around to find out why. He was met by a very frightened Mick who had gone as white as a sheet.

"Michael, what is wrong. Are you alright?" he asked worried by the look on his friend's face.

"Y-yes, Panos, I have just got a touch of heartburn," he replied, as the feeling passed.

"I think that I must have eaten something dodgy. I don't know. You Greeks, if you can't kill me off with your stupid little steps, you try to poison me." He shook his head and laughed nervously, relieved to feel fine again.

Panos was glad to see the colour come back into Mick's cheeks and laughed too.

"Oh Michael, you are a funny man." He put his arm around Mick's shoulder, and the two of them carried on down to the pool.

Ten minutes later, Danielle reappeared. She walked over to the lounger nearest the bar and put her things down. Mick was up at the bar talking to Panos, so she went over to join them.

"Don't say anything to Danielle about what just happened," whispered Mick to Panos.

"I don't want to worry her unnecessarily." Panos just nodded at Mick's request and focused on watching his beautiful Danielle walking towards him.

"So, what were you two whispering about? I'm not disturbing you, am I?" she asked sarcastically. She had noticed the two men talking close together and couldn't help feeling a little bit paranoid.

"N-no Dan, of course you're not," replied Mick quickly.

"P-Panos was just telling me how beautiful you are. Weren't you, Panos?" On cue Panos nodded, but Danielle wasn't convinced.

"Yes and that I love having you here very much," Panos added, colluding with Mick's plausible explanation. He took Danielle's hand and kissed it. Then, he pulled her to him and kissed her. Her doubts were suddenly quashed by the gentle touch of his lips, and she smiled.

"Oh OK, I'll let you two off the hook then, seeing that I was at the centre of your conversation. Now, I am going to top up my tan."

Kissing Panos full on the lips she walked over to her lounger. Both men watched her as she took off her clothes, and the vision of her gorgeous figure took Panos's breath away.

"She really is beautiful," he said, eyeing up her slim body.

"She sure is," said Mick completely forgetting himself.

Panos noticed the tone in his friend's voice and looked at him. "Michael, put your eyes back in your head, she is taken," he said sternly.

"Oh, oh, sorry Panos, I was just thinking," said Mick, realising his tone.

"I can guess what you were thinking, my friend," replied Panos laughing. "Now what was that about a lawyer?"

Two hours passed, and Panos was content with having Danielle in his sight. His heart filled with pride when he watched her swim, and a deep yearning for her stole his thoughts as he imagined her being in his arms. He couldn't wait to be alone with her and relished the thoughts conjured up in his mind.

Mick was now lying on the lounger next to Danielle; the warmth of the sun had taken him into a lovely sleep. Danielle looked over to Panos, who was busy serving a group of guests. The cluster of people made it difficult for her to see him, so she turned her attention to Mick. She spoke to him but then realised that she wasn't getting any response, so she shook his leg. He had been asleep for a while now, and she became quite worried when he didn't move, or respond in any way at all.

"Mick... Mick, wake up mate," she said, shaking him harder, but he remained still. "Mick, Mick!" she was shouting now causing Panos to look over from the bar. She stood up and slapped him on the arm. He didn't react. Now, she was concerned and very frightened.

Panos excused himself from the guests and ran over to Mick. He tried his best to wake him up, but with no success. He put two fingers to Mick's neck and was relieved to find that he had a pulse. It was rather weak, but it was there. Panos remembered what had happened earlier, and his heart dropped. He began to pray quietly.

Danielle, thinking about Tracey, went into Mick's pocket and pulled out his phone. Her hands were shaking as she went into his phone book and found her number. She pushed her finger down onto the ring button and waited for a connection. It took a few moments, but then it finally started to ring.

Come on, Tracey, come on, she thought, crossing her fingers. Then, to her relief, Tracey answered the phone. Danielle took a deep breath and explained calmly what was happening.

"Dan, try not to worry. This happens all the time. He'll eventually wake up. It's all part of his problem," said Tracey when Danielle had finished. "You do know that he's an alcoholic. It's one of the symptoms. He'll be fine, Dan, honestly."

The word, alcoholic, rang through Danielle's mind, and the reality of his problem consumed her.

"But he needs help Tracey. He has to stop drinking." She could feel the tears welling up, when she looked over at Mick's lifeless body. "What can I do?"

"Unfortunately, there's nothing anyone can do. Believe me, I've tried, but he has to realise that he has a problem. Until that day comes, Dan, we're helpless. It's called denial!"

Danielle couldn't believe what Tracey was saying, she sounded so calm. She knew deep down that he drank too much but surely, he wasn't an alcoholic. Her mind returned to the time when she had witnessed him drinking first thing in the morning. The severity of his problem overwhelmed her, and she could have cried. Tracey explained again that he would be alright and that she was not to panic. Afterwards, she said goodbye and hung up the phone.

Danielle was left holding the phone, feeling somewhat consoled by Tracey's encouraging words. She put the phone back in Mick's pocket and told Panos what Tracey had said. Mick's comatose state had caught the attention of all the guests, and a few of them came over to offer their assistance. Panos was reassuring them that it was all under control, when Mick began to move. He lifted his hand up to his head, and suddenly realised that a crowd had gathered around him.

"W-what's going on?" he asked feeling very confused. "Panos...Dan... Why are all of these people looking at me?"

"Oh Mick, you gave us such a fright. We couldn't wake you up. We tried, but you didn't move... Oh Mick." Danielle couldn't hide her distress and hugged him so hard that he found it hard to breathe. "Mick, I thought that you were dead!"

"I will be if you squeeze me any tighter, Dan," he squeaked, catching his breath. "I was just asleep." She let go of him and looked into his blood shot eyes. Mick could see the concern written all over her face and smiled.

"Dan, I'm fine, absolutely fine. I don't know what all the fuss is about, this happens to me all the time. It's just a deep sleep, that's all. Don't worry babe."

Panos directed the guests away from Mick, informing them that he was alright now. He told them that the panic was over and that they should get back to whatever they had been doing.

"Well I think that he should see a doctor," said one of the guests as they walked away.

"That isn't right, if you ask me. A healthy man shouldn't sleep like that in the middle of the day. No, it's definitely not right," she continued as she walked away.

Panos ignored the last part of the lady's comment and went over to Mick.

"Mick, you should see a doctor, my friend, especially after what happened earlier," said Panos noticing that Mick's face had turned an unusual shade of yellow.

"What do you mean Panos? What happened earlier?" asked Danielle clearly worried as she also noticed the colour of his skin. Mick was about to tell Panos to shut up, but he was too late because Panos got in there first. Danielle's heart dropped when he explained to her the earlier incident regarding Mick's chest pain. By the look on his face, she realised she had been right to be worried.

"Well that confirms it, Mick, you have to go and see a doctor," said Danielle sternly.

"No Dan, I'm OK. I just need a beer to calm my nerves. Panos, if you wouldn't mind."

"I don't think so, absolutely not!" responded Danielle harshly, turning to Panos for his support.

"Danielle's right Michael. I'll take you down there. It isn't far. You will be back, before you know it."

"But...but..." protested Mick trying desperately to be heard.

"There are no buts about it. For once in your life, you are going to do as you're told," said Danielle taking his arm. Panos took his other arm and they both lifted him up.

Mick was starting to feel very frustrated by his friends' behaviour. Then it occurred to him that if he didn't go, he'd never hear the end of it.

Besides, the sooner I get down there, the sooner I can get back to my beer, he thought, letting them lead him to the car.

"Like I said earlier, it's just a touch of heart burn. You're making a fuss about nothing," he said laughing. "You're going to feel really stupid Dan."

"I don't care; I want to hear that from a professional. Now, get in the car!"

Helen got into her hire car and turned the key. It started first time, and the soft purring of the engine filled the car. She sat there for a while with her foot hovering over the accelerator, her heart racing in her chest. The nervousness had re-emerged, and this was evidenced by the flutter of butterflies that danced around in her stomach. She took a deep breath, pushed her foot down and started to pull away from the forecourt. Following the road out of the town, she began to make her way up the picturesque hillside. The island's beauty stole her view, and she couldn't help wishing that she was there on holiday.

Oh, if only things were different, she thought, her mind ruled by her wishful thinking. She quickly refocused her thoughts back on to why she was there and sighed. Her eyes darted back and forth onto the map that was on the seat beside her, and then she came to a right turn. Feeling confident that this was the road leading up to the hotel, she took the turn and carried on. Driving carefully, she negotiated the many bends that awaited her, but found it very hard to concentrate. Her breathing was heavy, but she didn't let the narrowness of the road put her off. She came to a passing place on the road and stopped the car. As she picked up the map to study it, her hands shook uncontrollably.

If I'm right, then the hotel is just at the top of this hill, she thought to herself. Slowly, she pulled away to take the last part of her short journey. As she followed the bend round, she saw the Oasis hotel up ahead. Its name was displayed boldly on top of the white building. Her heart dropped. The traditional Greek hotel stood out like a sanctuary that only dreams were made of, welcoming her like a long, lost friend.

"Wow," she said out loud, admiring the pristine view. "It's beautiful." However, the reality of her purpose there made a sudden comeback, and she forced her mind to return to her mission.

She drove into a lay-by opposite the hotel and parked the car. Her heart was thumping, and she could feel her blood curdling through her veins, but this did not deter her. She stepped out onto the stony road. Peace and tranquillity filled the air, and the stillness that surrounded her made it possible to hear a pin drop. The hotel was protected by high metal gates, standing tall as if to guard this wonderful place. To her it was majestic, like a castle full of treasure, keeping safe its many riches, hiding its precious gems from prying eyes.

"Helen, what are you doing?" she asked out loud, claiming back her thoughts. The deception of the storybook view had tried to deceive her into believing this fantasy, but she was adamant not to let it.

No, the only thing that is in there is the secret behind who I am. Her mind went back to believing this reality, increasing the pain that she felt inside. She walked across the road and found herself in front of the gates. The gaps between the railings made it possible for her to see into the grounds. She looked through and as her eyes focused on the pool area she saw a group of people gathered there. It took her a few minutes to realise that they were crowding round a man on a lounger, and she couldn't help noticing the look of distress on their faces. She stood motionless as she witnessed a tall man shaking the lifeless body. Then she recognised a familiar face.

"That's Danielle," she whispered, watching her speaking on the phone. She focused her eyes back onto the man on the lounger, who was now moving, and the crowd began to disperse. Danielle came off the phone and the tall man went over and put his arm around her. Helen stared at the couple realising that this man must be Panos. She found that she couldn't take her eyes off him completely taken aback by how handsome he was. She felt mixed emotions pulling her in all different directions; she felt very confused. She wanted to be angry, but seeing her half-brother brought up a different feeling, and she couldn't help feeling sorry for him. This was not at all what she expected or how she'd planned it. These doubts began to scare her.

I didn't want to feel this way! I cannot afford to feel this way! she thought. Quickly wiping these unwanted thoughts from her mind, she tried to refocus. Looking around the pool for any sign of her father, her heart raced as resentment returned, releasing an inner strength that enabled her to face him for the first time. She was filled with regret when she couldn't see anyone who fitted his description, so she turned her attention back to Panos. He and Danielle were leading the man from the lounger towards the car. She could now see that the man was Mick. Sheer terror ran through her as she didn't want to be seen, so she ran back to her car and got in. She was confident that she hadn't been recognised, but, just in case, pretended that she was getting something out of the glove compartment. Moments later, the black Mercedes drove past her and she breathed a sigh of relief.

That was close, she thought, trying to calm her speeding heart. She sat looking at the hotel for a few more minutes.

She couldn't get over the place.

They must be worth a fortune, she thought to herself, smiling. This could get very interesting.

She started up the car, turned it around and began to make the short journey back to her hotel, the picture of Panos at the forefront of her mind.

Panos drove into the small, cobblestoned car park and skilfully parked the car in the one remaining space. The three friends got out of the Mercedes and began to walk towards the entrance. The big glass doors opened automatically, and they stepped inside.

"But what if they are too busy to see me?" asked Mick reluctantly.

"Don't worry Michael, the doctor will see you," replied Panos self-assuredly. He knew the doctor personally and was confident that when he had explained the circumstances, he would see him.

He told Mick to take a seat and went over to the reception desk. Danielle sat down with Mick and watched, mesmerised by the manner in which Panos conducted himself with the receptionist. His stature, and the way he presented himself was awe inspiring to her, and even though she couldn't understand a word he was saying, he came across as being very much in control. She smiled at the confidence that radiated through his words. She was impressed and couldn't help feeling admiration for this influential man. The receptionist remained silent until Panos had finished speaking, and then she picked up the phone. Her words were few, but after replacing the receiver, she nodded her head. Panos smiled at her and proceeded to sit down next to Mick.

"It is OK, my friend. The doctor will see you shortly," he said, patting Mick's back. "He is a good friend of mine."

"Blimey Panos, is there anyone on this island that you don't know?" He shook his head and smiled in answer.

"No Michael, there isn't. It is one of the benefits of being a very powerful man."

Danielle could detect arrogance in his voice that she had never heard before, and this unnerved her. Something changed in his eyes as he spoke, and she suddenly realised that there was more to this man that she had grown to adore. She couldn't help wondering if this was the real Panos, and he had been cleverly disguised by the displays of love and affection that he showed her. However, when he looked at her and smiled, her crazy thoughts melted away. His expression was so full of love, quashing any uncertainty in her mind so she smiled back at him. Feeling emotionally secure again, she got up to use the toilet.

Panos watched her leave the room and felt relieved to finally be alone with Mick. He had wanted to talk to him but found it hard to when Danielle was around. His conversation was to be a sensitive one, and he wanted it to be for Mick's ears only. He'd had his suspicions about Mick's drink problem but hadn't previously had the courage to broach the subject. The events of the day however along with what Tracey had said, confirmed his feelings, so he felt now the timing was perfect.

"Michael, I must speak to you. It concerns me that you drink too much. I care for you, and what I'm about to say comes from the bottom of my heart."

Mick tried to say something, but Panos put his hand up in the air and continued. "Michael, I believe that there is a God, and that he is there to look after us if we want him to. He is a God of love, and Michael, he loves you very much. Did you know that his son Jesus died on the cross so that you don't have to go through what you are going through?"

Mick looked at Panos and laughed.

"Panos, I am all for people that want to believe in something, everyone to their own, I say. But I'm not into that religious claptrap. I would be lying if I said that I was. If there was a God, then why do I have so much trouble with women? He is supposed to be a bloke, so he should understand," he said, now feeling quite agitated. "Sorry mate, but you're wasting your breath. So, I drink a little bit too much. My wife has just left me and I'm on holiday. So, to me it's allowed. I'll sort it out when I get home. It's not a problem. It's just my life at the moment. I'll change it. I know I can change it." Mick broke their eye contact and looked down at the floor. When Panos had mentioned God, his heart flipped in his chest. He knew that Greek people were very religious, but Panos had never mentioned God before, so Mick had assumed that he was different. In all the years he'd known him, not once had the subject of religion come up. He was rather put out by the conversation and thought Panos had a nerve to suggest that he had a problem.

What do you know, Panos? He thought. You're the one who plies me with all the alcohol.

Mick's expression changed as those thoughts went through his mind, and Panos couldn't help wondering if perhaps he'd overstepped the mark.

"OK Michael, I hear what you're saying. I just hope for your sake that you do. It's only that I care, and don't want to see anything bad happen to you," he said patting him on the knee. He wasn't however convinced by Mick's statement and just hoped that he was serious about sorting his life out when he returned home.

"I'll say no more about it."

At that point, Danielle came back just in time to hear the receptionist inform Mick that he could now go in to see the doctor.

Mick was grateful that the conversation had come to an end and began to walk towards the doctor's office door. Panos told Danielle to wait outside while he went in with Mick. She was rather put out that she couldn't hear the doctor's diagnosis for herself, but Panos reassured her that it was all in hand. Reluctantly, she sat down and passed the time by flicking through a magazine.

Mick strolled into the large room and was met by a short, stocky man wearing thick rimmed glasses. He was told to sit down, as the doctor shook Panos's hand.

"So, what seems to be the problem?" asked the doctor looking over the top of his glasses.

Panos explained Mick's symptoms, and Mick felt slightly intimated by this strange looking man who was staring at him.

"Look Doc, it's just a bit of heartburn, that's all. Just give me some medicine and I will be on my way. I've wasted enough of your time," said Mick shyly, forcing his eyes away. The smell of alcohol was evident on his breath, causing the doctor to shake his head.

"You've been drinking, yes?" asked the doctor abruptly.

"How many drinks do you have in a day?" He was starting to aggravate Mick.

What does my drink intake have to do with anything? He thought stubbornly. I don't have a problem.

The doctor tapped his pen on the desk waiting for Mick to answer.

"Like I said, it's just heartburn..." said Mick but the doctor interrupted him.

"Please answer the question."

"Yes, I have had a drink. I'm on holiday. That's what people do when they're on holiday. I don't have a problem with it, I can stop anytime. I've only had a couple."

The flippancy in Mick's voice was starting to annoy the doctor, and he soon came to realise that this man was in denial. He had seen it a hundred times before and knew the signs. He was disappointed that there was nothing that he could do for him.

"OK Sir, I'll give you some routine checks, and then you will be free to go. Just rest and try not to drink for the rest of the day. I'm sure that won't be a problem for you, especially as you can stop whenever you want," he said sarcastically. He took Mick's blood pressure and then listened to his heart.

"Your blood pressure is quite high, but your heart is strong. I'm going to put the pain down to anxiety, so like I said, just rest."

"I'm not surprised that I'm anxious with everyone going on at me," replied Mick laughing. "See, I told you not to worry, Panos."

Panos looked at the doctor and rolled his eyes.

"There's still life in this ole boy," said Mick as he got up and shook the doctor's hand. He couldn't wait to get out of there. "Thanks Doc, I appreciate you seeing me. Goodbye," said Mick as he turned and practically ran out of the room.

Panos shook the doctor's hand and thanked him.

"I'm sorry Panos, but that was all that I could do," said the doctor, shaking his head.

Panos thanked him again and walked out of the door. When he caught up with Mick, he was busy telling Danielle about what the doctor had said.

"So, I just need to rest, Dan. The doctor said it himself. I'm just a bit stressed, that's all. I told you it would be nothing," continued Mick smugly. "Now, let's get back to the hotel; all this fussing has made me hungry." He made his way to the entrance and continued to walk towards the car. Danielle looked at Panos confused.

"Well, at least I tried," said Panos putting his arm around her. On the journey back to the hotel, Mick had full control of the conversation. His sense of humour was in full flow, and both Danielle and Panos couldn't help laughing at his funny ways. Their worries were dispersed as they laughed, and Mick was confident that the earlier events of the day were now forgotten.

The sun shone brightly in the afternoon sky, and everything soon got back to normal. Panos was back behind the bar by the pool and Danielle was soaking up the glorious sunshine. She listened as Mick joked with one of the guests about his trip down to the doctor's surgery and was amazed that he could turn any situation into a funny story. She was still slightly apprehensive about him having a problem, but as she watched her comical friend, she found herself wondering if Tracey had perhaps been exaggerating. He insisted that he had his drinking under control, and surprisingly, when he'd ordered himself a glass of coke, she believed him.

Her focus went back to Panos, and all the love that she felt for him flooded her heart. Relieved to feel happy again, she closed her eyes and set her mind to enjoying this wonderful place. Mick took great pleasure in being the centre of attention. Already, he had a number of guests laughing at the top of their voices. The crowd eventually dispersed, and he was left alone with his glass of coke. He had cleverly disguised his need for a beer with his tale of misunderstanding, but now that he had stopped talking about it, the truth hit him like a tonne of bricks. His heart raced and his insides shook with so much force that he thought his body was going to explode.

He lifted his glass up to his lips in an effort to drink its content and had to force the fizzy liquid into his mouth. He looked around the poolside to see if anyone was watching as he gulped down the unwanted substance. His body shuddered when it reached his stomach, and he thought that he was going to be sick. Every inch of him seemed to cry out as his craving gripped his very soul. A picture of his wife came into his mind, and he could have cried.

See, this is what you've done to me, he thought angrily. This is all down to you! He tried to claim back his strength by pushing her out of his tormented mind, but he found it so hard. The only thing that made her image disappear was the thought of a nice, cold beer. Initially, he welcomed the exchange of images, but the picture of the beer was just as tormenting.

Well, at least I can cure this problem, he thought, breathing a sigh of relief.

He scanned the pool area and was pleased to see that no one was looking at him. Panos was busy serving behind the bar and Danielle was in her own world, sunbathing. Thankful for his segregation, he quickly slipped back into the hotel. Yannis was behind the bar, and Mick's racing heart calmed slightly when he thought about his long-awaited drink.

One beer won't hurt, he thought, walking towards Yannis.

"If you could be so kind," he said to him, smiling. "I'll have a pint of your finest."

Helen drove down the winding road, the Oasis Hotel fading into the distance behind her. The last thing she wanted to do was go back to her hotel, so she decided to go for a drive around the island. Patience was one of her strongest traits, but even she found her patience being tested because she wanted so much to go back and face her father. This overwhelming compulsion consumed her, but emotionally she knew that she was not prepared for that reunion yet. Consciously, she controlled this sudden urge to return.

After driving for half an hour, she stopped at a secluded beach. Stepping onto the white sand she shut her eyes and let the sunshine down on her face. The warmth of its rays gently kissed her cheeks, and she couldn't help feeling comforted by this ball of fire that hung high in the sky. Taking her time, she strolled down to the water's edge. The picture of Panos returned to her mind, but she quickly intercepted the guilty feelings that came with the image and set her mind on the next step of her plan. She made a mental note to call a colleague from her office, to ask their advice on the laws of entitlement. This was something that was alien to her because she was a criminal lawyer, but she wanted to know where she stood if she wanted to pursue any legal claims against her father. She wasn't quite sure this was the route that she wanted to go down but felt that she needed to be aware of all the facts incase she did decide to, and the situation should arise.

Bending down, she took off her sandals and let the waves lap over her bare feet and the coolness of the water took her breath away. Moments later, her flesh had adjusted to the temperature and she stared across the clear blue sea. The only thing that could be heard was the gentle sound of the waves meeting the shore, winning her mind into accepting being on this beautiful island. It occurred to her that she felt very calm, and she basked for a moment in the peaceful atmosphere.

The stillness around her caused her mind to wander, and she found herself thinking about how her life would have been if she had been raised here. More importantly, she thought about how different her mother's life would have been. The tears welled up and grief pricked her heart, when she thought about all the years that had been lost. She couldn't help feeling robbed; robbed of her identity, robbed of time, but most of all, robbed of a loving mother. Anger bubbled in the pit of her stomach, as she thought about her mother whose life and death had been so unnecessary. Strength was then birthed out of her rage, bringing her back into the reality of why she was there.

He has got to know what he has done, she thought, the tears now flowing down her cheeks. I have got to be strong. Wiping away her tears, she took a deep breath and walked slowly back to her car.

The second day drew to a close, and Mick and Danielle were the last two guests left in the bar. Mick was feeling very pleased with himself, having successfully managed to outwit Panos's attempts of keeping an eye on him. He had such fun sneaking in a few drinks, and he marvelled in his achievement. Panos washed the few remaining glasses, and then the three of them went up to their rooms. He'd waited all day to be alone with Danielle, and the thought of her lying beside him brought a childish grin to his face. He closed the door behind them, and then led her over to the bed. No words were necessary as they got lost in each other's arms, the world outside becoming a distant memory.

Mick walked into his room, and the emptiness of it embraced him like a blanket of loneliness. Despite the warmth of the summer's night, the coldness that hung in the air around him sent shivers down his spine. His confused state sent his mind into overdrive when he automatically thought about Tracey. He longed to be in his wife's arms and craved to feel her touch. He whispered her name into the darkness, but the sound of his voice was lost in the night. He had never felt so alone, and this unwanted feeling made him want to cry. He went over to his bed and sat down. Putting his head in his hands the tears began to run down his cheeks, a clear manifestation of the pain he was in. His heart ached as he yearned to be loved again. He lay down, feeling helpless in his sorrow. Pulling his legs up to his chest, his body curled into the foetal position, and he rocked himself to sleep.

CHAPTER
NINE

*D*aylight flooded in through the balcony door, and as the sun brushed against her cheek, Danielle was awoken by the gentleness of its rays. Panos's arm was wrapped around her, and the security of him being so close instantly brought a smile to her face. She turned to look at him and stared at his handsome face. It was still of any emotion, and the only sign of life was the tiny flicker of his eyelids. Her smile widened as she studied his perfect features. She felt honoured to be a part of this man's life. He was everything that she had ever wanted, and she found it hard to believe that he wanted her too.

Her mind wandered back to her conversation with Mick when he'd told her about Sophia. When she'd heard about how Sophia had left Panos, she had been filled with compassion for him.

She must have been crazy, she thought. Why on earth would anyone want to let go of this amazing man? Although this question baffled Danielle, she couldn't help feeling glad that Sophia had left him, because if she hadn't, she would never have had the opportunity to know him like she did.

Secretly thanking Sophia for her stupidity, she kissed Panos on the cheek. The feel of her soft lips on his skin brought Panos out of his sleep. He looked deep into her eyes and smiled. His heart skipped a beat when she returned the gesture, and he was instantly propelled into thinking he was the luckiest man in the world. Without the need to speak, he squeezed his arms tighter around her. The next step was inevitable as the ritual of love empowered their bodies to receive the other, bringing them to a place of one accord. He sighed heavily when the moment of passion came to an end and held her close to him. He was aware that he had to go to work, so made the most of every minute that was left by just holding her. Time soon crept up on them, and eventually he had to force himself to let go of her. It was a hard decision to make, but he had no choice, so reluctantly he got into the shower.

Ten minutes later Panos was dressed and ready for the day ahead of him. Danielle busied herself by looking for something to wear in the wardrobe. She found a suitable outfit and placed it on the bed. Next, she got her makeup out of her bag and put it next to her clothes.

"I don't know why you put that stuff on your face," said Panos seriously. "You look so much better without it. I like the natural look of a woman."

Danielle was taken aback by his comment. He went over to her and took her hand.

"And, I don't like that either," he said abruptly, pointing at her pink polished nails. The tone of his voice shocked her. The same arrogance that she had heard at the doctor's surgery escaped through his words, wiping the smile off her face. As he saw her expression drastically change, he could have kicked himself for expressing his opinion.

"I'm sorry Danielle," he apologised, his tone softening. "Sometimes I lose control of my mouth. I shouldn't have said that. It is, of course, up to you what you do." He kissed her hand and looked deep into her eyes.

Alarm bells started to ring in Danielle's mind and a feeling of De-ja-vu. The way that he had spoken to her and the things he'd said sent chills down her spine, because her husband had always tried to control everything that she did. For a split second, it was as if history was repeating itself, making her feel very uneasy.

Panos detected her concern and apologised again. He didn't like the look of distress that she wore on her face and cursed himself for his behaviour. He smiled at her; trying desperately to put things right and she sensed the repentance in his eyes. She soon dismissed her doubts and smiled back at him. Grateful to see his Danielle restored to her beautiful self again, he kissed her on the lips and went off to work.

"I love you," he said happily. "But now, I must work. I will see you very soon my darling." She nodded and watched him leave the room, spellbound by his loving tone.

Panos walked through the lounge and into the reception area. The sound of the phone ringing filled the room, and he was rather annoyed that no one else was around to answer it. His stern look and mild annoyance soon disappeared once he realised who it was. He finished off his conversation by saying goodbye and stating that he was looking forward to seeing them later that afternoon.

He couldn't wait to tell Danielle about his surprise visitor and was pleased to be able to show her off as well. This unexpected turn-around to his day, added to his joy, bringing the smile back to his face. The lounge became inundated with hungry guests wanting their breakfast, and Panos found himself rushed off his feet. Yannis had now joined him, and the two brothers worked together as a team, meeting the guests' every need. As they went about their daily routine, their professionalism could not be faulted. They made every effort to make each guest feel very special.

After the morning rush had quietened down, Panos told his brother about their visitor. Yannis's face lit up when he heard the good news, and he rushed into the kitchen to tell Anna, and his mother. The whole family were filled with excitement, so his mother planned a meal for their special guest.

Danielle closed the door to her room behind her and began the short walk down to the lounge. Her mind was distracted, wondering what the day would bring, when Mick came out of his room. The two friends followed the stairs down, and Danielle couldn't help noticing the sad look on his face.

"Are you OK, Mick?" she asked touching his arm. "You don't look very happy, mate."

Mick thought carefully about his answer. He did feel terrible. The vodka bottle had been empty, and the need to sustain his craving was unbearable, but he couldn't own up to this being the reason why he looked so miserable.

"You're not still getting that pain, are you?" she asked deeply concerned.

He looked at her and forced himself to smile. The concern in her voice touched him.

"N-no, Dan, I am OK. I just didn't get much sleep. I'll feel better when I've eaten something," he replied.

They walked into the lounge where Danielle was pleased to see Panos behind the bar. They took their usual seats and ordered their breakfast. Panos greeted her with a kiss and patted Mick on the back.

"Do you want a cup of coffee?" he asked Danielle, stroking her hand. She nodded. He turned to Mick, who felt himself cringe inside as he waited for the same question. He could feel the bile rise in his throat. Taking a deep breath, he swallowed hard. The last thing that he wanted was a cup of coffee.

"What would you like to drink Michael?" asked Panos looking him in the eye.

"Well, I don't like coffee," he lied. "So, I will have a beer. And, before you say anything, I'm a grown man and don't need to be told what to do, or what I can drink!" he replied determinedly. His craving overruled his need to be polite, giving him the courage to say those harsh words.

Panos didn't like his tone but poured him the requested drink anyway. He could see that Mick was unhappy, and didn't want to add to his unusual, bad mood. Danielle watched as Mick put the glass to his mouth and noticed that his hands were shaking. When he gulped down every last drop, her heart sank. His craving satisfied, his whole persona miraculously changed, and he suddenly relaxed.

"That hit the spot," he said triumphantly now smiling.

"Now, where's my breakfast?"

He was now feeling more like his old self, and this was apparent by the way he joked around with Panos. Danielle couldn't get over how one drink could completely transform a person, and she wouldn't have believed it if she hadn't witnessed it for herself. Sadness consumed her when she thought about his problem, and she remembered what Tracy had said about him being in denial. It all made sense now, and suddenly she understood what she had meant. Mick was acting as if nothing was wrong with him. She could have cried, but she did have to admit, he was a lot happier when he had a drink inside him. Panos interrupted her thoughts when he took her hand and kissed her cheek.

"My cousin is coming to the hotel this afternoon," he said with a glint in his eye. "His name is George, and I can't wait for you to meet him. He's coming over from the mainland." He proceeded to tell her all about his favourite cousin, and by the way he described him, she found herself becoming quite excited about meeting the man Panos spoke so highly of.

"I know he will like you," he said, kissing her hand. "We have the same taste in women. He appreciates beauty too. I'll have to be careful that he doesn't try and snatch you away from me," he laughed, and then kissed her again. "But I know that I have nothing to worry about, because you only have eyes for me."

A guest appeared at the bar, and Panos was drawn away from their conversation. Danielle thought that he couldn't be any nearer to the truth with what he had said, and felt an excitement rise in her belly. It was hard for her to imagine being with anybody else, but the reality of her real life back in England dampened the flame of love that flickered in her heart. It was as if she was living in a parallel world, where her hopes and dreams were temporarily allowed to come alive, giving her permission to live out this wonderful fantasy. Here, she was free to be who she wanted to be. Here there were no distractions, no demands that came with the responsibility of being a mother, no having to put herself last. It occurred to her that if it wasn't for her three children, she would never leave this amazing place. At this, she was suddenly overcome by an overwhelming sense of guilt, throwing her back into the reality of who she really was.

How could I be so selfish, she thought picturing her three children in her mind. My children are my life! The truth of the situation brought her back down to earth. She knew deep down that her future lay two thousand miles away, so she decided to cherish every moment left with the man of her dreams.

The afternoon arrived, and Danielle and Mick were lounging by the pool. The sun hung high in the sky, radiating its power through every ray of light. The intensity of the heat was too much for Danielle, so she went and cooled off in the pool. Panos kept a close eye on her, making sure that she was always in his view. The sound of the entrance gates opening distracted him from the vision of Danielle gliding through the water, and his heart filled with joy when he saw who had opened them. Seconds later, a tall man dressed in a navy-blue suit walked past by the pool. Danielle became aware of him and stopped swimming. He swaggered past her with so much confidence that he could easily have been mistaken for a member of the mafia. She watched him as he walked over to Panos, and by their embrace, she guessed that this must be George.

He was very tall and also very handsome. There was an air about him that led her to believe that he was a very wealthy man. Thick gold chains hung expensively around his neck, and the diamonds in his watch captured the natural sunlight, reflecting the nature of its flawlessness. Danielle was now mesmerised by the two gorgeous cousins. As they pulled away from each other, Panos called her over. As she got out of the water and walked over to the two men, she began to feel very nervous. George took one look at this beautiful lady and was stunned.

"George, this is Danielle," said Panos proudly. He was getting used to the way men reacted when they first met her, so the look on his cousin's face was of no surprise to him.

"Why Panos, she is adorable. Where did you find her?" he asked, taking her hand. Danielle felt her face go bright red and looked shyly away. Panos continued to say something in Greek and both men laughed. This made Danielle feel very uncomfortable as Panos had never acted this way towards her before, and this disrespectful display hurt her deeply.

"Panos you must be doing something different, my friend, because she is not like your usual girlfriends. This one is rather sweet." Danielle glared at Panos. She quickly grew to dislike George, and Panos could see it in her eyes.

"She is very special to me, George, and no, I have never met anyone quite like her," he replied hoping to counteract her angry look.

"OK, whatever you say, cousin. Now, where are my favourite aunt and uncle?" At that point a cry of joy came down from the terrace.

"George!" All three of them looked up to see Panos's mother standing there with her arms stretched out. George ran up the steps and embraced his loving aunt. Panos took this opportunity to talk to Danielle.

"I'm sorry about George. You'll have to excuse his manner: he is very outspoken. You'll get used to him. He's only here for one night," he said submissively, kissing her on the cheek.

"OK, if you say so," replied Danielle sarcastically. Panos ignored her tone and laughed when George picked his mother up and spun her around. Danielle took a deep breath, pacified by the fact that George wouldn't be staying long, and decided that she could tolerate him for a short length of time for Panos's sake. Moments later, she found herself laughing at Panos's mother's many attempts at telling George to put her down.

Mick was dozing, and the sound of a woman's screams brought him out of his sleep. Wondering what the hell was going on; the last thing he expected to see was Panos's mother being swung round like a rag doll. He sat up confused and scratched his head. He decided to find out what was going on, so he walked over to the bar. Panos explained who the man was who was responsible for his mother's shrieks of laughter. Her pleas for release were finally heard, and George put her down.

Panos took Danielle's hand and led her up to the terrace. Mick followed behind them, eager to meet Panos's cousin.

They were introduced and Mick's eyes widened as he stared at the man's thick gold chains.

"Hello, Michael; it is good to meet you. Any friend of Panos is a friend of mine." Mick shook George's hand, and his eyes nearly popped out of his head when he noticed his huge diamond watch.

"Blimey, George, that's some watch you've got there. It looks very expensive, my friend."

"What, this old thing? It is years old. I've got three better ones at home!" Danielle cringed at the arrogance of this man, but Mick was in awe of him.

"What about a drink, Panos? I could do with a nice, cold glass of beer," George asked, rubbing his hands together.

"You're a man after my own heart, George," said Mick smiling. "I like you already."

The rest of the afternoon was spent in George's company. His domineering nature made him the life and soul of the hotel as he captured everyone's attention with his tales of back home. Danielle found that, if she looked beyond his superciliousness, he was quite a nice guy. His sexist jokes still bothered her, but she was good at shutting her mind off to them. She had gotten a lot of practise in the past because Mick took great pleasure in sharing his chauvinistic anecdotes with anyone that would listen. To Mick, George was a godsend, and he was pleased to find that they had a lot in common. He quickly grew to admire this man and loved the fact that he had lots of money.

The afternoon soon evolved into early evening, and Danielle and Mick were invited to join the family for dinner. They both accepted the invitation and enjoyed being a part of their celebratory meal. The drinks flowed freely, the food was superb, and everyone was relaxed in each other's company. Danielle was amazed at how hard Panos's mother and Anna worked. They were so organised, and yet they still managed to eat with them. Panos's father was at the head of the table and it was the first time that Danielle had seen him interact with his family. She smiled as he joked with his nephew, and she had to admit that she did like this side of him. His eyes sparkled when he laughed, and Danielle saw a glimpse of Panos's good looks shine out of them. The conversation was flowing when George proposed that they all went into town. The night was on him, and he made this perfectly clear. Panos's parents declined, but his father encouraged Panos to go along. Yannis and Anna said that they would stay behind, so Panos took George up on his generous offer. He suggested that they went down to Nicos's bar, and they all agreed. George knew Nicos well, and he looked forward to seeing him again. Panos kept the news of Nicos's engagement to himself, as he couldn't wait to see the look on his cousin's face when he found out. The night ahead arranged, Panos couldn't have felt any happier. He was surrounded by people who were very dear to him, and he was loving every minute of it.

Helen's day had started off as a productive one. She had spoken to her colleague on the phone and was advised that all the relevant information that she had requested would be e-mailed to her later that day. The voice from home caused her to feel very homesick, but she quickly pushed aside these unwanted feelings. She had made up her mind to confront her father that afternoon, but her attempts to go through with this had failed miserably. She got as close as the hotel gates, but nerves had gotten the better of her, and she chose to drive away. She could have kicked herself for losing the courage to face this situation head on, but soon talked herself around, convincing herself that there was always tomorrow.

When she got back to the hotel, she asked the manager if she could use the hotel computer. She was pleased to be allowed to, and immediately went into her e-mail account. She spent the next couple of hours studying the many pages of documentation that she'd received, absorbing every word that was significant to her cause. Fortunately, she was blessed with having a photographic memory, so deciphering, and then remembering, the legal jargon wasn't a problem for her.

Her stomach was stung by hunger pangs, and she soon realised that she was starving. She was grateful that another day was nearly over, and she decided to treat herself to a nice meal. She hadn't eaten properly since she'd been on the island, and the thought of a nice steak tormented her rumbling tummy. A leaflet rack was hung on the wall beside the computer, displaying a varied range of general information. So, fingering through the leaflets advertising local restaurants, she pulled out one that caught her eye. Nicos's was displayed in bright bold letters, and to her, it looked like the perfect place to go. The leaflet indicated that you needed to reserve a table, so she took the liberty of asking one of the hotel staff to make a reservation, for her. Without hesitation, her request was carried out. Putting the leaflet in her bag, she went back up to her room to get showered.

An hour later, feeling refreshed, she left the hotel and headed towards the harbour. The evening brought with it the usual hustle and bustle of holiday life, and the atmosphere was electric. Everyone had a smile on their face, and the joy of being on this lovely island was evident in their eyes. Helen breathed in the friendly ambience and set her mind on enjoying the evening. Having put the thoughts of her father to one side, she carried on down the road feeling rather relaxed.

She reached her destination and looking at her watch. Realising she still had time to spare; she decided to have a drink at the bar. She was greeted at the top of the steps by a tall man wearing a tuxedo, and after checking his list, he let her though.

This must be some place, she thought, eyeing up the handsome Greek doorman. Her thoughts were confirmed when she walked in and was confronted by an exquisite restaurant. Quaint tables and chairs were neatly placed around the room and soft Greek music played in the background, making her feel very comfortable in her surroundings. She was met by the maître d' who was dressed in the same attire as the door man. As he led her over to the bar, he informed her that he would let her know when her table was ready. She politely thanked him, and he left her to order her drink.

As promised, twenty minutes later one of the waiters explained her table was ready and he escorted her to it. The service was excellent, and Helen congratulated herself on her choice of Taverna. The standards and quality were very high, highlighted by the price list. But the expense did not deter her, because this was all a part of the life that she had grown accustomed to back in England. Now feeling very much at home, Helen studied the menu. Many different dishes were on offer, making her decision of what to have a very difficult one. After a few minutes of debating, she finally decided on the sirloin steak. The waiter reappeared with his note pad and proceeded to take her order. She requested a glass of their best red wine to accompany her meal and was pleased to be told that it was on the house. It was a compliment from the host, and the waiter left Helen feeling very happy.

Her eyes scanned the perfect room. Because it was still quite early, only half the tables were occupied and she couldn't help noticing that most of the diners were couples.

Harry would love it here, she thought. She allowed her mind to wander back to her normal life that had been put on hold, and she could have cried. Harry was a very close friend of hers, but he wanted more from her than just that. He understood her decision to come to Skiathos and had reassured her that he was always there for her if she needed him. She had grown very fond of him, but she just couldn't commit to a long-term relationship. Her feelings for him were getting stronger, but the news of her father had rapidly quashed them. She missed the friendship that they shared, but she had to force herself back into reality. She couldn't afford to get side-tracked, so taking deep breath, she pushed him out of her mind. The waiter returned with her glass of wine, and she smiled at him when he put it down in front of her. Taking a sip, she focused on the beautiful music and waited for her meal to arrive.

Nicos came into the restaurant and went behind the bar.

He noticed a young lady eating alone, so went over to welcome her. As he introduced himself, Helen was taken aback by the attractiveness of her host. She couldn't help wondering if all Greek men were handsome, because she hadn't encountered an average looking one yet. After spending a few minutes in conversation, they were disturbed when Nicos was called over to the bar.

"I hope that you enjoy your meal," he said, kissing her hand.

Helen thanked him for his hospitality, and he walked away. She watched him walk across the room and was amazed by the friendliness that he had showed towards her. He went up to a very attractive lady who was standing up at the bar, and by the way that they embraced, she guessed that they were a couple. Then, the attractive lady left. Helen turned back to her meal and carried on eating. Finishing her dessert, she became aware that the restaurant was now a lot busier. The food was first-class, and she was content and feeling very full. The array of people gathered at the bar made it impossible for her to see the main door, so she didn't see the next group of guests entering the restaurant. Minding her own business, she sipped another glass of wine. Then, the sound of Nicos's raised voice caught her attention.

"Panos!" The sound of this name caused Helen's ears to prick up, so she strained her eyes to see who Nicos was talking to and her heart sank when she recognised her half-brother. She noticed that he was accompanied by Mick and Danielle. Furtively, she put her hand up to the side of her face and hid behind the menu, hoping that she wouldn't be seen. Her heart was racing in her chest, and she had a horrible feeling that she was going to bring up all the lovely food, she had just eaten. Taking deep breaths, she tried desperately to calm herself down.

Nicos welcomed Panos with a heartwarming embrace. George was standing behind Panos, and when Nicos saw him, he was taken by surprise.

"George is that really you, my friend," he said, quickly letting go of Panos. George nodded and stretched out his arms. The two men embraced, and Mick felt slightly hurt that Nicos hadn't seen him.

"H-hello Nicos," said Mick clearing his throat, but his words got lost in the sound of their laughter. Greek words flew back and forth through the air and he became quite agitated by their ignorance, because it was as if he wasn't even there! Eventually, Nicos turned to Panos's two friends.

"Danielle, ah Danielle, it is so good to see you again," said Nicos taking her hand and gently kissing it.

"And Michael, you have come back, my friend, it is good to see you too," he said finally.

Mick's faith in Nicos was soon restored as he shook his hand. Mick pulled him to his chest with so much force that Nicos thought he was going to squeeze the life out of him. The look on Mick's face said it all. He looked over to George and smiled. Nicos pulled himself away from Mick's bear hug and led them over to a table. He was so pleased to see George again that he ordered the waiter to fetch one of their finest bottles of champagne from the cellar. Panos kissed Danielle on the cheek, and taking her arm, they followed Nicos to their table.

No-one noticed the lady hiding behind her menu as they passed by her. Helen sighed with relief that she hadn't been seen and waited until they were all seated before making a quick exit out of what could have been a very awkward situation! Finally, as they settled at their table, she discreetly called the waiter over to pay her bill. The waiter took her credit card over to the bar, and she waited patiently for him to return. This would be one of the rare times that she could have cursed herself for not having any cash on her. She just wanted to get out of there. As time passed, she nervously tapped her finger on the side of her empty glass. Suddenly she felt an impulsive need to look over to Panos's table and forbid herself from doing so. She couldn't however help herself. As the compulsion grew too strong to resist, she decided to take a quick glimpse and she found herself staring at her half-brother, mesmerised by his handsome looks.

The sound of her name brought her out of her trance and she could have kicked herself because just at that moment Mick spotted her!

"Helen...Helen, it's me, Mick. We met yesterday, remember?" He flapped his arms around in the air in such an obvious way that she felt compelled to wave back at him.

"Come and join us Helen. You've got to meet my mate Panos. You know; the one I told you about," he continued eagerly.

Helen could feel her face go bright red. Mick's raised voice had unfortunately caught the attention of everyone in the room, and all eyes were curiously on her.

Oh no, she thought. How am I going to get out of this? She was just about to shake her head, when Nicos intervened.

"Yes, come on over," he said, gesturing for her to join them. "There's plenty of champagne to go around."

Helen looked at Danielle who returned her gaze with a big smile on her face, so she relented.

I suppose one drink won't hurt, she thought dismissively. The waiter returned her card, so she picked up her bag and went over to join them. Nicos put a chair between Mick and Danielle, and she sat down.

"This is just lovely," said Nicos, raising his glass.

"I'd like to make a toast, to family and long-lost friends."

Helen had just taken a mouthful of her drink. The words of the toast cut into her soul and she nearly spat her drink out across the table. She managed to swallow down the champagne, but nearly choked on it in the process.

"Are you OK Helen? You've gone as white as this tablecloth," observed Mick, concerned by the ghostly look on her face.

In response she just nodded and forced herself to smile, not wanting to draw any unwanted attention. Danielle gave her a napkin, which gave them the opportunity to talk. Danielle was rather relieved to have another female to chat to. Panos was preoccupied with George, so she welcomed this time spent with another woman.

As the two of them got engrossed in conversation, Mick took the opportunity to get Panos's attention. After many attempts of waving his hands, he finally succeeded.

"What's wrong with you, Michael? You look like a demented monkey."

Mick didn't have a clue what one of those was, but by the way George and Nicos laughed, he gathered that this must be a good thing.

"Panos, she's the lawyer I was telling you about. Isn't she hot? What do you think mate? Have I got a chance?" asked Mick. He spoke so quietly that Panos found it hard to hear what he was saying. He did, however, pick up on the words hot, and lawyer, so nodded his head in agreement anyway. He wasn't quite sure what he was agreeing to, but the cheesy grin on Mick's face assured him that he had given the right answer.

Panos looked at Danielle. She was deep in conversation, and to him, she was the most beautiful woman in the world. He felt slightly guilty for not giving her his undivided attention, but he knew that it was only temporary, because George would be gone in the morning. He knew that he would make up for this time, and after tomorrow, she would be the centre of his universe again. He put his hand on her leg and gently stroked it. Her eyes didn't stray from her conversation, but she did put her hand on top of his. This sign of her awareness was enough for him, and he turned his focus back to his cousin.

The drinks were flowing and naturally all their conversations were combined. Danielle was feeling quite drunk. Laughter rippled through the air, and George was the one responsible for their joy. The more drunk he got, the louder his voice was and Danielle found herself being drawn in by his chauvinistic views. The discussion became so heated at one point that it could quite easily have been mistaken for an argument. She managed to get her point across, and was pleased to find an ally in Helen, who was just as sure of her views as she was. The penny dropped when Panos realised who this woman was. By the way she spoke, she obviously knew what she was saying, and it suddenly dawned on him that she was the lawyer who Mick had met in the town. He looked at Mick and laughed. From the look on his face, and by the way he was hanging on her every word, he seemed to be absolutely besotted with this woman.

Panos turned to Helen and studied her face. She was very attractive, and he couldn't help feeling that she looked familiar. Racking his brains, he thought hard about where he might have met her before, but his mind drew a blank.

Oh well, she must just have one of those faces, he thought.

As the night drew to a close, Panos suggested that they went back to the hotel for a night cap. Mick invited Helen to come back with them and was pleased to get the approving nod from Panos. She couldn't believe she was still at the restaurant. The many drinks that were at hand resulted in her feeling very tipsy, so she said that she would think about it. The night had turned out to be a blast, and she was glad to have been able to show off her talent for courtroom boxing. Throughout the evening many times her words had been great ammunition, tying George's ludicrous comments up in knots and her justified statements packed a great punch, bringing him down a peg or two. She loved the banter, because it ignited a fire in the pit of her stomach, and she always enjoyed winning a good fight. Her competitive spirit made her feel like she was alive, and this was why she loved being a lawyer.

Her mind went back to Mick's invitation. She knew that the likelihood of her bumping into her father was high, but she felt strong enough to at least take a look. She didn't have to talk to him. Besides, nobody knew who she was, so they would be none the wiser.

I can have one drink and then I'll leave, she convinced herself laughing when she remembered that she had said this to herself earlier. Now here she was hours later, feeling rather drunk and actually contemplating going to the Oasis hotel. Her drunkenness had pushed her logic aside, so she decided what the hell.

"I will go with you, Mick," she said, slurring her words. "Yes, I would love to."

Mick thought that all his Christmases and birthdays had come at once.

See Tracey, I knew I could pull her, he thought his drunken state warping his mind into believing he was going to score with this classy lady

It took the next ten minutes to say goodbye to Nicos. Panos, who was the last to leave, held his close friend, and suddenly realised that Cassia hadn't been there. Nicos explained the reason for her absence, and reassured Panos that he would give her his regards. Panos had forgotten to mention his engagement. He apologised for his absent mindedness, and the moment had passed because George was now waiting in the taxi. The events of the night had pushed this good news out of his mind, but he vowed to tell George as soon as he got into the car.

"Tell him he has an invitation to the wedding," said Nicos patting Panos on the back.

"That will most probably be the next time I'll see him." Panos assured him that he would and went out of the door.

Danielle was waiting by the taxi. Mick and Helen were already inside with George, and Panos took this opportunity to take Danielle in his arms.

"Thank you for tonight. I know that we have not had much time together, but I will make it up to you, I promise." He kissed her lips, and once again she was lost in his embrace.

"I love you." With that they got into the taxi and were soon on their way the hotel.

The big iron gates opened, and the taxi pulled up by the entrance steps. George paid the driver, and Helen's heart began to beat faster as she got out of the car. Her drunken state had managed to push her nervousness aside, and all five of them walked up to the front door. She felt the need to hold Mick's arm and was somewhat comforted by using him as a crutch. Her actions confirmed Mick's earlier intentions, and he couldn't believe his luck. With Helen beside him, he felt that he could conquer the world, and the thoughts of Tracey were kept nicely at bay.

Panos opened the door and they piled into the lounge, which was free of guests. The only people present were Yannis and Anna. A big smile exploded across Yannis's face. He was delighted to be able to spend some time with his favourite cousin. George's loud voice bellowed across the room as he made his need for a drink known. Yannis quickly obliged his command and started to pour him a beer. Helen walked across the room in a daze. The simplicity of the hotel took her breath away, and she found herself in awe of its perfection. To her, it was the most perfect hotel that she had ever seen, and her mouth dropped as her eyes went around the room.

Mick noticed the dumbstruck look on her face and smiled.

"It's a nice hotel, isn't it?"

"Yes, it's beautiful," she replied, taking her hand out of his arm. Mick was bit concerned by her action, so quickly tried to think of something to say that would put her back in his clutches.

"Let's get a drink. Would you like some more champagne?" This was all that he could come up with, and he had to admit, in his head it was a good idea.

Helen nodded her head, still bewildered by her surroundings. Her thoughts were interrupted when the roar of laughter filled the room. She looked around to see what was going on. Mick had disappeared and she couldn't work out why the others were laughing, then it all made sense to her when she saw him sprawled out across the floor. She was reminded of their first meeting and couldn't help but laugh too. His response was the same as ever, as he cursed the little step that had contributed to his fall. Panos quoted each word in unison with Mick, and this added to their gales of laughter.

"Oh Michael, you are so predictable, my friend. You've got to be more careful," laughed Panos helping him up.

Danielle was reminded that those were her exact words and told the story of their first meeting with Helen. Helen backed up the account of the time they'd met, but she carried on the comical tale by saying,

"Well, at least this time you didn't end up covered in coffee and your hair is still intact."

Mick was hurt by her ploy to make him look silly. He was

quite capable of doing that himself and didn't need anyone else to point out his stupidity, especially not someone he had just met. Danielle noticed his troubled look. He looked so vulnerable and her heart went out to him.

"Come on, Mick, don't look so serious mate. If you could see yourself, you'd laugh..." she commented. "Have you ever noticed that you're always falling over? You're like a Weeble. Do you remember them?" she asked. She looked him in the eye.

"Weebles fall over but they just get up. That's you, babe. But I do wonder sometimes how you do get up," she said laughing.

"Well, it'll take a lot to keep me down, Dan," he replied positively.

"That's the spirit, Mick... but you do look funny when you go, especially when you're covered in coffee," she concluded. She just couldn't help herself.

"Well you know how important my hair is to me. It's my crowning glory. All the ladies love my hair," said Mick combing his fingers through his hair. "Now, where's my drink?" Reclaiming his confidence, he walked over to the bar, (minding the step) and took a big swig out of his glass. Helen walked up beside him. She felt terrible for being so mean, so apologised. He told her that it was ok, and that she needn't worry, continuing by saying that he was used to people making fun of him, and that it was water off a duck's back. She wasn't too sure of his answer, but she was glad, he was apparently back to being his usual happy self again. She kissed his cheek, restoring all his desires for her, and he smiled to himself.

She is putty in my hands, he thought.

Helen having put her mind to rest, continued to ask

about Panos. Her inquisitive questions took Mick by surprise, but he soon convinced himself it was her way of getting to know him. He quickly took her through their first meeting and was pleased to get in the situation between him and his ex-wife. He elaborated on the fact that Tracey was his ex, in the hope of using his sad predicament as a way of touching Helen's heart. His attempts to pull her heartstrings didn't seem to have the desired effect though, because she was more interested in Panos. George then stood up and motioned to Panos, and Mick was glad of the distraction from Helen's questions. Although he loved Panos, he didn't want to spend all night talking about him.

"Panos. A bottle of your finest champagne please. I want to finish the night off in style," said George excitedly.

Yannis took over the role of barman and went down to the cellar while Panos looked around and felt pleased to see that everyone was enjoying themselves. Mick took the opportunity to ask George about his work. George seemed reluctant to divulge too much information, and just told him that he dealt in property. This he said was where the money was, and making it quite clear that there was a lot of money to be made. This intrigued Mick who was always on the lookout for ways of getting rich. He felt that perhaps this was the perfect opportunity for him to get in on the action.

Yannis returned with the bottle of champagne. He poured out the required amount of glasses and handed them around. Panos was the one to propose a toast this time, raising his glass to the love of his life. The only person to leave their glass on the bar was George.

"But Panos she's not Greek," said George looking at him

puzzled. "You know that being with a foreign woman is frowned upon in our culture, so how can I toast to your future when you don't have one?" The whole room fell deadly silent. You could have cut the atmosphere with a knife.

"You do know that Danielle, don't you," continued George turning to Danielle. "Panos must have explained that you can never be his wife!" he said his eyes boring into hers in a hostile manner.

She had never been so embarrassed as he put her on the spot, and she didn't like it. She turned to Panos in the hope that he would say something on her behalf, but he stayed silent.

"Of course, Danielle knows that, George," said Yannis jumping to her defence. "But that doesn't stop Panos from having deep feelings for her. Look at her, George, she's gorgeous and there's no reason why they can't be very close friends." George threw his head back in disgust.

"Well, I hope you know what you're doing Panos," continued George ignoring Yannis's remark. "You must not disgrace the family."

Panos had the utmost respect for his cousin, but for the first time in his life he wanted to punch George in the mouth, and it took all his strength to control this sudden surge of anger. He breathed deeply to resist the urge and stayed silent in an attempt to contain his fury. He was frightened that if he opened his mouth, then the words would flow. After that, there would be no going back from the loathing that bubbled in his heart that was desperate to escape. He managed to calm himself down and looked at Danielle. The hurt look in her eyes melted his heart, and he smiled.

"I knew what was expected of me, George, but then this lady came into my life," he said, now fully composed his eyes still on Danielle. "I don't have to be reminded thank you... Anyway, I do not know what business it is of yours. I don't interfere with your affairs, and I expect the same respect from you," he said finally turning to George shrugging his shoulders. "And, Yannis is correct in what he says, she is gorgeous."

George stared at Panos but did not like what he saw in his eyes. The love for Danielle that they revealed seemed genuine, sending a wave of jealousy seething through his body. He had always envied his younger cousin, and this potent feeling had fed his desire to be better than him. The fact that George was older made it possible for him to manipulate his power of control, and from an early age he had always gotten his way where Panos was concerned. He knew that Panos had an angry streak and had always loved to provoke him into showing that side of his nature. He knew the right buttons to press and took great pleasure in instigating an argument, just to get him to the place of no return. He got satisfaction and felt rewarded by seeing Panos in such a state that he was nearly brought to tears. His title had been secured, so now it was time to put Panos back in his place. The respect that he gained fulfilled his insecure need to be the best, reassuring him into believing that Panos would never dare to defy him. But now, here he was confronted with a man whom he didn't recognise. He didn't like the fact that this woman was responsible for Panos's unexpected reaction, and on her head, he placed the blame.

George hated that Panos's life had always panned out for him; it seemed that everything he touched turned to gold. Even the women fell at his feet, and he found this frustrating because he didn't get a look in when Panos was around. Although his confidence had been shaken, when he came into money himself, he used this superficial power to help him in his quest to find love. But his wealth attracted the wrong type of women, who, he was to find out, were more in love with his money than they were with his character. This hardened his heart, giving birth to his arrogance and making him the man that he was today. But underneath his synthetic personality, still lived a timid man and he didn't like being reminded of this weakness. He did have to admit that Danielle was beautiful, and this added to the many reasons why he felt the need to destroy something that was special to Panos. Realising that his task was failing, he thought hard to find another plan to cause disunity between the couple. Then the revelation came, and he smiled slyly at his cousin.

"OK Panos, I know my place…" said George hesitating.

"Oh, by the way, I bumped into Sophia a couple of months ago," he lied. "You remember her, don't you? Well you should do, she was, after all, your fiancée. It's a shame that she left you the way she did. You did make such a lovely couple. She is just as beautiful as I remembered."

How could you have let her get away, Panos? And, I thought that she was the love of your life… Now, she is a gorgeous lady, sorry, a gorgeous Greek lady." His eyes reflected his triumph and his chest puffed up with pride. He knew that he'd touch a nerve when he mentioned her name.

The news of Sophia's sudden departure had swept through the family like wildfire. George had seen the devastation that it had caused and watched Panos's life crumble before him. He remembered secretly gloating at his cousin's misfortune back then, but he had managed to hide this sadistic side of him. This accomplishment proved to be a success, because he found that he could display the one of his two faces with the greatest of ease. Now Panos's life was restored, and he had managed to meet another beautiful looking lady, George's resentment had come back to life, in full force. He absolutely hated the fact that Panos had come out of his heartache unscathed.

The room went quiet. George's focus was on Panos, and the satisfaction that rose up in his eyes sent Panos's heart racing again. Panos couldn't believe that George could stoop so low. The bubble of anger in his stomach returned, bringing with it a compulsive need to hurt him. Panos tried desperately to understand why this man, whom he loved, would want to cause him pain. His fraught mind couldn't find an answer, baffling him even more. He made a conscious effort to keep the confused state from showing on his face and forced a smile to appear.

"That's nice, George," he replied keeping his anger at bay. "Now Danielle, I think that it's time we went to bed." He turned to Danielle and nodded his head. "OK, my darling?" Danielle agreed and Panos put his arm around her.

"Yannis could you please tidy up? I'm sorry but I need to get out of here." They were just about to walk away when George spoke again.

"Panos, I have to ask, my dear cousin."

You just don't know when to keep your mouth shut, thought Danielle. She was not alone because the same thought ran through everyone else's mind.

"After having Sophia in your bed," George continued. "How can you go to that?" he asked abruptly, pointing to Danielle. This statement was enough to push Panos over the edge. Unable to contain his rage, he ran over and hit George squarely on the jaw. The force of the punch knocked George clear off his stool, and he landed with a thud on the floor. Panos's anger flared. His control flew out of the window, but George got up and retaliated by hitting him back.

The two men fought furiously. Danielle tried to stop the fight by trying to get between them, but it was no use. The likelihood of her getting hit by the many blows that flew through the air was so high, that she got out of their way fast. She resorted to shouting at them in an attempt to stop the madness, but this was no good either.

Helen didn't know what to do. As Mick was encouraging Panos to hit George harder, one of the punches was misaimed, and he was struck on the jaw. The fist that felt like a missile knocked him to the ground, causing Helen to join in with the shouting.

The sound of shattering glass rang through the air, waking Panos's father up from his sleep. To his relief, his wife had not been disturbed by the noise, so very quietly, he put his dressing gown on, and went down to investigate. As he neared the lounge, the sound of hysterical screams could be heard, so he quickened his pace to see what was going on. When he entered the room, he couldn't believe his eyes. Mick was on the floor holding his chin. He was being comforted by a woman who he had never seen before, and George and Panos were now wrestling on the floor like wild animals. Yannis was running around like a headless chicken, and Anna was nowhere to be seen. The only person who was quiet was Danielle. She was now sitting up at the bar with her head in her hands.

"What is going on?" asked Panos's father whose voice was so loud that it made everyone jump. The fighting stopped instantly, and all eyes fell on him. Helen's mouth dropped when she looked at this middle-aged man, and a horrible feeling rushed through her body. Quickly focusing her mind back on Mick, she took deep breaths to get rid of this awful sensation.

"What are you two doing?" he asked looking straight at the cousins. "I'm surprised that you didn't wake up all of the guests. Your behaviour is disgraceful, do you hear, utterly disgraceful. Panos, you should know better than this. This is not what I expect from my son!" His voice was fired up with anger; and he was very disappointed by this despicable display.

"Blimey Panos, I meant hit George, not me...You really hurt me," said Mick accusingly still holding his chin. Panos's father's enraged stare went straight onto Mick. Helen's attention was on Mick's injury, when she noticed him looking over towards the restaurant door. She had heard the word, son, as clear as day, and her horrifying feeling returned more vigorously than before. She found some courage from out of nowhere, turned her head and followed his stare.

Panos's father was just about to look back over to Panos, when he saw her. His heart flipped violently, causing a dull pain to shoot through his chest.

"Elizabeth...Elizabeth?" he whispered. He brought his hands up, and rubbed his eyes, thinking he must be imaging things. When he looked again however the vision of his first love was still there. But it can't be, he thought disbelieving what his eyes were telling him, as he walked towards her.

Helen watched the man as he closed in on her. She wanted to run but found she couldn't, as it seemed as if her feet were stuck to the floor. Panos looked across the room and noticed that there was a handbag on the ground. He didn't recognise it as being Danielle's, so guessed that it must be Helen's. It had been thrown off the bar in the scuffle and its contents were strewn across the floor.

"Who the hell is Elizabeth?" asked Mick puzzled. "Her name is Helen," he said to no one in particular.

Helen wanted to agree verbally with Mick just to distract from the disaster she was sure was on the way. She also wanted to tell him to order her a taxi, but the words got stuck in her throat. She had lost the ability to talk and had a horrible feeling that she was going to be sick.

"Is that your name?" asked Panos's father as he got closer to her, his voice barely above a whisper. She nodded slightly, still unable to move. He stared at her face and couldn't believe how much she looked like his Elizabeth. His mind was taken back to all those years ago, bringing with it the love that he had locked away.

Panos looked over to his father. He didn't recognise the expression on his father's face, and he was filled with confusion. He was surprised that he had called Helen, Elizabeth. Suddenly he remembered the conversation they'd had privately, when his father had shared the story of his love affair with an English girl many years ago. He remembered that her name was Elizabeth, and this added to the confusion in his mind.

But she's about my age, he thought. That can't be her; that's impossible. He laughed at his stupidity and went over to pick up Helen's bag off the floor.

Mick sat nursing his jaw. He picked up his drink and gulped down the welcome liquid. George went over to join him, not wanting to be confronted by his uncle's wrath, so sat down quietly next to him. Danielle had also noticed Helen's bag on the floor. So, when Panos bent down to pick up the contents, she went over to help him. Helen was unaware of their actions because she had her back to them engrossed in standing face-to-face with her estranged father. She didn't have a clue what was going on behind her.

"I- I need to get back to my hotel," she said finally finding her voice. "Could you order a taxi for me please?"

Panos's father pulled himself out of his daze and nodded.

"Yes... yes, of course," he replied. He looked over to Panos, but he was busy gathering Helen's belongings together. Instead he told George to phone a taxi for her. George did as he was told and walked over to reception. The sight of her father standing before her induced a pain that clenched her heart, and suddenly she felt completely sober. She could have kicked herself for getting so drunk. If she hadn't, she wouldn't be in the position that she found herself in now. She was relieved to know that her identity was still largely unknown and felt that she wasn't in any danger of it being revealed.

"I'm going back up to bed, so make sure that this place is tidied up," commanded Panos's father as he headed for the door. "I'll deal with you two in the morning," he concluded.

Helen watched him walk away and breathed in a deep sigh of relief. The sooner she got out of there the better. This turn of events made her think twice about confronting her past, so she decided to get on the first plane back to England. She felt the need to get back to her life, and just wanted to forget that she had another family. She made a promise to herself to leave all this behind and focus her mind onto who she really was. She had come this far without a father, so she knew that she could live without him. All her plans to claim a part of his fortune flew out the window, as she just wanted to get back to the comfort of her own world, which suddenly seemed to be the most attractive option.

Danielle was now holding Helen's bag, and had carefully put all the contents back in, before returning it to her. Helen thanked her and went and sat down by the main entrance. She was desperate for the taxi to arrive and willed it to hurry up. Then, Panos noticed a brown envelope under one of the bar stools. He could see a piece of paper poking out and soon realised that it was a letter. He was just about to shout out to Helen, when he noticed his father's name on the front.

Looking suspiciously at it, he asked, "Helen, why have you got a letter addressed to my father?"

His question caught his father's attention just as he was about to go up the stairs back to bed. This caused him to stop in his tracks. When she saw the envelope in Panos's hand, Helen wanted the ground to open up and swallow her. Her mind went into overdrive, trying to think quickly of an explanation, but she was lost for words. She had no idea that the envelope had even fallen out of her handbag, and sheer terror ran through her as she considered the implications of this revelation. Her heartbeat so fast she thought that it was going to explode. Once again, she was rooted to the spot and just stared at the floor.

Panos's curiosity got the better of him, and he unfolded the letter in his hand. His eyes skipped down to the bottom of the page, and he froze.

"Papa, it is from Elizabeth. It is a letter to you from Elizabeth." His father walked over to him, puzzled.

Why would she have a letter from her? There must be some mistake, he thought to himself. It just didn't make sense to him. Panos handed him the letter and he began to read it.

Helen managed to stand up, but all that she could do was watch. She knew perfectly well what it said, and she cringed inside. It was the one explaining her mother's pregnancy. She had put it in her bag before she had come to the hotel earlier just in case she needed proof to back up her allegations. She could have kicked herself for not taking it out after she lost her courage to confront him, but there was no going back now. Tears stung the back of her eyes, but somehow, she managed to keep them from falling. Aware that she needed to be prepared for his reaction, she took a deep breath to summon up her strength. Miraculously, this seemed to work, bringing up the power to face this situation.

Panos's father finished reading the letter, and taking his time, he folded it back up. He needed to sit down so that he could take in what he had just read. He told Panos to get him a chair and by his expression, it was obvious to all that he needed one as the colour had drained from his face. In all the years that Panos could remember being with his father, he had never seen that look before. He was so deeply concerned that he reacted swiftly, carrying out his father's demand. The room went completely silent and everyone waited for someone to speak.

"Blimey Helen, what's going on here? Who's this Elizabeth, and what's she got to do with you?" asked Mick breaking the silence. Behind the bar, the same question went through Yannis's mind. He was confused and wandered how Panos seemed to know about this Elizabeth.

"Papa, what's going on, and yes, who is Elizabeth?"

Helen looked at Yannis and it suddenly dawned on her that he was Panos's brother. She previously assumed that he was just one of the hotel staff. Realising now that she had another brother added to the shock she already felt.

Oh great, now I have two half-brothers to deal with, she thought. Hearing her mother's name empowered her, so straightening her posture she waited for a reply from her father. When it wasn't forthcoming, his lack of words served as torture to her soul, and she found this unbearable.

"Well, aren't you going to say something?" she asked sardonically, staring at her father. "They're very keen to find out who she is. So, are you going to tell them, or do you want me to fill them in on all of the details?" The familiar fire in her belly reignited, making her feel relieved and glad it had returned.

"Are you the baby?" he asked quietly. He dreaded her reply, but deep down already knew what her answer would be. *That explains why she looks so much like Elizabeth,* he thought in a daze.

His question left everyone on the edge of their seats, and they all gasped when she replied.

"Yes, I am your daughter." There she had said it and couldn't help feeling somewhat relieved to have finally been able to reveal the truth. It was as if a big burden had been lifted off her shoulders, instantly lightening the load that had lain heavy on her heart.

"Blimey, that was not what I was expecting." The words just came tumbling out of Mick's mouth. He had tried to keep his statement in the comfort of his own mind, but it had reached his lips before he had time to control it.

"Oops, sorry Panos," he said noticing Panos's harsh glare. "That was supposed to have stayed in my head." Helen's earlier curiosity concerning Panos made sense to Mick now, and he smiled. *That's why she was asking all those questions,* he thought. *She's his half-sister. Great, that means I'm still in with a chance,* he thought selfishly. This time he made sure he kept his thoughts to himself.

Panos's father's mind was spinning. He would never have guessed in a million years that this could happen. This evidence of his past life had thrown the present into complete turmoil.

"So, where's Elizabeth? Is she on the island too? Does she know that you're here?" he asked, trying to keep himself calm.

"No, she's not here. She's dead, so you don't have to worry about her." The rage that bubbled inside of Helen was desperately trying to escape. But she was aware that she had to keep her cool.

"It was when she died that I found out," she explained. "Yes, it was a nice surprise. On the day that I buried my mother, I gained a father. How lucky was I?" she asked, the sarcasm in her voice evident. She couldn't help her tone but was proud of herself for being able to contain her anger. "So, here I am... Daddy."

Panos's father's face went even whiter. He could not believe what he was hearing. Her words were daggers in his heart.

"She's dead, but how, and when?" He couldn't take it all in. He felt sick to his stomach.

"Four months ago. The doctors put it down to a heart attack, but by what is written in all her letters, it would be truer to say that she died from a broken heart. Oh yes, there are many more letters like that back in my hotel room."

The distraught look on her father's face was enough for her to feel sorry for him. He seemed to have aged ten years in a matter of minutes, and she had never seen anyone look so vulnerable.

No, I've got to be strong, she thought, taking a very welcomed deep breath.

"She loved you so much... and I... I blame you for her death." A tiny hint of spite escaped through her words, adding another emotional wound to his heart.

"Now Helen that's unfair. You can't blame my father for your mother's death," Panos quickly intervened. "He had as much knowledge about you, as you did of him. I'm sorry for what happened to her, but it is not his fault. Look at him; he's devastated."

"Panos, now that's enough. I can fight my own battles, thank you," said his father raising his hand.

Unbeknown to everyone, Panos's mother was standing at the bottom of the stairs. She had woken up to find that her husband was missing, so went downstairs to find him. It was unusual for him not to be there beside her, and she was intrigued to find out the reason behind her husband's absence. When she got to the bottom of the stairs, she stopped. The sound of an unfamiliar woman's voice took her by surprise, so she listened to what this lady was saying. The announcement that she heard shook the very foundations of her life, propelling her into complete shock. Her first thoughts were that her husband must have had an affair, but when she looked closely at this woman, she began to get confused, because she looked older than Panos. This acknowledgement added to the confusion of her mind, so she stayed where she was, out of sight, in the hope of finding the truth behind this ludicrous accusation.

This has got to be a mistake, she thought in an effort of self preservation. But then when Panos intervened, she couldn't help wondering if what she had heard was actually true. By what Panos was saying, it was as if he knew all about this Elizabeth woman, and this act of secrecy hurt her deeply. She soon convinced herself that there must be a logical explanation. After all, she loved her husband, and she was secure in the knowledge that he loved her too. She decided to wait until she knew the facts before she jumped to any conclusions.

"Helen...Helen I am sorry that your mother is de... I mean, no longer with us," said Panos's father tactfully. "But Panos is right: I didn't know she was pregnant...This is just as much of a shock to me. If I'd known, then I would have supported you, but like I said, I didn't," he took a deep breath. "Helen, I loved her too, I really did, but it just wasn't meant to be."

"Oh yes, that's right, your father got involved. Apparently, he was really horrible to her, and from what she told my grandmother, he forced her to leave by threatening her."

Helen's strength was rapidly disappearing. The thought of her mother's heartache, and her having to endure such pain, made her want to cry. Panos's father's mind went back to that fateful day: the day that he had overheard his father talking to his uncle.

"No Helen, I'm sorry, but you're wrong. I was told that she wanted to leave. I knew my father was against us being together, and he had spoken to her about it, but she still left me. I was told she didn't even put up a fight. She didn't even say goodbye...I was going to give everything up for her." The pain of that day flooded back into his heart. It was all too much for him, and he began to cry.

"So, who told you that, your father I suppose?" she shouted. "Well, her letters don't relate to your version of events. All she had were words of love for you, she made that perfectly clear. It's all in there." Running over to him, she snatched the letter out of his hand.

"Look again, and read it for yourself, and this is only the last one!" Then waving the piece of paper in his face she said spitefully, "Look...Look, you can see it with your own eyes!"

"But Helen, I didn't know," he said now sobbing.

"How could you not know?" she screamed. "You were supposed to be in love with her!"

Now, Yannis was really worried. This whole situation and display of deep emotion disturbed him. He was in complete disbelief at what had just taken place. He really wanted to go to his father's aid, especially as he had never seen him look sad, let alone cry. He looked over to his brother for support, pointing to his father, but Panos shook his head, and then put up his hand to let his brother know he must stay where he was. Then Yannis eyes went over to the door, where he saw his mother standing there, tears streaming down her face.

"Mother," he said out loud. It broke his heart when he realised that she had been there all along. By the tears that rolling down her cheeks, it was evident that she had heard everything.

The whole room was filled with confusion. There was an eerie silence as everyone followed Yannis's glance and saw his mother standing there. Without thinking, Yannis ran over to her. Panos's heart filled with fury as he witnessed the same pain in his mother's eyes that Yannis had seen. He wanted Helen out of the hotel before she caused any more heartache to his family. The sound of a car sounding its horn could be heard outside, and Panos was pleased that Helen's taxi had finally arrived. The timing was perfect. He had never been so relieved to hear that sound, so taking charge he demanded Helen to leave the hotel.

"Don't worry, I'm going," she said hearing the aggression in Panos's voice. "I can't wait to get out of here. I'll make sure that I'm on the first available flight, so you can be rest assured that I won't be back." With that, she walked out of the door, leaving the Oasis Hotel well and truly behind her.

As soon as she left, Panos bolted the front door. Having done so, he stopped and looked around the room. Danielle was helping Yannis sweep up the glass and George was sitting down next to Mick. His father was still seated on the chair with his head in his hands. Panos's eyes went over to the stairs, but his mother was no longer standing there. He felt his heart drop when he recalled the expression on her face. His whole body filled with regret and he walked over to the stairs. Desperate to talk to his mother, he felt an irresistible need to comfort her into believing that everything was going to be alright. Even though he found this hard to believe himself, he just needed to be with her.

"Leave your mother alone," said his father firmly, looking over to his son. "I'll be the one to talk to her. You just stay here and help tidy up." He knew his son well and guessed that Panos would want to be with his mother, but that wasn't his place, it was his. He was the cause of this whole terrible situation, so it was his responsibility to try and sort out the mess. Wiping his eyes, he stood up.

The thought of having to explain his relationship with Elizabeth to his wife sent shivers down his spine. He would never have imagined being in this position, and he cursed himself for taking his past for granted. He was way out of his depth and felt that the rug of his life had been pulled right out from under him, but he knew that he had to face seeing his wife. She was, after all, his main priority. He temporarily pushed the fact that he had a daughter to the back of his mind. So, feeling totally helpless, without saying a word, he took the first steps to making his way to his distraught wife. The short journey leading up the stairs seemed to take forever. Just putting one foot in front of the other took a great deal of effort. The strength required to fulfil his tiresome destiny had abandoned him, and all that he had left was the bare-knuckle truth of a past life that he had known all those years ago. This unfamiliar sense of vulnerability cut him to the very core of his being, exposing the young man that he had chosen to put behind him. His defences were down, and this scared him. The fortress protecting his dignity had come tumbling down, revealing the same uselessness he felt when Elizabeth had left him. In his mind back then he was a failure, and now here he was experiencing the same feeling he thought he had successfully kept hidden. This reality added to his disposition, and he found it difficult to see a happy outcome to this earth-shattering situation. He was sure that all his future consisted of now was darkness. It was as if a blanket of gloom had snuffed out any remnant of hope. Finally, he came to the door of his room. Putting his hand out to open it, he noticed his hand was shaking. His nervousness reflected how he felt inside, but he couldn't turn back now. So, taking a very deep breath, he pulled the handle down and walked inside.

The task of getting the lounge back to its original state was now complete. Panos said, rather harshly, that it was time to go to bed, and no one dared to argue with him. George was the first to leave the room. He longed for his bed and couldn't wait to get on the boat back to the mainland in the morning. Even though his trip hadn't quite worked out the way he planned it, a deep sense of self-satisfaction caused him to walk out with his head held high. He had no regrets concerning his behaviour with Panos. It was like a game to him and in his mind's eye he pictured himself holding up the winner's trophy, just like he'd done all throughout his life. Only this time, it was bigger and better than before. Not only was he the winner compared to Panos, but he had won the ultimate prize of seeing this family fall apart right before his eyes. Pride pumped through his veins, and he revelled in the fact that he was going to be the one who broke the news of his uncle's estranged daughter. His ego was near to bursting when he imagined the look on his father's face, after he revealed the secret that would bring his uncle's credibility down like a lead balloon. Smiling smugly to himself, he carried on up to his room.

Yannis was the next to go up. Emotionally he felt drained but was relieved that at least, he had Anna to talk to. Panos had been unapproachable and had made it perfectly clear that he didn't want to talk about Helen. Nothing was new as far as Yannis was concerned because once again, he had been kept in the dark. Panos's enigmatic attitude frustrated him and it troubled him that his brother had chosen to keep the motive behind this woman's identity to himself. The torment that this secret had created played on his mind, and he feared that tonight was going to be a sleepless one.

Mick watched Yannis leave the lounge and his heart sank. Time had caught up with him, and the image of the empty vodka bottle that awaited him in his room presented itself boldly in his mind. The thought of having to wake up without his morning fix overwhelmed him. He couldn't go through that ordeal again, so had to think fast on his feet.

"P-Panos," he said nervously. "Is there any chance of me being able to take up a large vodka and orange with me? I... I didn't get much sleep last night, and...And, it will help me sleep. The...the doctor did say that I needed to get my rest," he said silently congratulating himself for coming up with this plausible excuse.

Panos nodded his head. Mick's problem had been pushed aside. All he could think about at that moment was the aftermath Helen had left behind her.

"Help yourself Mick, but be quick about it," said Panos walking over to the light switch. Mick ran behind the bar. He found the vodka bottle and poured himself a drink.

Danielle looked over to Panos, the sadness on his face made her heart go out to him. The usual twinkle in his eyes had disappeared, and all that they reflected now was deep hurt. The need to hold him grew stronger as she stared at this man she didn't recognise. He looked so lost. A cloud of vulnerability had attached itself around him like an old overcoat, covering up any traces of strength left in him. She couldn't ignore the impulsive feeling that dominated her heart and walked over to him. Panos watched her as she came closer. He looked down at the ground. Weakness was not a feeling he was familiar with, but somehow it had managed to overpower him. He didn't want her to see this unfamiliar side of him, so he kept his eyes firmly fixed on the floor.

What happened next took him totally by surprise when he suddenly found himself surrendering to her embrace. Her arms were like angel's wings, taking him to a place that was beyond his obstinate frame of mind, and for the first time in his life, he felt safe in the arms of another woman. All the love he had for Danielle flooded through his heart, washing away the debris of pain that had tried to reside there.

Panos was not the only person who was thankful for this loving gesture. Mick was just about to put the bottle of vodka down, when he realised that Panos's attention was elsewhere. Taking advantage of this opportune moment, he quickly slipped the bottle into his pocket. Guilt tried its hardest to convict him of this dishonest act, but the fear of not having anything to sustain his craving strategically overruled his conscience.

"Right, that's me done," he said, walking away from the bar.

Panos pulled himself away from Danielle and looked deep into her eyes. The warmth that radiated from them made him smile. "I love you," she said, smiling back at him. The sound of her voice was like music to his ears, but even he knew it would take more than words to fix this problem.

CHAPTER
TEN

Helen stepped out of the elevator and walked along the corridor to her room. The task of keeping her tears at bay had been a difficult one, but as she neared her door the floodgates opened, and they began to fall. Her vision was blurred, and it took her a few attempts to put the key in the door. Finally, she unlocked the door and ran inside. She'd never felt so relieved to be in the comfort of her room. Overwhelmed by a gut-wrenching pain, Helen dropped her bag down and threw herself on the bed. A deep sense of loneliness fuelled her tears, giving the ache she felt inside permission to escape. All the pent-up feelings that had lain dormant for the past few months were released, bringing with them an uncontrollable sense of fear that pierced her heart.

The image of her father's face came to the forefront of her mind. This unwanted vision added to her emotional state, throwing her deeper into the dark pit her life had now become. The accumulation of feelings that flowed stripped her of any strength she had left, uncovering a lost little girl who had always craved a loving mother. A lifetime of hurt spewed out onto her pillow, each tear representing a painful memory she thought had long been forgotten. Now here she was all alone, three thousand miles away from home, and facing the biggest rejection of her life. She had never felt so helpless. Up until now, who she was had been built on the strength that had kept her going, cleverly disguising her need to be a part of a family. Ignorance had been her comfort blanket, lifeline, and hope, but now that had been taken away, and she didn't like what was left.

She had never felt so vulnerable; the roots of her very being had been pulled up and exposed for all to see. Suddenly the muffled sound of a phone ringing brought her out of despair. Sitting up, she realised the noise was coming from her bag. Leaning over the side of the bed, she picked it up from the floor. Rummaging through the contents, she found her mobile phone and looked at the screen. Her whole body relaxed when she recognised the name displayed in bright green letters. Not noticing the time, she wiped away her tears and answered her phone.

"H-Harry...You don't know how good it is to hear your voice." With that, she broke down and poured her heart out.

Panos's father walked into his room. The natural light from the moon cut through the darkness, making it possible for him to see that the bed was empty. For a few moments he stood there, staring at the abandoned bed, confused by his wife's absence. The feeling of loss pricked his heart, but he managed to contain it before it found the power to consume him. The thought of losing the woman he adored was quickly disarmed, and he focused his mind on finding his wife. He was just about to walk back out of the room, when his arm caught a photo frame that was on the table next to the door. The sound of breaking glass made him jump, sending a tingling sensation to go through his body.

Oh no! Not that photo, he thought picking it up off the floor.

His fear was confirmed when he looked at the distorted picture in his hand. It was the one taken on their wedding day, and the shattered glass was like a reflection of his heart. Tears stung his eyes as he held the frame to his chest. The memory of that wonderful day became vivid in his mind, bringing with it the strength to try to salvage what was left of his marriage. Placing the photo down, he took a deep breath and walked out of the door.

Silence lay thickly in the air as he walked through the lounge. The quietness of the room couldn't hide the sound of someone crying in the distance, and he soon realised that it was coming from outside. The door to the terrace was open, so he walked over in the hope of finding his missing wife. His suspicions were confirmed when he was confronted with the woman he loved dearly. She looked over to him as he stood in the doorway, her teary eyes sparkling in the moonlight. His heart dropped when she quickly looked away. All he wanted to do was hold her in his arms, to comfort her. Frightened he might be rejected, he wanted to turn around and run away, and it took all his strength not to. Instead, he made the conscious decision to conquer his fear, and started to walk towards her. Finding the courage, he sat down next to his wife and took her hand in his. Aware she was shaking; he stroked her soft skin. Every part of her body was telling her to pull away, but she found she couldn't.

"Why didn't you tell me?" she asked accusingly unable to look into his eyes.

"Why did I have to find out like this?" Tears trickled down her cheeks and dropped onto his hand. "I thought you trusted me. I would have understood... then... then I wouldn't be feeling this pain… I would have been prepared for this day..." Her voice trailed off into a whisper, feeding the regret he felt in his heart.

"But it happened so long ago, and I thought it didn't matter. You are the one I love... You are the one that means everything to me," he said putting his hand under her chin and lifting up her face to look at him.

"How could you think that it didn't matter?" she asked pushing his hand away. "You were going to give up everything for her. You said so yourself."

"Back then, I was just a stupid naive young man. What did I know about love? Then I met you... And that all changed. Please believe me... I love you... and I had no idea she was pregnant...You and our sons are my life... You have always been my life... How can I make this right?" The desperation in his voice was evident, and his wife felt compelled to look at him. His expression went hand in hand with his tone, quickly neutralising the anger she felt inside, and filling her with compassion for the husband she loved so deeply. She found herself trusting his words, and at that point, realised just how much she loved him.

Frightened she would push him away again, he reached out his arms in an attempt to claim back his wife. Her reaction caused him to breathe in a deep sigh of relief, as she responded by submitting to his embrace. The couple held each other tightly, restoring the bond of unity that had kept them together for all these years. Silence fell once again, and after a few minutes, she pulled herself away.

"What was she like, Elizabeth I mean? You said you loved her; she must have been a very special lady?" He was taken aback by her question. Feeling apprehensive, he searched his wife's eyes for any sign of anger, but he was met with softness, reflecting curiosity and nothing else. All he could do was nod. He felt that if he backed up his gesture with words, he was sure to cause his wife pain, and he didn't want to do that.

"Well, I'm surprised you fell in love with an English girl, but going by the beauty of her daughter, I understand why you did. Please, tell me how you met, and what happened. You are my husband and I think I have the right to know," she hesitated and stroked his cheek. "Don't be afraid, I love you and this can only bring us closer together."

Hearing the sincerity in her voice, he shared his account of meeting Elizabeth. He took her through every detail of their time together, and when he came to the end, he noticed there were tears in her eyes.

"So, if it wasn't for her leaving like that, then… then you would have married her, and then there wouldn't have been us."

"But then I met you, and… and the love I felt for you was greater, even more special than I had ever known. I'm grateful for the part my father played… I know he only did it for my own welfare. He saw something in Elizabeth that I was blind to. He knew she would hurt me, and he was right. Like I said, I was just a naïve, rebellious young man who knew nothing about love. My father warned me against English women, but I was stubborn and thought I knew what was best for me… But he was right all along, and she did cause me pain. I'm glad because otherwise I wouldn't have met you, and I wouldn't have experienced the love I get from you."

Tears of frustration burned the back of his eyes. The thought of life without his wife cut him up inside. He couldn't bear the thought and took her hand. "Please believe me. I am nothing without you." She looked at him, tears still evident in her eyes, and smiled.

"I do believe you, and I'm also grateful to your father. I mean that from the bottom of my heart," she hesitated, suddenly understanding the way he reacted towards Panos and Danielle.

"So, that explains why you were so against Panos's relationship. It was as if history was being repeated." He nodded and looked down at the ground, feeling like a little boy who'd just been caught with his hand in the cookie jar.

"I'm sorry, but yes, you're right, I didn't want him to get hurt, and endure that same pain. My father knew what was right, and he passed that knowledge on to me."

"But what if your father was wrong? What if Helen was right and your father threatened her mother to leave? Helen said the evidence was written in those letters. If she is telling the truth, then your father lied, which makes you wrong. We can't change the past, but you can put things right with Helen, and also with your son."

He thought carefully about what his wife had said. The need to know the truth won over his mind, and he looked up and smiled.

"I'm sorry Helen left before I could explain. I should have stopped her. I made her angry, and I feel so bad," he confessed. She could hear the honesty in his words, and her heart went out to him again. Taking his head in her hands, she lifted his face, and kissing him on the cheek, she reassured him, telling him everything was going to be alright.

Panos's mind was whirling so much that he couldn't sleep and just lay there feeling helpless. Minutes passed and even though Danielle was lying beside him, he had never felt so alone. The shallowness of her breathing verified that she was asleep, and he couldn't help feeling slightly envious of her slumber. A little while later relieved that she was asleep, he got out of bed and got dressed. The need to get out of the confinement of his room became so strong that he decided to go downstairs to get some fresh air and clear his head. Pulling a cigarette out of the packet he walked across the lounge. He was just about to light it, when he heard voices coming from outside. Hearing the familiar sound of his parents, he went to the threshold and listened to what they were saying. After a few minutes of listening to their conversation, he was stunned by their words.

"You need to see Helen," said his mother. "She is after all, your daughter."

The sound of that woman's name was like a kick in the stomach. And he couldn't believe what his mother was saying. He was desperate to intervene, but knew it wasn't his place. Containing his feelings and keeping his mouth shut he concentrated on where this conversation was going.

"You can't let her get on that plane without telling her how you feel. It's bad enough that she's lost her mother.

You're the last link to her heritage... and I'll stand by you, like a good wife should stand by her husband." Her statement was food for thought for her husband. He felt honoured to have such an understanding wife, and all the earlier fears he had of losing this great lady were deflated by her words.

"But what if she won't speak to me? There's a high possibility that she won't," he said looking back down at the ground.

"Well, you'll have to cross that bridge when or if you come to it. She's the innocent party in all of this. You will have to be the strong one. There is enough love in this family to overcome this situation, whatever happens, and I don't want us to be responsible for her feeling any more pain than she has to."

The sincerity in her voice was touching, and Panos found himself in awe of this amazing woman he was fortunate enough to call his mother. He couldn't get over the fact that, even after everything that had happened, his mother still found it in her heart to put Helen's feelings before her own. This show of endearment highlighted his own lack of compassion for Helen's plight, and he cringed with shame. In all his selfishness, he hadn't once thought about how Helen must be feeling. He wanted to do the right thing now but was at a loss, as to what he could do. The answer came when his father spoke.

"But we don't know where she's staying. How can we find her before she leaves?"

"I will find her," butted in Panos boldly. "I can find out where she's staying," he continued. Both of his parents turned to look at him completely surprised to see him standing there. Bewildered by his son's presence, his father asked, "Panos how long have you been standing there?"

"Long enough to realise you are awesome parents," he replied smiling. "Just give me a few hours to make some calls. It's the perk of being a powerful man, and thanks, papa, for that. I'm my father's son after all." His father nodded his head with pride. He was grateful for having a supportive family but had to remind Panos of how late it was. They all needed to get some sleep, but he assured Panos he could do what he needed to do in the morning. Panos felt somewhat relieved to have been given the responsibility of finding Helen. He couldn't wait to get on it as soon as he got up. The relief he felt gave tiredness permission to creep over him, so he said goodnight to his parents and went back up to his room. Feeling confident in his quest of being able to track down his estranged sister, he got into bed.

Grateful for having Danielle to snuggle up to he kissed her on the cheek. A sudden gush of guilt sailed through him when he realised he had neglected this lady who had stolen his heart. He had not only allowed the situation with George to push her to one side, but also the fiasco with Helen. Taking those guilty thoughts captive in his mind, he made a promise to never let it happen again. Sleep soon got the better of him, and he drifted off, his arms wrapped around his Danielle.

Disappointment was the first thing to go through Danielle's mind when she opened her eyes the following morning. Not only was she disappointed to discover that Panos was gone, she woke up to find that it was raining. Feeling confused by

Panos's absence, she quickly got up to take a shower. Ten minutes later, she was walking down the stairs to the lounge. Her mind was plagued with worry, and she was eager to talk to Panos about what had happened the night before. His silence had been a warning to stay off the subject of Helen which she did. All she could do was hold him and she felt so helpless having to watch him in such despair. She hoped that now he'd had time to think, perhaps now he would talk to her. Confusion added to her worry as she walked into the lounge. He was at the reception and just as she entered, he put the phone down, and he had a big smile on his face. He said good morning and kissed her on the cheek.

"You are very happy, Panos, is everything alright?" she asked dubiously.

"Well, apart from the weather, everything is fine. I'll explain after I've made you a coffee."

She followed him over to the bar. Curiosity had now taken her thoughts captive, and she couldn't help wondering what the reason could be behind his happy mood.

"Now, my beautiful Danielle," he said placing her cup of coffee down. "I would like you to come with me to talk to Helen." She looked at him dumbfounded. That wasn't what she had expected him to say. He continued to recite, word for word, the conversation he'd had with his parents, and Danielle detected an excitement in his voice. He finished by asking her again if she would accompany him, and she nodded in response. At that point Mick came into the room and caught the tail end of the conversation.

"Panos, my friend, did I just hear you correctly, are you going to see Helen?" he asked. The expression on Mick's face mimicked the same look he had seen on Danielle's, causing Panos to laugh.

"Why yes, Michael, it's my father's wish to speak to her before she goes back to England," he replied proudly. "I don't know if she will listen, but as his son, I have to try."

Mick was surprised by Panos's loyalty but had to agree it did make sense. He really liked Helen and couldn't help sympathising with her predicament. After the way she left, he found it hard to imagine she would want to speak to Panos, so suggested he came along too. The few hours spent with her had been enough time for them to build up a friendship, and Mick was confident that, if Panos's plan failed, he'd be able to talk her round. He smiled to himself when he imagined her giving in to his charming ways.

She will not be able to resist, he thought. She will be putty in my hands. His alternative motive made his smile widen, bringing some sunshine into the otherwise gloomy day.

Panos thought about Mick's suggestion and agreed it was a good idea. He didn't want to waste any time, so told them to meet him by the car in five minutes. Kissing Danielle on the cheek, Panos walked back over to the reception desk. The name of the hotel where Helen was staying was written down on the pad. Panos tore off the piece of paper and put it in his pocket. Smiling furtively, he congratulated himself on his detective work and was relieved to have found the task of finding Helen a rather easy one.

Five minutes later, the three friends got into the Mercedes and headed towards the town. The humidity in the air was thick, and the low cloud made it impossible to see the tiny islands that usually dominated the view. It was now pouring with rain, and Panos had to be very wary of the winding road in front of him. Taking the bends with caution, he managed to get them onto the main road safely. Breathing a deep sigh of relief, Panos took a left turn. Rain on the island was scarce, and he hated driving in these conditions. Aware that he had to be extra careful, he slowed down to master the sharp bend that awaited them. He had driven down this road a thousand times and was used to doing it without having to think. Feeling confident that he was now in full control, he followed the bend round. Its sharpness restricted his view of any oncoming traffic when suddenly; the back wheels lost their grip, sending the car skidding out of control. Petrified, Danielle closed her eyes as a picture of her three children flashed through her mind. All Panos could do was try to stop the car from skidding, but it was no use. Mick screamed as he was flung from one side of the car to the other. The car finally skidded left, causing Mick's head to hit the side window. Shouting out his wife's name, he flew back across the back seat and thought he was going to be sick. The dream of being at his funeral replayed in his mind, and he was convinced this was the end for him.

The car spun around again, but this time Panos managed to gain control of the wheel. The sound of the brakes was deafening, and smoke came from the back of the car. Disorientated, Panos's heart beat faster as he suddenly become aware that the side of the hill was only yards in front of him. It was a hundred foot drop. The thought of plunging to their death, conjured up enough strength in him to turn the wheel in the attempt to swing the car round before it was too late. His empowered effort had the desired effect and the car skidded at a hundred and eighty-degree angle, stopping just inches from the edge.

Mick's kept his eyes closed as his face was pressed up against the side window. Aware that they had finally come to a standstill, he found the courage to tentatively open his eyes. Consumed by an indescribable fear, he looked down and saw the sea crashing against the rocks below. His body shook uncontrollably when he realised just how close they'd come to falling to their death. Terror struck, all he could think about was Tracey, and how he longed to be in her arms.

Panos turned to Danielle and asked if she was alright. Her face had turned ghostly white, but she assured him she was fine. Next, he turned to Mick, who was sliding his body across the back seat. The same frightened look was visible on his face, and the thought of being the one responsible for causing his friends harm sent shivers down his spine.

"Blimey Panos, that was close," said Mick clutching his chest. "I thought for a minute there that we were done for. I've never been so scared." The anxiety in his voice was obvious, and his need for a drink had never been so strong. He put out his hands and concentrated his mind on stopping them from shaking. His effort to control his trembling failed him miserably, justifying his need for a large, stiff drink.

Taking a deep breath, Panos started the car. Just as he was going to pull away, a coach full of people drove past him. His heart beat in a second wave of fear when he realised if it had been a few minutes later, they would have been right in its path. The car stalled and Panos put his head on the steering wheel. The thought of what could have happened was too unbearable to think about, so silently, he sent up a prayer of thanks for their lucky escape. The road was now clear. Shaken but not deterred, Panos restarted the car and very slowly continued his journey down to the town.

Daybreak came and Helen welcomed the start of a new day. It had been a long night, and she hadn't managed to get a wink of sleep. Unable to stop her mind from racing, she busied herself by packing her suitcase. Her next planned step was to book herself on to the first available flight back to England, so when she had packed the last of her belongings; she proceeded down to the reception desk. Stepping into the elevator, her thoughts went on to Harry. Hearing his voice had been a great comfort, and she couldn't wait to see him again. Their conversation had ended by him reassuring her he would be there to pick her up at the airport. He had also said he loved her very much. His heart had gone out to her and this was made evident by the kindness that flowed through his words. This display of compassion had touched her and helped her realise just how much he meant to her. She couldn't fault his loyalty towards her, rekindling the feelings she'd desperately tried to deny. A small smile escaped through her lips as she imagined being in his arms, and this positive outcome was welcomed into her heart, enabling her to find the strength to carry on.

Holding her head up high she stepped out of the elevator and continued to walk over to the reception desk. She was met by a crowd of guests all wanting the manager's attention, so she waited patiently at the back of the queue. Finally, after what seemed like an eternity the crowd dispersed, and she asked for the details of the next available flight to England. A veil of silence fell as the manager looked at her dumbfounded.

"But you just got here," he said, the same look staining his face. "Is everything alright? If there is a problem, I'll sort it out. We have a very good reputation, and our main priority is our guests. If you're not happy then it's my responsibility to make sure that you are."

Helen looked at the manager and shook her head. She was about to speak as he continued to pour out the many reasons why she should stay. Getting agitated, she found the only way to stop him from talking was to slam her fist down on the counter. This act of annoyance seemed to do the trick as he stopped in mid-sentence. His countenance changed dramatically as his amazement quickly turned to fear. Taking a step back, the manager put his hands up in the air.

"There is no need for that, madam," he said shakily.

"I'm sorry," she said forcing a smile. "It's just you wouldn't let me talk… It has nothing to do with your service: you run an excellent hotel… It's just that something has come up and I need to get home. OK?"

The manager was somewhat consoled by her statement and after regaining his composure, continued to tell her that the next flight out of Skiathos was at one o'clock. Her heart sank when she looked at her watch. It was only nine thirty, and the thought of what to do in the next few hours overwhelmed her.

"Would you like me to phone the airport and book you a seat on that flight?" he asked picking up the phone. "It is all a part of our service." She nodded and forced another smile. Her mind raced as she listened to him on the phone.

The conversation went on for a few minutes, and she was so pleased when he told her that her seat was now booked. Feeling relieved, she politely thanked him, paid her bill and walked away. The need to get out of the hotel was too strong to ignore, so she decided to return to her room, get her belongings and make her way to the airport, stopping for something to eat on the way. The hotel manager watched her walk towards the elevator and sighed. He didn't know what it was about her, but he couldn't help detecting a glint of sadness in her eyes. She was a very attractive lady and he found himself wondering what it was she needed to get home for. He had been struck by her good looks from the first moment they met, but something about her he felt was not right. Her beauty could not hide the air of loneliness that accompanied her, and he couldn't help feeling sympathy for this mysterious English lady.

His gaze was interrupted when a guest appeared, and his thoughts were quickly reverted on to his work. As the elevator doors shut, the main doors of the hotel opened. A wave of recognition washed over the manager's face as he looked up and saw one of the wealthiest men on the island walk in. Feeling very intimidated by this man's presence, he nervously averted his eyes back to his guest. A sense of inadequacy flowed through him and he couldn't help feeling in awe of his unexpected visitor. Sensing him getting closer, the manager quickly brought his conversation with the guest to a close and forced himself to look up. The guest walked away merrily, and the manager was left standing face-to-face with his influential visitor.

It wasn't until Panos was at the counter that the manager realised he was not alone. He was accompanied by a very attractive lady, and another man who looked a bit worse for wear. Aware that these two people were foreign, the manager turned his attention to the worried looking man and smiled.

"Good morning sir," he said nervously. "Can I help you?" The man was just about to answer, when he was interrupted.

"My family owns the Oasis Hotel, and I understand you have a guest staying here that I need to speak to," said Panos boldly. "Her name is Helen Stiller, and it is very important I talk to her."

Afraid to look this man in the eye, the manager, still focused on Mick, nodded his head. He did not like Panos's tone, and felt very uneasy, but the need to protect the English lady his guest, quickly overrode his fear.

"Y-Yes, she was staying here, but she's checked out. She left just minutes ago. I'm sorry, b-but you've missed her." He could feel the blood rush to his face as he spoke, and his body began to tremble. He knew all too well who this man was. He was a ruthless businessman with a reputation with the ladies, but this knowledge did not deter him from hiding the truth of Helen's whereabouts.

"Did she say where she was going?" Panos persisted, his tone staying the same. This time the manager kept quiet and just shook his head.

"Oh. That's great Panos, what are we going to do now?" asked Mick, disappointed. "I was hoping to get in a quick beer." Panos looked at him in disgust.

"Is that all you can think about?" he asked abruptly sounding very irritated. "There are more important things to worry about than alcohol. Now come on, we must find her." With that Panos thanked the hotel manager and walked away.

Mick was deeply hurt by Panos's comment. It was bad enough that he had nearly killed them all only half an hour before; now he had to add insult to injury by jumping down his throat. He was not a happy man but followed Panos out of the hotel anyway. The fact that he wanted to find Helen was the only reason behind his departure; otherwise he would have stayed for two beers, just to spite his so-called friend.

The hotel manager let out a big sigh of relief as he watched them walk out of the hotel. The arrogance in Panos's voice had confirmed his dishonesty, and he made a mental note to tell Helen about her visitors when she came down from her room. Suddenly, the reception area was inundated with people, and the manager became distracted by meeting his guest's every need.

Helen picked her handbag up from the bed and took hold of her suitcase. Feeling confident she hadn't left anything behind, she walked over to the door. Pulling the handle down, Helen took one last look around the room. A wave of disappointment swept through her when her mind went back to the first day of her arrival, and her heart grieved. The pursuit of finding out where she came from seemed so pointless now, and all the days spent on the island she concluded had accomplished nothing. She had hoped to have gone home with some answers about who she was, but she was still none the wiser. The only souvenir she had of this place was regret, and she could have kicked herself for pursuing her quest of finding the truth. Justice had been the instigator of her stupidity. Justice for her mother's life, justice for her mother's death, and most of all justice for having been robbed of a father she could call her own. Tears stung her eyes as a picture of her estranged father stole her thoughts.

Why couldn't you take some responsibility for me? She thought. Why did you have to lie and put the blame on my mother? Why didn't you fight for her? Where were you when I needed you? Suddenly the volcano of her heart erupted and all the hidden emotions around her fatherless years spewed out. Feelings of grief for the father she thought had died in an accident. Heartache for the thousands of kisses she had been cheated out of. Sorrow for the thousands of hugs and bedtime stories stolen from her. Anguish for the childhood which had been built on lies and deceit. The thing that had hurt her most was all the years of feeling responsible for her mother's illness…when it was all down to him! Tears flowed down her cheeks and she could take no more. Taking a deep breath, she swallowed hard and shut her mind off to the pain. Wiping her face, she took another deep breath and walked out of the room. She got to the elevator and pressed the button. Her patience took a leave of absence when it did not arrive immediately, and she decided to take the stairs down to the lobby.

She couldn't get out of the hotel quickly enough and hurried past the hotel manager, who was speaking to one of the guests at reception. Not acknowledging him, although he was waving his arms to try and get her attention, she pushed open the entrance door and walked out into the open air. The rain had stopped, and the sun was now desperately trying to break through the cloud. She was taken aback by the cool air brushing against her skin, and the feel of it on her bare arms sent shivers down her spine. Goose bumps spontaneously exploded on her flesh, so she stopped to get a cardigan out of her suitcase. As she bent down to undo the zip, a second wave of shivers cascaded through her body. Only this time, the weather wasn't responsible for making her shudder. Paralysed by fear, she was stopped in her tracks as she heard a familiar voice shout out her name.

Panos walked out of the hotel feeling rather annoyed. He was not only put out by Helen not being there, he was furious with Mick and his lack of understanding concerning his need to find her. Mick's main priority was Mick, and Panos concluded he had made a huge mistake in asking him to come along. He marched up the road and then stopped at the curb side. Danielle soon caught up with him, and noticing the distress on his face, took his hand.

"Don't worry we'll find her," she said stroking his hand. "She must still be on the island."

Mick walked up beside Danielle. He could see the fury in Panos's face, so thought carefully about what he was going to say.

"Yeah mate, she couldn't have gone far. Dan's right, we will find her," he said cheerfully, in the hope of bringing a smile to Panos' stern face.

"What is it to you Michael? All you care about is beer. Why are you even here?" asked Panos accusingly. "You know how much this means to my family, yet all you can think about is getting your next drink. Your selfishness goes beyond my belief."

Mick's first reaction was to hit out at Panos for talking to him like that and clenched his fist. But then he remembered the night before and soon thought better of it.

"Well, you did nearly kill us all," retorted Mick sarcastically, in his defence. "Sorry for being scared out of my wits… But any man would want a drink after what I have just been through… Selfish indeed. I have been called many things… but not selfish!" He put his hand on his chest feeling very hurt and turned away. Then, to his relief, he saw Helen bending over a little way down the road.

"There she is… Helen!"

CHAPTER
ELEVEN

Frightened to look up, Helen focused her mind on getting out of there as soon as possible. The sound of footsteps was in earshot, and she could tell that they were getting closer. Determined not to look around, she grabbed the handle of her suitcase, and with her cardigan still hanging out of it, began to walk away. As she quickened her pace, her heart beat hard in her chest, but her effort to escape the oncoming footsteps proved unsuccessful. The next thing she knew there was a hand on her shoulder.

"Helen, please don't run away, we only want to talk." The sound of this gentle voice startled her. Not being the same voice that had bellowed at her only a few moments earlier, she stopped and turned around.

"Just give Panos five minutes of your time." Danielle let go of Helen's shoulder and smiled. "He really needs to talk to you."

"I have a plane to catch," Helen said sternly, looking down to the floor, deliberately avoiding eye contact. "I haven't got time for this."

"He only wants to explain. Please, listen to what he has to say." Danielle placed her hand on Helen's arm again.

"He is so sorry for what has happened."

"I don't care how he feels. He didn't seem that bothered last night… I have nothing to say to him. Now, like I said, I have a plane to catch, so if you don't mind, I need to go." Frustration quickly replacing her surprise, she looked up at Danielle and forced herself to smile. Annoyed with herself for doing so, she could feel her anger resurfacing when she saw her half-brother over Danielle's shoulder.

Panos watched from a distance. He was only a few yards away from the two women, making it possible for him to hear their conversation. When Mick had first spotted Helen, Panos felt the irresistible need to run over to her, but Danielle soon convinced him otherwise, explaining she should be the one to speak to her. Every inch of his body wanted to rebel against his decision to let Danielle intervene, but he didn't want to scare Helen away. So, going against his instinct, he stood back and conceded to being just an observer. Mick was standing behind him. He had also been told to stay where he was and did not argue. Not wanting to give Panos another reason to shout at him, he did what he was told and kept his mouth shut.

"Just leave me alone," said Helen pushing Danielle's hand away. "Haven't you people done enough damage? I want nothing to do with you, do you hear, nothing!" With that, she turned and walked away.

Looking to Panos, Danielle shrugged her shoulders apologetically, and signalled at him to go after her. Helen was now practically running down the road. Without a second thought, Panos followed Danielle's command and ran after Helen.

"Helen, wait," he shouted, in the hope she would stop. "I have things I need to say to you!" His words were ignored. Their only use was to fuel her need to get away from him.

"Don't go like this," he continued, but she kept on going.

"Go away!" she replied, her pace quickening. "I don't want to talk to you."

"I'm not your enemy... I am you're..." Panos's words got stuck in his throat. His statement was instantly silenced by pride, and he found himself unable to finish his sentence. This caused Helen to stop suddenly and turn around.

"You are my what?" she spat at him. "See, you can't even bring yourself to say it... You're pathetic!" Her eyes bore into him as he got closer. "You're my sister! Is that what you were going to say?" she asked harshly.

Panos looked into her eyes and could see the fury they reflected. Her face was twisted with hate, but then something happened when she said, "I didn't think so! Why would you want to admit that?" Suddenly, her countenance changed when a deep hurt manifested itself right before his eyes. Realising her defences were failing her, she quickly reclaimed her strength, and the harsh glare returned.

"Now, leave me alone!" Turning away from him, she carried on down the road.

"You're my sister!" Swallowing his pride, he said it again. "Yes, you are my sister... and I want to... I want to get to know you."

She stopped again but didn't look round.

"And my... our father wants to get to know you too."

Still with her back to him, she remained silent. Her racing heart beat furiously. She was not prepared for this. His words tormented her mind as he repeated them over and over. Conflict induced a battle inside of her. Her heart was telling her to turn around and listen to what he had to say, but her mind was telling her to leave.

This will hurt you, the voice cried in her head. But this is the reason why you came, to find out who you are, argued the influence of her heart. She felt completely confused and could have screamed with the turmoil. The bubble in the pit of her belly returned, harbouring a profound bellowing that was desperate to escape. Taking a deep breath, she exercised her power of control, and once again regained her strength.

"I don't want to know. I have a plane to catch, and I don't ever want to see you again!" she said, walking away, her mind successfully triumphing over the voice of her heart.

Danielle and Mick had now caught up with Panos. They stood on either side of him, and both felt for him when Helen said those harsh words. Danielle put her arm in his. Kind words of comfort had gone astray, and all she could do was kiss him on the cheek. Mick's heart filled with compassion for the hurt in his friends' eyes, and for the first time since leaving the hotel, he felt sorry for Panos.

"There was no need for her to speak to you like that," he said, patting him on the back. "I'm so sorry it has ended this way." Panos's eyes bore into his. Mick did not like that look and became quite scared.

"Now what have I said?" he asked taking a step back. "I can't say anything right!"

Suddenly, a wave of confidence swept through Panos. Aware of his expression, his face softened when he said, "Michael, this is not the end, my friend, this is only the beginning." Mick looked at Danielle, made a strange face and shrugged his shoulders. He was confused by Panos's cryptic statement but was pleased to see his smile had returned.

"My job here is not done. She must know how my father feels, and then it is up to her. Then I have done what I came to do…You two stay here." He kissed them both on the cheek and ran after Helen. She hadn't completely disappeared yet, so Panos ran in front of her and put his hand out.

"I told you to go away," said Helen irately. "Don't you ever give up? I told you I'm not interested." Tears were evident in her eyes, and Panos smiled.

"What are you smiling at? These are not tears of joy you know!" she spat at him trying to push past.

"I'm sorry if you think I'm being insensitive, it's just that you remind me of me, and no, I never give up. Not when it is a matter of the heart."

"I'm nothing like you," she huffed. "And what do you mean - a matter of the heart? From what I have seen, you haven't got one. Now get out of my way!"

"I understand how you must be feeling," he said quietly, ignoring the cruelness of her words. "But whether you like it or not, we are family, and where I come from, families stick together."

"Ha, that's rich coming from you. Last night you couldn't wait to get rid of me," she said unable to believe what she was hearing. "You have a nerve. How could you possibly know how I feel?" Helen used every bit of her strength to stop her tears from falling, but it was no use. "You haven't got a clue!" The tears fell, but Panos was not deterred. Her strength had failed her where her tears were concerned but triumphed when somehow it flowed through her arms. Pushing him out of the way, she managed to get past him.

"No, you're right I don't know how you feel," he admitted sympathetically running in front her again. "But I do know how my father feels, and I know he's very sorry for his reaction last night. He told me so himself." There was something sincere in his voice, and this caused her to stop. Silence fell and finding the courage at last, she looked into his eyes.

"He wants to be a part of your life," continued Panos, taking her hand. "It was just a shock for him, a shock for us all. You must understand that." As he said these words, her heart softened.

Confused by the sudden change she felt inside, her mind went back to the previous night. Remembering the look of vulnerability on her father's face when he read the letter, for a split second she believed him. But she also remembered the outcome, and the humiliation she had felt quickly brought her back to reality.

"Well, I don't want to be a part of your so-called family," she said, forcing his hand away. "And yes, I do understand how shocked you all were… Now you know how I felt on the day of my mother's funeral!"

"I am sorry about your mother, but you have a father who wants… no needs… to speak to you. Helen, please come back to my hotel and talk to him." Panos's patience was beginning to wear thin. No one had ever dared talk to him like that before, and a huge part of him wanted to walk away. Taking a deep breath, he managed to summon up enough strength to continue. A few seconds passed and Panos smiled. Helen could feel her heart soften again, and she found herself mesmerised by his big, brown eyes. Aware that she wanted to smile back, a picture of her mother suddenly appeared in her mind. All the pain she felt coincided with the vision, and she managed to stop her expression from changing. Proud of herself for doing so, she suddenly concluded that all this family wanted to do was try and persuade her that her mother was wrong, and nothing else. These liberating thoughts reinforced her belief, bringing with them a surge of anger that came up from the pit of her stomach. Before she had the time to stop and think, she raised her hand and slapped him across the face.

"How dare you mention my mother!" she screamed. "She was ten of your father, and she was a drug addict! Now leave me alone!" Powered by rage, she took one last look at Panos and walked away. Panos just stood and watched her leave in complete shock. It took him a few moments to realise that she had struck him. The shock of what she did had been like an anaesthetic, keeping the pain at bay, but when the harsh reality kicked in, his face began to throb uncontrollably. Danielle and Mick came running over to him as he put his hand up to his cheek. They had witnessed the whole thing and couldn't believe that she had the audacity to hit him.

"Helen!" shouted Danielle angrily. "Get the hell back here!"

"Just leave her," said Panos quietly. "At least I tried."

A small smile escaped from his lips as he spoke. "I only wanted to help her but she's obviously angry. What else could I do?" A glimpse of sadness escaped through his words, and all Danielle could do was hold him. Mick was still in shock. The look on Panos's face tormented his mind, and he found himself feeling rather angry.

The poor bloke didn't deserve that, he thought. Maybe I had a lucky escape there, he thought sighing heavily as he imagined being the person on the other end of her anger and thought twice about getting involved with such a strong-willed woman. Not being able to think of anything constructive to say, he kept his mouth firmly closed. He was, however, surprised by Panos's attitude. After that assault, he had expected him to be furious but instead he seemed calm. This caused him to question exactly what was going on. Baffled, he racked his brain for an answer but couldn't find one. Eventually, he put it down to the fact that Helen was a woman.

Blimey, he thought. If that was me, Panos would have punched me to the ground, and he shuddered at the thought.

"Come on, there's no point in hanging around here, she's gone. We'd better get back to the hotel." Panos turned to Danielle and smiled.

"Panos, are you sure you're alright?" He kissed her on the cheek and nodded.

"Don't worry my beautiful Danielle, I'm fine. I have another cheek after all." He laughed putting an arm around her and they began to walk back to the car. On the surface he seemed to be in control of his emotions, but deep down he was really hurting. Not only physically bruised by Helen's actions, he was more upset that his pride had been wounded. He had let his guard down, and he didn't like the outcome. The only thing that had kept his anger at bay was the fact that he had done it for his father, and in a strange way that pleased him.

If you had been a man, he thought. I'd have left you lying in a pool of your own blood.

The ride back up to the hotel was spent in silence. Mick couldn't wait to get a drink inside of him. They were only halfway through the morning, and the thought of a nice cool beer was the only thing he looked forward to. What with the fiasco with George the night before, and now what had happened with Helen, he dreaded the atmosphere at the hotel. He guessed that Panos was only putting on a brave face for Danielle's sake.

Three arguments in twelve hours, that has got to be a strain for anyone, he thought. Relishing the thought of his long- awaited drink, he focused his mind on the positive side of his day.

The black Mercedes drove through the gates of the hotel. The sun had won the battle of the skies and was now shining victorious in its rightful place, and there was not a rain cloud to be seen. The three friends got out of the car, walked up the entrance steps and into the hotel, were they were met by a roomful of guests. Each one greeted them with a smile as they walked across the floor. Panos was gracious and returned the gesture but carried on past them, because he was eager to speak with his father. Kissing Danielle on the cheek, he told her to meet him at the pool bar, so she went up to the room to get changed.

Mick was relieved to see Yannis was busy serving his thirsty guests and went up to the bar. Through gritted teeth, he waited patiently to be served. Not realising his agitation showed, he looked at Yannis who was staring at him in an unusually strange way.

"What's up with you Yannis?" he asked quite innocently. "You look like someone's getting on your nerves." Yannis didn't say a word as he looked down the bar. Mick followed his stare, and realised that he was tapping rather loudly on an empty glass in front of him. He hadn't been aware of his actions, and his cheeks went bright red.

"What do I have to do to get a drink round here?" he joked in a desperate attempt to cover up his embarrassment.

"Well, you don't have to do that, Michael," answered Yannis aggressively. "I'll be with you in a minute."

"Easy Yannis, me ole mate," replied Mick hurt by Yannis's response. "I was only asking, and I thought you were the nice one... I don't know, you think you know someone."

Yannis ignored Mick's remark and carried on serving. The pressure of having to tend the bar by himself was taking its toll on him, and he could have cursed his brother for not being there to assist him with the morning rush. He couldn't help wondering why Panos had gone out so early, and why nobody had informed him of his whereabouts. Feeling rather put out by all the secrecy, he carried on catering for the guests' every need anyway. His brother had taught him well, and he was pleased to find that he was able to put on a professional mask, just as easily as Panos could.

The events of the night before had tried to steal his attention, but fortunately for him; he had managed to put the thoughts of having a half-sister to the back of his mind.

When Panos finally showed his face, Yannis gave out a big sigh of relief. Pleased to have his brother by his side again, he smiled graciously at him as he walked towards the bar. But Panos looked straight through him and continued out of the room. This act of ignorance sent Yannis's blood boiling, and it didn't help that Mick was tapping the glass to get his attention. Unfortunately, he had let his mask slip, and Mick had been the brunt of his anger. Feeling bad for speaking to him in that manner, Yannis looked back over to him. Mick was staring at the bar wall, and Yannis couldn't help feeling sorry for his English friend. He looked all forlorn, a look he hadn't seen in him before. Noticing his blood shot eyes, Yannis suddenly realised how much of a mess Mick looked. His face was a yellowy brown, and he could see tiny droplets of sweat on his forehead, highlighting the deep lines of stress just below his hair line. He didn't look at all happy, and this was not like Mick, he thought. Sensing that something was wrong, he finished serving his last guest and picked up a clean glass.

"A beer for my friend?" he asked happily. Mick looked over and saw the big smile on Yannis' face.

"Oh, you're talking to me. You soon changed your tune. I'm your friend now, am I?" he asked sarcastically. He returned to staring at the wall, but then panicked when he thought that he had missed his chance of getting a drink.

"Yes…Yes, a beer, and make it a pint," he said suddenly. He was now alone at the bar and the sound of the guests talking in various places around the room was evident. To Mick it was like a chant that only came from happy people, and soon he realised just how low he felt. Aware that Yannis was pouring his drink; he found himself watching the glass fill up with the golden liquid and couldn't wait to get it in his hand. He wanted to tell him to hurry up because his compulsion for a drink was so strong, but somehow, he managed to stay silent. He couldn't face another argument, so decided to keep his mouth shut. His drink soon arrived, and as the cold, fizzy liquid touched his lips, he let out a huge sigh. It was as if someone had let the air out of a balloon. He savoured the taste, and then as if by magic, the Michael that Yannis had grown to know and love, made a welcome comeback.

"Ah, that hit the spot, my friend," he said, having drunk half of the contents. "Now, what was the matter with you Yannis? You look like you've lost your wife but still gained a mother in-law," he continued, laughing out loud. Yannis didn't understand the logic of his statement but laughed anyway as it was good to see Mick happy again.

"I'm sorry Michael but I have a lot on my mind. I should not have spoken to you like that. It was just hard for me this morning, you know, without Panos here to help me?" said Yannis. Mick nodded his head but wasn't really listening. His mind was sabotaged by the thought of his second drink.

"Yeah, and I suppose last night didn't help?" he said carelessly.

Yannis's heart skipped a beat, and his first reaction was to tell Mick to mind his own business. It took all of his mental strength to stop those harsh words from escaping, instead he politely said, "Yes Michael, but that concerns only my family. It is between us, and no one else."

Mick heard every word this time, and smirked. Sensing that he had been told to keep his nose out of the family affairs, he decided to keep his comments to himself, just for now. He nodded his head and ordered another drink. Deviousness was not part of his nature, but Mick didn't like being told to keep out of something, especially something he was caught up in the middle of. It was obvious that Yannis didn't have a clue that they had just been into the town to try and bring Helen back, and Mick felt justified in telling him where they had been, and why. As Yannis poured the second glass of beer, Mick finished the last drop of his first, and put the empty glass on the bar. It wasn't long before it was replaced, and he took great pleasure in consuming a mouthful of the freshly poured drink.

"It's a shame that Panos couldn't persuade Helen to come back this morning," he said, prompting a reaction out of Yannis.

"What do you mean Michael? Panos has no authority to do that. My father wouldn't allow it. He wants nothing to do with that woman. You're talking rubbish, Michael. Why would you say such a thing?" Yannis thought that this was one of Mick's jokes and laughed. "Michael, this is no joking matter, my friend."

"But that's where you're wrong, Yannis. Panos was doing it for your father, he wanted him to go and get her. He told him to."

Suddenly something happened that Mick was not prepared for. Yannis's face filled with rage and he slammed his fists on the bar and said, "No Michael! Why are you saying that? You are wrong! Why would you be so cruel?"

Mick leant back on his stool instantly regretting what he had said.

Oh no, he's going to hit me, he thought. What have I done? The next thing he knew, Yannis had grabbed hold of the neck of his shirt and was holding it tightly.

"Why would you say such a thing?" shouted Yannis. "Why? Why?"

For the third time that day, Mick was frightened. Yannis had never shown any sign of anger before.

But, you're the nice one, thought Mick. Oh, what have I done? I've created a monster. He could see the veins protruding in Yannis's forehead and thought that they were going to explode. His face was distorted with hate, and saliva was coming out of his mouth.

"Yannis, it was a joke. You were right… I'm sorry. Yannis, Please don't hit me!" Yannis's grip tightened. He had never been so angry.

"It is not a joking matter!" said Yannis with his other hand raised above his head. "You're sick, do you hear, sick!" With that, he poked Mick in the middle of his forehead. "You're sick!"

His raised voice had caught the attention of the guests, and all eyes were on them. Anna and her mother-in-law came running out of the kitchen just as Yannis was about to poke him again.

"Yannis, what are you doing?" shouted Anna from across the room. Panicking, his mother turned back around and went to the office to get her husband. Mick was trembling, and secretly wished that the car had gone over the edge of the hill.

The fall would have killed me instantly and I wouldn't have felt a thing, he thought.

"This man is saying crazy things," said Yannis now clenching his fist. "He cannot say these things… He is mad!"

From where I'm sitting, you're the madman, thought Mick, but made sure that he kept these thoughts to himself this time.

"Yannis, I'm sorry… I was joking… If that makes me mad, then, yes, you're right," his eyes on Yannis's fist. "Please Yannis… Don't hurt me… I'm sorry for what I said!"

Yannis's eyes bore into Mick. Fury reigned, and Yannis pulled his hand back to punch him.

"Yannis… No!" said Panos running up behind his brother and grabbing his hand. "What did you say to him Michael?"

"I… I…" said Mick trying to explain but was cut short by Yannis.

"He said that you went down to see Helen… and that papa wanted you to bring her back. Panos, he is a liar, and I hate him for that!"

"Yannis, he's not lying. What he said is true. Now, put your hand down. You're making a show of yourself," said Panos calmly.

Yannis pulled his hand out of Panos's, let go of Mick's shirt and turned to Panos in complete disbelief.

"No, you're lying too. Why would you keep something like that from me? Panos, please tell me you are lying," he said, tears stinging his eyes as he looked at his older brother.

"It is true," Panos repeated.

"But I'm your brother; your flesh and blood. Why would you do that without telling me? No, I won't believe it. You wouldn't do that!"

"Your brother is telling the truth Yannis," their father intervened. "Now calm down, come into the office and I will explain," he said, putting his arm around his shoulder. He and Panos had been discussing about what had happened regarding Helen when his wife interrupted them. When she informed them of Yannis's unpredictable behaviour in the bar, they both ran down to put a stop to it.

"Panos, get Michael a drink, and calm the guests." With that, he walked his other son out of the room.

"Sorry about that," said Panos to the guests. "Families, who would have them," he said tossing his head back, smiling, in an attempt to lighten the atmosphere.

"I'll be down at the pool bar shortly." Everyone stayed silent and just looked at him. "And, you're all welcome to a free drink." The small crowd began to disperse, and one by one they headed off down to the pool.

Waiting until the last guest had gone, Panos turned his attention to Mick. He walked up behind him and patted him on the back.

"Michael, Michael, Michael. What am I going to do with you?" he said, continuing to pat his back.

"But… But Panos… Did you see him. He was going to hit me!" Mick said, trying to straighten out the neck of his shirt. "I don't deserve that… No one deserves that… He was going to hit me." He took a big swig of his beer.

"But what I don't understand is why you chose to tell him," he said as he walked behind the bar and picked up a clean, empty glass.

Mick looked at the glass in his hand. He had just managed to calm his trembling body, but it began to shake again.

"Please don't hit me Panos, I thought he knew, honestly I did."

The thought of hitting him never even crossed Panos's mind, and he looked at the glass feeling quite hurt.

"I wouldn't hit you... You're my friend... That's ridiculous. I do believe you, Michael. I was just going to pour you a drink, that's all."

Surprisingly, Panos did believe him. He knew that Mick wasn't a vindictive man, and he was positive that he wouldn't want to cause his family harm.

"Phew Panos, that's a relief. I don't want to fall out with you too." He eyed up his drink as Panos finished pouring it. The sight of the fresh pint looked even more welcoming than before, and as he took a gulp, he couldn't help thinking that it tasted so much better than the previous two.

"Yannis will be ok when my father explains, so you don't have to worry, Michael. When Yannis has calmed down, he'll apologise. I know my brother," he said laughing softly. "It takes a lot to get him angry Michael. He isn't hot headed like me."

"Well, it didn't take much for him to fly off the handle today, Panos. It was like a red rag to a bull, and I was the red rag!" he complained. Panos smiled.

"You're a funny man Michael, even when you're scared." Panos took hold of his hand. "See, you're still shaking my friend."

"Well even the toughest of men get scared... and that I most certainly was. I even wished that the car had gone off the road today... How crazy is that? Maybe Yannis was right. I am mad," he said letting out a small laugh. "Panos I'm so glad you came in when you did. I think he would have punched me right off the stool...Then I would have known how George felt last night," he said hesitating as he looked around the room. "Speaking of George...where is he?"

The sound of that name sent shivers down Panos's spine. Taking a deep breath, he said, "Michael, he has gone home, and I wish that you would never mention that name again. OK?"

"OK, OK. Sorry Panos, I don't want to get myself into any more trouble," he said taking another swig of his pint.

"Good. Now, we will get back to enjoying ourselves. Danielle will be down soon, and I don't want to worry her about any of this," continued Panos as he looked at his watch. "She should be down any minute now." Mick just nodded his head and carried on drinking his drink.

Painfully aware of their time spent apart, Panos was overwhelmed by a longing for his Danielle. He was so relieved that she hadn't come down in the middle of the Yannis situation. He knew how much she cared for Mick, and he was relieved that she hadn't witnessed the look of fright on his face. This would have hurt her, and he didn't want her to feel anything but love while she was staying at his hotel. The need to protect this precious lady prompted his heart to yearn for her, and he became quite agitated. He longed for her to be by his side, and to have her in his sight again.

His meeting with his father about Helen had gone well considering the circumstances. His father had been very understanding and had thanked Panos for trying. Thinking back to the trip into town, Panos touched his face. He couldn't help wondering if it had been a blessing in disguise that Helen was going home. Somehow, he felt relieved because now they could get back to normality as a family. He smiled as he remembered her slapping him across the face.

You are like me, he thought. This made him laugh out loud.

"What are you laughing at?" asked Mick feeling confused.

"Nothing, my friend, it was nothing... Ah Danielle, at last... My Danielle is back with me."

Danielle walked into the room wearing her bikini. A colourful sarong was tied around her waist, and Panos thought she looked even more beautiful than before. It showed off her slim frame, and Panos wanted to pick her up and take her back to the room. He refrained and, like a gentleman, took hold of her hand and kissed it.

"You look stunning, my darling, absolutely stunning. Doesn't she Michael? I'm a lucky man." Turning to Danielle Mick nodded his head.

Still holding her hand, Panos pulled her towards him and kissed her on the lips. She was taken aback by this show of affection and felt a little confused. She had expected him to be sad, considering what had happened with Helen only an hour or so earlier. However, falling into the spell of his embrace, she kissed him back.

"Panos, I don't mean to sound rude, but are you OK?" she asked pulling away from him. "You seem to be very happy.

I'm not knocking your loving kindness, but, but…" she was nearly too scared to mention it. "But you seem to be over the whole Helen situation."

Panos kissed her again.

"Thank you for your concern, but like I said earlier, it was her choice to leave. I did what I could. She'll be on the plane and on her way home soon. So now we'll get back to how it was before she came." Hesitating, he looked deeply into her eyes. "You're now where you belong again, at the centre of my universe. We've not got long left, and I want to spend every minute making you happy, OK?" Danielle was overwhelmed and just nodded her head.

This kind of flattery I could get used to, she thought, and kissed him on the lips. As she pulled away, her mind automatically went to the day of her departure and the sadness it would bring. Her thoughts were soon diverted when the sight of Mick caught her eye.

"What's wrong with your shirt Mick? You look like you have been pulled through a hedge backwards."

Panos thought that was a funny thing to say and laughed.

"You English people make me laugh. But don't worry yourself, Michael is OK. Yannis got the wrong idea and pulled his shirt. That's all. They are friends, so it doesn't matter. Isn't that right Michael?" he asked turning to him.

"Yeah, yeah, just a little misunderstanding, Dan, we are OK now babe," he said attempting to straighten his neckline again. The few beers consumed so far had begun to do their job, and Mick found he was now feeling very relaxed.

"We must go down to the pool now. I'll work and watch

you, my gorgeous Danielle, while you soak up the beautiful, Greek sunshine…You will come too Michael…Yannis will be out soon." Putting his arm around Danielle's waist, they walked down to the pool, Mick following close behind them.

CHAPTER
TWELVE

*R*esisting the urge to look back, Helen focused her mind on her escape. To her relief the image of a taxi loomed in the distance, guaranteeing her a passageway out of there. The sooner she was at the airport the better, and she couldn't wait to be in the safety of the airplane. Still trembling with rage, she ran up to the car, and was pleased to find it was available. Trying her best to calm herself down, she informed the driver of her destination and got in. It wasn't until the car pulled away that she found the courage to turn around and was relieved to find she hadn't been followed.

The five-minute journey seemed to take forever. Using all her energy to keep the thoughts of Panos, and what she'd done to him out of her mind, she centred them on seeing Harry and nothing else. Her sustained fury helped keep her mind free of any unwanted feelings, while she kept herself focused on the journey home. Finally, the car pulled into the airport grounds. The car park was near to overflowing, and it took a few minutes for the taxi to reach the appointed drop off area. Forcing a smile, Helen paid the driver and forgetting to thank him, got her suitcase and headed towards the main entrance. Her ignorance caused the driver to shout out something in Greek, but she was oblivious to his outburst of anger.

Once in the airport lobby, she studied the nearby sign and then followed the arrows pointing the way to the check in desk. The atmosphere was full of happy holiday makers eager to get home, and for the first time since being on the island, she felt a part of the crowd. Feeling comfortable in her surroundings she checked in and made her way to the airport lounge. Aware that she had time to spare, she decided to buy herself a cup of coffee, and then phone Harry to let him know the approximate time of her arrival. Comforted by the thought of hearing his voice, she walked over to the café. As she pushed her way through the many travellers, she was stopped in her tracks when she noticed a crowd of people pointing over to an area that was cordoned off. Following the collection of pointed fingers, her heart missed a beat, when she saw a man standing with his arms in the air with a gun aimed at his head. Her mind began to play tricks on her, when she could have sworn that it was Mick who the gun was aimed at. Blinking a few times, she shook her head and looked again. Locked in a trance, she was taken back to the day of her arrival, where the deception of her mind deceived her into believing that she had gone back in time. She could see Mick's face as plain as day. Then in a flash, she was quickly bought back into reality when the man was wrestled to the floor.

Disorientated by the vision of the past, she was consumed by an enormous sense of fear. The whole experience had freaked her out, so she closed her eyes, and took a deep breath attempting to calm her nerves. A picture of Mick exploded into her thoughts, bringing with it a deep sense of guilt that gripped hold of her heart. Putting her hands up to either side of her head she opened her mouth to scream. She wanted to shout so loud because she thought she was in danger of losing her mind.

'N…' the word "no" got stuck in her throat when she suddenly became aware of where she was. Frightened and confused, she opened her eyes and tried desperately to contain herself. Her head began to throb, so she closed them again. Only this time it wasn't Mick's face she was confronted with. There before her, in her minds eye, was Panos. The vision of him presented itself boldly in front of her, his big brown eyes pleading for her to listen to him. Her heart beat faster, pumping guilt through her veins when she remembered his face as she slapped him. The memory was too much for her to bear, so opening her eyes she scanned the room. Seeing the sign for the ladies' room, and holding back her tears, she fought her way through the horde of people, and pushed open the door. To her surprise, and relief, it was empty, so she went into the cubicle, and making sure the door was locked, sat down. Now all alone, she was once again confronted with a deep persistent guilt, which not only tormented her heart, but also her mind as it was bombarded with remorse.

Our father wants to see you, Panos's voice echoed in her head. He is sorry, he told me so himself… He wants to get to know you… You are family, and where I come from families stick together. His words rattled around in the confinement of her mind. It was as if they were trying to escape, but they had nowhere to go, so just repeated themselves over and over. The sound of his voice was torture to her soul.

"No," she said quietly. "No. No." Raising her voice she shouted.

"No. This can't be happening. I won't let it!"

Now it was doubt's turn to make an appearance. So, showing off its power, it overrode its adversary, and quickly added to the discomfort of her frail conscience. Suddenly, Helen couldn't help wondering if she had done the right thing by walking away from him.

But what if he was telling the truth, she found herself thinking. This could be the perfect opportunity to put things right, to have a father to love, to have a family to love me. Reigning triumphant, doubt congratulated itself for backing her into a corner. The battle was won! The tears began to flow; she had never felt so confused.

"Why did I come here?" she whispered. "Why did you have to die?" With no control over her tears she just sat there and let them fall. She was desperate to go home but felt a strange need to go back to the hotel, and this unnerved her. It was like she was being pulled by an invisible force, willing her, wanting her to return. Her mind didn't help as it went back on to Panos and the way he looked at her when she had left him by the road. Finding it hard to believe that she had actually hit him, she was soon convinced that he probably hated her now and would be happy if he never saw her again. She couldn't blame him for that.

I would hate me too, she thought.

Finding the strength, she managed to stop the flow of tears, and looked at her watch. Aware her plane would be leaving soon she took a deep breath and wiped her face.

No, I am going home. That is where I belong, she thought half heartedly, her doubts retreating in defeat. But the war was not over yet, because they still niggled at the back of her mind.

Panos walked Danielle over to her lounger. Taking one last look at her before he went to work behind the bar, he stroked her face and gently kissed her on the nose. Her beauty still astounded him, and he found it hard to have to walk away from her. He pulled her close to him and shut his eyes. The promise he had made to his father invaded his thoughts, and once again he cursed his heritage. He knew what was expected of him and secretly wished that things could be different. It felt so natural to have her in his arms, and a tear formed in the corner of his eye. It was as if she had been the missing piece of the puzzle, filling the hole in his heart, which now made him feel complete. Sighing deeply, he breathed in this special lady, and consciously pushed out the thoughts of having to let her go. Retraining his mind back into the present, he squeezed her tight.

I'll face that day when it comes, he thought. Pulling away slightly, he held her face and looked deep into her eyes. Using all his strength, he resisted the urge to make love to her, and kissed her full on the lips.

"I love you," was all he could say, and then he forced himself away from her, and went to tend to the guests who were waiting to be served. Danielle watched him walk away in a daze. The thought of having to leave him behind played on her mind, and she couldn't help wishing that there was a happy ending to this great love affair. Knowing she was in a no-win situation; she quickly wiped those thoughts out of her head before they could rob her of her joy. Deciding to make the most of every minute left on the island, she focused her mind on happier things. She couldn't wait to be back in Panos's arms, so looked forward to being alone with him again.

A few hours passed by, and things soon got back to normal. Yannis's father had explained the meeting with Helen, and Yannis was pleased to know that she was now on her way home. His fathers's explanation regarding his affair with Elizabeth was brief, but it was enough for Yannis to feel secure in knowing that the family was going to get over this little glitch. His mother had been by his father's side all the way through their conversation, which he found very comforting. Relieved to know that there were no more secrets, he left his parents in a much better mood and went back to his duties. Number one on his list of priorities was apologising to Mick. Filled with regret for his despicable behaviour, he was intent on putting things right with him. Whilst on the way down to the pool, he used this time to rehearse an apology, and went through it several times in his head. His groundwork had proved successful, because Mick was gracious enough to accept his plea of forgiveness, and both men were relieved to be friends again. Thankful that the misunderstanding between them had now been reconciled, Panos went about his business feeling both happy and relieved. Having put George and Helen out of his mind, he focused it on Danielle. Accommodating his guests every need, he kept her in his sight, a task he found easy to do.

The afternoon came and went, and the coolness of the evening air was a sure sign that the day was coming to a close.

Danielle and Mick dined in the restaurant, and after their meal they sat at the bar and talked to Panos. Mick was his usual comical self and had them laughing at his silly ways. The room was buzzing with excitement, and Mick silently congratulated himself for having stayed out of trouble.

The events of the past twenty-four hours had been forgotten, and Panos was pleased to find that everything had gone back to the way it used to be. Watching Danielle's face light up as she laughed, he longed to have her in his arms again. He was enchanted by her sparkling green eyes, but then suddenly he found himself thinking about her children. He knew how important they were to her, and a pain pierced his heart when he thought about her life back in England. Knowing that her life had been put on hold to be with him, he envied the fact that they were the vital link to the world she had temporarily left behind. Jealousy played a strong part in his mind as he imagined his life without her. Finding it a struggle to shake off these feelings, he tried to think past the pain, and tried to think of a positive outcome as to why he had met her. A few things came to mind, so following their path he searched for the answer. But they all led to the same conclusion. There was no answer, just a big void. His life was going to be unbearable without her. The result of the situation kick started him back into reality, and he could have cursed himself for letting it get the better of him.

I will cross that bridge when I come to it. I will concentrate on now, I will cherish and enjoy what we have now, he thought trying to stop himself from drowning. These empowering thoughts triggered his need to think only of Danielle's happiness, and not his own selfish desires of something that was obviously out of his control. So, taking charge of his thoughts, he put the smile back on his face, and carried on as before.

Darkness fell, giving the moon permission to rule the skies. Accompanied by thousands of stars, it hung majestically in the sky as if it was a king surrounded by his subjects. Panos and Yannis were now back together as a team, and both were pleased that the events of the past twenty-four hours hadn't got in the way of their relationship. Working simultaneously, they catered for their guests every need, and no one would have guessed that the bond between them had nearly been destroyed. All the family was now in the lounge interacting with the guests, and Panos was content with being surrounded by the people he loved so dearly. Having got through the unexpected start to his day, he was now pleased to know that the possibility of it ending well was high.

The plane to London travelled down the runway, escorting its passengers, who were now on a voyage back to their homeland. Delayed by only a few minutes, it began its ascent, and Skiathos was soon to become just a faint memory. Helen's heart missed a beat when the plane reached its peak, and her stomach somersaulted as it flew into the horizon. Looking at her phone she noticed Harry's name on the screen. Her finger was still hovering over the call button, but she hadn't found the courage to phone him.Looking up into the clear blue sky, she watched the plane disappear out of view. Unable to face talking to Harry, she reluctantly put the phone back in her bag. She couldn't explain why she hadn't boarded the plane to herself let alone to him, so she decided to take the easy option and tell him in a text that she wouldn't be on the plane. Carrying out her decision, she got her phone back out. After a few minutes of debating what to say, she found the words, and pressed 'send'. Regret hung over her like a veil, but there was no going back now. She was still on the island and she had no idea what her next step was going to be. Knowing that her phone would ring at any minute, she quickly turned it off.

Harry will understand when I explain, she thought, feeling guilty in her reasoning. I'll know by then why I'm still here in this Godforsaken place!

Night crept over the island, and Helen found herself sitting in the airport lounge. Frightened to get up, she sat there for hours wondering what to do. The thought of going back to the hotel terrified her, but after a belly full of coffee, she eventually concluded that it was an inevitable step she was going to have to take.

"I can do this," she said under her breathe. "I have got to for my own sake."

Suddenly having put things in perspective she realised that she was the one in control, and if she played her cards right, she would have this family eating out of the palm of her hands.

I'm a lawyer, and a bloody good one at that! She thought to herself. It's my job to prove the innocent not guilty and bring justice to those who can't defend themselves. Planting a seed of strength in her heart she sat up straight. My mother was blameless, and her only guilt was to fall in love.

I will prove her innocence and make them see that they're wrong. I will not leave until they know the truth, even if it's the last thing I do. Now feeling empowered, she put her bag over her shoulder and stood up. Confidence sprung up out of her strength and taking a deep breath, she got up and headed for the main entrance. The coolness of the night air touched her skin, energising her body, enabling her to carry on with her assignment of truth. Looking around the car park, she spotted the taxi that had brought her to the airport earlier. It was the only one in the vicinity, so relieved to see a familiar face; she walked over to the car. The driver was leaning up against the taxi door smoking a cigarette. He turned around and saw a figure walking towards him, and suddenly recognised it as being the bad-mannered passenger from earlier that day. Surprised that she was still around, he stood motionless as he watched her walk over to him.

"Can you take me to the Oasis hotel please," she asked politely.

The man looked at her but didn't say a word. His face showed no emotion, and he just stared at her.

"I said can you take…" she repeated, but then the man interrupted her.

"I heard what you said," he replied abruptly in a gruff voice.

Silence reigned again, and she began to get quite agitated. Then she remembered her mood earlier and guessed that's why he was acting that way.

"I'm sorry if I was rude earlier, but I had my reasons," she explained smiling sweetly. "I'd be ever so grateful if you could take me." Aware that this was the only taxi available, she kept her agitation at bay, and carried on smiling.

The taxi driver grunted threw his cigarette on the ground and nodded his head slightly. Pointing to the boot, he got into the car. She could feel her anger bubbling, but tried her hardest to overlook his ignorance, as she put her suitcase in the boot. After getting in the car, she suddenly realised she hadn't thought about her father for a whole ten minutes. But this distraction had only been temporary, because it wasn't long before he managed to take centre stage in her mind again.

I can do this… she thought feeling very nervous. I walk into the lion's every day and this is no different. But deep down she knew this would be the hardest thing she had ever had to do.

The car pulled out of the airport grounds and her heart beat faster with anticipation, as she wondered what fate had in store for her. The journey to the hotel soon came to an end. She paid the driver, and remembering to thank him this time, she got out of the car. The driver was kind enough to get her suitcase out of the boot this time, and then he got back in and pulled away. She was left standing at the gates, as she watched the car until it disappeared round the bend. Taking a deep breath, she said out loud to herself, "its sink or swim," and proceeded to walk up the steps to the entrance. The inside of her body trembled, but this did not deter her. Putting out her hand, she held the door handle and pulled it down.

The hotel lounge was alight with laughter. Guests were assembled in various locations around the room, and all were relaxing and enjoying their surroundings. Panos's family was gathered at the bar idly chatting, unaware of the visitor entering the hotel. Panos heard the tinkling of the bell that hung above the door and looked over to see where the noise was coming from. His conversation stopped suddenly when he saw a woman standing there looking at him. It took a few moments for him to recognise the identity of the unexpected caller, and his mouth dropped open.

"Helen," he said in astonishment. "Papa, Helen has come back." His eyes never strayed from her as he repeated those words. His father looked at his son confused. He noticed he was looking over to the main door and followed his stare. The last person he was expecting to see was Helen, and he wasn't sure whether it was excitement or fear that caused his stomach to suddenly flip over. Panos started to walk over to her, but his father stopped him.

"I'll see to her," said his father getting up from the stool. Turning to his wife, he looked at her and was pleased to see her smiling. She nodded her head in approval, and stroking his hand she said, "Go to her."

Panos, Danielle, Mick and Panos's family were the only people at the bar. Silence prevailed as they watched his father walk towards the front door.

"But Panos what if she has come to cause trouble," asked Yannis concerned for his father's welfare. As soon as he had laid eyes on her, his heart sank because her presence sent alarm bells ringing in his head, and he had a terrible feeling that something wasn't right. Panos looked at him and smiled to reassure him.

"Don't worry Yannis, Papa can look after himself," he said noticing the worried look in his brother's eyes. "I am as surprised to see her as you are. But it must have taken a lot of courage for her to come back. She was so determined to have nothing to do with us this morning and adamant that she was going home. Something must have caused her to change her mind."

Their eyes never strayed from their father, but Yannis wasn't convinced. The horrible feeling grew bigger in the pit of his stomach with his father's every step closer to her. He was desperate to intervene, to warn his father, to tell her to leave, but he knew he couldn't. His respect for his father overrode his need to protect, so he succumbed to the pressure of taking a back seat.

Helen could feel her hands shaking as she watched her father walk towards her. Studying his face, the anxiety she felt deepened, and she wanted desperately to turn around and walk away. The expression he wore was stern, and she couldn't help feeling slightly intimidated. She had seen that look many times before but was determined not to let it get to her. She had been up against the toughest judges in the industry, and always stood her ground, and this she thought would be no different. Gripping hold of her suitcase, she straightened her stance and waited for him to speak. Just then his whole persona changed, and he smiled. The hostile look disappeared, and his face lit up when he said, "Hello Helen, it is good to see you again." Putting his hand out to greet her, she felt herself responding to his gesture. The gentle sound of his voice caught her off guard, and the next thing she knew she was shaking his hand.

"I... I didn't come here for a social visit," she said quickly withdrawing her hand. "There are... There are just a few things that I want to say... no... I need to say."

Feeling confident and that she was now in control again,

she waited for his expression to change. To her surprise the smile remained on his face, and he nodded.

"OK Helen, but we can't talk here. Would you care to join me in the office? We'll have more privacy there."

She thought carefully about what he had said and looked around the room. All the guests were oblivious to her presence, and by the look on their faces they were having a great time. Not wanting to cause a scene, she nodded her head.

"Good, just follow me." He led her across the room towards the stairs. As she walked past the bar, she glanced over at Mick who was staring at her with a weird look on his face. Not wanting to catch his eye, she quickly looked away. It felt strange to see him again. It had only twenty four hours since she'd been at the bar talking to him. In fact he was sitting on the very same stool she had sat on when all hell broke loose. Stopping her mind from wandering back to that time, she kept her focus on her father and followed close behind him. They reached the door leading up the stairs, but then he stopped.

"Would you like a drink, or something to eat? You can take it with you if you want. It is no trouble," he said turning to her.

Helen thought about his offer. Contemplating the idea of a large drink to calm her nerves, she was tempted. But the need to keep her wits about her overruled her temptation, so she declined. Everyone at the bar was staring at her, and she could sense that all eyes were on her. Resisting the urge to look over to them, she kept herself focused on her father, and forced herself to smile. He responded by returning the gesture and carried on up the stairs. The few minutes it took to reach the office was spent in silence. As her father reached down to open the door Helen noticed that his hand was shaking. He had shown no signs of discomfort until this point, and it pleased her to see that he was just as nervous as she was. Opening the door, he invited her into the office, and asked her politely if she wanted to sit down. Nodding her head, he led her over to the desk and pulled out a chair. She couldn't help looking around the room as she walked over to him, and she was stunned by the décor. The simplicity of the layout caught her eye. The walls were painted white with only a few pictures of the island to add a touch of colour, but the main feature was the big oak desk that was strategically placed in the centre of the room. A filing cabinet was the only other piece of furniture to accompany the desk, and this was standing tall in the corner. The room screamed out perfection which made her heart sink, as she was reminded of her own office, back in England. Despite the fact hers was slightly smaller, and the pictures on her walls were abstract paintings, there wasn't much difference between the two. Being a perfectionist herself, she prided herself on this quality, and it was common knowledge around her workplace that she couldn't, and wouldn't, work any other way. Everything had its place, and it had taken her a great deal of time and energy to set up a system that went hand in hand with her professionalism. This trait reflected her personality and she couldn't help wondering what else she had in common with this man.

Returning her mind to the present, she ignored those thoughts and concentrated on why she was there. Finally, letting go of her suitcase, she sat down. Clutching hold of her handbag, she fiddled nervously with the clasp as she watched her father go behind the desk. Not wanting to be caught off guard again, her eyes never left him as he proceeded to pull out his chair and sit down. The room went deathly silent, and considering they both had so much to say, neither knew where to begin. A few minutes passed by. The remote sound of people talking by the pool could be heard from outside. Not being able to hear their words, she glanced over to the window. The distant fusion of voices caught her attention and she suddenly found herself feeling quite envious of their untainted joy.

Aware her mind had gone astray again she cleared her throat to speak, and turned back to her father. Before the words had the chance to come out of her mouth, she stopped suddenly when she noticed that he was staring at her. She could see the reflection of the light in his eyes, and he was smiling.

"You look so much like your mother. I can't get over the resemblance. You're a natural beauty, just like she was." Those words and the sincerity in which they were spoken took her by surprise. She had prepared herself for a battle, and expected to have a fight on her hands, but now she was staring into the eyes of a gentle man, whose only weapon was flattery. Shaking her head, she tried to think straight. He had managed to catch her off guard again. She wasn't used to this form of approach.

"Look, I haven't come here to listen to your bull crap, because that is all it is to me, crap. I've come here to tell you the truth, and whether you like it or not, (and I don't really care if you don't), you will listen to me." As soon as her mouth opened, the words just flowed. They came out with the greatest of ease, and she was pleased to finally be in control again.

Taking her eyes off him, she opened her handbag. After a few moments, she found what she was looking for, and pulled out the brown envelope.

"In here lies the truth," she said holding it up. "I hope you're ready, because this will blow your side of the story out of the water." As she took out the bundle of letters, the smile fell from her father's face. Noticing that her hand was shaking, a lump rose up in his throat. Aware that this was something he had to face; he took a deep breath. He'd had the utmost respect for his father, and it terrified him to think that he had been wrong for all those years. He'd hoped she'd been lying the night before, or at least had been mistaken. But seeing the determination in her face as she spoke, soon convinced him otherwise.

She wouldn't have bothered coming back, he thought noticing the fury in her eyes. If my father lied, then she has every right to be angry.

The thought of being deceived infuriated him, but he was aware that he had to keep his cool. Staying silent, he watched her every move as she undid the ribbon. His heartbeat increased when he realised how many letters there were, and he was thankful that he was sitting down.

"Well, I can see I've finally got your attention," she said, noticing the worried expression on her father's face. Then taking a very deep breath he said, "OK Helen, I'm listening."

The mood behind the bar was a sombre one. Panos and Yannis carried on with their work doing their utmost to hide their concern regarding Helen's visit. Keeping his mind from wandering, Panos kept it occupied by washing down the bar. Then he looked over to his mother. Every couple of seconds her eyes flitted over to the door and the anxiety in her face mirrored how he felt inside. Feeling helpless, he forced himself to look away from her and carried on with what he was doing.

Mick was sitting next to Danielle. His mind was also racing, and he couldn't stop it from imagining what was going on up in the office. Knowing Helen was an impulsive woman, he shuddered when he pictured her slapping Panos around the face. The image suddenly changed when it became Panos's father's face that had caught the end of Helen's fury. Panicking he said, "Panos I hope Helen doesn't hit your dad. She hit you, so there's no telling what she could do to him." This statement caught Panos's mother's attention and caused her to look over to Panos.

"What is he talking about Panos? What does he mean, she hit you?" she asked her jaw dropping.

"Don't worry Mother, it was nothing," he replied giving Mick an irate look. "It was only a little slap. She was angry because I mentioned her mother. I was wrong, and I deserved it." He walked round from behind the bar and put his arm around her.

"Papa is going to be alright, please don't fret." Wanting to comfort her, he squeezed her, but she pushed him away.

"I should go up there. Your father needs me. I shouldn't have let him go alone." Getting up from her stool, she started to make her way over to the stairs. Yannis quickly looked over to Anna and said, "I know mother, Anna will make a pot of coffee, and then you can take it up to them."

Panos looked at his brother and rolled his eyes. He didn't want his father to be disturbed. Also, unsure of what they were saying, he felt the need to protect his mother from hearing something that could hurt her feelings. Yannis suggestion caused his mother to stop. Turning to Anna she nodded her head, and as she looked away, she noticed the expression on Panos's face. She knew her son well, and recognised that look because she had seen it so many times before.

"Panos, I understand your reasons for wanting to look out for me, but it is OK son. I know all there is to know about Elizabeth, so it is you who should not fret." She walked over to him and took his hand. "This family has no more secrets, and I believe that. I am going to stand by your father's side, and that is the end of it, OK?"

Panos looked into his mother's eyes. All he could see was compassion, which led him to believe she was telling the truth. Pulling her hand up to his cheek, he smiled and said, "OK," and then let go of her hand. At that point Anna returned carrying a tray. Passing it to her mother in law, Anna kissed her on the cheek, walked behind the bar and stood beside Yannis. Not a word was spoken as she watched her future mother in law walk back over to the stairs. Then in an instant, she was gone.

Taking a mouthful of beer, Mick watched Panos's expression change when he saw his mother leave the room. The gentle look on his face soon disappeared, when he suddenly turned to him.

"Michael, why did you have to say that? It was not your place. Sometimes you can be so stupid!" Mick looked down at the bar. Once again, he had let his mouth rule his head, and he felt so ashamed for not being able to control his tongue.

"Panos I am so sorry," he said not being able to look him in the eye. Then he hesitated as he tried to think of a reason to excuse him from his outburst. Remembering his former defence regarding the situation with Yannis, he thought about using the same excuse. But even he knew Panos wouldn't fall for that one again, so soon thought better of it.

"Like I said, I am sorry. Sometimes what I think just comes out of my mouth," he said honestly. "I can't explain it, it just happens. I don't mean to do it. I guess it's a problem I have to sort out."

Panos could hear the sincerity in his voice, and this caused his expression to soften.

"Well it is done now; we can't change it. But please be more careful in the future," he said walking behind the bar.

"Now we must wait, and act as if nothing is wrong… Yes sir, what can I get you?" he continued, noticing a guest walking towards the bar.

Danielle sighed as she watched him serve. Aware his smile was just a disguise hiding his concern; her heart went out to him. She was getting used to seeing this charade, and she couldn't help wondering if he was right to be concerned. Surprised by Helen's behaviour earlier, she suddenly found herself feeling worried for his father's safety.

No, she thought. Helen wouldn't hit an old man. But even she wasn't convinced. Panos caught her looking at him, and she smiled.

"It's going to be OK," she mouthed, and he smiled back

at her, it being genuine this time.

"I know," he mouthed back and carried on serving his guest.

An awkward silence fell as Helen's father read the letter in his hand. He was now on the third one, and by the words he read, it was so obvious that his father had threatened Elizabeth to leave. Tears stung the back of his eyes, but he managed to keep them from falling. Suddenly, taken over by a wave of guilt, he read the last sentence telling him how much Elizabeth loved him, and carefully folded it back up. Not knowing what to say, he found the courage to look up.

Helen's eyes bore into his as he looked at her, and he had never felt so ashamed.

"See I told you she was forced to leave... I told you she had no choice, so... so why did you let it happen?" she spat at him. Her tone of disgust reflected the look in her eyes, and he was lost for words.

"I said, why did you let it happen?" she shouted suddenly getting up and slamming her fist down on the desk. "Why!" she shouted banging her fist again. "You were supposed to have loved her. You were supposed to have protected her. That was your job, but... but you let her down, you coward!" Her harsh words shot straight into his heart, forcing his tears to escape.

"But Helen, I told you before, I did not know. Please listen to me, please Helen. My father told me it was her choice to leave. He said she didn't love me anymore, and I believed that because she didn't say goodbye. I thought he was right. How could I have known any different? He was my father and I trusted him. Oh Helen, I'm so sorry!"

Putting his head in his hands, he began to sob. Unable to look at him, she walked over to the window. Furious by his tears, her heart beat faster, pumping her anger through every inch of her body. Aware she was slowly losing control she put her hands up to her head and squeezed her temples. Fighting the urge to go over and hit him, she squeezed them tighter in a desperate attempt to calm herself down.

"No, I don't believe you. How could you not know? Not only are you a coward, but you are a lying stinking one at that, and believe me I have come across many of them in my life, and you... you are the worst one of them all!" She turned to him, and walked back over to the desk, and raising her voice she said, "I hate you; do you hear me? I hate you and more importantly, I hate what you did to my mother!"

Panos's mother had reached the top of the stairs when she heard Helen's claim of hatred for her husband. Putting the tray down on a nearby table, she ran to the office. As she opened the door, she was confronted by Helen leaning across the desk, just inches away from his face. Tears were flowing down his cheeks, so she rushed over and put her arms around him.

"Oh great," Helen said retreating back into her chair.

"What are you doing Helen? Can't you see he is upset? We know you're angry, but this is no way to behave." Frustration soon replaced her fear, and this was evident by the tone of her voice.

"Helen, there must be some way of resolving this other than violence. I know what you did to Panos, and I'm sorry, but that is no way a woman should conduct herself." Seeing the determination in this woman's eyes, Helen found herself listening to her words, and she suddenly calmed down. Leaning back in her chair, she crossed her legs, and folded her arms.

"Well, I am sorry for what I did to Panos, and, yes you're right. I'm also sorry for raising my voice, but I'm upset too. I... I just wanted to prove that you're wrong, and that my mother wasn't to blame. Now I have proven my point."

Helen's father looked at his wife. Confusion was written all over her face, but then she noticed the letters on the desk.

"It's true, my father lied, and he did threaten Elizabeth to make her leave," he explained picking up the bundle of letters.

"For all those years I was led to believe that Elizabeth chose to leave, but... but it was him all along. If he wasn't already dead, I... I would have killed him with my bare hands." Feeling extremely hurt, he wiped his face with the back of his hand.

"Read them, and you'll understand why Helen is so angry. But I'm afraid that she doesn't believe my innocence. She will not let me explain." He handed the letters to his wife. Taking them from him, she held them in her hand.

"I don't need to read them to understand," she said placing them down on the desk.

"I'm sorry that your father lied to you, and I don't know why he chose to be so cruel," she said calmly to her husband, and then turning to Helen she continued. "But Helen, my husband is not a liar. He is a man of integrity, and I can say from the bottom of my heart. There is not a dishonest bone in his body, so if he says he didn't know, then he didn't know. I've known him for a long time, and I can vouch for his innocence in all of this. Now, can we please talk about this amicably, like adults?" she asked. Standing up straight, but still with her hand on his shoulder, she looked at Helen and smiled. "OK Helen, do you think you can do that?"

Even though her tone was firm, Helen couldn't help feeling a little more at ease. For some strange reason she found herself liking this woman, and this unpredicted feeling took her by surprise. The hidden undertone of her words revealed a kindness that reminded her of her grandmother, and suddenly Helen understood the truth behind why this lady was so likeable.

"OK, I can do that… But having read the letters, I don't see what else there is to say. I do believe you, but what good is that to me? It doesn't change anything, so I am happy to leave here knowing that you know the truth," she said picking up the letters from the desk. "So, I will get out of your lives, and continue on with mine." Putting the letters back in her bag, she stood up and grabbed hold of her suitcase.

"But are you happy Helen. I mean, are you really happy? Do you really want to leave knowing you have a father who wants to get to know you, with a family who wants to know you too?" Panos's mother asked sincerely, putting her hand over her heart.

Helen was somewhat surprised by these words, and the sincerity in which they were spoken touched her, but she found them hard to believe.

"But why would you want that? I'm sure that I'll be a disgrace to your family… You know me being half English… If the truth be known, that is probably why your father wanted to put a stop to the relationship in the first place… It's just a shame that it ruined my mother's life. So no, I wouldn't want to be a hindrance."

Yes please, I want a dad, her mind screamed, but the voice of her pride quickly overrode her need to be in a family. Taking a deep breath, she began to walk towards the door, but she was stopped in her tracks when her father asked, "Helen, what happened to your mother? I'm sorry if it is a sensitive question, but I need to know." Helen's heart missed a beat when he asked that question. She was desperate to get out of there, but her legs wouldn't move. The pain of her mother's life brought a lump to her throat, and the thought of how she spent her last years in that institute provoked her tears to flow.

Finding the strength to answer, she took another deep breath, wiped her eyes, and turned around to face him.

"Do you really want to know?" she asked catching the next flood of tears with her hand before they reached her cheeks. Her pain was evident, and both of her onlookers found it a struggle to contain their own tears.

"Yes Helen, it's obviously causing you a lot of heartache my dear," Panos's mother said walking over to her.

"Maybe talking to us will help. I am aware that you don't know us, but it breaks my heart to see you so sad. Please come and sit down. We don't want you to go like this. Helen, please." Panos's mother stopped only a few feet in front of her and put out her arms. Still wanting to run away, Helen looked into her eyes. Thinking carefully, she was at a loss as to what to do. She wanted to leave, just like she'd wanted to get on that plane, but the same force that drew her to the hotel was at work again, trying to convince her to stay. Looking into this woman's soft eyes, Helen cleared her throat.

"Ok, I'll tell you, but I warn you it's not a nice story." Resisting the urge to fall into her arms, Helen gained control of her emotions, and ignoring the welcoming gesture, she just walked past her. Her father, shocked by this show of disrespect, was just about to say something when his wife, realising his reaction, shook her head and put her finger up to her mouth. Her sign of silence was acknowledged, and swallowing his pride, he chose to keep his mouth shut. Even though he knew Helen was hurting, he still found it hard to contain himself. He loved his wife dearly, and it was only natural for him to pull someone up if their lack of respect was aimed at her, even if the circumstances were of a sensitive nature. Proud to have been able to control this impulsive response, he watched Helen walk over to him and sit back down. Suddenly remembering the tray of coffee she'd left outside, Panos's mother went out of the room to get it from the hallway table. Confused by her sudden departure, Helen and her father watched her leave the room, and were soon relieved when she walked back in moments later armed with the pot of coffee. Helen welcomed the need of a shot of caffeine to help her stay alert; because she had a feeling it was going to be a long night. Taking a sip, she looked at this couple and found it hard to believe that she was going to open up to them and explain the sordid details behind her mother's demise. Realising she did trust them, a good feeling in her gut prompted her to reveal the heart rendering account, not only of her mother's life, but also her death. Realising she had their undivided attention; she began to talk.

Finding it hard at first, she talked them through her childhood, and what it was like being raised by her grandparents. She delved deeper into her past, and pulling out all the stops, it soon became evident why her mother had left the responsibility of bringing up her daughter to her elderly parents. Initially she forgot to mention that her mother had lied to her, telling her that her father had died in an accident. Once she realised her error, she rewound her life story back to that time, nearly having them in tears again as she narrated the story of that unforgivable lie. Feeling it the most, her father studied her face as he listened, and his whole body became racked with guilt. Aware he needed to maintain his composure and stop the guilt from showing, he swallowed this emotion back down, and it took all his mental strength to keep it there.

She shared about her time at law school, and her father was consumed with pride as it was obvious that she was an intelligent girl, who knew what she wanted and had the willpower to get it. This was a trait that shone through both of his son's, and he silently congratulated himself for instilling this quality in them. Being a strong characteristic in his own personality, he felt honoured to know this was a hereditary ability that had also been passed down to Helen. Elaborating on the fact that it was her desire to help her mother overcome her addiction, that fed her determination to succeed, she couldn't have made it any plainer. The love for a woman that had abandoned her at a young age escaped through her words, and Panos's mother had to stop herself many times from giving Helen a hug. Thankful for having a tissue in her pocket, she spent most of the time wiping her eyes. Aware of the distress her tale was causing,

Helen kept her mind focused and carried on. Eventually she came to the time of her mother's death. Taking a breath, she excused herself and went over to the window. Not being able to face them as she spoke about this time, she looked out and noticed the guests by the pool. There were only a handful of people sitting by the tables, but just seeing them took her mind off her mother for a few moments. Then deciding to get it over and done with, she continued. When she came to the end of the tale, she raised her arms and said, "And here I am. The rest is history. I came looking for my father, and I found him."

Frightened to look around at the couple, she suddenly realised all the guests were gone from around the pool. The silence outside was as thick as the darkness, and Helen had been so consumed with her version of events that she hadn't even noticed them go inside. Feeling exhausted, she found what strength she had left in her, and turned around. She was met by two solemn faces and seeing the look of despair written all over them, she turned back to the window. Finding it impossible to contain her tears any longer, she began to sob.

"I am sorry I came here. I didn't mean to cause you any pain," she cried. "I just didn't know what to do. My hatred for you fuelled my strength, and I thought I could cope, but I can't." She turned to her father. "I wanted to hate you, it… it made me feel better, but… but you are a good man, I can see that… I just wanted justice for my mother's death. I couldn't help her when she was alive, so… so I thought I could make it up to her by putting things right… All I've ever wanted is a family, a proper family to call my own… Please don't get me wrong, I love my grandparents, and I'm so grateful to

them… but it wasn't the same… it will never be the same."
Looking at Panos's mother once again she cried, "I miss
having a mum… It's as if I have got a big hole in my heart,
and nothing I do can fill it… I feel so lost, so alone. It hurts
so much." Panos's mother ran over to her and once again put
out her arms. This time Helen took her up on her kind offer,
fell into her embrace and sobbed her heart out.

"There, there, there," she said stroking Helen's hair. "It is
going to be alright; I promise. If you will have us, we will be
your family. There is enough love in this family, for you and
your grandparents. It will be OK. We won't let you down."
The tears were also flowing down her cheeks, but she
couldn't help that. This lady in her arms was precious to her,
and she had meant everything she said from the bottom of
her heart.

"Yes, my wife is absolutely right. I'm your father, and I
know I was not there for you at the beginning, but… but I
am here for you now." He walked over to her and put his
arm around her. He'd never felt so much pain for another
person in his life, and he couldn't help feeling responsible
for the heartache she'd had to endure.

"I'll make it up to you Helen, I promise you that. No one
will ever hurt you again; I'll make sure of that." Holding her
tight, he kissed her head. "I mean no one!" Pulling herself
away slightly, Panos's mother let go of her, and Helen
looked at her father. Tears were streaming down his cheeks,
and the same look of vulnerability she saw the previous
night was evident on his face.

"You promise," she asked staring into his teary eyes.

"I promise," he replied smiling.

"Thank you…Dad." With that, she fell into his arms and squeezed him tight. She spent the next ten minutes in her father's arms. It felt so good to finally feel at peace, but then reality bowled in and tried to snatch it away from her.

"But what about Panos, and Yannis, what will they say?" she asked pulling away. "I don't think that I'll be able to face Panos, especially after what I did to him this morning. He must hate me." Tears came to her eyes as she remembered hitting him, and she felt so ashamed.

"Helen you don't have to worry about Panos, he'll understand when we explain," said her father taking her hand. "He can't complain, from what I am aware of, you are very much like him. He is very hot headed as well. So please get those thoughts out of your mind young lady. Papa will talk to them, and they will soon get used to the idea of having a sister, even if you are a half sister. I'm confident that they'll welcome you into the family, just like we have." He turned to his wife and smiled. "Isn't that right my darling?"

Panos's mother nodded her head. Dabbing her eyes, a huge smile swept across her face when she said, "oh yes, they'll grow to love you just like we will, and I hope you will grow to love us too."

Glowing with pride, Helen tore herself away from her father, and went over to her suitcase.

"Thank you both of you, you are so kind. I feel a big weight has been lifted off my shoulders, and I'm sure I will. Now I had better find a hotel. I should get some sleep; all this emotional talk has drained me. I'm absolutely shattered."

"What do you mean find a hotel," her father exclaimed. "I don't know whether you noticed, but we own a hotel," he laughed. "You'll stay here. I insist. Please don't insult your father by saying you will stay in another hotel," he said jokingly. "I will not hear of it. We have room; we'll make room, so that's final." He laughed again and looked at her.

The kindness displayed across his face was genuine, and Helen was touched by his generosity.

"OK, OK, I will stay, but only if I can cook you breakfast." Their hilarity filled the room, bringing with it an abundance of joy that made itself at home in each of their hearts.

"Now we must go downstairs and tell Panos and Yannis of our good news. Who knows what's been going on in their minds since we have been up here?" said her father walking over to the door. Opening it, like a gentleman, he let the ladies leave first. Suddenly anger tried to raise its ugly head when the thought of his father's deceit came back into his mind. Not being able to comprehend his father's motive behind the lie, he was suddenly reminded of what Helen had said earlier, "You know, me being half English. That's why your father probably put a stop to it in the first place." Those words repeated themselves in his mind, when suddenly Panos stole his thoughts. Thinking about his son's relationship with Danielle, his mind wandered as he pictured them getting married. The thought still went against the grain of his heart, and he panicked. Still wanting him to find a nice Greek girl, his heart became saddened when he remembered Elizabeth.

Well I suppose if he loves her, I could get used to the idea, he thought to himself. But then he smiled when he remembered her three children.

My father might have been wrong about Elizabeth, but

I would have to be six foot under before any son of mine takes on another man's child, especially three of them. Pleased to see his son with a Greek girl rose up out of his worst nightmare and this caused him to feel happy again.

"I can tolerate her whilst she's here, but when she goes home, I'll have to have a seriously long talk with him about his heritage, and what it means to be a Greek man!" Confident of this inevitable outcome, he followed Helen and his wife down the stairs, feeling very pleased with himself.

Helen walked down the hallway beside Panos's mother and couldn't help looking at her. A huge smile was displayed across her face, and she realised that the same expression was evident on her own face. Sensing the joy that radiated through her smile, she laughed softly. Remembering how she felt earlier when she walked through that very same hallway, she had never have guessed in a million years, that her attitude would have taken a hundred and eighty degrees turn. Hearing her laugh, Panos's mother looked at her and was pleased to see she was happy. Glad to see this unexpected turn around, she put her arm through Helen's and pulled her close to her side.

"It's so good to see you this way, you are a beautiful lady, and it lifts my heart to see your beauty enhanced by your smile. I'm so glad you chose to stay." Then lowering her voice to barely above a whisper, she said, "To tell you the truth, I always prayed for a daughter, this wasn't how I expected my prayer to be answered though. But I promise you I will regard you as one of my own. I know I will never replace your mother, and I wouldn't want to, but I look forward to becoming close friends." Helen was touched by her honesty.

"Thank you and I am looking forward to that too," she said patting her hand. The two women walked down the stairs arm in arm, and Helen had never felt so at home.

Yannis had been ushered over to the reception desk and was dealing with a guest when his mother walked into the lounge with Helen on her arm. This display of unity distracted him from the couple querying their bill and he looked at his mother in complete disbelief. Watching them walk over to the bar, he quickly diverted his attention back on to the irate couple in front of him and focused his mind, on resolving their problem as quickly and as smoothly as possible. Feeling agitated not only by this couple, his anger was bumped up a level as he remembered the look on Helen's face when she walked into the room. Eager to find out the motive behind Helen's smile, he took a deep breath to keep his agitation at bay, as he tried to focus on the guests who were obviously mistaken.

Panos however, was over the moon to see his mother and Helen walk in looking extremely happy. He couldn't wait to hear the outcome of their meeting, and guessing by the look on Helen's face, it had been a good one. Then his level of joy increased when he noticed his father walk in only a few paces behind them wearing a smile that went from one ear to the other.

"Panos, Helen will be spending the night, so can I leave her in your capable hands as I go up and prepare a room for her," said his mother leading Helen over to the bar.

"Why Yes, it would be a pleasure, she will be safe with me." He laughed as he watched his mother walked away.

"And get her a drink, we have a lot of explaining to do," stated his father boldly, putting his arm around Helen's shoulder. Kissing her head, he suddenly caught Yannis out of the corner of his eye and could see he was having trouble with a couple at reception. Taking his hand away he said, "But first I must go and see to your brother, by the look on his face he needs my help. I won't be long." Pulling himself away, he made his way over to Yannis. Aware that she was now alone at the bar, Helen began to feel very nervous. Not being able to face speaking to Panos, she turned to Danielle.

"Hello again," she said nervously.

Danielle could hear the tension in her voice but found it difficult to respond to her. Disorientated by this change of attitude, Danielle couldn't believe this was the same woman that had left them by the road earlier that day. Feeling loyal to Panos, she looked at him and shrugged her shoulders. Panos could see the concern in her face and nodding his head, smiled. Helen was aware of their silent communication and sighed. Then finding the courage to look at Panos, she took a deep breath and said, "I'm so sorry for slapping you this morning. My behaviour was disgraceful, and please believe me when I say, I am deeply sorry." Only finding enough courage to say these words, she looked down at the bar.

"Helen it is ok," said Panos putting his hand on top of hers. "I understand how upset you were, so no hard feelings. I would have reacted the same way if I were you, so please, it is forgotten. Honestly it is." The pressure of having to convince Panos of her remorse quickly disappeared, so looking back up, she smiled.

"That's such a relief. I didn't think you would ever want to speak to me again."

"I am a hard man Helen, but even I cannot find it in my heart to dislike you. From the look on my parents faces you've made amends, and if they are happy then..." he hesitated as he tried to find the words, "Then that's all the proof I need to forget what happened earlier. It's in the past, so now we'll just enjoy the moment. Who knows, maybe having a sister won't be so bad after all." Helen could detect the humour in his voice and suddenly laughed.

"Ha, it's like that is it? I think it's me that has the greatest challenge ahead of me, there being two of you," she replied, proving that she was just as capable of outwitting him with her sense of humour as he was.

"Yes, I agree that Yannis is a challenge, but you're so wrong about me Helen. My charm will see to that," he chuckled and bringing his hand up he tapped her on the chin.

"Charm you say..." she replied scratching her head. "I would say it was more like wishful thinking, or maybe delusion. Yes, that's more like it; you're definitely a man who resides in fantasy land." Unable to stop her sarcasm, she suddenly had a horrible feeling that she had pushed him too far. The dark cloud of fear soon lifted when he said, "Why Helen, you've got me there. I'm impressed with your answer. I do believe that I've found the female version of me." The bar erupted with laughter, and following suit, she gave out a huge sigh of relief.

"Well your father did say I was a lot like you, so maybe he was right. Nice to meet you at last, but I do think you are more female than I am male." Helen smirked putting out her hand.

"I'm afraid to say you're wrong, oh so wrong. After the way you hit me this morning it's true to say that it's the other way around," replied Panos, cheekily, shaking her hand.

She could feel her face burning with embarrassment. Remembering that time and being consumed by guilt, she felt her insides quiver with shame. Taking her hand away she looked down at the floor.

"I can vouch for that!" shouted Mick suddenly. "You certainly gave him a good slap."

Loving the banter flying between them, Mick couldn't help but intervene. Then realising what he'd done, the smile fell from his face. Proud of himself for having kept his mouth shut up until this point, he cringed as he waited expectantly for Panos to jump down his throat. But it didn't happen. Feeling confused, he tentatively looked at Panos and was relieved to see him still smiling.

"Now, now Michael, don't encourage her, she might decide to hit you too," Panos laughed. "Helen, I wouldn't blame you if you did, I have come close many times." Looking at Helen he winked. "Believe me I have."

"Hey! Did you forget about last night Panos? You did hit me. It may have escaped your memory, but I remember it as clear as anything." Mick took a mouthful of his beer with one hand and rubbed his jaw with the other. "You really hurt me; I can still feel the lump."

Helen smiled as she remembered nursing him the night before. The vision of yesterday was so clear in her mind, and she still felt sorry for him. Looking over to Mick she said, "Well you didn't deserve that Mick, but Panos most certainly did this morning, he did have it coming." Then turning to Panos she smiled sarcastically at him. "You seem to forget that I am a lawyer and defending the weak is my job." Her confidence made a welcome comeback, and she was pleased it had returned.

"Oh yes, so you are. I'd better be quiet. I want to stay on your good side. I would be a fool to argue with you." Panos took a step back and put his hands up in the air. "I wouldn't want to get on the wrong side of you Helen. You're as tough as they come."

The air was once again filled with laughter. Mick's amusement was the loudest, but then he suddenly realised what Helen had said.

"Hey Helen, what are you saying? I am not weak." The smile dropped from his face, and feeling quite hurt he said, "I don't know, you stick up for someone and then they discredit your manhood." Unsure if he was joking, Panos patted him on the back.

"Michael, what is that sad look for, my friend. It is only a bit of fun." Noticing his glass was nearly empty, he picked up a clean one and said, "I know what will put the smile back on your face," and started to pour him out a fresh pint of beer.

"Well if you insist," Mick said eyeing up his next drink. "It would be rude not to." Proving Panos right, his smile soon returned. Then rubbing his hands together, he asked, "Right, what's everybody having?"

Helen spent the rest of the night, getting to know her newfound family. Considering she was from another part of the world, she soon realised that she had a lot in common with them, especially Panos. So, deciding to spend a few more days at the hotel she relished in the love they freely demonstrated, and at last, finally felt a part of something special. Yannis soon came around to the idea, of having a half-sister when his father explained the situation, and after taking time out to talk to Helen, he found himself liking her. The mood behind the bar was now restored, and the sound of their jolly conversations was a sure sign of new beginnings yet to come.

As the night drew to a close, Panos smiled as he remembered his earlier prediction. Having Danielle by his side prompted his smile to widen, and not only being blessed by her presence, he now felt honoured to have two beautiful English ladies in his life. Even he was surprised by the bond that was evident between him and Helen, considering they had spent all those years apart, but he sensed that this was the beginning of something special. Confident that the last twenty-four hours were now in the past, he silently congratulated himself for having the best family, and proposed at toast.

"To Helen," he said raising his glass. "Welcome to the family." Her name echoed around the room as everyone followed suit. Being totally overwhelmed by this show of unity, Helen could feel her eyes filling up with tears. Thankful for them being provoked by joy this time, she put her glass down on the bar and took a bow.

"Thank you for being so kind. I am honoured that you

have found it in your hearts to accept me. It is a privilege to be a part of your family."

Their father watched Helen's face light up as she responded to his son's statement, and felt a lump rise in his throat. Now that the shock of having a daughter had disappeared, he found himself looking forward to spending the next few days getting to know her. Although he knew he had a task on his hand, when he had to explain her to his extended family, he smiled,

If I can accept her, then so can they, he thought. If they don't, then it's a burden they shall have to carry. These inspiring thoughts stirred up his courage to face the situation when it arose, but until then he decided to focus his mind on making up for lost time. Relieved by the outcome of her visit, he went over to Helen and gave her a hug. Welcoming his embrace, she knew this was the start of the next chapter of her life, and she had never felt so happy.

CHAPTER
THIRTEEN

*T*he time to depart was fast approaching. Lingering on the horizon like a bad smell, their final day together loomed in the distance, and everyone did their best to ignore the inescapable consequence of its presence. The past few days had flown by so fast, and Helen couldn't believe that in less than twenty-four hours time, she would be going home. Panos had booked her a seat on the same flight as Mick and Danielle, and it pleased her to know that her journey home wasn't going to be a lonely one. She had spoken to Harry and after a long detailed, discussion she came off the phone feeling on top of the world. Harry had been very understanding about the whole thing, and once again assured her that he would be there to pick her up at the airport. Relieved and pleased by this show of consideration, she decided to make the most of every minute she had left on the island with her family.

Panos however, was finding it very hard to ignore the calling of time. Aware that it was rapidly running out, he couldn't stop his mind from imagining his life without Danielle. Having trouble controlling his thoughts, he tried to focus them on his work. This proved to be just as difficult, and he suddenly found himself feeling very angry.

Frustration rose up from the pit of his stomach, and he could have screamed.

Why does it have to end this way? he thought clenching his fist. Trying desperately to ignore these unwanted feelings, he looked over to Danielle. She was sitting on a lounger talking to Helen and seeing the innocence in her face as she spoke, added to the torment in his heart. Conscious that he had to keep his feelings from showing, somehow, he managed to overpower them. Setting his mind on her happiness, he decided to make her last night a night to remember. Just then the promise he had made to his father invaded his mind, bringing with it a deep sadness. Knowing that this was the last night he was going to spend with her, he suddenly had the overwhelming need to explain something to her. Deep down in his heart he knew that they could never have a future, but he wanted to tell her how much she meant to him, and that he did truly love her. A horrible feeling of dread flowed through his body, but he knew this was an inevitable step he was going to have to take. Not only out of respect for his heritage, but also out of respect for her. Taking a deep breath, he left the bar and began to walk over to her.

Lost in her conversation with Helen, Danielle was oblivious that Panos was walking towards them. Having spent the last couple of days in Helen's company, she soon realised she had a lot of time for her. They hit it off immediately, and by the depth of their conversations, the sign of a good friendship flourishing was evident. Her heart went out to her as Helen talked about her life, and when the sorrowful tale came to an end, Danielle realised how lucky she was. Guilt pricked her heart when she thought about her own mother, and how she'd taken for granted the fact that she had always been there for her. This feeling doubled in size, when her mind automatically went on to her children. Not being able to figure out how anyone could choose to give up their child, she suddenly found herself missing them terribly. She felt a longing for them in her heart and knew then that her need as a parent was greater than her need to be loved by a man. Knowing this loyalty outweighed her selfishness as a woman, she was confident that this truth was going to help her get over Panos. Aware that walking away from him for the final time was going to be extremely hard, she kept that thought in the forefront of her mind.

Helen noticed the smile disappear from Danielle's face. Feeling concerned by the sudden change of her appearance, she was just about to ask her if she was OK, when she saw Panos walking towards them. Becoming distracted by his presence, she couldn't help noticing that he also wore the same glum look on his face. Confused by this unexpected transformation, she said, "Come on you two, it can't be that bad." Disguising her concern, she laughed. Then in a second attempt to revive their smiles, she laughed again. Realising her effort to lighten the mood was failing; she quickly gave up and lay down.

"Danielle, could I please speak to you in private?" he asked quietly, resisting the urge to answer Helen's statement. Danielle looked at him, taken aback by his tone. Detecting seriousness in his voice, a horrible feeling bubbled in her stomach. His tone went hand in hand with his expression, and this unnerved her. Noticing her lack of enthusiasm, Panos managed to raise a smile.

"Please, I really want to talk to you, it's important." His smile defused her worry slightly, and she nodded. Putting out his hand, she took hold of it and he helped her up. Then the two of them walked away.

Mick came over from the bar and sat down next to Helen.

"Where are those two going? They didn't look very happy," he asked apprehensively.

"Panos wanted to speak to her," replied Helen sitting up. "Mick, there is something I don't understand. They've been all over each other like a rash, so what has happened? They were so happy together just a short while ago. It just doesn't make sense."

"It's probably because she's going home tomorrow. This will be their last night together, so I'm guessing that is what's wrong," he replied taking off his t-shirt.

"But they're in love, that's obvious. He can't just let her go, that's crazy," she said unable to believe what she was hearing.

"Well, from what I know, Panos's father, sorry your father, doesn't want them to be together. It goes against their religion or tradition; I'm not sure which one, but apparently that's the way it is."

"But... but surely after everything that's happened things are different now?" she asked frowning.

"Look Helen, I don't know the logistics, all I know is to stay out of it. I've had enough arguments to last me a lifetime, and I've learnt to keep my big nose out." He took a mouthful of his beer and lay down. "And I suggest you do the same."

Helen could feel anger bubbling.

I will not do the same, she thought defiantly. I will not let this happen.

"Oh, and it's because she's got children,"he suddenly remembered. "Apparently taking on someone else's children is unheard of in the Greek culture. Dan knows about it though, so she's aware. Doesn't make sense to me, but hey, who am I to argue," he continued closing his eyes.

"Oh," said Helen thinking carefully about what he'd just said. "That is a shame, because they do make such a lovely couple. I'd hate to be her tomorrow." Relaxing back on her lounger she sighed.

Even I can't fight that battle, she thought, and refrained herself from interfering. Not wanting to rock the boat, she focused her mind on topping up her tan.

Pulling Danielle to his side, Panos walked them back into the hotel. Aware the guests were either by the pool or down in the town, he decided to talk to her in the restaurant. His body was tense, and his stomach was wound so tight, he felt that at any minute, it would snap. Entering the restaurant, he led her to a table, pulled out a chair, and told her to sit down. Filled with apprehension, Danielle followed his command and sat down. Her nervousness took over and it was like a sign of consent, giving her butterflies permission they needed to have full reign of her tummy. Then a dull ache rose up out of her heart, authorising her tears to well up in her eyes, and she had to use all her will power to stop them from escaping. Frightened to look away, she watched as he pulled out the chair opposite her and sat down. Silence filled the air, as he struggled to find the right words to say. The last thing he wanted to do was hurt her feelings, and he was aware that he had to choose his words carefully.

"Danielle, my Danielle," he said breaking the silence. "I'm so grateful that you come back to me." Taking her hand, he looked into her eyes and continued. "I can honestly say you are the best thing that has ever happened to me, and I... I have never felt this way about anyone before in my life. You're so special, and... and..." hesitating, he looked down at the table. Frightened to set his words free, he sighed heavily. "And I will never forget you."

"Panos, thank you, but you don't have to explain. I understand," she said squeezing his hand.

"But you don't understand Danielle!" he said raising his voice. "I love you so much, but I have to let you go. You're everything I want in a woman, everything I need in a woman, and... and it breaks my heart to imagine you not being here." Looking back up at her, his tone softened. "I don't want to let you go Danielle, but... but I have no choice." Tears stung the back of his eyes, and his body was riddled with pain, but finding his strength, he carried on.

"I am a strong Greek man with strong Greek family values, but it is in times like this that I wish I'd never been born into this way of life. It hurts me Danielle to say that, but it hurts me more losing you. I'm sorry, but that is the way I feel. I know your children are important to you, I do know that, but... but if it wasn't for them, we'd have had a chance. The reality of this whole situation causes me so much pain." Lifting her hand to his mouth he kissed it. "I'm sorry I can't be the man you want me to be. I'm sorry I can't fight for you, unfortunately it's out of my hands." A single tear rolled down his cheek. His honesty yanked at her heart strings, and seeing his pain she said, "Panos, my darling Panos, I know how hard it will be. I feel the same way. I don't want to leave you either, but I know this is the way it's meant to be." Finding it difficult to hold back her tears, she brought his hand up to her lips.

"Yes, you're absolutely right, my children are my world, and I would do anything for them, and… and that includes walking away from the best thing that has ever happened to me too. So yes, I do understand." Then kissing his hand, she finished by saying, "And I will never forget you." Her words echoed her pain, and her heart was near to breaking, but then she was reminded of her hidden weapon. Thankful for having an ally in her children, this seemed to ease her pain.

"I wonder what our children would have looked like," said Panos suddenly out of the blue. "I know one thing, they would have been beautiful just like you," he said softly looking at her and smiling.

"And they would have been hot headed just like you," she replied laughing.

"There is nothing wrong with that," he said complacently taking her other hand. "They would have had beauty and brawn, what a perfect combination," he laughed cheekily. "Now come over here." Letting go of her hands, he patted his legs. Understanding his command, she got up and went and sat on his lap.

"I do love you, my heart tells me so, and you'll always be

my number one." Pulling her close, he put his head to her chest and squeezed her tight. Finding it very hard to stay focused on the present, Danielle's mind wandered to the following day. She dreaded it coming, and a tear rolled down her cheek.

I have got to be strong, she thought, stopping the flood of tears from falling. But it's going to be so hard. Kissing the top of his head she closed her eyes.

Oh, what have I done?

A short while later they walked back down to the pool. Panos had insisted that nothing was going to spoil their last night, and Danielle did not argue. They agreed to cherish every moment they had left together and promised to save their tears until the following day. Sealing this pact with a kiss, Panos took great pleasure in telling her about the special night he had planned. Wanting it to be perfect, he suggested they started the evening off in the hotel. Colluding with his mother earlier that day, he had asked her to cook something extra special for their last night. She loved the idea, and agreed, happy to be involved. Danielle's chest puffed up with pride when he shared his proposal, and she felt honoured to know his mother would go to the trouble of doing something like that just for her.

Next the plan was for them to go into town, giving her the choice of either going to Nicos's or a club. Having already been to Nicos, she chose to go to the Borzoi club in the high street. Knowing that place held good memories of her last visit to the island, he was very pleased with her choice. He also planned on asking Mick and Helen to join them at the club.

She was over the moon they were all going to be together.

Mick was back up at the bar talking to Yannis when the couple reappeared. He was pleased to see that they were both looking a lot happier than when they first left.

"Panos my friend," he said putting his hand out to greet him. "It's good to see you smiling again. You had me worried." Shaking his hand, Panos's smile widened.

"Why Michael, that's one for the record my friend and I thought the only thing you worried about was your beer. I must say, I'm very touched by your concern." Mick wasn't sure how to take this statement but smiled anyway.

"Well there's always a first for everything," he said raising his glass. "Cheers."

Kissing Panos on the cheek, Danielle left him to ask Mick if he wanted to join them at the club later. She also took on the task of asking Helen the same question. Pleased to see the smile had returned to Danielle's face, she took great pleasure in accepting her invitation. Having spent all her time at the hotel, she thought it would make a nice change to go into the town. Although she felt a bit guilty for leaving her father, she soon convinced herself that it was only for a few hours, which eased her conscience slightly. Looking forward to the night ahead of them, they spent the rest of the afternoon in one another's company and enjoyed their time together. Once the sun began to set, Panos carried out his daily routine of shutting down the pool bar. Keeping a close eye on the time, he suggested that Danielle went up to get changed whilst he catered for the evening rush. Helen chose to do the same, and both ladies giggled like teenagers as they went up to their rooms.

Mick, being Mick, decided to spend his last few hours up at the bar, and used this time interacting with the guests. Whilst sitting there, he couldn't help noticing that Panos kept flitting between the bar and the restaurant. He became somewhat surprised and curious about the look of secrecy written all over his face.

"Panos, what are you up to?" he said suspiciously on Panos's fifth trip back to the bar. "Slow down mate, you're making me feel sea sick," Panos didn't have time to answer, so just tapped his finger on the side of his nose.

"Oh, it's like that is it?" he asked disturbed by Panos's sign of confidentiality, but soon got over his disappointment when he realised that he had better things to think about. So, putting his mind on more important things, he picked up his glass and carried on talking to one of the guests. Panos continued with his work. With Danielle in the forefront of his mind, he took every opportunity he had to check on his mother's progress with the meal. Having been assured by his mother on numerous occasions that she had everything under control, he was pleased to know that everything was going to plan. Thankful not only to his mother, but also for having plenty of things to keep him occupied, his time apart from Danielle passed quickly. He couldn't wait to see the look on her face when she entered the restaurant, causing his chest to puff up with pride.

Before long, she was back in his sight, looking absolutely gorgeous. Wearing a figure hugging black sequinned dress, he watched mesmerised as she walked over to him. Taken aback by her beauty all he could do was smile, feeling as though he was the luckiest man in the world.

Mick was in the middle of a discussion about his wife with a guest, when he realised that his conversation had become very one sided. Noticing that his talking partner's attention had suddenly gone elsewhere, he turned to see what had caught this man's eye. Taking a mouthful of his beer, he turned around to find out the culprit behind this interruption and spat out his drink.

"Blimey Dan, you look gorgeous!" he said, soon understanding the reason for the man's sudden lack of interest in his tale of woe. Wiping his chin, he said "That dress should carry a health warning Dan because it nearly gave me a heart attack." Putting his hand to his chest, he hit it with his fist. "I think it has stopped working, blimey Dan you're going to kill me."

"Don't be so dramatic, Mick," she said coyly looking down at the floor, going red in the face.

"But he's right, you do look gorgeous. I didn't think it could be possible, but I was wrong. I have never seen you look so beautiful." Panos walked around to her stunned. "Oh, how I love you." Lifting her chin, he looked deep into her eyes and kissed her. "You are so perfect," he whispered, kissing her again. Her butterflies returned more vigorously than ever, and she felt her heart would stop as she dared to kiss him back. All her emotions flooded to the surface, and she could have cried. Putting his arms around her, he held her tight. Aware that his emotions were also trying to escape through his tears, he closed his eyes.

"We have to be strong," he said quietly in her ear. "We have to be strong."

Losing the power in her voice, she just nodded. Forcing himself to let her go, he cleared his throat and said, "Right, a drink for the lady before dinner." Then he went back behind the bar and began to pour her a drink.

The flow of conversation soon returned, and the air was full of cheerful chattering again. Yannis came into the lounge and informed his brother that he was needed in the restaurant. Feeling a rush of excitement, Panos excused himself and practically ran out from behind the bar. Confused by his sudden departure, Danielle looked at Mick. He was just as confused as she was, and noticing her puzzled look, he shrugged his shoulders.

Turning to Yannis she asked, "What's going on? Why did Panos rush out like that?" Confronted with the same motion as Mick, Danielle's heart sank. Then just as quickly as his exit, Panos returned.

"Danielle, if you could come with me please. I will show you to your table," he said grinning from ear to ear. Cupping the air with his hand, he swung his arm as a signal for her to lead the way. Picking up her glass, she got off the stool, but then Mick grabbed her arm.

"Danielle, before you go, there's just one thing I need to say," he said as she looked down at his hand.

"Panos is a lucky man, you do know that don't you?" Taken aback by his statement she nodded. "And I know... I know tomorrow will be hard for you, but... but I just wanted you to know that I'll be there for you. OK?" Looking into his eyes, she smiled.

"You are beautiful, and... and I know Panos will not be there to remind you, so I'll make it my job to tell you, and

I'll tell you every day, I promise." She could see his eyes filling up with tears, and she could feel hers doing the same. Aware of her tears, he was conscious not to make her cry, so he said, "Now go on and enjoy your meal, before you see this old man cry." Touched by his words, she kissed him on the cheek. He had never said anything like that to her before and she was totally overwhelmed by this show of affection.

"Thank you, Mick, you are a true friend, and I love you for that." With that, holding back her tears, she took a deep breath and walked away. Quickening her pace, she made her way over to Panos, who was standing in the doorway to the restaurant. Still overwhelmed by Mick's lovely words, she was led over the threshold. Halfway across the room, she suddenly noticed Panos's mother standing in front of a table in the corner. A huge smile was displayed across her face, and Danielle was surprised to see her standing there. Not being able to see the table, Panos's mother moved to one side, and Danielle's heart suddenly somersaulted in her chest. A vase of freshly cut flowers took centre stage, and a ring of tiny candles were placed neatly around the base. Their flames danced around like miniature ballerinas, highlighting the bouquet as if it were a work of art. Unable to contain her tears, Danielle looked at his mother, and then looked at Panos. Putting his hand to her face, he gently wiped her cheek and said, "Danielle, my beautiful Danielle, you made a promise."

"I… I know, but… but I wasn't expecting this. It… it is so lovely," she replied taking hold of his hand. "You knew this would make me cry. You did this on purpose." Out of her sadness came a hint of joy, and she laughed. "You're a wicked man Panos."

Seeing her teary eyes sparkle in the candlelight, he said, "If making you feel loved and appreciated makes me a wicked man, then yes you are correct. You wait until you see what's coming. Then you will think that I am downright nasty." They both laughed and bringing up his other hand he held her face and kissed her.

"I love you so much." The gentle feel of his soft lips on hers sent a tingling sensation through every part of her body and she wanted to be in his arms forever. But knowing that she had to let go, she pulled herself away and smiled.

"I love you too, from the bottom of my heart." Captured by her dazzling emerald eyes he smiled back at her.

"I know my darling, but now we must eat."

Panos's mother fighting back her own tears pulled out a chair for Danielle to sit down. She was just about to walk away when Danielle grabbed her arm.

"Thank you for your kindness," she said stroking her hand.

"Why Danielle, you do not have to thank me, it is me who should be thanking you." Then smiling at her, she walked away.

"Right, now for the second surprise," said Panos reaching down under the table. A few moments later his hand came back up, and he was holding a brightly coloured gift bag.

"This is for you. I hope you like it. I brought it for you when I knew you were coming back to me." Handing it to her, her eyes widened. Frightened to look at what was inside, she hesitated and said, "Panos you know I don't like surprises; you shouldn't have." Ignoring her words, he hurried her up with his hands.

So, taking a deep breath she opened the bag and pulled out a blue box.

"Go on, open it," he said smiling. "It doesn't bite."

Aware that her hands were shaking, she nervously unclasped the latch, and gasped when she saw what was inside.

"Do you like it," he asked getting up.

"Oh Panos, I love it," she replied fondling her present.

Panos walked behind her and taking the gift from her, he pushed her hair to one side, and hung it around her neck. Then kissing her head, he returned to his seat. Looking at her he smiled, and graciously said, "It suits you, a beautiful diamond for a beautiful lady."

Unable to resist touching it again, Danielle brought her hand up to her neck. "It sure is beautiful. Thank you." Leaning across the table she kissed him. "I love you so much, Thank you."

"You are welcome." He leant back in his chair and admired the huge diamond that dangled neatly between her breasts. It hung perfectly on a gold chain, and the flickering of the candles reflected every intricate detail, making it as dazzling as her eyes. The smile across her face was a sure sign that his night had started well, and he couldn't have wished for a better beginning to his last night spent with her.

The first course came and went, and Danielle felt on top of the world. Only a few guests dined in the restaurant, and she noticed that they kept looking at her smiling. Aware that their table was the only one with candles and flowers, this made her feel incredibly special. The main course came, and Danielle could see another gift bag on the tray. Panos's mother handed it to Panos, and he proceeded to give it to her. Giving him a strange look, she took it from him, and without any hesitation this time, she opened it.

"Panos," she shrieked. Pulling out a bracelet that matched the necklace she said, "Panos, this is too much. It's beautiful."

"Now you nearly have the set."

Looking at him confused, she realised that there was another box inside the bag. So, pulling out the box she opened it, and shrieked again.

"Oh, my goodness earrings as well you are too kind."

"Now you do have the set. My, my what a wicked man I am."

Letting out a laugh, she kissed him again, totally overwhelmed by his generosity. "Yes, you are a wicked, wicked man," she replied still laughing.

They ate the main course, and Danielle was almost too frightened to finish it. Not knowing what else to expect, she took her last mouthful and thanked him again for the lovely night. His mother returned and took away the plates. Before Danielle had time to think, she came back with the dessert, but this time it was accompanied by four gift bags, two of them blue, and two of them pink. Overwrought with joy she took each one, but then she noticed that three of them had names on them. Looking closely at the labels, she suddenly recognised them as being her children's.

"I hope you don't mind, but I took the liberty of buying a gift for each of your children. I know they are special to you, which makes them special to me. I hope they like them. I must admit that the credit should go to both my mother and Anna, because I don't know the first thing about what children like. They chose them, but I asked them to." Noticing the tears in her eyes, he hesitated. "I'm sorry to upset you, but… but I really wanted them to know how much I care. Not only do I care about their mother, but I care about them too. Really I do." Not knowing what to say, Danielle just stared at the bags. This was all too much for her and she began to cry. Watching her tears flow down her cheeks, Panos suddenly felt he had done the wrong thing.

"Danielle, I'm so sorry, I shouldn't have…" he said taking her hand.

"No… No please don't be sorry," she said finding the courage to look up at him. "It's just… It's just so kind of you. They will love them, I love them, and I don't even know what they are." Trying to stem her tears she got up and ran around to him.

"I love you; I love you; I love you," she said kissing his face. Relieved by her response he put his arms around her waist.

"I love you too special lady, from the bottom of my breaking heart." Holding his face, she looked into his eyes and smiled. The pain in his eyes was evident, and she found herself believing him.

"I am going to miss you so much," she said kissing him again.

"Now, now young lady," he said holding on to his tears. "Don't forget there is a fourth gift bag."

Leaning back, she noticed him pick up the bag.

"Oh Panos, this is definitely too much. My heart can't take any more of your generosity."

"Nothing is too much for you, if I could afford the world, I would buy it for you." He handed her the bag and smiled. "This is the last one, I promise."

"You promise?" she asked looking into his eyes. He nodded and she took it from him. Putting her hand inside, she was suddenly met with something furry. Surprised, she pulled it out and laughed. In her hand was a soft cuddly bear, and it was holding a big love heart with 'I love you,' written across the middle of it.

"Oh Panos, I love it," she said holding it up next to his face. "It is cute and cuddly, just like you," she laughed. "I'll take it to bed with me every night and it'll remind me of you." Bringing it away from his face she hugged it. "Words can't express how I'm feeling right now. I just don't know what to say."

"You don't have to say anything. The look on your face says it all. I was hell bent on making you the happiest lady alive, and I'm now content, knowing that my mission is complete." Pulling her close to him again, he squeezed her tight. Forcing away her tears, she took a deep breath and breathed in this incredible man.

I don't ever want to let you go, she thought, but she knew that there was no other way. Fate was going to take him out of her life just as quickly as it had brought him into it. Suddenly, reminded of her secret weapon, strength rose up out of her weakness, and she let go of him.

"Ok my darling Panos. What's next?" she asked now fully composed.

The authority in her words pleased him. Turning this very sad moment on its head, he felt comforted to know he was now strong enough to see this night through. He was aware that his emotions were almost ripped to shreds, but the power behind her small statement reinforced his belief in knowing he was now in control of his feelings again.

"Now my darling we shall go back into the bar. There, I will book us a taxi, and we will enjoy the rest of our night by each other's side. Is that OK with you?" he asked kissing her lips.

"As long as I'm with you, then yes, it's OK," she replied. Now that she'd stopped crying, he was pleased to see a big smile sweep across her face.

"Good. Now we must go. I can't wait to have you all to myself." Getting off his lap, she put the cuddly toy back in the bag. Then taking it and the other three in one hand, she held Panos's hand in the other, and they made their way to the bar.

Helen was now up at the bar talking to Mick. She had come down from her room not long after Danielle and Panos had left to go into the restaurant, and Mick had explained their absence. Relieved to know that their love had interrupted their sadness, she spent most of her time talking to her father, who on this rare occasion was working behind the bar. Thankful for having some extra time with him, their conversation flowed as if they had never been apart. Regrettably for them both, he was called away from the bar, so she sat with Mick and talked to him whilst waiting for the love birds to reappear.

Danielle came into the bar holding Panos's arm, and the huge grin on her face was a sure sign that her time alone with Panos had gone well. As she walked over to them,

Mick was the first to notice her display of diamonds and said, "Blimey Dan, you look a million dollars." Turning to Panos, he said shrewdly, "and I bet they nearly cost that much too." Panos just looked at him and smiled.

"Why Michael, I commend you on your observation, but even I haven't got that sort of money my friend," he replied modestly. "But if I did, then I would have no problem spending it all on this special lady." Taking Danielle's hand, he kissed it. Then excusing himself, he walked over to the reception to phone a taxi.

Helen looked at Danielle's beaming face and couldn't help but smile. Not only happy for her obvious state of mind, she felt privileged to have known this exceptional lady. It surprised her to feel this way, because she usually found it hard to relate to other women. Living in a male dominated world, her status had prevented her from becoming close to any other females. The women she did know were either power hungry bitches who did anything to climb up the corporate ladder, or they were so weak that they were treated like door mats. She didn't have anything in common with either of these types of women. Having a good eye for authenticity, she soon realised that Danielle was neither of these things, and even though she was raising three children by herself, the strength that she portrayed shone out of her like a light in the darkness. Recognising this outstanding quality, she felt only admiration for Danielle, and was so glad to have met her.

Panos confided in her earlier that day and told her about his surprise. She was sworn to secrecy, and seeing his face shine with excitement, she had assured him that his secret was safe with her. Having said he wanted to make it a night to remember, she'd been somewhat confused. But after her little chat with Mick by the pool, she soon realised why it was so important to Panos. Her heart filled with sadness when she thought about how tough tomorrow would be, and she couldn't help feeling for them. She knew that it would be hard for her, because she had to leave this lovely place too, but it made her feel better to know that at least she would be coming back. The thought of never being able to return made her heart bleed, and she found this burden too hard to bear.

Danielle, I'd hate to be in your shoes tomorrow, she thought miserably. Trying her best to hide her concern, she pushed those thoughts to the back of her mind and concentrated on making the night a memorable one, not only for her but also for Danielle. A rush of joy flowed through her, washing away her sorrow, causing her to smile.

"Why Danielle, they are beautiful," she said as Danielle pulled back her hair, uncovering her diamond earrings. "Panos certainly knows how to spoil a lady. They go so well with your ring. You would think they were part of a set."

Danielle lifted her hand and looked at the dazzling solitaire. Suddenly realising that it was a perfect match she said, "Oh yes, so it does. He must have got them from the same shop."

"Are you saying that he brought the ring for you too? What a romantic. If we weren't related, I would be quite jealous," said Helen and they both laughed.

Rewinding her mind back to her first visit, Danielle took great pleasure in telling her all about that time.

Not wanting to take all night, she purposely left out the part about Stuart, and just took her through the amazing story of how she met Panos. Helen was absolutely mesmerised by this tale of love, and found herself feeling quite envious.

Maybe it wouldn't have been so bad being in her shoes, she concluded. I've met lots of men, but none of them have made me feel like that, not even Harry, she thought. Ignoring those stupid thoughts, she concentrated her mind on what Danielle was saying. Seeing her eyes light up as she spoke, Helen could see why Panos had fallen in love with this lovely lady.

Twenty minutes later, the taxi arrived, and the four friends made their way into town. Panos was under strict instruction to keep a close eye on Helen. Their father made it perfectly clear that he must under no circumstances leave her on her own. Aware of his concern, Panos had promised to look after her, and assured his father that he would bring her back in one piece.

The taxi stopped outside the Borzoi club, and they all got out of the car. Panos paid the driver and thanked him for the lift. He knew the driver well, so gave him a generous tip in a show of appreciation. Putting his arm around Danielle he led the way and walked them through the entrance. Just as before, the room was heaving with happy holiday makers who were making full use of the limited space on the dance floor. Looking over the crowd of people, Panos searched the room in the hope of finding the manager. Spotting him talking to a group of girls at the bar, he told his guests to wait by the door, and proceeded to walk towards him. Danielle watched in amazement as he spoke to the manager, and by the expression on his face it was evident that he knew Panos. Then following closely behind him, the manager went over to a table that was occupied, and Danielle couldn't believe her eyes when the collection of people picked up their drinks and went elsewhere. Turning around, Panos waved them over with his hand. So, responding to his command, Danielle made her way over to him. Helen walked behind her, and she had also seen what had happened over at the table. Gobsmacked by this show of respect, she turned to Mick who was beside her and said, "Is Panos some kind of a king around here?"

"More like a god," he replied his tone full of pride. "Panos knows everyone. How do you think he found you? It wasn't just luck you know."

Feeling smug, she suddenly felt six foot tall.

I certainly did fall on my feet, she thought, her face glowing with pride.

They reached the table, and Panos took the liberty of buying the first round of drinks. The manager, still at the table was just pulling out a chair for Danielle to sit down, when a look of shock went across his face. Insistent that the drinks were on him, he felt quite hurt by Panos's lack of understanding. Panos didn't argue, so both he and Mick followed the manager up to the bar. Once again, Danielle and Helen giggled like teenage girls. Pointing out Panos's influential power, Danielle took her through the time in the high street on her previous trip, and Helen was once more amazed by the high opinion that these people had of him. Halfway through the conversation, they were rudely interrupted when a drunken man sat on a chair next to Danielle.

"Hello gorgeous, are you up for a good time?" he asked cheekily putting his arm around her.

Panos had ordered their drinks and was getting quite agitated having to wait. The manager had disappeared, and this didn't help the agitation he felt. Noticing that he was back talking to the group of girls, he couldn't help but smile. All of them were attractive ladies, so understanding the managers desire to get back to them, he decided to look past his annoyance. Aware that he had been a while up at the bar, he turned around to look at Danielle just to make sure she was alright. Seeing a man groping her, a surge of pure anger erupted up from the pit of his stomach. Unable to contain his fury, he pushed his way through the crowd, and forgetting his behaviour, he shoved the obstacle of people out of the way. Not thinking about their safety, their drinks went up in the air, and the sound of breaking glass filled the room as they hit the floor. But Panos didn't care; all he cared about was Danielle's safety, and the thought of some other man touching her made his blood boil.

"Get your hands off her," he said running towards him.

The man was oblivious to his aggressor and had no idea that he had put himself in serious danger, until someone grabbed him.

"I said… get off her!" he said grabbing the man by the shirt and lifting him off the chair. He threw him on the floor, and kneeling over him, he pulled the man up by his collar and punched him on the jaw.

"Don't you ever touch what is not yours to touch do you hear me?" Wanting to hit him again, still holding him, he drew his hand back and clenched his fist.

"I… I'm sorry… I… thought she was on her own," the man said apologetically, as he shook with fright, now feeling completely sober. "Please… please… I am sorry. Don't hit me again."

The look of sheer terror in this man's face caused Panos to bring his hand down. Taking a deep breath, he pushed him back to the ground and said, "You are one lucky man, so you had better thank your lucky stars that I didn't kill you. I don't ever want to see you again. … now get out of here." The man got up off the floor and ran out of the door. The whole club had gone deathly silent, and all eyes were on Panos. Straightening his shirt, Panos noticed the manager looking at him, the same look of fright evident on his face. Putting his hand up in the air Panos said, "Sorry about that, but you should not let that type of person in here, they could give your club a very bad name." Then turning to his onlookers, he said, "And sorry for spilling your drinks. But don't worry, they'll be replaced. Now return to what you were doing and have a great night." The music started up again and the people went back to their business. The fracas was soon forgotten and Panos was pleased to see that everyone was now having a good time again. He walked over to his table. Seeing the look of horror on Danielle's face he said, "Danielle, are you alright?"

"Y…Yes Panos, I'm fine, just a bit shocked… you didn't… why did you?" Still in shock she was unable to string a sentence together, and just stared at him.

Taking her by the hand she stood up. Pulling her to him, he squeezed her so tight, that he was in danger of crushing her ribs.

"I'm so sorry, but I couldn't help myself. Just seeing you

with another man, makes me crazy… but… but Danielle he touched you, he actually put his filthy hands on my beautiful Danielle, and I couldn't let him get away with doing that. Once again I'm sorry." Taking her face in his hands he kissed her passionately on the mouth.

"I can't bear to see you with another man. I know it will break my heart."

The manager came over with a tray of drinks, followed by Mick, so Panos forced himself to let her go. Pleased by his timing, because the thought of her being with someone else was too much for him to think about, the two men spent a few minutes talking to each other in Greek. Then the manager left looking extremely happy.

"Right may the night commence," Panos said handing round the drinks. "Here is to us." He looked at Danielle and smiled. "And to the most precious and most beautiful woman I know." Raising their glasses, they made a toast, and then he turned to Helen. "And to Helen, the second most precious and beautiful woman I know."

Helen could feel her cheeks burn up with embarrassment. Then trying desperately to hide her awkwardness she said, "And to Panos, the most hot-headed man I know, and believe me, I have met many of them in my time." Raising their glasses for the third time, Panos was relieved to find that he was at last feeling calm. So, wiping the incident out of his mind, he focused it on his friends and decided to enjoy the rest of his night.

Time passed by so quickly, and it was now time to leave. Gathering their things together, they all walked out of the club feeling very happy. The night had turned out to be a brilliant night, and all were content to know that it had ended a lot better than it had begun. Panos had kept his promise to Danielle, and she was filled to the brim with happiness, because she had been the centre of his attention all through the night. Showering her with compliments, he was always the gentleman, and the thought of it being her last night was put safely on the back burner of her mind. As they walked down the steps on to the high street, Panos noticed a group of young men to the left of him. Holding Danielle's hand, he pulled her to his side, when one of the men shouted out something in Greek. The remark was in very bad taste and was aimed at Danielle. Knowing that the comment was designed for his ears only, he let go of her hand and ran over to the man.

Oh no, not again, thought Danielle as Panos punched him. Greek words flew as the man fell to the ground, but this time Panos just kicked him in an attempt to scare him away. This forceful gesture seemed to work, when the man got up and scurried away with his friends following behind him.

"Blimey Panos, what did he say?" asked Mick dumbfounded "You should see someone about your anger you know, it is bad for your health my friend, and anyone else's who happen to get in your way." Panos ignored Mick's stupid remark and put his arm around Danielle.

"Now, where were we?" he asked carrying on down the road.

"But Mick is right Panos, you do have a short temper," she said laughing. "And yes, what did he say?"

"He said something about your sexy legs," he replied seriously.

"But... but Panos it was a compliment, you had no reason to hit him, you should be proud to have a lady who has legs like these," she said jokingly lifting her right leg.

"I know, and I am, but he should have known better than to talk about you like that. Men can think those things, but they cannot say them, especially not in ear shot of me." He kissed her on the head and said, "Anyway, he was a fool, and he deserved to be hit. And yes I do have a temper, and yes I do get very jealous, but I do have good reason to be, you are the most beautiful girl on this island, and thank God, you just happen to be with me. Anyway, he will get over it. I know his family, and if I know his father, he will get another kick up the behind, if he is stupid enough to tell him that is," he said flippantly.

Danielle had felt sorry for the man when Panos attacked him, but now after he had explained the reason behind his burst of anger, she was left feeling quite angry herself. Flattery soon replaced her annoyance, and she said, "Thank you Panos for looking out for me, I'm so grateful that you care."

"You are most welcome my darling, you are most welcome." Kissing her on the head again, they walked arm in arm to the taxi rank.

The hotel was consumed by silence when they walked into the lounge. Mick was feeling very restless as he imagined the lonely room that awaited him. Finding the nerve, he asked Panos for a night cap. Panos refused to serve him at the bar, and Mick was very disappointed by his answer. Feeling like a child that had been deprived of its sweets, he hung his head and sulked just out of pure frustration. Not having the power to help himself to the drink that he craved, he walked over to one of the settees and threw his agitated body down on it. Sensing Mick's irritation, Panos added that he could take a drink up to his room, and his mood miraculously lifted as quickly as it had taken over him. Wanting to be alone with Danielle, Panos poured out a large vodka and orange for him as quickly as he could. Handing it to him, he said goodnight, and went over to turn off the light.

Helen was the first to go up. She was dead on her feet, and the many drinks she'd had all through the night had turned her legs to jelly. Picturing her bed, she could feel her eyes droop with tiredness, and she wanted to get a full night sleep before her last hours spent with her father. So, saying goodnight, she went up to her room. Now it was Panos's turn to get agitated when Mick suddenly declared that his water works were playing up. Not having been told of this problem up until now, his finger hovered over the light switch while Mick rushed to the toilet. Unbeknown to him, Mick had an ulterior motive behind his sudden need to go to the gents. He was confident that if he played his cards right and took his time, then Panos would get fed up with waiting and go up to his room, leaving him to help himself to the vodka bottle that he could have sworn was calling his name from behind the bar. So, he hung around in the toilet until Panos and Danielle had gone up too. Not having the faintest idea of Mick's cunning plan, Panos, after waiting for what seemed like an eternity, found that his patience had abandoned him, and so decided to leave Mick to his own devices. Not wanting to waste any more precious time, he took Danielle by the hand and they went up to his room.

Mick waited patiently by the toilet door, making sure he kept himself out of sight, and let out a huge sigh of relief when he heard the couple leave. His whole body shook because of his dishonesty, but the thought of waking up and starting his day without his morning fix soon swayed his mind into believing that it was ok to steal from his friend.

Of course, I'll pay for it, he thought. I'll just get Panos to add it to my tab. This warped truth eased his conscience enormously, so he sealed the deal with a smile. Happy to feel in control of his ethics, he picked up the bottle of vodka and took it up to his room feeling very pleased with himself.

Panos opened the door of his room, but suddenly hesitated before going in. Taking Danielle in his arms he kissed her hard on the mouth. Frightened to take the next inevitable step, he held her tight for a few moments more. He thought that by prolonging their embrace he could somehow stop time, because if he shut the door behind them, this would be a sure sign of having to surrender himself to the powers of providence, and then he would have to turn her over into the hands of fate.

"I love you," he said quietly looking into her eyes. "I love you so much." Kissing her again, he was now left with no other choice but to give up his power of control, so led her across the threshold. Kicking the door with his foot, it shut with an almighty thud, and from that very moment, the minutes leading up to her departure began to silently tick away.

CHAPTER

FOURTEEN

*W*atching the sun rise out of its sleep, Panos held Danielle so close to him. His arms were wrapped around her so tight; he was frightened that if he took them away, if only for just a second, she would disappear. They had spent what was left of the night making love, holding on to every moment of passion as if it was the end of the world. Now just holding her in his arms, he sighed deeply, and the predicted appearance of daylight brought a tear to his eye. The day they had been dreading the most, had now finally arrived. Brightening up the room, it began its slow climb up into the sky. Stretching its rays out from its silent slumber, in all innocence it rose up to its glory, oblivious to the pain it was going to inflict on this couple.

Burying his face in the back of her neck, he kissed her soft skin, and breathed in the lovely scent of his Danielle. Feeling the gentle touch of his lips, she moaned softly, and the sound of her pleasurable groaning sent shivers down his spine. Her eyes were closed as she concentrated on his tongue caressing her neck, and fighting back the tears, she focused her mind on the intensity of his kisses. Suddenly she could feel his teeth sink softly into her skin. This unexpected act of love sent a wonderful sensation through her body and, taking her breath away, she impulsively opened her eyes. Without thinking, her concentration was suddenly disturbed when she saw the cuddly bear, her gift from Panos, sitting on the bedside cabinet beside her. Reading the expression of love, it displayed so boldly, the tears began to flow. Not being able to contain her hurt, she closed her eyes and swallowed hard to fight against the pain. This, she found, was a useless attempt to win over the sadness that had successfully dominated her heart, and the continuous flow of tears confirmed that it was now in control as it reigned triumphant. Stripped of all her power, she wept uncontrollably, and turning her head she closed her eyes and cried into her pillow. Panos could hear the faint sound of her sorrow and, feeling her pain, this prompted his own tears to escape. Turning her over to face him, he could see the tracks of her tears and began to kiss her dampened cheeks. Finding the strength, she opened her eyes. He reached her lips, and seeing his tears made her sob even more.

"Danielle, my beautiful Danielle, I love you so much," he said still kissing her. "I love you," he repeated those words over and over with every kiss, and the pain of having to let her go, gripped hold of his heart like a vice. "Oh Danielle, I'm in so much pain, I… I am afraid that my heart will really break." Kissing him continuously, the onslaught of tears kept coming, and she had never felt so afraid.

"What am I going to do?" she sobbed. "How am I going to get over losing you? It breaks my heart to think of you so far away."

Pulling her as close to him as he possibly could his kisses grew more passionate with every touch, when suddenly he could take no more.

"I can't do this. I haven't the strength to let you go. I want to hold you in my arms forever," he said angrily. "But there is no other alternative. Every which way I turn; I still have to let you go."

"Yes, you do, and I have to let you go too. We both know there is no other way. So... so this is the way it has to be," she said kissing his face. "I wish there was, but... but there isn't."

The reality of his birth right brought him back down to earth, and he calmed down. Taking a deep breath, he said, "Oh Danielle, I wish I had the power to make this right, but I don't. Once again, I am so sorry." This time it was Danielle that kissed his tearstained face.

"It's ok Panos. We're both very strong people so we can get over this. I am sure of that." Then wiping her face with the palm of her hand, she laughed. "It's just as well, because I think that this would have killed me."

Panos laughed. Then, squeezing the top of her arms he said, "Yes my strong, powerful lady, it is just as well, because rather than letting you go, I would have had to kill you."

"Oh, is that so?" she replied punching him lightly on the arm. "You haven't seen my bad side yet; I can fight too you know. But you would have to catch me first." She said jumping off the bed.

Panos jumped up and ran after her. Giggling hysterically, she managed to escape his many attempts to catch her, by jumping to and fro across the bed. Her final effort to outrun him failed her miserably when she tripped up and fell to the floor. Taking advantage of this unfortunate mishap, he grabbed her by her waist, picked her up and threw her back on to the bed. Then adding insult to injury, he started tickling her. Squealing like a pig, she found that she couldn't get up, so just lay back in surrender. Relieved to see that the joy had returned to her beautifully tanned face, Panos sat across her stomach and took hold of her wrists. Putting her arms behind her head he said childishly,

"Oh, so you say you can fight. OK then little miss warrior, let's see you fight your way out of this."

Holding her wrists tighter, he leant over and kissed her hard on the lips. He could feel her squirming beneath him, and this caused him to kiss her harder. Then leaning back, he smiled and said, "I didn't think so young lady, maybe you're not as tough as you think."

That statement caused her anger to rise, and she tried her hardest to push him off. Nearly breaking free from his grip, he suddenly panicked, so he bent back down and blew a big raspberry in the side of her neck. Unable to contain her anger anymore, she giggled and shrieked out at the same time, and told him to stop, but he did it again.

"Do you give up," he said pulling away, still holding her wrists.

"Never!" she shouted through her laughter, so he did it again.

"Now do you give up?"

Still she shook her head. He was just about to do it again when she said, "OK, OK I give up! I can't bear it anymore. You win. Please let go of me, you are hurting my arm."

Letting go of her wrists, he kept a close eye on her.

She smiled at him so innocently; it was as if butter wouldn't melt in her mouth. He turned away for just a second, and she saw her opportunity going for his stomach and started tickling his sides. Falling to the bed because she'd taken him by surprise, he suddenly found himself laughing. One of his pet hates was being tickled, and he loathed the feeling that it provoked, so the unexpected joy he felt was somewhat of a surprise to him. Overpowering her again, he caught her arm and pulled her towards him.

"Oh, OK so you want to play dirty, do you?" With that he tickled her again. Deciding to take her by surprise this time, he slowed down the speed of his hand, and ever so gently, he started to slide his fingers up her legs. Making their way up the side of her body, he could see the reaction his touch was having on her, as goose bumps erupted all over her skin. This went on for a few more minutes, and then he lay down by her side, his fingers having reached the inside of her arms.

She stopped laughing and looked deep into his eyes. Seeing her desire for him in the twinkle of her stare, he impulsively smiled back at her. Then succumbing to the power of her magnetism, he fell into her embrace. The birthing of the new day outside suddenly slipped miraculously from their minds, and it was as if they had all the time in the world.

Mick carrying his suitcase, walked into the lounge feeling very apprehensive. Up until now he had managed to ignore the prospect of his holiday coming to an end. As reality kicked in, he suddenly found himself dreading going home. The thought of having to go back to his lonely life depressed him, but even he knew that this was something he was going to have to face. Hanging his head in sheer disappointment, he walked over to the bar. Yannis was busy serving, when he saw Mick coming towards him. Noticing him looking very down, he finished catering for his guest and then gave him his full attention.

"Michael, it upsets me to see you looking so sad. I thought you'd be looking forward to going home. I know how important your work is to you. Your business can't run all by itself you know."

Picking up a clean glass, he waved it in the air. Understanding the purpose of Yannis's gesture, Mick nodded and said, "Thanks Yannis and make it a pint, you know for my nerves... and yes you're right, I do have to get back to the car yard," he lied, letting go of his suitcase. The last thing on his mind was his business, but Yannis statement prompted him to think about this reality and what a failure he had become. He didn't want to admit the reason behind his shortcomings to himself, let alone to Yannis, so he quickly pushed such thoughts and feelings aside, choosing to focus on his beer instead. Moments later his drink was in his hand. Taking a big mouthful, his spirits lifted slightly, and he smiled.

"Well, here we are again Yannis," he said taking another mouthful. "It only seems like five minutes ago when we got here, and now it's time to leave...Well I suppose they do say that time flies when you're having fun, and it's so true. I can't believe we've been here for a week." Looking up at Yannis he felt his smile fade. "I'm really going to miss being here." Seeing the sadness in his face, Yannis suddenly realised that he felt the same way. As always, it was fun having Mick around, and it was hard to imagine life without his crazy friend.

"Michael, it will seem strange you not being here too, my friend, but no doubt you'll be back. You're like a bad penny," said Yannis laughing and patting him on the back.

"Yannis what are you saying? I'm not sure that I will, after that remark. I think I'd rather spend a penny than come back here!" Recognising Yannis humour, Mick laughed.

"All jokes aside my friend, I've had a great time, and yes I'll be back, even if it's just to annoy you," he sniggered, pulling a funny face. Aware that the bar had started to fill up with guests, Yannis replied, "Oh Michael, you're a funny man. I'm going to miss you my friend," he finished as he walked off to serve the other guests. Mick watched him retreat to his duties, and soon realised he was now feeling a lot better. Not knowing if it was down to the beer or whether it was the thought of coming back that made him feel that way, he was just pleased to be smiling again. He drank his drink and waited for the others to come down.

Helen came out of the shower and looked at the time. Disturbed to find that she only had a couple of hours to go until her flight, she got dressed and began to pack her suitcase. Not wanting to waste any more time than she had to, she finished in record time and then made her way down to the lounge. As she walked down the stairs, it suddenly dawned on her that she was going home. This realisation caused her to stop suddenly. Her mind went back to the day she first set foot on the island, and she still couldn't believe that she had found the courage to come to Skiathos in the first place. Remembering how nervous she felt as she stepped off the plane only seven days before, her heart missed a beat at how angry she had felt. She hardly recognised herself as being the same woman, and just how bitter and twisted her outlook on life had become. Back then, the only thing that dominated her mind and her heart was hate for the man whom she thought had destroyed her mother's life. It was only because of those tormented feelings that she'd had a reason to come to this place. It had been the only thing worth living and fighting for!

She shuddered as she remembered how desperate she felt only a short while ago and it was hard to believe that she was the same person now walking down the stairs to meet her father. She could feel her heart fill up with guilt, as she thought, I was so wrong! He was just as much a victim as my mother was! Then a picture of her mother came into her mind, and the love she felt for a woman she hardly knew, flushed all those guilty feelings away. Now all that dominated her heart was love for a man she hardly knew, but this she was convinced, was going to change. Now her future looked a lot brighter, a total contrast to her past, and this made her smile. For the first time ever, the memory of her mother failed to bring a tear to her eye, which to her was a very liberating moment and one she would remember for a long time to come.

Oh mum, I think everything's going to be alright, she thought closing her eyes. Feeling a fluttering in her heart as that thought went through her mind, she knew then that she was right. The woman who came to Skiathos was dead and buried along with her mother, and the new Helen

Stiller was born. Having passed through the storm of emotions that had managed to stop her in her tracks, she took a deep breath, and continued down the stairs.

Eventually Panos and Danielle came out of the room. Holding on to her suitcase with one hand, he held her tight with the other, and then they began their last journey as a couple, down to the lounge. Neither of them spoke as they walked down the first flight of stairs, but the pain of knowing this was their last time together, was evident in their eyes. Knowing that the time to say goodbye was getting closer by the second, Panos was adamant that this word would not pass his lips until she walked away from him at the airport. His heart was weighed down with sadness, but he was determined to hold his pain inside for as long as he possibly could, until she disappeared out of his life forever. The thought of having to let her go ate him up inside, so he used up every spare moment by holding her tighter than he had ever done before. Unable to stop his mind from wandering, once again he found himself thinking about her life without him. This not only tormented his mind, but also his heart especially when he imagined her in the arms of another man. Trying desperately to hold back his tears, he kissed her head then he stopped. Turning her around to face him he went against the grain of his heart and said, "Danielle, I know I should not be saying this, but… but I know that I will see you again." Knowing full well that this was very unlikely to happen, as soon as his mouth opened, something in his heart made him believe that what he was saying was true.

"Panos please, you know that will never happen…We've talked about this… Please don't, this is hard enough as it is," she said trying not to cry. "It has taken me all morning to get my head around this situation... and... and I am now strong enough to let you go... so please... please, you're being very unfair." Seeing her eyes fill with pain, he brought her hand up and gently kissed the back of it.

"I'm sorry, you're right, I shouldn't have said that." Taking a deep breath, he said, "I don't want to cause you any more pain. It was just wishful thinking."

They proceeded to take the last flight of stairs down, but Panos just couldn't shake off that feeling. In his mind he knew that this could never happen, but something in his heart was telling him otherwise. Trying his utmost to ignore this fantasy his heart had created, he decided to set his mind on what was real. Pleased to know that he had more control of that than he did his heart, the feeling finally disappeared. Now focused, they walked into the lounge and were pleased to see everyone gathered at the bar.

"Ah Panos," his father said smiling. "And Danielle, come and take a seat. I will get you a coffee before you go."

Panos and Danielle were both taken aback by his kindness, especially as he had hardly said two words to her whilst she was there. She guessed it must be because she was going home. Nodding her head, she watched him embrace his son, and then watched as he poured out her drink in complete amazement.

The next twenty minutes flew by, and Panos looked at his watch and announced that it was now time to go. Helen spent a few minutes saying goodbye to her father. Their farewell was a very touching one, and Danielle was surprised to see that he had tears in his eyes.

"Now Helen, you make sure you keep in touch, do you hear," said her father reaching out his arms. "I want to see you again, so don't leave it too long."

Danielle watched as Helen fell into his arms and cried. Suddenly, finding herself racked with jealousy, she forced herself to look away. It took all her mental strength to stop her tears from falling, and she couldn't help wishing that Panos's father was saying that to her instead. Taking control of those feelings, she walked over to Panos. Unbeknown to her, the same thoughts were going through his mind. He couldn't bear to watch, so they went over to fetch her suitcase. As he grabbed the handle, his mother came over. She had said her goodbyes to Helen, and now it was Danielle's turn. Reaching out her hand, she took hold of Danielle's and held it tight.

"Goodbye Danielle. It was so lovely to see you again… I know Panos… I am aware that Panos… and you can't…" She just couldn't find the words. "Oh Danielle…Thank you…Thank you." Unable to contain her tears, she let go of her hand, looked at her son, and shaking her head she walked away. Panos with tears in his eyes, looked at Danielle and said, "Come on Danielle, it's time. Are you ready?"

No, no I'm not. I won't go, I don't want to go, the voice in her head screamed. I can't bear the thought of leaving you! Ignoring these thoughts, she smiled and like a lady she replied, "Yes Panos, I'm ready."

The journey down to the airport was spent in silence. Even Mick was quiet. He could see that Helen was really upset, and his heart went out to her as she sobbed next to him in the back of the car. Aware that Danielle was trying her hardest to be strong; his heart went out to her too. He was sure that it wouldn't last long, and he was prepared for her flood of tears when they got onto the plane. Feeling bad for both of them, he put his hand on their shoulders. Still remaining quiet, he patted them both on the back in a show of support, and then took his hands away.

The car pulled into the car park and Panos found a place to park. Taking a very deep breath, he got out of the car. An array of holiday makers waiting to go home filled every inch of the floor space, and the usual hustle and bustle of airport life carried on around them, oblivious that two people's hearts were breaking right in the midst of them. Walking over to the check in desk, they were told by a pretty Greek lady that their flight was on time, and this caused Danielle's heart to sink. She had hoped that it had been delayed, and then she would have had more time to spend with Panos. The lady continued by saying that they would be boarding in approximately half an hour. Suddenly grateful that they had to hurry, Danielle just wanted to get their goodbyes over and done with, because the strain on her heart was getting unbearable. Taking up more of their time, they finally checked in, and Panos walked with them over to customs. Knowing that this was as far as he could go, he stopped and turning to Mick he said, "Well Michael, it was good to see you again my friend. Take care, and look after yourself, I mean it." Shaking his hand, Mick nodded his head.

"And you too my friend," replied Mick smiling. Not being able to find any words of encouragement to say, this was all that he could say. Next Panos turned to Helen.

"Helen, Helen, I'm so glad to have met you. Take care."

Pulling her to him they embraced, and whispering in her ear he said, "I hope to see you again."

His words brought tears to his eyes. He longed to be able to say the same thing to Danielle, but he knew that he couldn't.

"Yes Panos, I'm so glad to have met you too." Understanding his heartache, she wiped her face and pulled away. Sensitively she turned to Mick and said, "Come on Mick, we need to give them some time alone."

Nodding his head, he was just about to walk away when Panos grabbed his arm. Taken aback by this, he looked at him confused, and questioned, "Panos?" Pulling him to towards him, Panos embraced him.

"Please Michael, look after my Danielle," he whispered in his ear. "Please don't let anyone hurt her."

This was all too much for Mick, and a tear rolled down his cheek.

"OK, OK Panos, I will see that she is alright, I promise." With that Mick tore himself away and left them to be alone.

Taking a very deep breath, Panos closed his eyes. Unable to fight his pain, his tears began to flow, and finally he turned to Danielle. Opening his eyes, he looked at her and was met by a flood of tears streaming down her face.

"Well Danielle, this is it my darling," he said letting his tears fall. "This is…" he couldn't bring himself to say it; it was just too hard for him to let this word out of his mouth. It would make it too final, and there would be no going back. He knew however that the terrible moment had arrived, so it had to be said. There was just no time to put it off any longer. Taking another deep breath to try and control the pain in his heart. He took her hands and looked deep into her eyes as he heard himself say simply, "Goodbye my darling." With that she fell into his arms and he sobbed as he continued, "I love you. Please remember that I will always love you. You will always be my number one." Bringing his hands up, he held her face and kissed her. "I will always love you."

"Panos, I will always love you too. You are so special. Thank you for everything." She fell back into his arms and cried.

"How am I going to get over this…? I can't bear it Panos; I'm so scared my heart is going to break." Choked up by his own tears, he hated that he couldn't give her the answer she so desperately wanted. Holding her tighter, they spent their last moments as one, but then the hand of fate came down as an announcement for boarding her flight filled the air. Knowing that there was nothing more to say, he kissed her for the last time, and then watched his Danielle walk out of his life just as quickly as she had entered it. Danielle, racked with pain, ran over to Mick. She couldn't bring herself to turn around; she just couldn't risk seeing Panos's handsome face again. If she did, she knew that she'd have to go back to him, unable to stop herself. Reaching Mick, she took a deep breath. Focusing her mind on her children, she stood up straight, wiped her eyes and said, "Come on, we've got to get out of here, before I do something stupid."

Nodding his head, Mick put his arm around her, and they began to make their way over to the boarding lounge. Panos watched helplessly as they caught up with Helen. All three of them went through the double doors that closed with a sudden thud, disguising the sound of his heart breaking, and then his Danielle was gone.

Part Two

CHAPTER

FIFTEEN

The next two months went by, and Danielle carried on as if she had never been away. Having locked her memories of Panos away in the vault of her mind, she had now conceded to the fact that life could, and would, go on without him. It had been very hard at first, and had taken a few weeks to adjust, but the normality of parenthood, and the strife that came with it, soon brought her back down to earth. Knowing that her children were her main concern, she put her heart and soul into their wellbeing, and her time in Skiathos was buried so deeply, it was as if it had all been just a wonderful dream. Every so often her mind would betray her though, when the memory of Panos would try and steal her thoughts, but the reality of her real life kept those thoughts from invading her mind. Having finally got through the test of time, Danielle was now content in knowing that life was back to the way it was before the days of Panos.

Having spent the last couple of months focusing on her family, she fell back into the routine of being a mother. Unbeknown to her, a cloud of devastation loomed on the horizon, and this time she was not prepared for the chaos it would cause. Totally unaware that something terrible lingered in the path of her destiny, a chain of events began to unfold that would not only change the course of her life forever but would also have an everlasting impact on her children's lives too!

The time bomb began ticking when Billy came home from school early one day. She had received a phone call from his form tutor whilst at work, and she panicked when he told her that Billy had been sent home. He also added rather harshly that she needed to phone the head teacher regarding disciplinary action as soon as possible. He finished the conversation by warning her, that the seriousness of this type of offence usually carried the penalty of temporary exclusion, so she should be prepared. Not knowing the actual length of time regarding his exclusion, he left her holding the receiver in complete shock.

Her shift at the pub was nowhere near finished, so she asked if she could leave early. Not wanting to go into too much detail, she blamed her need to get home on feeling unwell. She was pleased and relieved to be told that she could. This lie brought with it a deep feeling of guilt, but she soon realised that it was nearer to the truth than she had first thought, because the news of her son's despicable behaviour towards his teacher, made her feel sick to the stomach.

Her mind raced with worry all the way home, but by the time she reached her house she was feeling very angry. She couldn't figure out why Billy's attitude had suddenly taken a turn for the worse, because she was sure that the pain of losing his father had subsided. Since her time away, his behaviour had improved enormously. She thought that they had put those bad times behind them. Listening however to the distress in his form tutor's voice had now proven otherwise.

Her heart sank when she remembered back to the time of her husband's abandonment and could have cried because of the devastation he had callously left behind. Once again, she was faced with having to pick up the pieces and the thought of having to go through all that again made her want to scream. Trying to calm herself down, she decided to give Billy the chance to explain himself, and then she would take it from there.

So, walking through her front door, and feeling somewhat calmer, she made that unavoidable phone call to the school. Just after she got off the phone, Billy came strolling in. She wasn't surprised to see her son walk in with a big smile on his face as if he didn't have a care in the world. He was however more than surprised to see that his mother was home, and his smile soon disappeared when he saw the look of anger on her face.

"Well?" she asked as he threw his bag down. "What have you got to say for yourself?" Knowing full well the reason for the premature finish to his day, she stood glaring at him waiting for a reply.

"What?" he asked walking into the kitchen. "I haven't done anything wrong." Opening the fridge, he looked inside for something to eat.

"Don't lie to me Billy," she said slamming the fridge door narrowly missing his fingers. "I just got off the phone to Mr Crowley, and he made it very clear that you did do something wrong. So, tell me the truth young man. Why were you so rude to your teacher?"

Realising that he had been backed into a corner, he forced his way past his mother and tried to walk away.

"Don't you dare walk away from me; do you hear!" she said raising her voice. "Now tell me why you disrespected your teacher like that." Grabbing his arm, she swung him around to face her. "Billy?"

"Well I don't like him, he's always picking on me, and I swear he hates me," he replied pushing her arm away. "He's had it in for me from the beginning, so I shouted at him. So, what!" he asked turning on the TV. He sat down and started to change the channels.

"What do you mean, so what?" shouted Danielle snatching the remote control out of his hand. "You've been excluded for a week, that's so what." Without thinking she added, "If your father was here…"

"Well he's, not is he?" retorted Billy. "So, what are you going to do?" The sarcasm in his voice made her blood boil.

"How dare you speak to me like that! I'm still your mother. You might think you can get away with speaking to your teacher that way, but… but you will not get away with talking to me like that." Storming over to the TV, she turned it off.

"Hey, what are you doing? I was watching that," he said looking at the blank screen.

"Oh no you're not young man. You're going to your room. Now go upstairs until I tell you to come down."

Billy stood up and looked at his mother.

"That's just it Danielle, you said it yourself. I am a young man, and you can't tell me what to do." With that he walked out of the room and slammed the door behind him.

Seething with anger, Danielle sat down. He had never called her by her Christian name before, and she knew then that something was terribly wrong. Then her whole body flinched when she heard the front door slam close. Realising that he was no longer a child, she put her head in her hands and began to cry.

This incident was only the first of many, and she could feel her son begin to slowly slip out of her hands. She tried her utmost to use her authority as a mother, but it was no use. It was almost as if he was deliberately going out of his way to defy her, and this hurt her so much inside. Having to carry on providing for her children, she still managed to go to work, but the strain of having an uncontrollable teenager was taking its toll on her.

Mick hardly came into the bar anymore, and when he did, he was so drunk that she couldn't make any sense of what he was saying, so she couldn't talk to him about her worries.

She couldn't really talk to her mum about things either as her visits were becoming less and less. She had met a man on a night out, so now her time with Danielle and her children became limited.

She couldn't blame her for that, especially as she had spent many years looking out for her. By the look on her mum's face, she was happy at last, and Danielle couldn't find it in her heart to burden her with her own troubles. However, on the rare occasions that she did come to visit, Danielle put on such a brave face that her mother would never have guessed that something was seriously wrong.

Now an expert at hiding her pain, she dragged her way through every day in the hope that things would get better, but they didn't, they just got worse. Finding it hard to cope with the way life was going and what it had become, she began to relieve her stress by having a glass of wine in the evening before she went to bed. This seemed to help her sleep at first, and she found that after a good night sleep, she could cope with the next day ahead of her. The amount she drank however increased over time, and the next thing she knew she was getting through a bottle a night.

Billy had now been permanently excluded from school and spent most of his day in bed. As she had lost total control of his comings and goings, she thanked her stars every morning when she got up and saw his trainers by the door. At least she knew where he was, and even though he was asleep, it eased her mind to know he was safe all the time he was under her roof.

The start of a new day dawned, and Danielle got up feeling very groggy. Aware that she had nearly polished off two bottles of wine the night before, her head was banging. Dragging herself into the shower, she got dressed and went downstairs. Noticing Billy's trainers by the front door, she went into the living room and was pleased to see that Marie had taken the liberty of doing Charlie's breakfast. Relieved to have one less job to do that morning, she kissed her daughter on the head and went in the kitchen to make herself a strong cup of coffee.

Whilst waiting for the kettle to boil, she opened the fridge and noticed that the half empty bottle of wine had gone. Confused by its disappearance, she went over to the bin and saw two empty bottle necks sticking out of the top. At that point Marie came into the kitchen and looking very worried she said, "I emptied it out when I came down mum. It was on the table and… and I didn't want Charlie to get hold of it."

"Marie, it wasn't on the table, I distinctly remember putting it in the fridge. You had no right to throw it away," she snapped. The tone of her voice was stern, causing Marie's eyes to well up with tears.

"No mum, it was on the table. I'm not lying," she said desperately. "Honestly it was."

"Marie, I know what I did," she spat at her. "I am not losing my mind you know. Don't you defy me too? I have enough of that with your brother!"

Unable to stop her tears, Marie started to cry. "But Mum…"

"Don't but mum me young lady! Now go and get ready for school."

Danielle was fuming as she watched her daughter walk away. Thinking back to the previous night, she tried to retrace her steps. The more she thought about it, she realised that she couldn't remember going to bed. The last recollection she had was sitting on the settee watching a film, but then her mind went blank. Trying desperately to set her mind on the ending of the film, she found that she couldn't remember that either. Shaking her head, she put her fingers to her temples and squeezed them in a desperate attempt to jog her memory.

Charlie came in carrying his breakfast bowl. Putting it in he sink he said, "Mummy why did you shout at Marie. She wasn't lying; I saw her pick the bottle up from the table and put it in the bin."

A wave of guilt flooded through her body, and looking at the empty bottles, she brought her hands down and put them over her mouth.

"Oh Charlie, what have I done?" she asked, tears stinging her eyes. "Go and tell your sister to come down, I need to speak to her." As Charlie ran out of the room, she started to cry.

How did my life come to this? she thought, the pain in her head increasing by the second. 'How could I go from being so happy, to being so miserable? When did I lose the strength to persevere?' Her tears continued and she suddenly realised that this was the first time she had cried since leaving Skiathos. This realisation was the key to unlock the safe place in her mind, and the combination of walking away from the man of her dreams, and the fear of losing her first born son, suddenly unleashed a flood of emotions that she had desperately tried to deny.

I've already lost someone dear to me. I can't risk losing another, she thought sobbing. Tearing her eyes away from the bottles in disgust, she turned around and jumped back when she saw Marie standing in the doorway.

"Oh Marie, I'm so sorry," she said noticing her teary eyes. "I shouldn't have shouted at you like that; I was wrong. I'm so sorry that I upset you. That's... that's the last thing I wanted to do."

She raised her arms up into the air and smiled.

"Come here sweetheart." Marie ran to her mother and fell into her arms.

"Mum, mum I'm so scared," she sobbed. "I don't like you drinking, it changes you. Please mum, you don't need it. I know you're hurting… but mum… it hurts me to see you like that. I don't want to lose you."

Kissing her head, Danielle cradled her daughter in her arms. Holding her like a precious doll for a few minutes more, she pulled away and held her face.

"Marie, please don't be scared. I'll stop, I promise darling. Everything is going to be alright," she said reassuringly, wiping her tear stained face. "I promise. Please believe me."

Marie nodded her head, smiled and said, "I believe you." The fear of what would become of her mother lifted, and she now felt secure in believing her words of encouragement.

Looking at the clock on the wall, Danielle let go of her daughter and said, "Good, now we'd better get ready for school. We don't want to be late!" She walked Marie to the bus stop, and then took Charlie to school. She couldn't get the look on Marie's face out of her mind. When she'd shouted at her earlier, there was a distinct look of fear in her eyes. Thinking about it made her go cold inside.

I'll be ok, she thought trying to wipe the image out of her mind. I've gotten through worse. I'll make things right with Billy, and we will be a proper family again.

Those thoughts caused her strength to return, so she set her mind on her son. Knowing that she had an hour or so till she had to go to work, she decided to cook him a big breakfast. Then she would tell him how much she loved him, and that she would do anything to try and help him get over this little hitch in his life. Determined to salvage what was left of their relationship, she went home feeling very much in control again.

Billy responded well to his home cooked breakfast and was now downstairs watching TV. After taking time out to talk to him about his life, Danielle was relieved to know that he was just as sorry about the situation as she was. He promised to do more around the house, and told her that he would curb his tongue, and show her more respect in the future. He also promised to pick Charlie up from school for good measure. She was so pleased to see a glint of hope on the horizon that she left for work feeling a whole lot happier than when she had first got up. The joy that reigned in her heart was evident, and every one of the customers commented on her happier frame of mind. Not realising how miserable she had been, she laughed because she had been so conscious of trying her best not to let it show!

Confident her life was now back on track, she suddenly thought about Mick. She hadn't seen him for a couple of weeks, so decided to give him a ring when she got the chance. Feeling slightly guilty for letting their friendship slip away, she thought that she would make it up to him by asking him round for dinner. She was unsure of what state he would be in by the time her shift ended but decided to cross that bridge if or when she came to it.

She spent the next half an hour rushed off her feet. After serving the last of her customers, she got her phone out of her bag and rang Mick. The voice on the other end informed her that his number was unavailable, so she put it down on the bar looking very confused.

"Hey Dan, are you having problems with your phone?" asked Jimmy noticing the concerned expression on her face. "You can use mine babe."

"Thanks Jimmy, but it's not my phone. I'm having trouble getting through to Mick. Have you seen him lately?" she asked feeling quite worried.

"Dan he's in Skiathos. He went back a couple of days ago. Did he not tell you?" By the look on her face it was obvious that he hadn't, and Jimmy was quite shocked, and embarrassed to be the one breaking the news.

"N…No, I haven't seen him for a while, so… so I wouldn't have known." Putting her phone back in her bag, she felt like crying. Confused and hurt, she couldn't believe that he had kept something like this from her.

"Listen Dan, between you and me," said Jimmy quietly. "Mick's been acting very strange lately, and if I were you, I wouldn't worry about him. I think that he has got a problem with drink. Every time I saw him, he was always drunk, and he kept talking a load of gibberish. I know he's your mate, but he kept saying how you ignored him while you were away. He got quite nasty Dan. I know it was down to the drink, but believe me, he was telling anyone who would listen."

Danielle's brain could not take in what he was saying. Shaking her head disbelievingly she said, "No Jimmy, Mick wouldn't do that, we're friends."

"Dan, I'm telling the truth babe. He said the same thing to me. Like I said, I know it's the beer, it's pickled his brain," he said touching her arm. "Sorry to be the bearer of bad news, but it's true. You don't need that; you've got enough worries of your own to think about."

Stunned, she looked into his eyes and asked, "Has he gone back to the Oasis hotel?" Already knowing the answer, she braced herself anyway. He nodded, and her heart sank.

Another customer came up to the bar, so pleased by this distraction, she went over to serve him. The thought of Mick being back at the hotel tormented her mind. She told herself that Jimmy was exaggerating, and soon convinced herself that he hadn't said anything to her for her own protection.

He didn't want to hurt my feelings, she thought. No that's it. He didn't tell me for my own good. We both know I can't go back, so that's why he kept it from me! Those thoughts made her feel much better. "Thank you, Mick you're a good friend after all." She focused her mind back on to her work and put thoughts of Mick being with Panos safely locked away.

It had been a tough day, so she was relieved when her working day finally came to an end. She got in the car and took the short journey home. Remembering just at the last minute that Billy was collecting Charlie, she took the turning and drove up her road. Having put Mick to the back of her mind, she walked into the house and was glad to finally be home. As she walked into the kitchen, the curtain in the front room caught her eye. For some strange reason it was moving, which was unusual, so she went into the room to investigate. As she got closer, she realised that it was flapping in the wind. Under her breath she said, "Oh Billy, what are you like? You forgot to close the window." Suddenly she noticed that the catch was on the hook! Confused, she pulled back the curtain, and saw a big hole in the glass. "Oh no, someone has broken in."

Turning around, she suddenly noticed that the stereo had disappeared. Running over to the now empty gap on the wall, she froze.

What if they are still in the house, she thought, and strained her ears for any unusual noise. She was met by silence, so she ran into the kitchen and picked up the phone. She was just about to dial 999 when Billy and Charlie walked into the house. Charlie spotted the glass on the floor and said, "Mummy, what's happened to the window?"

Billy saw his brother point over to the window, and his heart dropped.

"Mum, Mum. Don't phone the police," he said running into the kitchen. Gesturing she didn't want to be disturbed she ignored Billys plea and began talking on the phone. Totally unprepared for what happened next, Billy snatched it the phone out of her hand and put it back down.

"Billy, what are you doing? Someone has broken in, so I need to tell the police," she said shocked he had the audacity to cut her conversation off.

"Mum please. Don't tell the police. I know who did it, and they will think that I'm a grass and come looking for me. Mum please," he pleaded. Unable to look his mother in the eye he looked down to the floor.

"What do you mean you know who did this? How the hell do you know Billy? Come on, I'm waiting."

Still looking at the floor, he began to explain how he had got in with the wrong crowd of boys. Danielle could not believe what she was hearing!.

"I realised they were trouble when they wanted me to do bad things," he continued. "But…but I refused mum. Honestly, I did, and I came home instead. But they said that they would get me back by breaking into our house, and if I told the police…then… then they would come after me and hurt me, so mum… you can't phone the police… Please… please mum. I'm so sorry."

Hearing the fear in his voice, she relented. The last thing she wanted was to see her son get hurt.

"OK son, I won't phone them, but they cannot get away with breaking into my house. Do you know where they live?"

Billy shook his head and said, "No, but I know whereabouts."

"OK, that will do. I'll phone Uncle Tony, and I'll go with him to get our stereo back. That was a present from your Nan. Don't worry. Tony will explain, and tell them that the police haven't been told, OK?"

"But Mum…" He was just about to say something when Charlie came running down the stairs.

"Mummy, Mummy, they've been in Marie's room and took her DVD's. Mine have gone too," he said beginning to cry.

Danielle turned to Billy looking really angry.

"That's final Billy, I am phoning your uncle Tony." Picking up the phone, she began dialling.

Tony responded quickly and was soon knocking at the door. Danielle let him in, and he flew into the front room.

"Dan, what the hell is going on? Louise said that someone broke into your house. What have they taken?" he said his face red with rage. "Don't worry, I'll get the bastards!" Danielle took a few minutes to explain the situation and had quite a job trying to calm him down.

"Look Tony, you can't go in there all guns a blazing. They've threatened to hurt Billy, so I just want to get back what they've stolen." Tony wasn't pleased with the way she wanted to handle it, but the look on Billy's face soon convinced him otherwise.

"OK sis, I wont hit anyone I promise. Now let's go."

They left Charlie with a neighbour, and Danielle, Billy and Tony got into Tony's car. Billy directed the way and they drove into an estate that had a very bad reputation

"There are two of them," Billy said quickly spotting two of the boys walking down the road. Tony pulled up beside them and got out.

"What's this about you breaking into my sister's house," he asked shouting at the top of his voice.

The boys stopped suddenly and turned around. Billy ducked down, but was not quick enough, because one of them spotted him in the back of the car. Tony guessed the boys were about sixteen years old, but this didn't stop him from losing his temper.

"I said, what is this about you breaking into my sister's house?" Pushing one of the boys, his coat flew open and a load of DVD's fell out.

"I don't know what you're talking about; we didn't break into anyone's house,"said the other boy unaware that his friend had already given the game away.

"So how do you explain this then?" asked Tony picking up one of the DVD films and waving it in his face.

Danielle got out of the car just as Tony was about to grab the boy and managed to stop him before he did something stupid.

"Look, we don't want any trouble," she said trying to keep herself calm. "I just want my stereo back."

"You can't go around accusing people of theft lady," blasted one of the boys. "We know our rights you know," he continued.

Danielle went up to him, and the rudeness in his voice caused her anger to flare, so right up in his face she said, "You had no right breaking into my home. Now I'm not asking you, I'm telling you, you'd better get my stereo back to me by tomorrow, or you'll be sorry. Do you hear me?"

"OK, OK, I'll see what I can do," said the boy going a ghostly shade of white.

Tony was picking up the DVD's when she said, "Good, I'm glad that's sorted. Come on Tony. Let's get out of here." With that they got back into the car and drove away.

"Blimey Dan you had me scared then," said Tony driving onto the main road. "I must say, you surprised me. I didn't think you had it in you."

"Neither did I, look I'm shaking."

"That's my big sis!" he laughed patting her on the leg.

In next to no time were back at the house. Charlie was up at the neighbour's window, and when he saw the car pull up, he ran out to meet them. After thanking her neighbour they all walked inside, and Danielle was pleased they had all got back in one piece.

Marie came in from school and was surprised to see the broken window. Danielle explained what had happened, whilst Tony fixed the gaping hole with some plywood. When Danielle had finished Marie burst out crying.

"But they were my favourite films. You and Nan brought them for me. It's so unfair," she said crying harder.

Danielle tried to console her daughter pulling her to her chest as she said, "I know sweetheart, but we did get most of them back."

"But what if they come back?" she sobbed. "Can I sleep in your room tonight?"

"Yes of course you can darling, but please try not to worry, your uncle and I have got it all under control."

"OK Dan, that's done," said Tony putting his tools away. "But I really do think Billy should come home with me tonight, you know, just in case there are any repercussions." Danielle agreed so told Billy to get his things together.

"You're more than welcome to stay too," he said putting his arm around her. "There's plenty of room." Danielle declined his kind offer, and soon convinced him that she was better off at home.

"OK, but phone me if you need me. I'm only a phone call away." Danielle assured him that she would, and then kissed her son goodbye. Watching them leave, she bolted all the windows and doors, and began to cook the dinner.

After a long drawn out conversation with her mother on the phone, Danielle decided to get an early night. It had taken her an hour to convince her mum that she had nothing to worry about, and that she and the children were quite safe. Promising to keep her phone tucked under her pillow, Christine finally said goodnight, and Danielle went up to bed.

Unable to sleep, she spent the first couple of hours tossing and turning. She felt powerless over the thoughts tormenting her mind, so soon gave up on getting any kind of sleep. Sitting up, she looked down on the floor and the sight of Charlie and Marie cuddled up together on the mattress made her feel all warm inside. Leaning over, she kissed them both on the cheek, and then lay back down. Still feeling very uneasy, she tried to take her mind off the earlier events, but she couldn't get the frightened look of that boy's face out of her head. Suddenly thinking of Panos she said quietly under her breath, "See, little miss warrior is as tough as she thinks," and laughed.

Letting her thoughts run free, she opened her mind, and giving it her full consent, she rewound it back to her time in Skiathos, and cried herself to sleep.

CHAPTER
SIXTEEN

The day began just like any other, but this time Danielle got up feeling as bright as a button. Having kept her promise to Marie, not one drop of alcohol touched her lips, and she felt that it was nice to wake up with a clear head for a change. Noticing the difference in her attitude, she went downstairs singing at the top of her voice. Welcoming the new day with a song, it was a great relief for her to know that all her cares and worries were now put behind her.

Start as I mean to go on, she thought smiling, feeling confident that the worse of her fears were now in the past where they belonged. The sound of her voice travelled around the house like a symphony of hope, bringing with it the great expectations of things yet to come. At last, she felt at peace and by a leap of faith, her past bowed down in defeat, and the bright future that lingered on the horizon came forth and took over the reins of her day.

The sun was shining, and determined that nothing would spoil this wonderful feeling, she went about her business as if she didn't have a care in the world. But little did she know, hanging on to the tail end of her victory, hid the face of **Disaster.**

Biding its time like a prowling lion watching its prey, Disaster waited patiently in the background, so when the right moment came, it was ready to pounce.

Marie and Charlie went to school as usual grateful to have their mother restored back to her old self, and they went off feeling very happy. Danielle pottered around the house, and then decided to phone her sister in law, to check on Billy before she set off to work. She was pleased to be told that he was fine, which added to her joy. She started her shift at the pub, content to know that everything was going to be all right after all.

Unbeknown to all of them, only a few miles away on a nearby council estate, two teenage boys left their homes with only one thing on their mind; revenge. Walking side by side, they met up with a third boy. Wanting to put things right, the three of them left the comfort of their surroundings, and without even considering the consequences of their actions, they walked boldly on to the main road.

Poking its head out of its hiding place, Disaster watched the three boys as they neared their target and smiled. Radiating pure evil, Disaster called on his right-hand man, and then Destruction showed its ugly face. Knowing that death was not too far behind him, Disaster managed to stop him from appearing, because now wasn't the right time for him to intervene. Retreating into its hiding place, Death disappeared, but not of his own accord. He was very disappointed that his time to shine had been put on hold.

The boys continued relentless in their mission. The only time they stopped was to get what they needed from the petrol garage which, fortunately for them was on route to where they were going. As soon as they armed themselves with the right tools, they carried on with their mission, and five minutes later their target was in sight. They walked up the alley way as bold as brass, found the right garden they were looking for, and then two of them jumped over the fence.

Like bats out of hell, Disaster accompanied by Destruction, flew over the boys and watched their every move as they started to pour petrol around the back of the house. Lighting the match that was to give Disaster its glory, one of the boys threw it on to the damp trail. As the tiny flame took hold, the boys ran and jumped back over the fence to make a speedy get away. Disaster hailed out a cry of victory as the flames increased, but Destruction took a step back. This was only the beginning of its reign. Its plan was now underway.

The atmosphere in the Kings Head was vibrant, and the collection of happy customer's conversations filled the air. Danielle catered for their every need and was proud to be a part of its joy. Laughing at Jimmy's tales from his past, she was nearly brought to tears, and had to admit he was capable of telling a great story just as well as Mick was. Thankful for the banter that flew across the bar, she couldn't have wished for a better place to work.

Looking at the clock, she noticed the time. Having got through the first half of her day without any problems, she now looked forward to spending the next half in the company of her crazy customer. Jimmy had had his operation and was pleased to be told it was a success. He was glad to finally be on the mend, and this was evident by the way he joked around. Happy to have been given a new lease of life, Danielle was relieved to know that his illness had been cured. She was sure that he had many more of his stories up his sleeve.

Pausing for breath, Jimmy took a mouthful of his drink. The phone behind the bar started to ring so Danielle walked over to answer it.

As always, she put on her polite voice, and said, "Hello Kings Head, can I help you." Aware that Jimmy was mimicking her posh accent, she laughed, and turned around to make sure that she couldn't see him. Repeating those words, the smile fell from her face when she listened to her neighbour, who was obviously distraught, on the other end of the line. The conversation came to an end, and Danielle hung up the receiver in complete and utter shock.

"Dan, what's the matter?" he as he witnessed the colour drain from her face. "Dan you look awful, what's happened babe?" His concern stopped everybody else's conversations, and the bar went deathly quiet.

"Oh Dan, what's wrong," another customer asked noticing her expression. "You look like you're going to be sick."

Danielle walked back over to Jimmy in a daze.

"My... My house... I... I... There's..." She couldn't get the words out.

"OK Danielle, try and relax," encouraged Jimmy as he walked around the bar. Putting his arm around her he led her to a stool and told her to sit down.

"Jimmy," she said looking at him, tears stinging her eyes. "Jimmy my house has been set alight. Oh my god, Jimmy, there's been a fire." Taking a deep breath, she managed to contain her tears, but then she began to panic. "I've got to get home; I can't just sit here."

Getting up, she ran around to the back of the bar, and gathered her things together. Fortunately, the land lady was eating her lunch in the kitchen. Danielle quickly explained why she had to go, and before the land lady had time to answer, she was out of the door. Throwing her bag on to the passenger seat, she started the car and pulled away. All the way home her mind raced, and a deep gruelling sense of fear took over her whole body. Not knowing what she was going to be confronted with when she got home, she tried desperately to control her body that was now shaking. Trying to stabilise her fraught mind, she swayed her thoughts from thinking the worse, and thanked her lucky stars that no one had been in the house when the fire started. This seemed to ease the anxiety slightly. She concentrated on keeping such thoughts in her head, conscious she couldn't allow negativity to get the better of her. She turned up her road and her heart flipped when she saw a fire engine parked in the middle of the road outside her house. The street was an array of people just being nosey, and this caused her to feel quite angry.

Oh, you're all out now, she thought. Where were you an hour ago?

Not being able to go any further, she calmed herself down, and then got out and ran to her neighbour who was talking to a fireman by her wall.

"What's happened?" she asked stopping in front of him, trying to catch her breath. "I live here, is anyone hurt?"

Paula her neighbour, took her hand as the fire chief explained what had happened. He told her that it had started at the back of the house, and fortunately for her, the fire was contained before it consumed the whole building. Their job now was to find the cause. Apparently, they had the top experts going through the damage, hoping to rule out foul play.

After some further questions, she found the courage and explained about the break in from the previous day. Feeling very weak, she explained that her eldest son knew the boys, and she could have kicked herself for listening to him, and not reporting the incident to the police.

"OK Miss," said the chief looking somewhat dismayed.

"The police are on their way, so you can tell them exactly what you've told me." Then his face softened as he continued. "Please try not to worry. I have a teenage son myself, so off the record, I do know how irresponsible they can be, so as a parent I do understand why you didn't call the police, but I must say it's no excuse. Your whole house could have gone up in smoke, and then where would you be?"

If I wasn't so irresponsible, then my son wouldn't be either, she thought hanging her head in shame.

Another fireman walked out of her house and shouted out something that Danielle didn't understand. Then the chief turned to her and said, "OK, it's safe to go in, but I have to warn you, even though the fire didn't get into the main part of the house, the smoke did cause a lot of internal damage, so brace yourself. Right, just follow me." Danielle let go of Paula's hand and taking a very deep breath, she walked into her house.

The pungent smell of smoke hit her as soon as she walked through the door. Putting her hand over her face in an attempt to stop the burnt odour from making her gag, she found that it was too late, and she began to heave. Now being able to taste the disgusting smell too, she managed to stop herself from breathing in, and looked around the room. Everything was covered in black ash, and the sight of how her lovely home looked brought tears to her eyes. When she was led into the garden, she literally froze. A little room that backed onto the house was completely gutted, and all that was left was the metal carcasses of what were once a washing machine and a tumble dryer. Looking at their remains she could have cried.

"Most of our clothes were in there," she said pointing to the remains of her washing. Looking into the little room, she noticed the boiler had a big red sticker across it.

"What does that mean?" she asked reading the word condemned.

The chief officer explained that it could no longer be used, and it had to be replaced before she could even think about turning on her gas.

"B… but where does that leave my children and I? We can't stay here without any gas," she said trying to contain her tears.

"I'm sorry, but until this is sorted out, then nobody will be able to stay here. Have you got somewhere else you can stay?"

"But for how long?" she asked unable to comprehend what was going on. Shaking his head, he was called away, and left her feeling very distraught.

Putting her hands up to her head, she wanted to scream, but knew she had to pull herself together because her children would be home very soon. Looking at her watch, she suddenly thought about Charlie but couldn't face walking up the school to pick him up. She got her phone out of her bag instead and called her mother. When Christine heard the news of the fire, she dropped what she was doing and rushed out of the door to be by her daughter's side. Danielle asked her to pick up Charlie on the way, and she was only too happy to help.

Danielle sat on the garden wall and just stared at the mess that her home had now become. This disaster was just about to take a grip of her very being, when a police officer came out of the house and began to ask questions. An influx of firemen kept coming and going, and she didn't have time to think about the impact this was going to have on her and her family. The thought of becoming homeless never even entered her mind, so she just focused it on answering the police officer's questions as specifically as she could. The expert who worked for the fire department stole the police officer's attention and explained that the fire had probably been caused deliberately. Danielle, overwhelmed by this conclusion, couldn't believe what she was hearing. Putting her head in her hands again, she began to cry.

The police officer turned back to Danielle, and ignoring her sorrow, resumed his questioning. Twenty minutes later, Tony came in with Billy in tow. He couldn't believe what had happened to Danielle's house.

"Oh Dan, this is terrible," he said interrupting the policeman's next question.

"Yes, it is Tony. So how did you find out? Mum I presume." Nodding his head, he went back into the house and began to speak to one of the firemen.

"Oh mum, I'm so sorry," said Billy sitting on the wall next to her.

"Billy this is just as much my fault sweetheart. I should have phoned the police," she replied putting her arm around his shoulder.

"So, is this your son?" asked the police officer sternly, interrupting their conversation. Danielle nodded, and squeezing Billy tight she said, "Yes, and he knows the names of the boys who we think started this."

Two hours later, the last of the firemen left the house, and Danielle and her family were left to pick up the pieces of their lives. Christine was adamant that they all stayed with her, and Danielle had no choice but to take her up on her offer. Living in a privately rented house, her next step was to inform her landlord, so before she and the children left, she made that important call. There was no reply so she left a message on the answering machine.

Gathering the children together, with just the clothes on their backs, they left the house. Marie being an absolute star took it upon herself to look after Charlie, who could not stop crying.

Billy was also very helpful which meant that Danielle managed to keep this disaster from ruling her mind. She even found the strength to stay positive! She decided that the first thing she would do in the morning, was to go up to the local council offices. She was confident that they would help her in her hour of need. Bearing this optimistic view in mind, she and the children spent the night away from the home they were brought up in. Little did they know, they were never to spend a night in that house again.

Danielle spent the next few days trying to sort out a place for them to stay. She had spoken to her landlord, and after assessing the situation, he informed her that it was very unlikely that she could move back in any time soon. Not sure himself of the exact time it would take to get her home back to how it was, all he could do was apologise for the inconvenience. Their relationship had always been a good one, and in all the years of her tenancy this was the first time she'd ever come close to being evicted. Grateful that it hadn't come to that yet, her heart sank when the prospect of being homeless during this time became more evident. Holding on to the hope that things would soon be back to normal, she tried her best to stay positive. It was just as well, because her trip to the council had proven to be a very disappointing one. After spending hours pleading her case, she was told by a very unsympathetic lady, (whose job it was to help people in dire need), that it would take a couple of weeks to process her claim! She unhelpfully pointed out that Danielle's situation was not an emergency, and that there were plenty more people worse off than her, and as Danielle left her office she found herself feeling rather guilty!

Having no other alternative but to stay with her mother, Danielle soon accepted her position, and focused on her children. Their well being was her main concern, so using her skills as a loving mother, she did everything in her power to keep things as normal as she possibly could.

Two weeks passed, and unfortunately Danielle wasn't any nearer to being back under her own roof. The works on her house had been put on hold for a few days due to financial trouble, and the pressure of them all living in a one-bedroom apartment, was starting to get her down. Christine spent most of her nights away, which eased the overcrowding slightly, but having to sleep on the floor, was really taking its toll. She tried to ignore the frustration that came from not knowing how long this would go on for, but her patience began to grow very thin. She caught herself snapping at the slightest thing, but she couldn't seem to help herself. The weight of this burden pressed down on her like a concrete block, and she thought that at any minute she would break. The only thing that kept her going was her job, and she was grateful to be able to take time out, to escape from the nightmare.

Her life had once again been put on hold, but this time there were no loving gestures to cling on to. No words of passion to help her through. Now all she had to hold on to was the hope that the bond that tied her family together was strong enough to keep them together. The mortar that was also her foundation, however, began to show signs of stress. She stood firm though, believing with all her heart that it was only temporary. She was confident that the stability of having her home back again, would be enough to smooth over the cracks, and this gave her the strength to persevere.

The news of Mick's homecoming had been brought to her attention, but she still hadn't seen him. She had called him several times since he got back, but each phone call had resulted in her feeling more frustrated than the one before. The sound of his phone constant ringing was now getting on her nerves. After leaving numerous messages she decided to put the ball in his court and left contact down to him. She had more than enough worries of her own to occupy her mind, and just knowing he got home safely was enough to satisfy her curiosity.

Three weeks later, Danielle's day started out like any other. As usual, the first few hours were busy getting Charlie and Marie to school, and then cleaning the tiny apartment. The only upside to living in such limited space, was that it didn't take long to tidy. Grateful for this small mercy, she said goodbye to Billy, and headed towards the front door.

"Mum," called Billy just as she was about to open it. "Can I come to work with you? I get so bored, and it would be good for me to get out for a little while. I won't get in your way, I promise." She thought carefully about what he said. Having him in her sight did but her mind at rest, so had to admit it was a good idea. She practically ran the place, so as long as he behaved, it wouldn't be a problem. She was just about to answer, when Billy spoke again.

"At least then you can keep an eye on me," he said ironically. She had no idea that he had extrasensory powers, and this caused her to laugh.

"OK, but you must promise to be good," she said opening the door. Billy ran up the hallway.

"Why mother, what are you saying?" He said putting on his coat. "I am always good."

"Oh, is that right?" she answered ruffling his hair. "You've got, 'make it up as you go along,' powers too," she laughed.

"Now conjure up the power to hurry, because I'm going to be late."

Billy didn't have the faintest idea what his mother was going on about but did as he was told anyway. Five minutes later they were in the car, and on their way.

Halfway through her working day, Danielle received a phone call from her landlord. He was desperate to see her, so they arranged to meet at her house once she had finished her shift. Having failed to mention the reason for their meeting, she presumed it was to discuss a date for her to move back in. Even though his tone didn't show any signs of hope in that department, she wasn't surprised, by his request. On previous occasions before the fire he had made it quite clear that he needed to speak to her, but she could never tell if it was good news or bad, because his tone was always the same. Every time it caused her to worry, but he always had something good to say, and this led her to believe that this time was no different. Now enlightened by this fact, she carried on working feeling a lot happier.

Jimmy had Billy's full attention. He was showing him how to make a bar mat disappear, when the bar door opened. Danielle was busy serving, and with the music from the jukebox blaring, and the chatter of customers trying to compete and be heard over the song, she didn't hear the door close. Then walking back from the till, she froze.

"Mick," she said taken aback. "Mick, where have you been? I've left countless messages for you to phone me. I was so worried." As the reality of seeing her friend standing in front of her began to sink in, she suddenly noticed how awful he looked. His eyes were puffy, and she had never seen them looking so red. Her heart sank, and she couldn't get over the state of him. Instinctively she put her hand on his.

"Mick, what's happened to you? You look dreadful."

"Dan, you're not my mother," he huffed. "There was no need to worry. This is the face of a man who's had a heavy few days," he said slurring his words. "Blimey, can't a man enjoy himself?"

Danielle withdrew her hand. It was obvious he was drunk, which didn't surprise her, but the tone of his voice she didn't recognise.

"Alright Mick excuse me for caring," she retorted, unable to control the sarcasm in her voice. "Did you have a good time in Skiathos?" she continued.

Miraculously his face softened, and he smiled.

"Why yes Danielle, I had a great time with Panos thank you. Sun, sea, beer and women…Yes, and we had plenty of the above," he said rubbing his hands together. "Well I must say, Panos soon got over you! Now can I have a pint of your finest?"

Confused by his statement, Danielle got a clean glass from the shelf and began to pour his drink, and it took all of her mental strength to ignore his comment.

"What do you mean Mick, Panos has gotten over me?" she asked curiosity getting the better of her.

Looking around the bar, Mick moved closer to her and took a mouthful of his beer.

"Sorry babe…" He said making eye contact. "But… but Panos has found another English girl. He was all over her… I was shocked Dan, but he told me, actually told me to my face, that he was over you. He said that you didn't mean that much to him, and you… you were now in his past and this woman was now his future. Well, all the time she was staying at the hotel anyway. Just like you!"

He took another mouthful.

"Sorry Dan." He patted her hand. "But I think he played you for a fool." Then taking his hand away he spotted Jimmy at the other end of the bar. "Ah Jimmy, my good mate Jimmy, I need to have a little word in your ear." With that, he turned around and walked toward him.

Danielle was stunned as she watched him stagger away. The thought of Panos with another woman pierced her heart. Finding it hard to believe, a picture of him appeared in her mind's eye, bringing with it a deep hurt that she found impossible to ignore. Aware that tears were stinging her eyes, she took a deep breath and forced the image out of her mind.

How could you do that to me, she thought closing her eyes. And with an English woman, you lying bastard! This time the only emotion conjured up was anger, and she could have screamed. It had taken weeks for her to come to terms with losing him, and now all that effort, she felt, was wasted.

I should have listened to my head, she thought. I knew he was too good to be true.

Billy looked over to his mother, and by the expression on her face he knew something was terribly wrong. Concerned, he left Jimmy talking to Mick, and went over to her.

"Mum, are you OK? You don't look right," he said taking her hand. Her thoughts were suddenly diverted when she heard the alarm in his voice.

"Yes sweetheart, I am fine. I just had a rather big reality check that's all," she said raising a smile. "I'm alright now." Squeezing his hand, she took another deep breath, and suddenly realised that she did feel fine.

Oh well, it was good while it lasted, she thought wiping Panos out of her mind, for good.

Danielle's shift finally came to an end. Mick had hardly said two words to her since spilling the beans on Panos's newest conquest, and she couldn't help feeling that their friendship was slowly coming to an end. It was obvious to her that his love for alcohol was greater than his love for her, and this was proved by not showing the slightest bit of interest when she'd mentioned the fire. His lack of concern bothered her at first because they had always been so close. But by the end of her shift, she decided that she'd had enough of being battered emotionally. Her mind was made up; she couldn't and wouldn't put her trust and love, in a man ever again. This realisation hardened her heart, but she was tough, she was strong, and the only people that mattered now were her family.

The glare of the afternoon sun came through the windscreen forcing Danielle to put on her sunglasses. Considering it was mid-September, it was still very hot. Autumn was only a stone's throw away, and the only sign of its arrival was that the evenings were starting to draw in.

Pulling up outside her house she smiled when she saw her landlord's car parked just a few spaces up the road. Confident that her worries were now coming to an end, she felt good as her and Billy walked up the path. The front door was open, so with Danielle leading the way they walked inside. The air still bared signs of the fire, but to her relief the smell was nowhere near as strong as before. Hearing her landlord's voice coming from the kitchen, a huge smile swept across her face as she walked into the front room. But as quickly as it emerged it disappeared, and her heart sank. There, in front of her written across the wall in bright red paint were the words 'Billy's dead!'

Turning around she realised that it was not only written on just the one wall, but every single one displayed the same cruel words. Fear not only caught her breath, but also Billy's as his eyes went around the room.

"Mum, I'm scared. How did they get in?" He asked grabbing hold of her hand. "What do they mean I'm dead? What if they come back to get me?"

"It's OK Billy," she said squeezing it tight. "No one is going to hurt you, I will make sure of that," she said trying to reassure herself as much as her son. It was at this point she knew they could never come back to this house again. The realisation came down on her like a tonne of bricks, but something deep down inside of her told her that she had no choice. The power to overcome this situation was taken out of her hands, and she had never felt so helpless.

The sound of her voice caught her landlord's attention. Seeing her and her son standing there, he put his tools down and walked towards them. The expression on his face was a mixture of sadness and fury, so Danielle waited with bated breath to see which emotion was going to come at her first.

"Danielle, I'm sorry but I cannot put up with this sort of behaviour," he said pointing to the graffiti on the walls.

"This is my house after all, and it is my responsibility to look out for my investment, so this… this is not on." The anger in his voice was evident, and Danielle couldn't blame him for that. It angered her too, and it wasn't even her house, but it had been her home.

His tone softened when he saw the look of despair in her eyes as he said, "Sorry but I have no other alternative but to cancel your tenancy agreement. It hurts me to have to say this, it really does, but… but I have no choice. I'm sure you understand Danielle."

She nodded her head. Usually she would stand up for her rights, and fight tooth and nail for her family, but even she couldn't find the right words to justify this unforgivable act of criminal damage.

"I've called the police, but they're no closer to catching the thugs that did this. They did say they arrested the boys whom you thought were responsible for starting the fire, but of course they denied it, so unfortunately it is your word against theirs. Like I said, I'm sorry that it has come to this, but in my opinion the possibility of this happening again is very high, and I cannot risk losing a house that I have put a lot of money into." Hesitating, he stared at her for a few moments, but then he forced himself to look away. Seeing the sadness in her eyes tortured him, but he continued. "You can arrange to pick up your things. You have three days to sort it out, but then you will have to give me your key."

Wanting to cry out in her defence she knew she had been backed into a corner, and unfortunately for her she had to take his demands on the chin. Aware that this now left them permanently homeless, she swallowed down her hurt and anger, and focused her mind on going back to the council. Reaching way down to the depths of her being, she found what was left of her dignity and smiled at him.

"Yes, I do understand. It's not fair that we are the ones who have to suffer because of this injustice, but obviously…" hesitating, she took a deep breath. "Obviously bricks and mortar are more important to you than our lives, so I'll take you up on your kind offer and collect my things that haven't been damaged, and then… and then in three days we'll be gone. It will be as if we'd never been here." Holding her head up high, she put her arm around Billy's shoulder and said, "Come on son, we have a life to rebuild." With that, they turned around and walked out of the house.

Danielle was true to her word, so three days later all the signs of her having lived there were gone. Practically on bended knees, she had taken time out from the gruelling job of cleaning the house and gone back up to seek help from the council. Now that her circumstances had changed, another lady she spoke to was more than helpful this time, and her claim was processed. It still took a few weeks to go through, but she was assured that after that time she would without a shadow of a doubt, be placed in some sort of temporary accommodation. She was also offered a place to store what was left of her furniture. She was so relieved to know that at least she had somewhere safe to keep her belongings.

All her family pulled together, and she was overwhelmed with gratitude for their help and support in her hour of need. Now having put her memories of yesterday away in the depths of her mind, she carried on regardless. Keeping one step ahead of this disaster that could have easily destroyed her; she managed to stay focused. She knew that for whatever reason, this whole situation was going to turn out to be a blessing in disguise. This was a great comfort to her, so holding on to this hope with all her might, she pushed through this terrible time the best she could.

Disaster snarled as it looked down on Danielle. Fuelled by hatred, it was forced to take a step back, and its assignment to destroy her life was now put on hold. At one point, certain that its crowning glory was at hand, it stood tall ready to claim it. Using all its power to drag her down into the depths of hopelessness, its attack was suddenly disarmed, when a tower of strength rose up out of the blue and proceeded to steal its glory. Totally unprepared for this turnaround, it retreated in defeat, but all was not yet lost. Deciding to use another strategy, it waited patiently on the side lines, and when the time was right, it was ready to strike.

CHAPTER
SEVENTEEN

*A*utumn had finally arrived, and the cold breeze that shook the leaves off the trees was a sure sign that summer was well and truly over. Yet another three weeks had gone by, and Danielle and her children were still living in the confinement of her mother's apartment. She had just got back from taking Charlie and Marie to school, and when she walked through the front door the sound of her mother's voice coming from the kitchen made her smile. She hadn't seen her for a few days, and it always cheered her up when she paid them a visit, especially if it was an unexpected one. Hanging up her coat, she noticed a pile of letters on the floor. Picking them up, she walked into the living room. Billy was watching the TV, and his eyes were glued to the screen. He did however greet his mother by waving his hand in the air.

"Hello sweetheart," said Christine poking her head out of the kitchen door. "I've just put the kettle on. Do you want a cuppa?"

Danielle went up to Billy who was silent and tickled the top of his head.

"Well at least I get a hello out of you mum. Billy seems

to have lost his voice, and yes please I am gasping." Billy brushed her hand away and grunted. Laughing, she tapped him with the pile of letters and then walked into the kitchen.

"Here mum, these are for you," she said handing Christine the letters. "I don't suppose there is anything in there for me. I think the council have forgotten about us."

Christine fingered through the usual batch of bills, when she noticed an envelope with Danielle's name on it. Easily mistaken for another miscellaneous load of junk mail, Christine re-read the front, and sure enough it was addressed to Danielle.

"Dan, Dan there is a letter for you," she said excitedly. "This could be the one you've been waiting for." Frightened to take the letter out of her hand, Danielle just stared at it.

"Mum you open it, and if it's bad news I don't want to know," she said not being able to face yet another disappointment.

Christine opened the envelope and pulled out a letter that was three pages long. Skimming through the papers, she came to the last page. Keeping a close eye on her mother's face, Danielle watched for the slightest change in her expression. Christine finally looked up, and then, as if by magic, a big smile swept across her face.

"Dan, they have offered you a place," she said now laughing. "It's only bed and breakfast, but... but Dan, it's a start." Danielle took the letter out of her mother's hand and began to read through it. Christine's smile was infectious, and the same beam of joy was now on Danielle's face.

Billy was now by his mother's side. Having been drawn away from the TV he waited with baited breath for

Danielle to finish reading, and his heart sank when the smile slowly slipped from her face.

"I knew it was too good to be true," he said retreating to the settee. "Nothing good ever happens to us."

Danielle looked at her mother and began to shake her head. Christine's joy soon deflated along with Danielle's smile.

"What's wrong, what's with the sad face? Its good news isn't it?" she said taking her hand.

"No mum, it's not, it's far from good news. You were right though, they have offered me a place, but… but its miles away from anywhere. How am I going to get Charlie and Marie to school?" Tears stung her eyes, but she managed to keep them at bay. Folding the letter back up, she put it back into the envelope. Then turning to Christine, she shrugged her shoulders. "When's this nightmare going to end? I don't think I can take much more. From what they've said, I have no choice but to take it. Oh mum, my life is such a mess."

Christine put her arm around her and embraced her. Hearing the desperation in her voice made her want to cry, but she knew she had to be strong for her daughter. Trying to find the right words, she searched her mind for something positive to say.

"Oh sweetheart, I'm sure things will turn out for the best. If its petrol you're worried about, then I'll help you out. I'm sure that it won't be long before you get a proper place to call your own. Come on darling, it's going to be OK." Taking Danielle's face in her hands she looked deep into her teary eyes and smiled.

"Danielle you're going to get through this. You are strong young lady and sorry, but I am going to take credit for that. You're made of tough stuff just like me."

Nodding her head, Danielle laughed. Her mother's words of encouragement were food for thought for her. She did have to admit her mother was right. She'd been through a lot in her thirty or so years, and she had always pulled through. The love in her mum's voice was evident and she realised how fortunate she was to have such a supportive mother.

This made her think about Helen. The last conversation they'd had was at the airport when they'd arrived home. Knowing that the only thing they had in common was Panos, both said goodbye for the last time and went their separate ways. She had been tempted to get Helen's number, but the thought of her staying in touch with Panos was just too much for Danielle to cope with. Thinking back to when Helen shared her sad story by the pool, Danielle was reminded of how sorry she had felt for her. This memory backed up her own reasons for never taking her own mother for granted, and she not only felt blessed, but she felt honoured to have such a great mum who was always there for her.

Kissing Christine on the nose, her smile returned.

"Yes, you're so right, I am tough, and I will not let this get the better of me! OK, where's the phone? I am going to phone the council and book an appointment for a viewing." Hesitating she took a deep breath. "Looks like I'm my mother's daughter after all." Seeing strength rise out of her doubts, Christine smiled.

"That's my girl," she said handing her the phone.

No sooner than Christine had made the tea, Danielle had taken the first step, and an appointment to view the property was booked for the following day. Having successfully turned this negative situation into a positive opportunity, she actually found herself looking forward to seeing her new home. Temporary was still the operative word, but she knew it was the first stage of the process. She was confident that in a few weeks she would finally have a place to call home.

The prospect of not knowing where they were going to end up was still slightly daunting for her, but something in the core of her being, led her to believe that everything happened for a reason. Welcoming this feeling, it became the pole that kept her balanced, as she walked along the tight rope of life. As long as she kept looking forward, she was sure not to fall. Bearing all of this in mind, her day carried on as before, but this time the light at the end of her tunnel was beginning to get brighter.

The warm autumn sun claimed the new day, and Danielle woke up feeling like a new woman. As far as she was concerned, this brand-new day was filled with hope and nothing else. All her dreams of being able to get on with her life were now becoming a reality. Confident that in just a few hours her existence would have gained some purpose again, she followed her usual routine, feeling very happy.

Having arranged to meet the housing officer at noon, she was left with no choice but to book the day off work. The response she got from the landlady of the King's Head took her by surprise. She had expected her to be supportive. Instead however, she was met by a very irate employer who seemed very put out, because her situation was now affecting her work. Shaken by her unsympathetic attitude, Danielle was not deterred. Determined that no one was going to spoil her day, she carried on despite her landlady's attitude.

Accompanied by her mother, Danielle put all her worries concerning work to one side, and they set out to meet the woman who held the keys to the next chapter of her life. After travelling some distance, and following the directions given in the letter, they pulled into a road that was in the middle of nowhere. Danielle checked the address and sure enough they were in the right place. She parked the car outside the terraced house that was to become her new home, and they got out.

"Oh, my goodness mum it's tiny," she observed focusing on the slim building. "But I suppose it's a start."

Opening the gate, she walked up the short path and looked through the window. Her view was restricted by the reflection of the sun and as she took a step back, the sound of someone calling her name startled her.

"Danielle, Mrs Danielle Green?" asked the voice out of the blue. She turned around and suddenly recognised the face that was responsible for making her jump.

"Oh hello," answered Danielle smiling, putting her hand out to greet the lady from the housing department. "It is good to see you again."

The housing officer smiled courtly and remarked on the weather. After a little small talk, she soon got down to business. The lady searched through her bag for the front door key. Holding her breath for a few seconds, Danielle let out a huge sigh.

"Well this is it," she said nervously, looking at her mother. Christine, recognising the anxiety in her tone, smiled reassuringly.

"Yes, I guess it is sweetheart. Don't worry, it will be just fine," she said patting Danielle's arm.

Moments later the door was unlocked, and in single file the three women walked into the house. The smell of recent cooking hung in the air, and this confused Danielle because it was if someone else had been in the house. Realising that she was obviously mistaken, she blamed it on the neighbours and continued into the front room.

"This is the living room. As you can see it is quite spacious, and I'm sure there is adequate space for you and your children to share with the other tenants," the housing officer said pointing to the miserable looking three-piece suit. "And as you can see, it leads out into the kitchen."

It took a few minutes for her statement to sink in, but then Danielle answered rather sharply, "Hang on a minute. What do you mean 'the other tenants?' Are you implying that we will not be living here alone?"

"That's correct Mrs Green. You'll be sharing the property with another family. Did you not know? It should have been explained in the letter you received."

"Well it's quite obvious that I didn't know, I wouldn't have asked otherwise, would I?" replied Danielle sarcastically. "So no, it didn't say anything about that in the letter I received." She could feel her anger rising and she was finding it very hard to control.

"I'm sorry Mrs Green, but you must be mistaken.

I'm sure that it did state that you would be sharing the accommodation," the lady replied sternly. "So, there is no reason for you to take that tone."

"Look lady, I'm not mistaken," replied Danielle, her blood now at boiling point. "And it is you who should be minding their tone. How dare you talk to me like that? You're not the one that is homeless!" Using all her strength to control her temper, she put her hand up to her forehead.

"Okay Dan, calm down," Christine intervened. "This lady is just doing her job."

Turning to the housing officer she said calmly, "My daughter was not mistaken. I also read the letter, and it didn't mention anything about her having to share. I'm sorry but it is you who has got it wrong."

Taking a deep breath, the housing officer, unable to give a plausible explanation for this misunderstanding, swallowed her pride, smiled and politely said, "I'm so sorry Mrs Green, in that case, you can be rest assured that this error will not go unnoticed, and the person responsible will be disciplined. I will see to it personally. Now, shall we go upstairs?"

No, I don't want to bloody go upstairs. I just want to go home! thought Danielle. She wanted to scream at her. Aware that she had to keep her cool, because she still didn't have a home to go to, she managed to keep her thoughts to herself and just nodded.

"Okay. Just follow me."

Following her up the stairs, Danielle could not get her head around having to share this tiny house with another family. This whole situation lowered her spirits, and she could have cried. But once again, she swallowed down her disappointment, and just focused on the fact that it wouldn't be forever.

"Right, this is the bedroom your children will be sleeping in," said the housing officer cheerfully, interrupting her thoughts as she opened the door. "As you can see there's a bunk bed, and also a single bed that will be more than sufficient for them," she said enthusiastically.

Looking around the room, Danielle's heart sank.

You're right about how many beds there are, she thought, but you couldn't swing a cat in here. I can't expect them to share this tiny space. They would end up fighting every five minutes! She kept her thoughts to herself for the time being and followed the lady to the second bedroom. This room was even smaller. A single bed and a single wardrobe were crammed into its limited space, and the thought of having to sleep in there brought tears to Danielle's eyes. "This is ridiculous," she said out loud, picturing her old bedroom in her mind.

"We can't live here. We've come from a lovely spacious house, and now... and now it has come to this. It's so unfair. We did nothing wrong, and we don't deserve this!" she said finally exploding! Anger now replaced her frustration, as she thought of the boys responsible for putting her in this situation, as well as the fact that they seemed to have got off scot free. This added to her fury.

"Danielle, I do sympathise with your predicament, honestly I do," the housing officer said genuinely. "But you have got to remember, it's only temporary. Unfortunately, this is all we can offer you now, but... but eventually you will be re-housed. You'll just have to be patient." The sincerity in her voice was apparent, and the power of her tone quickly neutralised Danielle's temper.

"So how long is temporary?" Danielle asked, feeling a lot calmer. "How long are we expected to stay here?"

"Anything up to six months, but…"

"Six months! We can't stay here for six months! It's miles away from my kid's school, and not only that, it's miles away from their friends," Danielle interrupted, again putting her hand up to her forehead.

"This can't be happening… Mum?" Turning to Christine, she used every bit of strength she had in her to stop her tears from escaping, but it was no use, and they began to flow.

"Oh sweetheart," was all that Christine could say as she put out her arms.

Conscious she had to keep her feelings on a professional level, the housing officer took a deep breath in an effort to ignore Danielle's understandable outburst and continued with what she was going to say.

"But that doesn't necessarily mean you'll be here for that length of time. I've known families to be re-housed after four months."

Then taking a few moments to think about Danielle's situation she suddenly asked, "Is it too unbearable living with your mother? If not, that could be the solution for now. The six months would still apply."

Danielle laughed.

"That's not an option; her place is even smaller than this, if that's possible," she replied sarcastically.

"It was just a thought. At least then, your children would be near their school and their friends. I'm sorry Danielle, but that's all I can say. So, am I right in thinking that you accept our offer?"

Unable to find the strength to argue, Danielle just nodded.

"Okay, you can move in as soon as you like. There's just a form I need you to fill in, and then the keys are yours."

Disaster watched closely as Danielle signed the appropriate forms. The tears flowing down her face were the ammunition it needed to fuel the arsenal of its empty soul. Confident that its plan was now coming into play, Disaster summonsed Destruction in order to gloat over their victory, which was getting closer by the minute. Destruction stood beside his commandant and smiled.

"Is it time to call on one of our snipers?" asked Destruction as it drooled at the mouth. Its hot molten eyes still fixed on Danielle. Disaster nodded in reply. Imagining her lifeless body in its talons, its hollow chest puffed up in sheer delight.

"This is going to be so easy," it whispered, the stench of its breath stunning the tiny air particles as it spoke, leaving them suspended in animation.

"It's going to be like taking candy from a baby."

Laughing hysterically, it levitated off the floor, and then circled around the house. Then, landing on the roof, Destruction returned, but it was not alone. Raising its right wing, Disaster gave the command, giving Depression permission to proceed. Its mission was now in progress. Letting out a blood curdling scream, Depression

swooped down and flew into the house. Reducing in size as it flew; it homed in on its target, circled Danielle's head a couple of times, and then attached its scrawny talons into her skull.

"Ha ha, she's mine," it squealed as its talons sunk deeper into her skin.

"Get out of this one, little miss warrior!"

Danielle, her mind in disarray, felt she couldn't cope with driving back, so Christine, who was only too happy to help, got into the driver seat. Danielle's earlier positive mentality had now been snuffed out like a candle, and any flicker of hope left on her horizon had disappeared. Feeling as though her life had been downgraded yet again, she had an overpowering need for a drink. Trying desperately to ignore this sudden urge, she tried to set her mind onto something constructive, but all she could think about, was spending the next few months in this godforsaken place. This domineering thought not only tormented her mind, but also her soul as she remembered the lovely home that had been so cruelly snatched out of her hands. The memory of what used to be exhausted any trace of strength left inside her.

Now she was left with no other choice but to bow down to her situation. Having lost the last bit of hope, she began to cry.

I must have done something really bad in a past life, she thought, letting the tears flow. That has got to be the only explanation to why my life has gone so wrong.

Attempting to claim back her strength, she turned her thoughts to the boys who had got her to this point of desolation. She hoped that her anger would somehow lift her out of this incredibly dark place. This failed to have the desired effect, because the added thought of them getting away with this injustice, just plunged her deeper into the depths of despair. The ability to fight for her family at whatever cost had abandoned her, feeding the inadequacy she felt as a mother, enhancing her need for a drink. Somehow, she managed to put this urgency on the back burner of her mind, as she noticed that she was nearly back at her mother's apartment, so focused on telling her children the bad news, as sensitively as she could. Swallowing down her pain, she stopped her tears and wiped her face. The feeling of doom still clouded her mind, and she could honestly say she had never felt so helpless.

Christine, aware of her daughter's suffering, drove into the car park, completely lost for words. The journey had mostly been done in silence, and as a mother, she felt crippled emotionally to see Danielle in so much pain. Having searched deep into the core of her very being for the right words to say, it broke her heart to find it empty. There was nothing she could say, that had the power to comfort her at this time, so all she could do was cling to the hope that this terrible nightmare would one day come to an end.

The telltale signs of being consumed by the affects of this situation were written all over Danielle's face, and Christine feared that it would take her daughter down the slippery path of destruction. She had never seen her looking so distraught, and this unnerved her. In the past, she'd had her problems, but they had never been of great concern to Christine. She knew her daughter was a fighter, and this had always pulled her through, hardship. This time however, something in Danielle's eyes told her that this time was different and could actually push her over the edge!

Previously, even when her husband had left her, she had always seen a glimmer of hope in her eyes. It had taken some time, but she always managed to find the strength to rise above her circumstances. Now however looking at her daughter, who would once have fought the world if need be, it was like looking at a completely different girl. Her eyes were like pools of muddy water, reflecting emptiness and nothing else, and Christine had never been so afraid. Knowing that she had to be strong for her daughter, she put her own fear to one side, and using all her own strength, focused her mind on helping Danielle in whatever way she could.

Taking a deep breath, she stopped the car. Then turning to face her daughter she smiled and said, "Come on sweetheart, it's going to be alright."

"We both know that it's not!" Danielle spat at her. "How can you be so sure? And I don't know what you're smiling about. Unless… Unless. You can't wait to get rid of us!" With that she got out of the car, slamming the door as she walked away. The door shut with so much force that Christine was certain that the windows would break. Thankful that they didn't, she chose to ignore her daughter's harsh words. After locking the car, she followed her up to her apartment, trying her hardest not to cry.

Danielle broke the news to Billy, and he was somewhat confused by the aggressive person who was now standing in front of him. Bewildered by his mother's angry attitude, he went and stood next to his Nan, who to his relief was behaving in a calm manner.

"Okay mum, there's no need to be so destructive," he said as she started to throw his things into a black sack. "Be careful, that's not even mine." Picking up a computer game, she turned to her son and glared at him.

"Be careful!" she bellowed at him. "Be careful?" If it wasn't for you, we wouldn't be in this mess!" Turning back around, she threw the game on the table.

Billy grabbed hold of his Nan's hand and was just about to retaliate when Christine gently squeezed it. Confused, he looked up, and stared at her. Christine smiled and shook her head. Putting her arm around her grandson, she said, "Danielle, please darling, this is not Billy's fault. We're all to blame. I should have made you go to the police... Tony should have made you go to the police, but we... none of us expected it to end like this... Now come on. Please calm down. Throwing things around isn't helping now is it?" she reasoned.

"No, but it makes me feel a bit better," she lied. "Nothing is going to help. Nothing is going to take this uselessness away! I've let everyone down. Some mother I am!" Feeling the tears well up in her eyes, she swallowed hard to ease the pressure, and they stopped. Letting the black sack fall out of her hands, she sat down on the settee and put her head in her hands.

"No sweetheart. Don't say that," said Christine letting go of Billy's hand. "You're a great mum. You have always done your best. No one can fault you on that," she said sitting down next to Danielle and taking hold of her hand. "There's one thing I'm absolutely sure of. I know I can't make things any better, but... but one thing I do know, I'll do everything in my power to help you and the children...

That, I can promise you!" she said sincerely.

Billy plucked up the courage and sat down on the other side of his mother.

"Mum, I know you must hate me, but... but mum we will get through this... I'm so sorry. Nan's right; you're a great mum... even when you're angry." Suddenly, regretting his statement, he kissed her on the cheek. "And that isn't very often," he concluded trying to soften his words.

Danielle looked at her son. Finding it hard to believe she had said those harsh words just a few minutes ago, she said, "Oh Billy. I don't hate you, and I'm sorry too. I shouldn't have said what I did. It's just so hard for me." Looking down at the floor she continued. "I feel so helpless, and so angry. I've let you all down. I... I should have been the responsible parent, it's my job. I shouldn't have let it get this far... I'm the one to blame, not you." In an effort to shake off the tormenting feelings of worthlessness, she tried to smile, but all her attempts to rid herself of the guilt that filled her mind, failed her miserably. Taking a deep breath, she stood up.

"Right, there is no getting out of this, so come on, let's get our bags packed. We'll have to get some shopping, and then we can go straight to that house when we've picked Marie and Charlie up from school." Picking up the black sack, she continued to fill it with Billy's things, and he was pleased to see that she was being more careful this time.

The light at the end of Danielle's tunnel began to slowly fade away. Now there was just a tiny flicker on the horizon, with just enough power to keep it burning. Although the disaster that had taken Danielle's life hostage nearly

dampened the flame, an unknown life force was at work striving to keep it alight. Still a long way off in the distance, as slowly as it had begun to disappear, the flame retained its energy and began to rise.

After finally packing all their belongings, Danielle and Billy left the comfort of the small apartment and drove to the nearby supermarket. Disappointed that Danielle had told her to stay behind, Christine watched them drive away, and all her pent-up tears begun to flow. Danielle had promised to phone her as soon as they were settled, and when the car disappeared from her view, she set her mind on finding things to do whilst waiting for the call that was going to put her at ease. She felt it was going to be a long wait.

They got the necessary supplies from the supermarket and then collected Charlie and Marie from school. Charlie came out ten minutes earlier than his sister, so was picked up first. He had been given strict instructions to wait by the main gate until his mum arrived, and then it was Marie's turn. Trying her hardest to keep the atmosphere a happy one, Danielle put on a brave face and forced herself to smile. She tried to turn this move into an adventure and put on an act to the best of her ability, but the charade was not very convincing. Marie saw straight through the falseness of her mother's carefree attitude. Quickly recognising that this was all a show to ease the discomfort of them not knowing where they were going, Marie played the game and went along with her mother. Just seeing Charlie's little face light up when he was told that there was a park nearby, was enough for Marie to feel free to get in on the act.

"Oh Charlie, we're going to have so much fun. We can play pirates on the swings, and you can be captain hook," she said cheerfully.

Catching a glimpse of her daughter's smiling face in the rear-view mirror, Danielle found herself smiling too. Pleased this was the first genuine smile she'd managed since getting in the car, she began to feel a little bit better.

Maybe it won't be so bad after all, she thought, taken in by Marie's imaginative thinking. Her glimmer of hope soon vanished when they finally pulled up outside the house.

Well that didn't last long, she thought, the image of her new home deflating her optimism as fast as it had appeared.

"Well here we are," she said taking the keys out of the ignition. "This is our new home for the next few months. Now everyone, grab a bag."

Being the oldest, Billy was insistent that he carried the heaviest one of them all, and no one argued against his decision.

"Wow mum the people next door has got a dog," said Charlie excitedly hearing the distinct sound of barking coming from the neighbouring house.

Oh great, that's all we need, thought Danielle grumpily.

"So, they have," she replied forcing a smile as Charlie looked at her.

"Great, maybe they'll let me stroke it," he stated, picking up a bag of his toys. "I like it here already."

Seeing the excitement in his face, she tried to use this as an excuse to like the place, but even his boyish grin couldn't bring up any feelings of joy.

"Yes, maybe tomorrow sweetheart," she replied, putting the key into the door. "But now we must concentrate on getting our things moved in."

Thankful that all her furniture was in storage, all four of them walked into the front room holding their own bag of belongings. All that remained in the boot of the car were the bags of shopping. Apart from Charlie's toys, the main contents of the bags were clothes, so moving into this house had been easy compared to all those years ago when she first had the task of moving to a new home. This sudden flash back caused Danielle's heart to drop, bringing with it a terrible feeling of loss that jolted her mind into the reality of why they were there. Tears stung the back of her eyes, but conscious not let them escape, she again swallowed down the pain of yesteryear.

Hearing footsteps coming down the stairs, all of them stopped what they were doing, and focused on the living room door. As it opened, the children gathered around Danielle, surprised to see a big burly man walk into the room.

"Oh, you must be the new tenants," he said in a strong Irish accent. "So, is this all of you?" he asked walking over to the window.

"It's just that there are five of us, and anymore people would be ridiculous. I don't know how we are all supposed to live under the same roof. Anyway, we eat down here at six o'clock sharp, and then we, as a family watch some TV, so I don't know what you're going to do. We were here first, so those are the rules," he said arrogantly. "I just needed to get that out of the way. We've been here for a month, so it's only fair."

Danielle could feel her blood pressure rise. She had only been in the house for two minutes, and already she hated this place more than when she first walked through the door. Before she could say anything, it was if a herd of elephants were running down the stairs. Then three children came in followed by a lady, who Danielle guessed was the rude man's wife.

"This is my clan," said the man smiling. "And this here is the missus. Kieran get down from there!"

Feeling Charlie grab hold of her hand, Danielle watched in amazement as one of the man's sons jumped along the three-piece suit!

"Kids, who would have them," he said as the boy continued to bounce, blatantly ignoring his father's command. "I said, get down!" His deep voice bellowed around the room, causing Charlie to jump two foot up into the air.

Now I know why that settee looks so battered, thought Danielle as she squeezed Charlie's hand, reassuringly.

"Oh, by the way, it's stated that this is bed and breakfast. Just ignore the breakfast part, because that's just a fallacy, there's not even a kettle," said the man laughing at the top of his voice.

Danielle could feel herself sinking deeper into depression, with each passing minute. She quickly grew to despise this egotistical man and the thought of having to share a house with him and his family darkened her thoughts of the future even more. His two other children soon put in an appearance joining their brother, so now there were three children bouncing across the furniture.

"Ok, Billy grab what you can, and you too Marie. Let's get our things upstairs," said Danielle before the man voiced any more concerns.

"Come on Charlie. That's it sweetheart; get your toys… Charlie?" Mesmerised by the three children using the settee as a trampoline, Charlie stood there gawping at them. "Charlie! Come on," she repeated, finally getting his attention. Her three children walked out of the door, and she was not far behind them. She couldn't wait to get out of that room, so rushed out of the door.

"Stuck up cow," said the man as she left the room. She heard his comment as clear as day, and it took all her mental strength to stop herself from throwing down her bag and retaliating to his nasty remark. Confident that her children were too far ahead to have heard him, she carried on up the stairs, feeling extremely angry.

Even though their bedroom was small, neither one of Danielle's children complained. Having found a place for their clothes, she decided to buy them fish and chips for their tea. Since it was their first night, she explained that this was a special treat, because they had all been so good. Noticing a fish and chip shop just around the corner when they first arrived, they all went out to fetch their tea. On their arrival back to their new home, Danielle ushered them all back upstairs, and sitting in the children's bedroom, they ate their food.

The noise of the children fighting downstairs filled the house and Danielle couldn't believe that she was going to have to spend the next few months, sharing a house with a bunch of hooligans! The thought was an unbearable one and made her want to scream.

But what choice have I got, she thought trying to keep herself calm. Eventually, the noise downstairs quietened down, and after some persuasion, she left her children and went into her own room. Lying down on her bed the realisation of where she was, kicked in and she felt like crying again.

The need for a glass of wine reappeared, and she suddenly remembered the bags of groceries in the car. Her sudden appetite for a drink that had been put on hold jogged her memory and she realised that there was a bottle of wine in one of the bags. She waited for half an hour, then went quietly down the stairs, carrying on out to the car. She had no choice but to walk through the lounge to get to the kitchen, so putting her head down low, she went in search of a glass. To her surprise, 'the whole family,' were sitting quietly watching TV, so as quickly as she could, she went straight into the kitchen, without pausing. The only thing that she found was a mug.

That will have to do, she thought as she proceeded to go back up to her room. Grateful that she had been ignored, she sat on her bed and poured out a mug of wine.

This will be just for tonight, she thought feeling rather guilty. I need something to make me sleep. Taking a mouthful, she sighed as the liquid went down into her stomach, and for the first time that day, she relaxed. Staring at the black sack that held her belongings she decided to make use of the wardrobes and began to put her things away. In next to no time the first bag was empty, so she began to unpack the second. Now feeling quite tipsy, she found her walkman, so very quietly, she put on some music. Out of the blue, a pain gripped her heart when she pulled out the cuddly toy that Panos had bought for her. Looking at the big love heart on the front of the bear, the tears that she had resisted all day began to well up in her eyes.

"Oh Panos," she whispered pulling the bear to her chest. This is so hard. I miss being in your arms. With that, she lay back down, and squeezing the memento that was from a lifetime ago, she began to sob. A vision of him flooded her mind, and the pain in her heart increased.

Oh, Panos, I miss you so much...God, if you are really there, please help me. Moments later, the sound of her mobile phone distracted her from her despair. Noticing her mother's name displayed in bright green letters, she took a deep breath, wiped her face and answered it. The concern in her mother's voice was evident, but after five minutes of Danielle reassuring her that she and the children were just fine, her mum began to sound more at ease. Promising to phone her in the morning, Danielle explained that she needed to get some sleep. So, reluctant to let her daughter go, Christine said goodnight and then hung up the phone.

Watching the screen saver appear on the screen, Danielle's heart dropped. Feeling totally alone, she pulled the teddy bear to her chest and closed her eyes. The image of Panos re-emerged in her mind, and the familiar sense of hopelessness prompted her tears to return. Giving way to the agony that came with the vision, she cried with so much passion, she feared that she would never stop. Eventually, the bottle of wine she'd drunk won over her tortured mind and aching heart, and she finally drifted off into a restless sleep.

CHAPTER

EIGHTEEN

*D*anielle woke up with a start and sat bolt upright in her bed. The sound of a boy screaming had brought her out of her sleep, and her first thought was that it was Charlie. Jumping out of her bed, she ran over to the door and opened it. Suddenly, she realised that the tremendous noise was coming from down the hallway and sighed a huge sigh of relief when the mother of the other family came out of her bedroom.

"Shut that bloody boy up!" her husband shouted out from their room. "What do I have to do to get a good night sleep around here? Why does he have to scream like that? It happens every bloody night. I have to get up in a couple of hours." The woman quickly glanced at Danielle, a look of terror washing over her face. She stared at Danielle for a few seconds more, but then the sound of her husband's bellowing voice made her jump.

"Woman, what are you doing… I said, shut him up!"

The boy's screams had now turned hysterical, so the woman, taking her eyes off Danielle, quickly ran into her son's bedroom to calm him down. Danielle, thankful that it didn't wake any of her children, or so she thought, just stood on the threshold of her bedroom in complete disbelief. Aware that it was still very early, she couldn't believe the nerve of the man.

How can you be so insensitive? she thought. We live here too.

Deciding to check on her own children, Danielle went into the neighbouring bedroom. Conscious not to wake them, she slowly opened the door, and looked inside. The dull light of the beginning of the day made it possible for her to see them, and grateful that their sleep hadn't been disturbed, she began to close the door.

"Mummy, Mummy please don't go, I'm scared. I don't like it here," Charlie said, poking his head out from under the covers.

"Neither do I mum," said Marie sitting up. "That man is horrible, and… and I want to go home!" Hearing the sadness in her children's words, Danielle walked over to Marie and kissed her on the head. Suddenly, realising that the boy had stopped screaming, Danielle stroked her daughter's forehead and said, "it's OK sweetheart, I'm certain that the boy has gone back to sleep now, so you do the same, we have got an early start."

Marie lay back down, and Danielle was just about to go and see to Charlie, when the boy screamed out again. The almighty shriek cut through Danielle's body like a laser beam, sending shivers down her spine. As before, the blood curdling scream was followed by the bellowing of the father's voice, but this time it made Charlie cry.

"Mummy, Mummy, I hate this house," he sobbed. "Do we really have to stay here? Why can't we go back to

Nanny's?" Danielle, desperate to console her son, pulled back the covers and got in beside him.

"Mum, please can we go back," asked Billy from the top bunk, feeling very angry. "If that man doesn't shut up, I'm going to hit him." Fully understanding Billy's outburst, Danielle put her arms around Charlie and pulled him close to her.

Feeling at a loss as to what to do, she suddenly remembered what the housing officer had said earlier that day. Even though she knew that her mother's apartment was a lot smaller, the thought of having to endure the same torture every night soon convinced her that out of the two, going back to that poky little flat was the far better option. Knowing that the six months would still apply, Danielle thought hard about her decision. Then the man shouted out even louder than before, bringing the verdict to her troubled mind. His deafening tones confirmed her need to get out of there, so in the morning she decided to re-pack their bags, and then they would be gone. Feeling somewhat relieved by this conclusion, she relayed the good news to her children. She held Charlie in her arms, and she spent the next couple of hours wishing they would hurry up and pass.

Unable to get back to sleep, Danielle kept a close eye on the time. Pleased that the screaming had finally stopped, she was relieved to find that her children had at last managed to drift back off to sleep. Her head began to throb and dismissing the fact that she had finished off the bottle of wine, she blamed the inconsiderate man who had kept her up most of the night for causing the pain. Knowing full well that the boy had also contributed to her sleepless night, she couldn't help feeling sorry for him.

It isn't his fault that his father is a heartless man, whose only concern seemed to be his own selfish needs, she thought. She put full responsibility on the head of the brash Irish man.

The minutes soon ticked away, and the distant sound of her alarm clock confirmed that it was now time for her to get up. Conscious not to wake Charlie, very slowly she got out of bed. Her head was still being tormented by a dull ache, and as she stood up the pain got worse, and was soon accompanied by nausea. Closing her eyes, she took deep breaths in an attempt to stop herself from being sick. This seemed to do the trick, and to her relief the queasiness subsided. Her head was still banging, so pushing through the pain, and picking up her wash bag, she made her way to the bathroom.

A nice hot shower will help, she thought. The whole house was quiet, and the stillness in the air tried to convince her that last night had all been just a terrible nightmare. Forcing her thoughts onto the reality of what had really happened only a few hours before, her mind overruled the silence, and she walked into the bathroom.

Ten minutes later, feeling a little bit better, Danielle got out of the shower. Putting a towel around herself, she went over to the sink and began to brush her teeth. Her mind was distracted by thinking about phoning her mother, so she was oblivious that someone was trying to get in to use the bathroom.

"Hurry up in there!" said the broad Irish man, banging his fists on the door. "I need to use the toilet," he said not bothering to hide the irritation in his voice. The sudden loud noise made Danielle jump three foot up in the air, and nearly choke on the toothbrush.

"I can't put up with this every morning," he complained. "I live here too you know!" he continued.

Catching her breath, Danielle clenched her teeth so tightly together she could hear them squeak. Counting to ten, she breathed deeply and said, "I've just got out of the shower, so you'll have to wait." Her anger had got the better of her, and this was evident by the tone of her voice.

"I don't bloody believe this!" he replied. "And who the hell do you think you're talking to, you stuck up bitch."

Danielle was fuming and couldn't believe the audacity of the man! Once again, she found herself fighting the urge to give him a piece of her mind. Hearing his bedroom door slam shut, she got dressed, grabbed hold of her belongings and opened the door. Relieved to find the hallway empty, she made her way back to her room. As she passed her children's bedroom door, Billy opened it peeping his head out cautiously.

"Was he talking to you mum?" asked Billy rubbing his eyes. As the words came out of his mouth, the man came back out of his room and looked straight at Danielle.

"About bloody time too. You really know how to take the piss," he said glaring at her. "You women are all the same. You're all selfish."

"Hey, don't you dare talk to my mum like that," said Billy walking towards him. "You're the one who is taking the piss mate, you ignorant p…" Before he could finish his sentence, Danielle grabbed her son's arm.

"Billy!" she said pulling him back. "Don't bring yourself down to his level, it's not worth it."

The man's jaw dropped. Taking a step closer to them, he was just going to retaliate when Danielle, unable to control her tongue any longer, spoke out.

"You come anywhere near my son, I'll have you arrested," she spat at him. "Do you hear me? You are just a big bully who gets his kicks out of intimidating people smaller than you. Well I'm not having it! And yes, my son is right, you are an ignorant pig. Now get back to what you were doing."

The man stood frozen on the spot. No one had ever raised their voice to him, let alone a woman. Seething with anger, he just looked at her.

"Come on Billy," said Danielle pushing him into his room. "We're going to get our things together, and then we are out of here."

The man watched as Danielle closed the door, and a smile escaped through his lips.

Another one bites the dust, he thought, now laughing. "Good riddance to the lot of you," he shouted. "We got no time for the likes of you! What kind of a person brings up their kids by themselves anyway? Good bloody riddance is what I say." With that he went into the bathroom, laughing at the top of his voice.

A little later, Danielle and her three children were putting their bags back into the car. The need to get out of that house was so strong, that Charlie and Marie were still dressed in their pyjamas. After explaining that they would get ready for school at their Grandmother's apartment, they didn't argue.

Now, with everything packed in the boot, they all jumped in the car. Putting her foot down on the accelerator, Danielle made a speedy getaway from the house.

"Good riddance to you," she said, looking in the rear-view mirror. "Thank God we won't ever see that place again," she continued letting out a huge sigh of relief, the house disappearing behind them.

Seeing her mother's apartment block in the distance, Danielle quickly realised just how much she had missed being there. Pleased that there was still plenty of time for her to get Charlie and Marie ready for school, she drove into the car park. Noticing her mother's car parked in her designated space, she breathed in another huge sigh of relief because her mother was at home. Turning off the ignition, the children got out of the car, and grabbed their bags. They were pleased to finally be somewhere they could call home.

Christine came out of the kitchen when Danielle came into the apartment. Taken aback by the sound of her front door opening, Christine froze. Suddenly, a smile appeared on her face when her grandchildren came running down the hallway.

"What are you doing here?" she asked noticing that Charlie and Marie were still dressed in their night wear. "And why are you still in your pyjamas?"

Danielle followed in behind them and shared her account of the previous night. After explaining the many reasons why she chose to leave that place, Christine was left gob smacked.

"Oh dear Danielle, that man sounds absolutely horrible. You certainly made the right choice in coming back here."

"So, you don't mind then? Anyway, why aren't you staying at Phil's house," asked putting her bag down.

"No… No of course I don't mind, sweetheart, I couldn't bear the thought of you staying there with that family. It will only be for six months, so if you are happy with living in these cramped conditions for that long, then so am I," she replied, hugging her daughter.

"Oh, and Phil and I were having a few problems, so I decided to call it a day."

"Ah, that's a shame, but I guess you know what you're doing, and thank you for letting us move back in," said Danielle, a tear coming to her eye. "I think if I'd stayed there any longer then I would have gone crazy. We will be gone before you know it."

Squeezing her mother tight, Danielle looked over to the clock hanging on the wall. Realising the time, she pulled away from her mother's embrace and said,

"OK you two; it's time to get ready for school. I have got to go up to the council offices before going to work, so, chop, chop."

There was a break out of arguing about who was going to use the bathroom first, until Danielle intervened, and told Marie to get washed. Sulking Charlie slumped down on the settee, as he looked pitifully over at his grandmother trying to win the sympathy vote. Danielle couldn't help but laugh.

"Well, it didn't take long for things to get back to normal, did it mum?" asked Danielle putting her hands up in the air. "Are you sure you want us back?"

"God help me," Christine replied sarcastically. "I think I am going to need it," she laughed.

"That's funny, because that's what I said last night," said Danielle, thinking back to how desperate she felt, not so long ago.

"Maybe there is a God after all." Laughing again, Danielle picked up her bag and walked out into the hallway.

"Mum, I can't find my toothbrush!" Marie cried out from the bathroom. "What have you done with it? Mum, Mum!"

Taking a deep breath, Danielle turned around and looked back at her mother. "Or maybe not," she huffed. "Okay Marie, I'm coming. It's a good job my headache has gone."

Depression could feel its grip loosening. Holding on for dear life, it managed to cling on for a few minutes more. Then hearing the sound of a mighty wind, it began to panic. Its evil eyes flitted to and fro looking for the source behind the unwanted noise, but nothing could be seen. Aware that whatever it was, it was getting closer, Depression's hearing suddenly became impaired. Confused, it shook it's head in a desperate attempt to re-establish its bearings. Failing to do so, it froze as the noise began to get louder. Suddenly, a gush of wind that sounded like a torrent of water came out of nowhere. As it blew through Depression's soul less body, every bone rattled, enhancing the emptiness of its very being. Determined not to abandon its mission, Depression dug its claws in deeper.

"No, she's mine," it screeched into the air. "She's mine." Noticing a rumbling in the distance, Depression closed its haughty eyes. Then, armed with flames of fire, a

second gush rose up with so much force it dislocated the bones in Depression's scrawny talons. With no choice but to let go, it flew across the floor. Disorientated, Depression nursed its injury, and feeling embarrassed by its defeat, stood up. Looking over at Danielle, it was clear that she was being protected by this now known life source, and as it flew past her, it cursed her with every breath it had left in its conquered body.

"You might have won this battle," it screamed, flying into the darkness of its horizon. "But the war isn't over yet." Then, just like that, it disappeared.

Danielle, feeling more like her old self, drove Charlie and Marie to school. Her mind that had been plagued by a deep sense of fear was now free from this torment, and she was pleased to find that she was finally able to think straight. An unexpected sense of excitement bubbled in the pit of her stomach, which left her somewhat confused. Finding it hard to relate to this strange feeling, she soon put it down to being in control of her life again. She knew that the next few months ahead of her were going to be difficult, but the excitement she felt led her to believe that everything was going to be alright.

Her faith in seeing the positive outcome of her situation was heightened when the trip to the housing office proved to be a successful one. Having been told that it was perfectly fine to return to her mother's apartment, it gave her great pleasure to hand back over the keys to the horrendous house. She left the building feeling a whole lot happier. Seeing the glimpse of hope on her horizon again, she welcomed its return, wiped the memory of the previous night from her mind, and made her way to work.

Falling back into the stability of her routine that had very nearly been snatched out of her hands, she parked the car and walked around to the back entrance of the Kings Head. Sylvia, the landlady was in the kitchen making up the rolls for the lunchtime rush, and when Danielle walked in, she couldn't help detecting a bad atmosphere in the air.

"Morning Sylvia," she said, putting her bag down. "Is everything OK?" She was met by silence. Confused by the woman's ignorance, she repeated the question. There was still no response, so accepting Sylvia's lack of communication, she made a cup of coffee and went out into the bar. Determined to keep herself on an even keel, she blamed her employer's bad mood on the stress of running a pub and carried on with her work. Having been met by this attitude several times before, and aware that Sylvia was a volatile lady, she found it easy to ignore. In next to no time the bar was ready for opening. Managing to maintain her happier frame of mind, she unlocked the front doors, and her smile widened when Jimmy came strolling in. Walking straight over to the bar, he ordered his usual pint of bitter and asked her how she was. Taking five minutes to explain the sordid details of her night spent in that awful house, she finished by telling him that she and her children were now back at her mother's apartment.

"Well, I've got to say Dan, I take my hat off to you girl," he said, taking a mouthful of his beer. "You've certainly been through it, but yet you still manage to smile. You are one strong lady." Danielle could feel her cheeks burn up with embarrassment.

"I'm surprised you didn't hit him; I know I would have," he continued, screwing up his face.

Danielle was just about to reply, when another regular walked through the door. Picking up a clean glass, she began to pour his drink.

"Did you hear about Mick?" the customer asked, watching the glass fill up with beer.

Both Danielle and Jimmy shook their heads. Waiting to hear about another one of Mick's antics, Danielle listened half heartedly. Nothing surprised her where Mick was concerned.

"Well, I was just having a conversation with Sam, you know the bloke from the pub up the road, and he just told me that Mick's in hospital. He was taken in a couple of days ago. I don't know the details but apparently, he's in a bad way. He collapsed outside his parent's house."

Danielle's heart dropped.

"Oh my god, that's terrible," she said, panicking. "What hospital is he in?" Suddenly a wave of guilt flooded through her body. "I need to see him." Her mind went back to Skiathos, and picturing Mick's lifeless body by the pool, she remembered how scared she'd been then.

"He's in the infirmary," said the customer, watching the colour drain from Danielle's face.

"I'm sure he'll be alright though Dan. You know what Mick's like; he is as tough as old boots."

Turning around, the only thought on her mind was going to the hospital, so she went into the kitchen to fetch her bag.

"What do you think you're doing?" asked Sylvia angrily.

"I'm sorry, but Mick's in hospital, so I have to go and see him," replied Danielle putting on her coat.

"Oh no you're not young lady, you can't just leave. What about my customers?"

"Like I said, I'm sorry. He's my friend, and from what I have just been told it sounds really serious. Please understand."

Danielle looked deep into her employer's eyes and searched for any sign of sympathy, but to her horror she was met by a look of disgust and nothing else.

"Friend," she huffed. "That's rich coming from you. After the way you treated Mick on holiday, I would be very surprised if he wanted to see you."

Those spiteful words cut through Danielle like a knife. She couldn't believe what she was hearing.

"W…What do you mean?" asked Danielle trying desperately to stop her tears from escaping. Once again Danielle was confronted by silence. Knowing that the pub environment was a breeding ground for Chinese whispers, she chose to disregard the land lady's remark.

"Oh, I haven't got time for this," she said, feeling frustrated by the woman's ignorance. "I'm going. Mick needs me. I'm sure that Maggie will cover my shift."

With that, Danielle picked up her bag and walked out of the door. Leaving her responsibility at work behind, she got into her car and headed towards the hospital. The thought of Mick dying, made her take leave of her senses and forget about the consequences of her sudden work absence. She put her foot down and drove as fast as she could.

In no time at all she was in a queue at the hospital reception. Feeling very agitated because she had to wait, she nervously tapped her fingers on the desk. Finally, it was her turn to be seen, and after being told which floor Mick was on, she flew up the stairs. Confronted with a long corridor, she quickened her pace and went in search for the relevant ward. Panting for breath, she reached the end of the corridor, and to her relief, there it was. Her finger hovered above the buzzer as she hesitated. She was almost too scared to press it. She took a few seconds to take a deep breath and push her fear to one side. Some how she managed to find the strength and pushed the button down. After waiting anxiously for a few minutes to be let in, the door clicked open, and she found herself walking down another corridor. The distinct smell of the hospital overwhelmed her, bringing back the deep sense of fear that could have easily made her turn around and run away. Knowing that she had to be strong, she tried to ignore her need to escape, and just focused her mind on being there for her friend.

Danielle felt at a loss as she looked around. There were so many beds, and she couldn't see anyone who looked even remotely like Mick.

"Can I help you?" a young African nurse asked politely.

"Y...Yes... I am looking for my friend Mick... Mick, I mean Michael Fletcher," replied Danielle, her eyes still scanning around the room.

"He is just down there at the end of the ward. It's the last door on the left." Danielle thanked her and began to make her way down the corridor. Reaching the door, Danielle stopped. Concerned about not knowing what state she would find Mick in when she walked into his room, her heart began to beat faster in her chest. Searching for more courage to open the door, she took a very deep breath and reached out her hand. Gripping hold of the handle, she was just about to pull it down when the sound of someone calling her name stopped her. Turning around she let go and managed to raise a smile.

"Tracey," she said, taken aback to see Mick's wife walking towards her carrying two cups of coffee. "Tracey, I… I didn't expect to see you."

"Well I must admit, I didn't expect to see you either Dan," Tracey replied, smiling. "Mick will be so pleased to see you. He's been in here for two days, and no one else has bothered to come and visit him. This is such a nice surprise."

"I only found out today, and as soon as I did, I came straight up here," replied Danielle, quite shocked that she was his one and only visitor. "So, how is he? I was told that he collapsed."

"Yes, he did. He scared the life out of his poor mum and dad."

Putting the cups down on a nearby table, Tracey took Danielle's arm and led her away from the door. Lowering her voice, she said, "Danielle, Mick has had a lucky escape. From what the doctors have said, he's lucky to be alive. Don't be alarmed," she said reassuringly, seeing the look of fright rise up in Danielle's eyes.

"He is going to be okay as long… as long as he gives up drinking. It is seriously damaging his liver, and the consequences if he carries on are…." Hesitating, she shuddered. Then taking a deep breath she forced the words out of her mouth. "Fatal."

Danielle gasped. "But he does know that, right? The doctors have explained the seriousness of what he is doing to his body, haven't they?" asked Danielle, tears stinging her eyes.

Tracey, seeing the concern on Danielle's face, nodded.

"Yes, they have, and I know he would hate me telling you this, but…but he is so scared. I've never seen him so frightened, but I'm hoping that the shock will keep him away from that wretched poison. He says that he will give it up, he wants to give it up, but that's okay all the time he is in here. The real test will be when he goes home. He needs lots of help Dan, and good friends around him that can give him that help, not the low lives he usually hangs around with."

"I will do whatever I can Tracey, but…but how are his parents going to cope. They can barely look after themselves. No disrespect to them, but…but they are old." Tracey laughed.

"Oh, Dan, I know you mean well, and you are right to be concerned, that…that is why I have decided that he should come home with me. After all, I am still his wife, just about, so it's only fair that I take the responsibility of looking after him." Overwhelmed with compassion for Mick and gratitude to Tracey, Danielle smiled.

"Mick doesn't know how lucky he is to have a wife like you."

"Well who else would put up with him," laughed Tracey.

"I wouldn't wish him on my worst enemy." Tracey's comment made Danielle's smile widen.

No, me neither, she thought. Returning to the table, Tracey picked the cups back up.

"Okay Dan, shall we go in? Apart from the colour of his skin, he looks just the same, so don't worry. I know he will be so happy to see you," she said, walking over to the door.

Danielle nodded, and noticing Tracey's hands were full, she opened the door for her.

"Mick look who I found lurking around outside," said Tracey, walking over to the bed.

"Blimey Dan, you're a sight for sore eyes."

Disaster stood in the corner of the room. Its very being was filled with hatred, and he cursed the day that he gave Depression the responsibility of dragging Danielle into the pit of desolation. That callous fool can't do anything right, it thought picturing Depression's unpredicted demise in its shallow mind. Turning to Danielle, it became aware of a dim light around her body. It was just a hint, but even that was enough for it to know he had no choice but to leave her alone. Cursing the force that had snatched her out of its clutches, Disaster suddenly smiled.

You might have saved her for now, it thought slyly. "But what about him? Most of my work has already been done.

Turning its focus to Mick, it let out a blood curdling laugh. It's time for a new strategy, thought Disaster, its wicked smile widening. She will be putty in my hands my friend after what I do to you.

"Death!" it cried out, its rancid breath as potent as the grave, sucking the life out of the air around it.

"Get ready my friend, it won't be long now!"

CHAPTER

NINETEEN

A couple of days later, Mick was finally allowed home. Tracey took on the role as the perfect wife and catered for his every need. Grateful she had found it in her heart to let him back into the house, for the first time in years Mick felt that his life was worth living again. Having been prescribed some tablets to help him overcome the cravings, he was feeling like a new man. Not only did the medication help keep his addiction at bay, it kept the tormenting thoughts from coming into his mind. Tracey monitored all his calls, which she found a very easy task to carry out. Only two other people showed any concern for Mick's health, and one of them was her sister. The other was an old friend of the family, and Tracey had no qualms about this lovely man wanting to spend time talking to Mick. Tracey let out a huge sigh of relief. Things were finally getting back to normal.

In the space of two weeks, Mick seemed to be on the mend. Tracey had gone back to work, but he found himself feeling very lonely having to spend hours on his own. Danielle came to see him as often as she could, sometimes accompanied by Billy, but her visits were always short and sweet. Having worked most of his life, it was if his right arm had been cut off, as he found it very difficult to adjust. The car yard had been forced to shut down, and he was at a loss as to what to do. He not only felt lonely, but he was beginning to feel very bored.

Into his third week, the need to fix cars was just too strong to ignore. He therefore decided to do something about it and began to make some phone calls. When Tracey came home, he told her about his plan, and she froze.

"What do you mean, you are going back to work?" she asked in amazement. "You can't, the yard is closed so it's impossible. Unless…Unless you are thinking of doing it from here."

"You have just hit the nail on the head," he said, his face lighting up with excitement. "It would only be small jobs like changing the oil etc, and getting cars through their M.O.T's. I get so bored; it's driving me stir crazy cooped up in here all day."

Hesitating, he watched Tracey as she began to shake her head.

"Come on babe, it will be good for me, and it will bring in a little bit of extra cash, and… and I've even thought about getting Billy to help me. He has nothing to do either, and it will keep him out of trouble. Tracey, please. You know it makes sense." Taking her hand, he looked deep into her eyes. "Please. Pretty, please." Seeing the boyish grin on his face, she soon relented.

"Okay, but…but you must promise me that you will stay away from the pub. Most of your old customers drink in the Kings Head."

"I promise," he said, kissing her on the cheek. "Right, now I am going to phone Danielle. Oh, where did I put my phone?"

Danielle was over the moon when Mick asked if Billy could help him out. Even though she found him plenty of things to do whilst she was at work, she knew that he was bored. Her many attempts of trying to get him back into full time education proved to be unsuccessful, and she felt so frustrated because she always seemed to hit a brick wall. No other school would take him, and she feared that his lack of education would be a stumbling block to his future. But knowing that he loved working with cars, she felt that this would be a great opportunity for him to learn something constructive. Maybe one day he could even make a living out of it! Billy jumped at the chance when she told him the good news, and at last they felt things had started to go their way. Life was still difficult living at her mother's, but she was confident that it wouldn't be for long. Just as they were lulled into a false sense of security, things took a turn for the worse.

Billy loved spending time with Mick. He had only been working with him for a couple of days, and already he knew the mechanics of a car. Finding the workings of an engine easy to pick up, Billy woke up each morning eager to learn more. Confident he had at last found his niche in life; Billy began his day as normal. After finishing his breakfast, he kissed his mother and grandmother goodbye, and proceeded to go down to the bus stop. As he got into the lift an excitement stirred in the pit of his stomach. Welcoming the feeling, he smiled. His life finally now had some purpose to it, and he was convinced that in spite of everything that had happened in the past, things were going to be alright.

The lift reached the ground floor and after a few seconds, Billy began the first part of his journey to Mick's house. Looking at his watch, he was pleased to find that he was on time. His bus wasn't due for another five minutes, so he took a casual stroll over to the bus stop. After waiting for a few minutes, he could see his bus in the distance. Putting his hands in his pocket he searched for his fare. Pulling out a handful of change, he was just about to count out the exact amount, when a few of the coins fell out on to the floor. Realising the bus would be there at any minute; he cursed himself for being so clumsy, and bent down to pick them up. Suddenly he was consumed by fear, and froze as a familiar voice shouted out angrily, "Look who it is!"

"It's Billy the big mouth Green. I was wondering what happened to you." Recognising that the voice belonged to one of the boys who had set light to his house; Billy's heart began to race in his chest.

"Oh, so it is," said another voice. "It's payback time Billy boy!" Aware that the boys were getting closer, Billy found the courage to look up. The two boys were only yards away from him. Frightened they would hurt him; he dropped the coins in his hands and began to run back towards his grandmother's apartment building.

"Get him!" Shouted one of the boys, running after him.

"When I get my hands on you Billy, I am going to kill you."

Billy ran as fast as his legs could carry him, making his way over to the main entrance. To his relief, another tenant had just walked out of the building. Before the door closed, he ran inside, and with all his strength, he forced it to close.

"BILLY!" shouted both boys said in unison, banging their fists on the heavy security door.

"You can run, but you can't hide. We know where you live now," one of the boys continued, laughing loudly. "And I promise you we will be back."

Billy, without a second thought, ran up the stairs. His dreams of a new life were shattered, and the only thing on his mind was being in the safety of his grandmother's apartment.

Danielle was in the kitchen preparing two pack lunches, when she heard the doorbell go.

"It's OK Dan, I'll get it," shouted Christine as she came out of the bedroom. Danielle thought no more about it and carried on with what she was doing. Then the continuous sound of someone knocking on the door caused her to stop.

Who the hell is that? she thought.

Putting the knife down on the side, she walked out of the kitchen to investigate.

"Mum, what's going on?" she asked feeling confused.

"Billy, what on earth is the matter?" Billy came running down the hall and went straight over to his mother. Panting for breath he tried to explain but found that trying to talk whilst gasping for air was useless.

"It's OK Billy, just calm down sweetheart," Danielle said, putting her arm around her son. "That's it, deep breaths." A few minutes later Billy, feeling a lot calmer, began to explain what had happened at the bus stop. The whole family had now gathered around him, and when Billy mentioned that the boys had threatened to kill him, Charlie clung to his brother's legs and began to cry.

"I don't want you to die," he said, now sobbing.

Christine grabbed Charlie's arm.

"Nothing bad is going to happen to Billy sweetheart," she said, trying to prize his hands off Billy. Unable to force him to let go, Christine looked over at Danielle. Noticing that her daughter's face had gone red with rage, she took a step back.

"Yes, you're Nan is right Charlie," said Danielle desperately trying to keep her anger under control.

"Mum, hand me the phone. I am going to call the police. Those boys are not going to get away with this."

Danielle and Billy were left alone at the apartment to have a little time to process what had just happened. She was thankful that her mother had taken on the job of getting Marie and Charlie to school. She needed time to think! Shortly afterwards, there was a knock at the door. Danielle walked down the narrow hallway and opened the front door. Relieved to find two uniformed police officers standing outside on the landing, she forced a smile and invited them in.

With some persuasion from his mother, reluctant to speak, Billy took them through every detail of his ordeal.

"So, Billy," said the male officer when Billy had finished explaining. "Were you alone? Was there anyone else at the scene? Any witnesses there you can remember?" Billy, thinking hard, shook his head.

"Okay son. We will be in touch," he continued, putting his notebook into his pocket.

"What, that's it?" asked Danielle angrily. "Aren't you going to arrest those boys? Can't you see that my son is frightened?"

"Look Mrs Green, it's not that simple. There are no witnesses so I warn you now, it will be Billy's word against theirs. We know the boys well, but we will need proof to back up Billy's accusations. Of course, we will look into it, but whether they will be charged or not is another matter. I'm sorry, but that is the way it is."

Danielle felt like screaming.

"So yet again, those boys get away with ruining our lives. Some justice that is," she retorted sarcastically.

The officers, ignoring Danielle's remark, stood up and began to walk towards the front door. The other officer hesitated, turned around and said, "Off the record, if I were you Mrs Green, I would look for somewhere else to live. I understand you are temporarily homeless, so given your circumstances you stand a good chance of being re-housed by a different council. This call out will be recorded, so that is an option. Phone the station and they will give you a crime number. I know it will be a difficult choice to make, but it could be the best one for you and your family. Just think about it."

With that, the two officers left the apartment. Danielle shut the door and leant up against the wall.

I don't believe this is happening, she thought miserably. When is this nightmare going to end?

Mulling over in her mind what the police officer had said she suddenly found herself tempted by his suggestion. The need to get away from this place was beginning to over rule her need to stay, so walking back into the front room she decided to ask Billy what he thought. Not surprisingly, he agreed with the police officer and encouraged her to think seriously about moving away.

Looking at her son, she smiled.

"Okay, Billy I will, but now I have to get to work. Do you want a lift to Mick's?" Without any hesitation, he nodded his head.

"I love you mum," he said, giving her a hug. "Who needs a dad when I have got you?" She laughed.

"Yes, your father would have had a mental break down by now. Come on, let's get on with our day. Those boys might have taken our home, but they will never take our dignity."

Mick walked into the kitchen, his mind in a daze. He had spent most of the night tossing and turning and blamed his lack of sleep for causing his head to throb. The pain was so severe that it was beginning to make him feel sick. Opening the medicine cupboard, he pulled out a packet of pain killers. Confident that the pills in his hand were the answer to restoring him back to health again, he opened the adjacent cupboard in search of a glass. Suddenly a deep sense of fear gripped hold of him when he noticed the name of his favourite beer displayed across the pint glass in front of him. The word seemed to jump out at him, and then with no control of his thoughts he suddenly imagined it full to the brim of the substance it boldly advertised. The forbidden liquid conjured up in his mind brought with it a need for a drink that was so strong, he could actually taste it.

The overpowering urge warped his mind, to believe that this was the cure to overcome his physical state. In an instant he had forgotten about the pain that had brought him to the cupboard in the first place. Terrified that the image would take him right back to square one, he slammed the door shut with so much force, the sound of it echoed around the house. In a desperate attempt to rid his mind of the picture that tormented his sanity, he shook his head.

"No," he said, out loud determined to clear his head of this unwanted desire. "You've not going to get the better of me!"

Looking around the room, he suddenly remembered the medication the doctor from the hospital had prescribed for him. Now focused, he returned to the medicine cabinet, setting his mind on finding them. His heart sank when to his horror he found they were nowhere to be found, and he panicked. The feeling of dread fuelled his need for alcohol with so much intensity, it left him feeling deflated. It robbed him of the strength to push through this setback and his whole body began to shake uncontrollably.

"No!" he screamed. "I will not give in!"

His mind, now in complete disarray, began to play tricks on him, and he couldn't remember the last time he had taken his medication. Racking his brains, he tried to think, but it was no use, his mind was blank. Frustrated by his lack of memory, he sat down at the kitchen table and put his head in his hands.

Think man, think, he thought massaging his temples. Lifting his head up he noticed his mobile phone on the kitchen side, and out of sheer desperation he thought about phoning Tracey.

Yes, she will know what to do, he thought as he got up to retrieve his phone. Aware that his hands were shaking, he managed to find her number, and after a few attempts he pressed the call button. Tapping his finger on the work top, he waited for her to answer.

Out of the blue a voice cried out in his head.

She can't help you. No one can help you. Go on, you know what will help you…One drink won't hurt. Ignoring the taunting thoughts, he hung on to his sanity for dear life.

"Come on Tracey, answer the damned phone…Ah, Tracey," he said, relieved to hear the familiar sound of her voice.

"I'm sorry, but I cannot come to phone right now. If you just leave your name and number, I will get back to you as soon as I can." Realising that he had got through to her voice mail, he screamed and threw his phone on to the ground.

"Where are you when I need you?" he cried. "It's so bloody typical! You're work always comes before me!" Feeling as though his world was crumbling around him, he sat back down.

See, I told you she didn't care, the voice in his mind said calmly. What harm can one drink do? It won't kill you.

All of a sudden, the fretting stopped, when he suddenly recognised that it was his voice he could hear. Looking out of the window, he smiled.

What am I getting in such a state about?' he thought his smile turning into a grin.

Of course, one drink won't kill me. The doctors were exaggerating. They only say that to scare you. What do they know? I bet half of them enjoy a drink themselves.

At that moment, a picture of Tracey's face came to the forefront of his mind.

"What Tracey doesn't know can't hurt her. It will only be one after all… Now where's Billy?" No sooner had the words come out of his mouth, a wave of peace washed over him. All the traces of fear disappeared; leaving him convinced that he had at last gained control of the situation. Noticing his phone on the floor, he bent down to pick it up, when there was a knock at the door.

"Ah, there you are Billy," he said, thankful that his phone was still intact. "You're timing is perfect."

Unable to contain its excitement, Death hailed out a presumptuous cry of victory. Knowing that Addiction had been in control of Mick's worthless life for years, Death hadn't been the least deterred by Mick's few pointless days of sobriety. To Death, it had only added another element to his joy, and it was a bonus seeing this defenceless man fight against something that was way out of his control.

"Oh Michael, you are so predictable my friend," it said under its rancid breath. "The commandant was right; you will be putty in my hands." Leaving Mick in the capable hands of its Comrade in arms, Death, confident it's time to shine was only a dog's breath away, flew off triumphant to tell Disaster the not so long-awaited good news.

Mick opened the front door, and ushered Billy into the hallway. Relieved that Danielle didn't come in to say hello, he gave her a quick wave of acknowledgement, and shut the door behind them.

Confused by Mick's eagerness to get him inside, Billy looked at the man standing in front of him and suddenly became very concerned.

"Mick, what's the matter mate, you look like death warmed up."

"Oh, oh Billy it's nothing for you to worry about matey. I… I've just got a touch of flu that's all," lied Mick, grabbing his coat. "Now come on, I've got to meet a potential client in five minutes, so we had better get our skates on." Not only confused by Mick's unhealthy appearance, Billy found himself questioning his unusual choice of words.

"Potential client," said Billy mimicking a posh voice. "You sound like you have swallowed a dictionary."

Ignoring Billy's cheeky remark, Mick checked that he had his front door keys, and opened the door.

"Yeah, yeah, whatever you say Billy. Now get a move on. I can't be late," said Mick, desperate to get his hands round a pint of beer.

"OK, OK. So where are we meeting this potential customer," asked Billy walking towards the road. "Buckingham palace?" continued Billy laughing, but Mick was not amused.

"No Billy," answered Mick, abruptly. "I'm meeting him in a pub in town. That was the only place where we could meet."

Taken aback by Mick's tone, Billy came to a sudden halt. Turning around to face him, he said, "But Mick, you can't drink. How…how…"

"Billy, before you start telling me what I can and can't do, I can have a coffee. It's not unheard of you know. Anyway, just be quiet, you are beginning to sound like my wife. Now come on!"

Finding it hard to imagine Mick sitting in a pub drinking coffee, Billy wanted to laugh. Then remembering what his mother had said about his terrible brush with death, he suddenly felt really sorry for him.

Well I guess he knows what he is doing, he thought. He is a grown man after all. Putting his trust in Mick's faithful words, he caught up with Mick and they practically ran down to the town.

Mick finally stopped outside a pub that was unfamiliar to Billy. Looking sheepishly up and down the road, he grabbed hold of Billy's arm and pulled him inside.

"Right Billy, my client isn't here yet, so you go out into the garden, and I will bring out a coke to you."

Before Billy could argue, he found himself being pushed towards the back entrance of the bar. Even though it had been raining earlier, there was still a damp chill in the air. The thought of being outside in the cold garden at a place he had never been before sent shivers down his spine. Obeying Mick's instructions anyway, he opened the door and went and sat down at one of the tables. Realising that he had forgotten to ask Mick for a bag of crisps to go along with his coke, he got back up and went back inside.

Mick was totally unaware that Billy had returned, and Billy's heart dropped when he witnessed Mick gulping down a pint of beer, which was followed by a shot of vodka. Not knowing what to do, he just stood there and watched in horror and amazement, as Mick put the now empty glass down on the bar.

Mick what are you doing? he thought feeling sick to the stomach.

"Ah that hit the spot," said Mick, still oblivious to his observer. "I'll have another pint of your finest. Oh yes, and also can I have a coke for my young friend in the garden."

Billy couldn't believe his eyes and couldn't believe that Mick could be so stupid. Frightened that he would be seen, he ran back outside. All his dreams of becoming a mechanic were quashed there and then. He felt angry at Mick for giving him the false hope that he could help him actually become someone. He was so disappointed that he could have cried.

Why do men always let me down? He thought, suddenly reminded of his father. I can't trust anybody.

Pushing away the thoughts of a dad who had abandoned him for another family, he sat back down on the cold seat. Totally unprepared for coming face to face with Mick's problem, he closed his eyes, took a deep breath and swallowed down the pain that had brought up the memories of a childhood scarred by hurt and mistrust. An overpowering need to escape suddenly flowed through him. He opened his eyes and was just about to stand up when Mick came into the garden carrying his glass of coke. "Here you go Billy boy," said Mick putting the drink down on to the table.

"I won't be long mate. My client will be here any minute now."

The smell of Mick's breath was so strong; Billy thought he was going to be sick. Thankful that Mick had turned away, he suddenly said, "Don't lie to me! There is no so-called client, you just want a drink." His statement of truth caused Mick to stop in his tracks. Frightened to look him in the eye, Mick began to shake his head.

"Whatever gave you that idea? I have got a cup of coffee waiting for me at the bar," he replied guiltily.

Before another lie could reach his lips, Billy said angrily, "I saw you Mick, just now, pouring that pint down your throat, it was disgusting, and your breath reeks of alcohol. I…I thought you were different Mick, a true man, but…" Looking down at the ground he said, "But I was wrong, you are a lying bastard just like my old man."

Now it was Mick's turn to stand there in amazement.

"Look Billy, I'm sorry I lied to you," he said, finding the courage to sit down next to him. "It's just that…" Unable to find an excuse for his behaviour, he hesitated.

"So, I like a beer, what's wrong with that? You are far too young to understand Billy, but when you're old enough to enjoy a pint of beer, you will know exactly how I feel. I'm sorry I've made you angry, honestly I am, but…but old habits die hard. And you have got to admit, I am old… I am only going to have one drink, honest. Tracey will only nag at me, so I thought it was best to do it in secret. I am not like you're dad. I do actually care about you."

Mick put his arm around Billy's shoulder in a meagre attempt to comfort him into believing his words of honesty.

"But you could die, the doctors said so themselves," protested Billy shrugging off Mick's arm. "I hate you, you're selfish, and I don't want anything to do with you, do you hear!" Billy got up and began to walk away.

"Billy, where are you going? Please come back and talk to me."

"I am going to see my mum. At least I know I can depend on her."

With that, Billy disappeared back into the bar.

"Oh, to hell with you Billy, do what you want," Mick shouted out angrily. "Don't forget to give my regards to your mother!" Miraculously, his anger suddenly turned to joy, and he felt quite relieved that Billy had gone and left him on his own.

Good riddance to bad rubbish! Now, where was I? Getting up, he lost his balance and fell on the floor. Giggling to himself he managed to get back up, and after brushing himself down, he walked back into the bar.

"Barman if you would be so kind."

Danielle was passing a plate of sandwiches to one of her customers when Billy walked into the King's Head.

"Billy, what are you doing here?" she asked putting the plate down onto the bar. "Why aren't you at Mick's?" Ignoring his mother's questions, Billy went over to a table and sat down. Noticing that he did not look at all happy, Danielle began to panic. By the expression on his face something was obviously wrong, so after handing over the gentleman's change, she walked out from behind the bar.

"Billy, sweetheart what on earth is the matter?" she asked sitting down next to him. "Where is Mick?" Unable to look his mother in the eye, Billy stayed focused on the table and began to play with one of the bar mats.

"I don't know where he is," he lied. "And I don't care," he continued shrugging his shoulders.

"But... but Billy, Mick will be worried. Please tell me what has happened."

With his eyes still fixed on the table, Billy stayed silent. He knew full well that Mick was playing Russian roulette with his life the moment the pint of beer had passed his lips, but some how he felt a strange sense of loyalty towards him. Finding himself caught between a rock and a hard place, he decided to give Mick the benefit of the doubt in the hope that his gluttonous behaviour was just a one off. This optimistic outlook eased his conscience slightly, causing a smile to creep across his face.

"It was nothing mum," said Billy eventually looking up at Danielle. "I...I just couldn't get the hang of doing something, and it annoyed me, that's all. I just lost my temper." Something in his voice led her to believe that he wasn't telling the truth. But before she could say her piece, she noticed a customer up at the bar looking at her with a very distressed look on his face.

"Well if that's the case, I'll give you five minutes to calm down and then you can call Mick and apologise. Then you can get back to him. OK Billy?" she asked standing up. Billy showed no sign of a response, so she asked him again. "I said, OK Billy?"

This time Billy nodded his head slightly. Frustrated by this measly act of acknowledgement, she shook her head to show her disappointment, and made her way back over to the bar.

"OK Fred," she said to the now irate looking customer. "There's no need to look so worried mate. Now, what can I get you?"

Billy watched his mother walk away. Knowing that she was angry with him, he couldn't help feeling that he had done the right thing by hiding Mick's latest misdemeanour. Dealing with the brunt of her anger he felt he could cope with. She was his mother after all, and he was used to her bouts of moodiness. Most of the time she had every right to be upset with him, but knowing how much she cared for Mick, this time it was different. The thought of seeing the disappointment in her face was enough to justify his need to lie to her, and he didn't want to cause her any unnecessary pain. As far as he was concerned Mick's lapse was only temporary, and he was confident that when Mick realised the error of his ways, he would soon come to his senses and stop drinking for good.

Preoccupied by his thoughts, Billy suddenly became aware of his mother's presence when she put a glass of coke down in front of him.

"There you go Billy. You can drink this and then it's time to go. In the meantime I will phone Mick and then you can explain your lack of patience and hopefully he will understand and accept your apology. Then things can return to normal," she said, walking away from the table.

"But, Mum, I…"

"No excuses young man," she said raising her hand. "You will do as you are told and that's final." Billy cringed as he watched her walk behind the bar. Putting his hands on his lap, he crossed his fingers, willing Mick not to answer her call. Danielle pulled out her phone. Going into her contacts, she found Mick's number and pressed the dial button. Still feeling very angry with Billy's behaviour, she tapped her finger on the bar and waited patiently for Mick to pick up. After a few moments, she let out a sigh of relief when he finally answered.

"H… Hello, who's this?" Mick asked bluntly.

"Mick, it's me, Danielle," she replied, confused that he did not recognise her number. "I have got Billy here, and he wants to say s…."

"B…Billy's with you?" he said, before she could finish her sentence. "What the hell has he said? I bet the little sod has put me right in it."

"What are you talking about Mick? Billy told me what happened, and he just wants to…"

"Dan, he is lying. That boy is nothing but trouble… I told him that it would only be one, but he didn't listen… he never listens."

Danielle, confused by Mick's cryptic statement, tried to work out what he was saying. Then, hearing music playing in the background, her heart somersaulted in her chest.

"Mick, are you in a pub?" Afraid to hear the truth, she braced herself for the answer.

"Yes Dan, I am in a pub," he spat at her. "So, what if I am… It's a free country you know."

Danielle could feel every bone in her body weaken. She had not been prepared for this and had to sit down.

"So, when you said only one, you were talking about only one drink. Oh, Mick what are you doing, you know it will kill you. The doctors said so themselves."

"Oh, don't you start Dan; you're as bad as Billy! I would have only had the one if Billy hadn't been so controlling. I tell you Dan, that boy could push Mother Teresa into having a drink. Anyway, I do know what I am doing; besides the doctors always exaggerate. Now what was it you wanted? You are interfering with my drinking time!"

Sitting down on a stool, Danielle could have cried. Certain that his drinking days were well and truly over, she would have bet her life that he had put his past behind him.

How wrong could I have been? she thought, holding back her tears. Silence hijacked the phone line, and she was at a loss as to what to say. Her mind was telling her to shout at him for being so nasty about her son, but the shock of actually hearing his cruel words stunned her.

A few moments went by, and then Mick said, "Look Dan, I've got a lovely pint of beer sitting here with my name on it, so if there is nothing else, I am going to go… Goodbye." With that, the line went dead. Holding the phone in her hand, Danielle looked over to Billy, who was staring at her, looking very sad. Noticing that his eyes were glistening, she suddenly understood why Billy had left her so called sober friend. Her thoughts then went onto Tracey, and the devastation his drinking was going to cause, and her heart felt as if it was going to break. Feeling totally helpless, she took a deep breath, and walked over to her son.

"Sorry I didn't tell you mum, I just couldn't," he said, looking down at the table. "I thought it was just a one off, honestly I did. I can't believe he would be so stupid." Unable to contain his tears, he began to cry. Sitting down next to him, Danielle put her arm around his shoulders, and it took all her mental strength to stop her own tears from escaping.

"I should have stopped him. It's my fault," he sobbed.

Feeling every inch of his pain, she cradled her son in her arms.

"No Billy, it is not," she said, kissing the top of his head, feeling very angry for Mick's misplaced blame.

"Mick has a problem, and if anyone is to blame it is him. You are not responsible for what he does, he is a grown man and it is his responsibility, not yours, sweetheart."

Once again, Danielle was distracted by a customer standing up at the bar. Taking her hand away from Billy's shoulder, she held his face and looked deep into his eyes.

"Billy, I love you so much, you do know that don't you?" Unable to look his mother in the eye, he looked back down and nodded.

"You, Marie and Charlie are my responsibility, and my main priority. We need to concentrate on getting a new home. You know how much I care for Mick, but...but I have concluded that it's his problem, not ours. OK? We cannot help him, only he can help himself, so... so you sit here whilst I finish my shift, then we will go to the council offices together." Hearing her name being called for the third time, she kissed Billy on the cheek, and left him to serve her customer.

At last it was three o'clock and finally time for the shift to end. The past few hours seemed to drag by at a snail's pace, and Danielle thought her shift would never come to an end. Relieved that home time had arrived at last she and Billy left the pub and took the twenty minute journey, to the council offices which were in another borough. Confident that this new approach to her housing dilemma was going to be a good one, she put thoughts of Mick to the back of her mind, and walked arm in arm, with Billy into the building.

She explained her circumstances to the receptionist, and after taking down some details, she was directed to the homeless department on the first floor. Feeling very nervous, they walked up the stairs to the next floor where they were met by another receptionist who told them to take a seat and that someone would be out to see them shortly. Time managed to expand itself again, and after what seemed like hours, Danielle and Billy were called into one of the offices, a stone's throw away from the reception desk. Taking a deep breath, Danielle took hold of Billy's hand, squeezed it tight, and they walked in.

They were greeted by a tall African man, who offered them both a seat.

"Hello Mrs…" the man said, looking through his notes. "Mrs Green. Danielle, can I call you by your first name?" The polite manner of this man caught Danielle by surprise, so she nodded. "Great. My name is Samuel. I am the head of the homeless department. Now, what can I do for you?" The soothing tone of his voice instantly put Danielle at ease.

She quickly grew to like this man and began to tell him all about her situation. Taking him through the terrible ordeal of how her family had become homeless, she couldn't help noticing him shake his head. His expression, along with his action, portrayed pure disgust towards the perpetrators who had forced them into losing their home, and this led Danielle to believe that this man could help ease the burden of finding somewhere for them to live.

After a lengthy discussion, he was pleased to inform Danielle that she did have a case. Because of the near assault on Billy earlier that day, there was reasonable cause for them to be accepted onto that council, and as soon as an available property came up, he would let her know.

"It was nice meeting you Danielle," Samuel said, putting out his hand.

"What, that's it?" asked Danielle shaking his hand. "Don't you need proof from the police first?"

"I will sort that out, so you don't have to worry. You have been through enough. It's all a part of my job."

Showing off his pearly white teeth, Samuel smiled.

"Off the record, you seem a genuine person, and I am in no doubt that you have been one hundred per cent honest with me. It's disgraceful that those boys got away with what they have done to you, but I am a great believer in a higher power. Everything happens for a reason!"

Danielle looked into his dark brown eyes, when something strange happened. A wave of peace swept through her body, and she felt as though she could take on the world. Studying his face, she suddenly found herself wondering if she had seen him before. He had a familiar look about him, but she couldn't put her finger on it.

Feeling stupid, she ignored this strange sense of familiarity, and just nodded.

"OK Danielle, I will speak to you in a few days." Leading them to the reception area, they said their goodbyes, and Samuel walked back into his office. Danielle, putting her arm around Billy, left the building feeling very happy. She didn't know what it was about that man, but it was as if she was saying goodbye to an old friend.

Samuel walked behind his desk and opened the drawer. As he pulled out a leather-bound book, a multi coloured beam of light flew out of the pages and surrounded him. Closing his eyes, he smiled, put the book up to his chest, and started muttering something under his breath. The more words that came out of his mouth, the brighter the light became, filling the room with its glorious glow. Totally unaware of this presence, he did however feel a great power flow through him. Sensing the authority of his words, he found himself engrossed in their meaning and couldn't help but laugh. A few minutes later, he opened his eyes and the feeling disappeared. Still smiling, he whispered Danielle's name and took the book away from his chest.

"Amen," he said, placing it back into the drawer. 'Now, who's next?'

CHAPTER
TWENTY

*D*anielle spent the next few days trying to live her life as normal as possible. Having learnt from her past experience concerning how the council worked, she had now acquired a very pessimistic view over her situation. Convinced that it could take weeks to be re-housed, she kept herself busy and put the prospect of moving to the back of her mind. She hadn't heard from Mick, so Billy was back to having plenty of time on his hands, stuck in his Nan's apartment again.

Danielle had however, heard through the grapevine that Mick was once again, back at his parent's house. This didn't surprise her. The gossip mongers in the Kings Head were having a field day, and Danielle was becoming sick and tired of the constant talk of Mick's drunken exploits. The final straw came when one of the customers, who had no qualms in pulling Mick's name through the mud in front of the whole bar, joked about how he had seen him trying to chat up a young girl. Unbeknown to Mick, she was a drug addict who was just after his money to feed her daily habit. Mick's drunken attempt to woo this gold digger had ended up with him being totally taken for a ride, and it seemed the only person who couldn't see this was Mick.

Laughing at the top of his voice, the customer aired his views with so much spite; Danielle had to resort to shouting at him to shut up. Even though she still felt rather angry with Mick, she couldn't stand back and listen to this man's malicious opinion of him. Subsequently, there was deathly silence in the bar.

Hearing Danielle's raised voice from in the kitchen, Sylvia gave her a verbal warning, and in front of the all customers, Danielle was reminded of her place in the Kings Head. Ignoring Sylvia's public show of humiliating her, Danielle still found the strength to carry on working, despite her need to tell her just where she could shove her job.

As promised, three days after her visit to the council offices, whilst driving home Samuel phoned her with the news she had been waiting for. A two bedroom maisonette was now available, just for her and her children. He pointed out that it was still only temporary. He assured her that he would do everything in his power to find them somewhere with a secure tenancy. He continued by saying that it would take two months at the most, but he was confident that after that time her and her family will finally be settled in their new home. Suddenly feeling extremely happy again, Danielle couldn't thank him enough.

At last, she could see an ending to the nightmare that had taken over her life, and her future was looking bright again. Hearing the excitement in her voice, Samuel, conscious not to burst her bubble, took her through the minor details, and warned her that the accommodation was far from being a palace. Having only two bedrooms, he told her it would be a bit of a squeeze, but it was still in driving distance from her children's school. This didn't bother her in the slightest, she was just glad to have a place of her own. They finished off the conversation by arranging to meet the following day, where he told her he would take great pleasure in handing over the keys.

Danielle's next inevitable step was to call Sylvia. Knowing that she would not be happy with her for having to take another day off to move, she took a very deep breath, and made the call. Expecting to hear the wrath of Sylvia the moment she broke the news, Danielle braced herself. Then, as predictable as the sun rising, Sylvia began to rant and rave about being left short staffed yet again. Taking the phone away from her ear, Danielle couldn't help but laugh when the sound of Sylvia's fury came screeching out of the phone. Giving her a few minutes to let off steam, she quickly put the receiver back to her ear and had to raise her voice in order to ride over Sylvia's angry tone, to apologise. Her apology was ignored, because all Sylvia could think about was having to serve the customers herself. Trying her hardest to get her point across, Danielle suddenly gave up and went silent when she was told that her job was on the line if she didn't get her act together. Stunned by yet another bout of verbal selfishness on Sylvia's part, Danielle could take no more, so put the phone down.

"That woman is unbelievable," concluded Danielle, turning to her mother who had heard every word that come out of Sylvia's mouth. "I am starting to hate my job."

The following day after taking Marie and Charlie to school, Danielle, Christine and Billy headed off to meet Samuel. They had arranged to meet at the property, and

Danielle was pleased to find him already there. Being in the middle of autumn, a cold chill hung in the air, but thankful that it wasn't raining Danielle embraced this new day full of the joys of spring. She got out of the car and looked up at the house that was to become a stepping stone into the next chapter of her life. From the outside it looked like a normal semi-detached house, and it wasn't until Samuel led her around the back of the property that she realised it was split into two. Leading the threesome up a flight of steps, Samuel opened the front door and walked inside.

"Well at least we have this place to ourselves," Danielle said out loud, following closely behind him. Christine and Billy stayed silent, but they nodded their heads in agreement.

Samuel's short tour of the property began in the kitchen. The room was tiny, but Danielle was not put off. As soon as she had walked into the hallway, for some strange reason she felt right at home. It had an air of warmth about it which led her to believe that she was going to like living there. Her gut feeling was confirmed when he showed her the rest of the property. Even though Samuel had been right in saying it was small, the thought of having to spend the next couple of months in this cosy little maisonette appealed to her.

Noticing that the property was fully furnished, Danielle suddenly became confused. Knowing full well there was not enough room for her own furniture, she began to panic. As if to read her mind, Samuel explained that he had spoken to the manager of the storage company responsible for holding her belongings, and that he was more than happy to keep them there until further notice. Thankful for having one less thing to worry about, Danielle's anxieties instantly disappeared, and her excitement returned.

"So, what do you think Billy, could you put up with living here for a couple of months?" asked Danielle cheerfully putting her arm around him.

"I suppose so," he answered, looking around the room. "No disrespect Nan," he said turning to Christine. "But it will be good to have my own bed to sleep in, even if I am sharing a room with my smelly sister." The whole room lit up with laughter.

"OK then Danielle," Samuel said, reaching into his briefcase. "You just have to sign a form, and then the keys are yours." Five minutes later the form was put back into his briefcase, and Samuel, as promised, gave her the keys.

"I will be in touch as soon as a permanent property becomes available, but until then, enjoy your new home." Samuel shook Danielle's hand and smiled. Having complete trust in his words she looked him in the eye and smiled back at him.

"Thank you, Samuel, for all of your help; you don't know how much this means to me. I am so grateful for what you have done for my family."

Her statement of gratitude touched him, and seeing the genuineness of her smile, he felt compelled to hug her. Knowing that wouldn't be a professional thing to do, he refrained, and resorted to just tapping her on the arm.

"It was my pleasure. I was only doing my job, and it gives me so much satisfaction when a plan comes together. It makes it all worthwhile just to see the smile on your face."

Taking a deep breath, Samuel grabbed hold of his briefcase and began to walk towards the front door.

"God bless you Danielle and have a great day." With that, he walked out of the property.

"God bless?" said Billy laughing, as the front door shut. "Is he some kind of a religious nut? If there was a God, we wouldn't be in this mess!"

Ignoring Billy's remark, Danielle turned to her mother.

"Right, now we had better go back to your place mum. Time to get our things packed again. I must admit, I am looking forward to spending the night in a proper bed." Christine looked at her daughter and smiled. For the first time in weeks she saw the old Danielle resurface, and breathed in a deep sigh of relief.

"I know you are sweetheart," she said, pleased to see that she had returned. "I've got a good feeling about this Danielle, and I think that everything is going to be alright." Then turning to Billy, she said, "Anyway Billy, what if Samuel believes there is a God, you never know he could be right."

"Oh Nan," Billy said laughing. "You are such a geek. Of-course there isn't a God. That's probably the silliest thing I have ever heard you say. Please, those boys would have been put away for what they did if there was."

Danielle found herself agreeing with Billy, but the hurt look on her mother's face made her think twice about sharing her opinion. Instead, she grabbed hold of her mother's arm and said, "At least now you can have your life back Mum. I bet you can't wait to be able to watch what you want on the TV." Christine, diverted away from giving Billy a good telling off, suddenly laughed.

"You are right there, sweetheart," she said, patting Danielle's hand. "All of those children's programmes were beginning to drive me mad." Pleased to see the quick transformation in her mother's face, Danielle laughed.

"Come on then, let's get this show on the road."

Danielle and her children spent the first night in their new home. It had been hard saying goodbye to her mother, but deep down, Danielle knew it was the step in the right direction. She loved her mother dearly and wouldn't have a bad word said against her. But having left home at the tender age of seventeen, Danielle was used to having her own space, and being back under her rules and her ways again was like taking a step backwards. Danielle would never have dared let her feelings show; she loved her mother too much for that. Besides, now she could at last look forward, and was pleased to know that their relationship had not been affected by their 'forced' time spent together.

The next morning, Danielle got Marie and Charlie up for school. Marie had no qualms about getting up, but getting Charlie motivated proved to be a lot more difficult. Ignoring his pleas of wanting to stay in bed for five minutes more, Danielle struggled to get him to the breakfast table. He was not a happy little boy, and this was evident by his constant whingeing about having to go to school. Finally, after fighting an uphill battle, Danielle won him round by promising to take him swimming at the weekend. This seemed to do the trick when miraculously a smile replaced his pouting, and he ate his breakfast. By the time she returned from doing the school run she felt as if half the day had gone. Aware that her shift started soon, she managed to get the washing up done, and then went off to work. She felt really guilty for leaving Billy to fend for himself, but he assured her that he was OK as he had his computer to play on.

Pulling into the driveway besides the Kings Head, Danielle noticed that Maggie, another one of the barmaids, car was parked in the drive. Confused because she usually started her shift after Danielle's had finished. She couldn't help wondering what she was doing there so early. Noticing that she was five minutes late, Danielle got out of the car and walked quickly entering in by the side entrance of the pub.

"Hello Maggie," she said, noticing her making the lunchtime rolls. "I'm surprised to see you here so early. Where is Sylvia, she usually does that," she continued, pointing to the work surface covered in breadcrumbs.

"Err... I... S...Sylvia asked me to cover your shift," Maggie replied, surprised to see Danielle standing there. "She said that...."

"What do you mean cover my shift? She knew I would be in today," Danielle interrupted harshly. "Where is she? I need to talk to her."

Taking her eyes off Danielle, Maggie carried on buttering one of the rolls and said rather sheepishly, "S...Sylvia has had to pop out. She said she wouldn't be long...Sorry Dan, I didn't think you were coming in."

"It's OK Maggie, you weren't to know. I will wait for her in the bar."

Danielle made herself a cup of coffee and went out into

the bar. Surprised that the pub was ready for opening, Danielle's heart dropped. Knowing that the last conversation she'd had with Sylvia was a heated one, she suddenly found herself wondering if she still had a job.

Maggie came in carrying the tray of rolls and looked at her watch.

"Do you want me to open up Maggie?" Danielle asked forcing herself to smile.

"N…No, it's OK Dan," Maggie replied awkwardly. "I…I had better do it." Not being able to look Danielle in the eye, Maggie walked over to the main entrance and unbolted the door. She knew full well why she had been called in on such short notice, because Sylvia had spent half the night telling her the many reasons behind her sudden need for her to work. Maggie however didn't have the heart to tell Danielle about their employers backstabbing remarks. After all, she liked Danielle, and she knew that she was having a bad time lately, so left it to Sylvia to tell Danielle the bad news. She couldn't help feeling that Sylvia was wrong in her decision and found it hard to understand why she had been so harsh, but she had two young children of her own to support, and she didn't want to risk losing her job too.

Ten minutes later, the bar area was occupied by the many regulars who took great pleasure in coming into the Kings Head for their morning pint. Danielle sat at one of the tables and was surprised that no one had come over to talk to her. It was if she wasn't there, and she had a horrible feeling that something was very wrong. She even asked Maggie if she needed any help serving when she noticed that she was rushed off her feet, but all Maggie could do was shake her head. Looking up at the clock on the wall behind the bar, Danielle felt very uneasy. Knowing that Sylvia would be back at any moment, her nervousness grew with every minute that ticked away.

Hearing the back door close, she braced herself when Sylvia walked into the bar.

"What are you doing here?" Sylvia shouted across the room when she saw Danielle sitting there.

"After the way you spoke to me the other day, I am surprised you have the nerve to show your face in here!"

Danielle couldn't believe what she was hearing and stood up. Sylvia glared at her as if she was a piece of dog's muck on her shoe, but this did not deter her from retaliating.

"What do you mean, after the way I spoke to you?" asked Danielle walking towards her. "You're the one who as screeching down the phone; I couldn't get a word in." Trying to stay calm, Danielle proceeded to walk over to the bar.

"How dare you speak to me like that? I have bent over backwards to help you and your family, and all I get in return is your bad attitude. I have had enough of your feeble excuses. I told you your job was on the line and you overstepped the mark the minute you put the phone down on me. No one has ever, I mean ever, got away with doing that. I don't know who the hell you think you are. Now get out!"

Conscious that tears were stinging her eyes, Danielle used all her strength to stop them from escaping.

"But… but I have worked here for over a year and have never put a foot wrong. Who the hell do you think you are talking to me like that?" Her anger successfully overriding her tears.

"I know that Danielle. You were a good girl until you went away to Greece. That place changed you. You weren't the same when you came back, 'miss high and mighty.'" The spite in Sylvia's voice coincided with the look in her eyes, causing a pain to stab Danielle's heart.

"Maybe I have changed because of losing my home, did you ever think about that!" asked Danielle raising her voice. "That disastrous situation would be enough to change anyone, you, selfish, uncaring bitch!" Danielle could not help herself, because she was so angry. This woman had been her friend, or so she thought. She knew Sylvia could turn at any given moment, but she didn't think she would turn on her.

Ignoring her cry for sympathy and understanding, Sylvia laughed and said, "That's a joke, from the way you have been parading yourself around here you would have thought you owned this place," she continued. "Now, get out!" she said calmly.

Disaster looked on from the side lines and smiled. Showing off his greyish yellow fangs, it was in his element. Seeing this lady rip shreds out of Danielle, it revelled in the fact that it had instigated this ambush. Rubbing his scrawny talons together, it focused his stare on to Sylvia. Noticing one of its faithful servants clinging to her back, it ran its black ravenous tongue over its sharp razor like fangs and let out a blood curdling cry.

"Poor little miss warrior," Disaster said childishly under its stale, rotten breath. "What are you going to do

now? First Mick and now Sylvia, I wonder who will be next? Poor, Danielle." Knowing full well that it didn't have the authority to touch Danielle, it laughed again. Gloating, it prided itself on the fact that it could use this very obnoxious human being as bait and was certain to bring Danielle to her knees.

"And you have a nerve to call yourself a woman," Disaster said, its poisonous statement aimed at Sylvia. "Ha, ha, now that is a joke."

Digging its talons deeper into Sylvia's flesh, Pride looked over to its commandant and smiled. Having been born into a very controlling family, Sylvia had been easy pickings for Pride from an early age, and it was in no doubt that was where it would stay, until the day she left this gloomy world. Feeding on the anger that bubbled in her selfish heart, Pride turned its attention back to its host and concentrated on the job at hand.

"I knew you could be a miserable cow," Danielle said, resisting the urge to thump her one. "But I didn't have you down as a selfish, vindictive, malicious one too." Finding the courage, she went behind the bar to fetch her bag.

"Oh, no you don't Danielle," Sylvia screeched at her, putting out her hand. "Maggie give this woman her bag, she is leaving."

Both women's eyes locked together, Maggie leant down and picked Danielle's bag up from the shelf. Hesitating, she held it in her hand for a few moments more, and then gave it to Danielle.

"Now, get out of my pub!"

The whole room went deadly silent. Danielle grabbed her bag and stormed out. She had never felt so humiliated and could have cried.

Just when things were beginning to go my way, she thought getting into her car. Why is this happening to me? She looked up into the air. What have I ever done to deserve this? Putting her head onto the steering wheel, she began to cry.

"When is this ever going to stop?" she whispered, feeling cut up inside.

She was suddenly distracted when there was a tap on the window. Nearly jumping out of her skin, Danielle looked up and recognised a familiar face.

"Dan, Dan. What are you doing in there, babe? Is everything alright?"

Wiping her eyes, she wound down her window.

"Mick, oh Mick, no everything is not alright. Everything is such a mess," she replied, a new flood of tears flowing down her cheeks.

Mick walked around to the passenger side and got into the car.

"Oh babe, please don't cry. It will be alright, Uncle Mick will look after you," he said taking hold of her hand.

Out of her pity, she laughed and said, "You can't even look after yourself. I've heard all about your antics with that young girl."

"Oops, you have got me there Dan. I could have done with you that day. She was another woman just after my money. You would have sorted her out, I am certain of that.

But she was a good-looking girl, well through my beer glasses, she was anyway."

Danielle couldn't help but laugh again. Even though he had gotten himself in a right mess, she still loved him, and missed having him around. Smelling the alcohol on his breath, she looked him straight in the eye and boldly asked outright, "So you're still drinking then?"

Turning away from her in shame he nodded his head.

"But what about what the doctors said, you could die."

Looking back at her, he saw the concern in her face, and smiled.

"They exaggerate Dan, there's years left in me. Besides, I have cut down. I am in bed by nine o'clock."

Putting his arm around her, he pulled her to his side.

"Dan, I am so sorry about what happened with Billy. I feel terrible. The need for a beer was too overpowering, and I think it sent me a bit crazy. I have cut down since then honestly, I have. I stay well clear of the vodka now. Realising how it had jeopardised our friendship, I decided to calm it down a bit, and I don't get so drunk now. I have more or less cut out the vodka. That stuff was sending me mental; I was waking up in all sorts of places. I must admit though, I still have to have one or two, in the morning to get me going, but that is it. I stick to the beer during the day, it's better for me."

Searching deep into his eyes, Danielle was touched by his honesty and smiled. Seeing her big teary eyes sparkle, he was reminded of their time in Skiathos. Suddenly overcome with guilt, he brought his arm away and took hold of her hand.

"Danielle, I am so sorry that I wasn't there for you. I heard what Sylvia said to you, and I was halfway up the road.

Blimey, that woman has got a mouth on her."

Realising he was digressing he hesitated, took a deep breath and continued. "I made a promise to Panos to look out for you, and… and I let you down. I let all of you down. It is because of that evil vodka, and it is evil, believe me Dan, that I forgot all about your situation. At the time, all I could think of was myself."

All the honesty made him suddenly lose control over his emotions, and he began to cry.

"I am such a mess Dan, and…and I miss you so much. Please believe me when I say how sorry I am."

Now both of them were crying. Hearing the genuine sincerity and compassion in Mick's voice, the tears just flowed down Danielle's face. Seeing her pain escape through her tears, Mick suddenly laughed.

"Look at the pair of us," he said wiping her cheeks with his hand. "If only Panos could see us now?"

Unable to stop herself from following suit, Danielle chuckled and said, "He would think you were a right sissy."

Laughing out loud, he suddenly realised what she had said. "Hey, what do you mean he would think I was a right sissy; you're crying too babe."

Danielle let out a laugh that came from the bottom of her stomach.

"That's better Dan, you look so much better when you laugh. You are a beautiful young lady," he said seriously.

"Now I know you are drunk Mick," Danielle exclaimed. "You must be to say that."

"I told you I would tell you that every day, didn't I? So, I am a few months too late, who cares... Seriously Dan you are, and Panos thinks you are too. He told me so every day that I was out there with him."

Once again, consumed by guilt, Mick had to look away.

"But... But Mick what do you mean? He had another English girl on his arm. You told me so yourself, so why would he have told you that?" Confused, Danielle shook his arm. "What do you mean?"

Feeling the urgent need for a beer, he said desperately, "Let's get a drink first, and then I will explain. I need some Dutch courage; actually, I need a lot of Dutch courage. Come on, I will buy you a coffee." Curious to find out what he meant; Danielle nodded.

"Good, I will take you to the posh pub across town... Now let's get out of this hell hole." With that, Danielle pulled out of the Kings Head, and made her way to the other end of town.

Unbeknown to either of them, two entities were standing across the road watching their every move.

"Oh Michael, you are such a sissy," Death said howling out a cry of strength. "You cannot escape your destiny my friend."

"And what a destiny he has got," Disaster said smugly. "You are destined for a fall my friend and you won't be falling onto any rocks. But you will fall into the sea, a sea of fire!" Both entities cried out in unison, sending the birds fleeing out of the trees.

"And you, beautiful Danielle, won't be far behind him. We will see to that!"

His mind and body tormented by shame, Mick took their drinks over to where Danielle, was sitting at one of the tables. He dreaded having to explain what had really happened in Skiathos, but he really felt that she had the right to know. Placing her cup of coffee in front of her, he sat down opposite, and took a big mouthful of his beer. Looking at Danielle he smiled.

"It is only one sugar, isn't it, Dan?" he asked handing her a sachet of sugar.

"Yes, thank you Mick. So, about what you said earlier. What did you mean; Panos told you every day that I was beautiful? How could he when he was with her, his new girlfriend?" asked Danielle finding it hard to say those words.

"There was no her," admitted Mick taking another mouthful of his beer. Looking suspiciously at him, she put her spoon down, loudly on her saucer.

"What?"

"There was no girlfriend. I lied."

Completely dumbfounded she said it again, "What?"

"Panos wasn't seeing anyone else. All he spoke about was you. I was so out of it, babe. I think I had finally lost the plot."

Looking down he hesitated. "I…I told him that you had a boyfriend too. He was heartbroken, really heartbroken. I feel so ashamed for lying to both of you. I can't explain why I chose to lie. Before I had time to think, it just came out of my mouth. I suppose I was feeling guilty because I hadn't seen you. I hadn't kept my word to look after you. So, every time he asked after you, I said that I hadn't seen you, and he kept asking me why, so…so I lied and said it was because you had a new boyfriend."

"So not only did you lie to him, but…but you lied to me too. How could you do that? It broke my heart too you know, imagining him with another woman. It almost put me off men for life. I thought you were my friend."

Danielle was in shock at what she was hearing. It was hard to believe that some of the pain had in fact been needless!

"I know you must hate me Dan, but…but I have no excuse. After that, I felt so ashamed and worthless, so I tried to drink myself into an early grave. That's when I collapsed. I was mortified when I woke up. And… and then you came to see me in hospital, and I vowed never to drink again. I wanted to make it up to you somehow. Then I came up with the idea of Billy helping me, and that made me feel a little bit better. But then all my effort to stay sober went down the pan. I was one drink away from the pit I had managed to pull myself out of…one drink away Dan."

Hesitating again, he took a mouthful of his beer.

"And then it, gripped hold of me again. Just seeing a pint glass pushed me over the edge. How stupid is that Dan? A stupid pint glass, and now here I am. I'm left without a wife; without a home, and without a purpose. What a waste of space I am?"

"Mick you're not," Danielle said stroking his hand. "You are one of the loveliest people I know. Please don't say that."

"But I am Dan. How could I have lied to the two-dearest people in my life? I need to get my head tested." Tears welled up in his eyes, but conscious of not wanting to make a fool of himself in public, he took a deep breath to keep them at bay.

"But you're better now; well you're staying away from the vodka. I know you have had a drink, but this is the soberest I have seen you in ages. I know what drink can do to people; it makes them lie. Billy's aunt was an alcoholic, and she was forever lying. It's all a part of the problem."

Danielle took hold of his hand. "Mick, I forgive you babe. Actually, you did me a huge favour. It helped me get over Panos quicker, so no harm done."

"Do you mean that Dan," Mick said, looking up hopefully. A huge smile swept across his face when she nodded her head.

"I mean it Mick, from the bottom of my heart."

His happier expression prompted a smile to form on her face.

"You haven't got any more things you want to own up to do you?"

"No Dan, I don't." He lifted her hand up to his lips and gently kissed it. "Now what was big mouth Sylvia ranting on about earlier?"

Danielle proceeded to take him through the past couple of months of her life. When she finally finished, Mick was left stunned.

"Oh my God Danielle, that's terrible. You shouldn't have had to have gone through that on your own. What an idiot I am. See, that is exactly what I was talking about. I promised Panos, but, where was I? I was in the pub getting wasted. Oh Dan, I am so sorry. And that Sylvia, how dare she talk to you like that. I feel like going around to the Kings Head and giving her a piece of my mind, the old bat."

"Mick calm down. You will give yourself a heart attack. Anyway, I wasn't enjoying working there anymore. It was only fun when you were around. I have got over that now besides, I can find another job." Hearing her own words cheered her up. She had always found bar work, so she was confident it wouldn't be a problem for her.

"And the place where I am living isn't too bad. It will only be for a couple of months. You will have to come around for dinner. I know Billy will be pleased to see you."

"I will take you up on that," Mick said, feeling happy again, having forgotten about Sylvia.

Taking a sip of her coffee, Danielle suddenly thought of Panos.

"So Panos was heartbroken when he thought I had a boyfriend?" she smirked.

"Ah Dan, he most certainly was. I caught him with a tear in his eye many a time, well the times I can remember anyway. He was gutted."

"When was the last time that you spoke to him?" she asked as curiosity got the better of her and she just had to ask.

"A few weeks ago, I think. He was telling me that he and the family were moving to the mainland for the winter and opening up a travel agent there, or was it an estate agent," he said scratching his head. "Anyway, it was some kind of an agent. He has asked me to go over next March, but I don't know. I could be dead by then."

"Shut up Mick," Danielle said quite angrily. "You've got years left in you, you said so yourself. So, don't say stupid things like that," she said telling him off.

"Ok Dan, you're the boss. I'm sorry. Now, where was I?

Oh yes, Panos. He invited me over to his new house. I probably will go. It would be good to see him again. The only problem is, it won't be sunny, but hey, I can always go again in the summer."

"So, does that mean they have sold the hotel?" Danielle asked inquisitively needing to find out more.

"Oh no Dan, it's just for the winter. It would be interesting to find out what he does for a living there though. You never know, he could be a secret agent."

Danielle burst out laughing.

"Oh Mick, you are still a funny man...I have missed having you around," she said, her laughter quickly replaced by a deep sigh.

"Yes, me too Dan, me too. It's been so lovely talking to you, and I am glad we are friends again."

Danielle looked at her watch and suddenly realised the time.

"Mick, I have got to go," she said, drinking the last drop of her coffee that had gone stone cold. "Thanks for the drink, and thanks for your honesty. Give me a call, and we can arrange that dinner, OK?" Danielle kissed Mick on the cheek and said her goodbyes.

"OK Dan will do babe." He watched her walk away, and just as she was going to walk out of the door, he called out her name.

Danielle stopped and turned around.

"What is it Mick, I have got to go," she said tapping her foot.

"Are you sure you are going to be OK babe?" He shouted out across the room. Seeing her nod her head, he said one final thing.

"You look a million dollars Dan, and you are an absolute diamond. Don't you ever forget it? You were too good for the Kings Head anyway. Take care."

Waving her hand up in the air, Danielle walked out into the cold autumn air. Mick watched her walk away and smiled. He was so relieved to have gotten that cruel lie off his chest, and he was glad to have his dear friend back in his life again. Drinking down the last drop of beer, he went up to the bar to order himself another one. Resisting the urge to ask the barman for a large Vodka to go with his beer, he got his phone out of his pocket. Finding the appropriate number, he paid the barman and then walked back over to his table. Looking at the number on the screen, he decided to make the call that he had been putting off all day. Pressing the call button, he put the phone up to his ear and waited for the person on the other end of the line. To his relief a familiar voice answered, so Mick said cheerfully, "Hello Panos my ole friend, there is something I need to tell you. I hope you are sitting down."

CHAPTER

TWENTY-ONE

*I*t had been two months and Danielle had got used to living in the small maisonette. Having found another job in a nearby bar, she spent the weeks leading up to Christmas doing as many shifts as she possibly could.

Christine and Phil had sorted out their differences, and Danielle was pleased to see her mother happy again.

Things were looking up for the whole family, and the added bonus came when Danielle received a call from Samuel. He took great pleasure in telling her that a three-bedroom property had come up. The only problem was it was another half an hour away from Charlie's school. The thought of having to get up any earlier was too hard to imagine, so thinking carefully about her decision, she decided it would be easier to change his school. Samuel explained to her that one of the terms of the agreement of helping her get the tenancy was that she had to accept the offer, so left with no other choice, she broke the news to Charlie. He didn't seem to be put off in the slightest, so a viewing was arranged.

Christine accompanied Danielle to view the property, only this time she had to pick the keys up from Samuels's office. After giving her directions and the keys, she went off in search of their new home. Having to go out further into the country, they finally found the small town and the place they were looking for. She hadn't even heard of this place, let alone been there. It was a small block of flats and as she searched the letter for the house number, she suddenly realised that they were going to have to live on the second floor. The distinct smell of rubbish suddenly hit her as she walked onto the main entrance, making her feel very queasy. Putting her hand over her nose, Danielle and her mother walked up four flights of stairs. Her new home was along the short balcony, and finding it difficult to stay positive, once again she felt like crying. Being on the top floor was the only thing that pleased her.

At least we haven't got anyone living above us, she thought opening the front door. Christine, just as shocked as she was, put her arm in hers and they both walked in together.

Surprisingly the property was very spacious, and even though it was put down as a maisonette, it had two floors.

If it would have been a house, it wouldn't have been so bad, thought Danielle looking around the large kitchen.

"Well, I am in the middle of nowhere," said Danielle turning to her mother. "And I don't know anyone, but apart from that, I suppose I could grow to like living here," she said trying to convince herself.

Not quite sure if she could hear sarcasm in her daughter's voice, Christine chose to ignore her tone.

"It does seem a nice area though," she said, looking out of the window. "Maybe a new start in a new place is just what you and the children need," she commented turning back around, as she pointed to the kitchen wall. "It won't be that bad sweetheart. With a lick of paint, you could turn this place into a palace."

"If only it was that simple," Danielle huffed. "It would take more than that to make this place feel like home."

Christine walked over to Danielle and put her arm around her shoulder.

"Don't be disheartened Dan. Knowing you, it will be like home before you know it. Just give it a few months, and it will be as if you haven't lived anywhere else, I promise," Christine said, eager to bring a smile to her daughter's face.

"I wish I had your faith mum," Danielle said resting her head on her mother's shoulder. "I can't see it myself. But what choice do I have? I suppose I will just have to make the most of it. Come on let's see what else this potential palace has to offer." This time the cynicism is her voice was too hard to ignore.

"Don't be like that Danielle. Everything will work out just fine. I know you can't see it now, but...but it could be a blessing in disguise. You never know, you might have a single handsome man as a neighbour." Danielle laughed, and moved away from her mother's reassuring hold.

"Yes, you could be right there, a potential husband to go along with my potential palace," Danielle said, following through with her sarcasm. "Oh mother, please take off those rose coloured glasses." She walked out of the kitchen and went into the living room.

"Well, you never know," Christine shouted out, feeling quite hurt by Danielle's uncalled for remark. "I was only trying to help."

"I know you were. I'm sorry. Now, are you coming? Or are you going to stay there and conjure up any more silly ideas out of your warped imagination?"

Deciding to see her own wishful statement from Danielle's point of view, Christine smiled.

Well I suppose a sarcastic sense of humour is better than nothing, she thought, following Danielle's voice.

After viewing the rest of the property, Danielle locked the front door. Sighing deeply, she looked at her mother and forced herself to smile. Seeing the disappointment in her face, Christine couldn't help but sympathise with her daughter's situation. Knowing that Danielle had come from a lovely home, she found it hard to believe that it had actually come to this. She never imagined that her life could have changed so dramatically in such a short space of time, and she suddenly found herself resenting the boys that had brought her daughter to this place.

"Oh sweetheart, I really do wish I could make things right. I know it will be hard at first, but you will adjust. Look how far you've come? Anybody else would have cracked under the strain," she said holding her daughter's hand. "But you my girl are a fighter, and I am so proud of you for being so strong."

"Well I don't feel very strong. In fact, I could cry."

Danielle, aware that tears were stinging her eyes, looked down to the floor. "I am sick of fighting. Since their father left, that's all I seem to have done. Even leaving Panos was a battle I had to contend with. It's been nothing but heartache and pain with a whole lot of misery thrown on top. I'm sorry mum, but it's been so hard."

Sensing her pain, Christine put her fingers under Danielle's chin and lifted her face up to look at her.

"I know it is sweetheart, and it breaks my heart to see you in so much pain. Everything will work out, I promise. Don't give up. I will help, you know I will. Like I have said before, you are tough, just like me. It runs in the family you know." Danielle, searching for her hidden strength, looked at her mother and smiled.

"I know you are right, and I won't give up. What else could possibly go wrong?"

"That's my girl," Christine said, kissing Danielle on the cheek. "It's all downhill from now on."

Danielle and Christine soon arrived back at Samuel's office. Danielle signed the appropriate forms, and Samuel informed her that he would arrange to get her furniture delivered the day after next. He also explained that because she was coming from another council, the tenancy was only secure for two years. After the two years were up, her name would automatically go down on the permanent housing list, and then, if there were no problems, she would be re-housed in a three-bedroom property.

"I know two years seems a long way off, but believe me Danielle, it will fly by," he said placing the forms in her file. "I have got a good feeling about this Danielle. One day you will look back on what has happened, and you will be grateful that it ended well. I'm convinced that it will all turn around in your favour. I would bet my life that this is a blessing in disguise." Remembering that was what her mother had said earlier, she sighed. Still not convinced, Danielle forced herself to smile.

"If you say so Samuel," she said glumly. "So, I will be moving into the property in two days. Is that correct?" Samuel nodded his head.

"At least you will be moved in before Christmas. I know that two thousand and one will be your year Danielle. New beginnings bring along new blessings." Danielle couldn't take any more of his happy outlook on life, so without any more delay, she said goodbye.

"Goodbye Danielle," Samuel said, as she rushed through the door. "And good luck. Not that you're going to need it!" With that, the door slammed shut, and Samuel was never to see Danielle again.

Danielle spent most of the following day sorting out Charlie's new school. The exchange was easier than she had anticipated, and she was relieved to find that Charlie wasn't the least bit upset with having to make new friends. To him it was just another adventure, which seemed to ease the guilt she felt for disrupting his young life. The past few months had proved only too well how easily he had adapted to change, and this was evident by his demonstration of the carefree attitude that he showed.

Danielle had thought about changing Marie's school as well, but it just stayed at that, a thought. Doing some research into her soon to be neighbourhood, she was pleased to discover that there was a large shopping complex only a few miles away from where they were going to live. So, being a strategic place for commuters, it was only one bus ride away from Marie's school. Now that she was at secondary school and very grown up for her age, Danielle knew Marie could be trusted with using this method of transport. Grateful for this small blessing, she spent her last night wandering what the future held for her and her children. The thought of being so far away from everyone was really daunting for her, but the reality of why they were moving to the middle of nowhere, managed to stall her anxieties from ruling her mind.

The following morning, Danielle and her children said goodbye to their cosy little maisonette and set out to pastures anew. Whilst on their journey into the unknown Charlie, being Charlie, spent most of the time asking questions. His inquisitiveness took centre stage, and Danielle found it hard to concentrate on the road. Unable to find all the answers to his "but what if this mum, and but what if that," she soon became quite agitated especially as she had a million unanswered questions of her own! Sensing his mother's struggle and need to keep focused, Billy quickly intervened. She smiled as she listened to him taking great pleasure in sharing his views on the new computer game that had just come out. For the first time ever, she was thankful for having an ally in that blasted computer consul that had managed to take over both her son's lives.

Marie, however, was very quiet, and Danielle couldn't help wondering what was going through her daughter's mind. Having enough things going on in her own mind she blamed Marie's silence on yet another upheaval, and focused her thoughts on seeing her furniture again. Visualising the layout of the house her children had grown up in, she was somewhat surprised that this picture had somehow managed to manipulate her thoughts, and out of the blue, a deep sense of sorrow washed over her, to the extent that she suddenly felt like crying.

Confused that a three-piece suite and a dining room table had the power to bring her to tears, she tried to figure out why these inanimate objects made her feel so sad. Then just as unexpected as her initial train of thought, she suddenly came up with the answer. Harsh reality kicked in wearing size nine boots when she realised that her furniture was the only tangible piece of evidence left, of a life that seemed too long ago. This formidable conclusion was enough to bring her to breaking point, but she was aware that she had to stay strong. Not only did she have to keep up appearances for her own state of mind, but she had to keep on top of things for the sake of her children.

Trying her utmost to push these feelings aside, she deliberately refocused her mind onto the positive side of her situation. Finding this a very hard task to carry out, her thoughts were suddenly interrupted when Charlie asked if they could get a dog. Thankful for this diversion she laughed, and very politely told him "no."

Looking into the rear-view mirror, she caught a glimpse of her now sorrowful looking son and smiled. He didn't seem at all worried about where they were going all that bothered him was the fact that he couldn't get his way.

"Charlie, the last thing we need is another mouth to feed," she said, her concentration going back onto the road. "Having a dog is a big responsibility sweetheart, and it's hard enough looking after you three." There was a moment's silence. Returning to the reflection of her son's face in the rear-view mirror, Danielle's smile widened. Reading the look on Charlie's screwed up face, she instinctively knew what was going on in his mind. Waiting patiently for a response in defence of his claim for a pet, she took a deep breath and prepared herself for the oncoming debate. Then, just as unpredicted as his last comment, his face softened when he said, "OK, can I have a fish then?" The whole car roared with laughter.

"Oh Charlie, you are so funny," Marie said, unable to keep a straight face. "You go from one extreme to the other."

Charlie looked across at his sister, confused.

"I don't want one out of a stream," he said seriously. "I want one out of a pet shop." Once again, the atmosphere in the car lit up with laughter. Thankful that the heavy mood had lifted, Danielle set her mind back onto where they were going, only this time she had a smile on her face.

Driving up a winding country lane, Danielle's heart began to beat faster as she neared her destination. Although she had been there before with her mother, somehow, she had managed this time to come in on a different route. Relieved to be going in the right direction, she carried on up the small hill. Silence quickly replaced the juvenile chit chat that had recently ruled the air waves, as all three of her children were captured by the tree lined landscape. Not a word was spoken as she reached the top of the lane, and even she found herself taken in by the view. The picturesque landscape was short lived when Danielle turned the corner and was met by a row of houses that resembled a council estate not far from her original home. The beautiful scenery that had captivated her imagination only a few moments ago had managed to hide what lay ahead, and Danielle's flit of a happy ending disappeared as fast as the winding road behind her. Deciding to take this harsh reality on the chin, Danielle carried on through the small village until she reached the block of flats, she was now to call home.

In next to no time, carrying her bag of belongings, she led her children up the stairs to their front door. Still in silence, she opened the not so welcoming door that had seen better days, and they walked in. Throwing their own bags down, Billy and Charlie ran up the stairs to put a claim on their bedroom. Marie was not as willing as her brothers to venture out into the unknown, so followed her mother into the kitchen.

"Well Marie, what do you think?" Danielle said looking around the empty room. "Do you think you will grow to like it here?"

"I hate it," Marie replied angrily. "I will never like it here, never!"

"Oh, please don't say that sweetheart," Danielle said putting her arm around her daughter. "I know it will be hard to adjust, but…but you will make new friends. I know you will. You just have to give it time."

Not quite sure who she was trying to convince, Danielle walked over to the window. Fully understanding Marie's lack of enthusiasm, her mind wandered to only a few months ago, and for the first time in months she remembered how safe she had felt in Panos's arms. Now feeling as if he had been just a figment of her imagination, she found it hard to believe she had actually lived that wonderful dream. Somehow the thought of Panos having another girlfriend had eased the burden of having to leave him behind, but since Mick had revealed the lie that her strength had been built on, she found it hard to shake off the tiny piece of hope that had manifested itself out of this unwanted truth. Shaking her head, she quickly brought her mind back into the present.

As far as she was concerned, feeling secure herself wasn't an issue anymore. It was now her job to be the safety net, her job to keep the wolf from their door, her job to keep them safe, and no memory of what used to be would ever change that. Pushing Panos out of her thoughts, Danielle sighed.

I have got to stay strong, she thought, still looking out of the window.

As she stared out over the tops of the houses opposite, she noticed a lorry pull up outside. Hoping it was the removal van that contained her furniture, she stood motionless, and watched two men jump out and look up at her kitchen window. Holding a piece of paper in his hand, the driver nodded and made his way over to the main security doors. A few seconds later, the sound of a buzzer coming from the hallway startled her, and she was pleased to discover that her furniture had finally arrived.

A short while after the two men began the tiresome job of hauling her belongings up the four flights of stairs, Christine showed up raring to get stuck in. She had come dressed for the part, so without any hesitation she began to help Danielle get organised. The task of finding a new home for Danielle's furniture was a long drawn out process, but by the end of the day everything was in its place. Her next step was to empty the many boxes that were scattered around her living room, and Danielle was pleased to know that sorting them out would keep her busy for the next couple of days. Being surrounded by the remnants of a past life that had slipped from her mind, she at long last felt at home.

She had now accepted that this was where she was supposed to be and made a promise to herself to look only to the future and to leave the past behind. The disaster of losing a home she adored, had pulled the rug right out from under her, and that she knew, could not be changed. But somehow that did not matter now, because even though she was in the middle of nowhere, the ball was in her court again, and she was now in control. This liberating feeling strengthened her ability to override the storm that had brought chaos into her life, bringing with it the distinct impression that everything was going to be alright.

Christine stayed until the children were tucked up safe in bed. The day had definitely taken its toll on everyone. Danielle said goodbye to her mother and had a long soak in the bath. The only thing that dominated her mind was the thought of getting into her own bed, and this she found was a great comfort to her. Having washed away the evidence of a day's worth of labour, she pulled back her covers and got into bed. The smell of fresh linen danced up her nostrils as if to welcome her back into its comforting arms, and for the first since being with Panos, she felt safe.

This heartwarming feeling prompted the memory of Panos to enter her mind, causing her to squeeze the quilt tighter.

"I wonder if I will ever see you again," she whispered, allowing her mind to wander. Then closing her eyes, she imagined it was him she was holding, and drifted off to sleep.

Destruction, knowing that its time to shine was getting closer, came out of its hiding place and began to glide up the stairs. The peace and quiet that hung in the air made its scaly skin crawl, but this did not deter it from reaching the top. Entering the smallest of the bedrooms, it went over to Marie's bed and stood beside the pine frame.

"Aw, so you hate it here do you little girl?" it said in a sickly voice, watching her take small intakes of breath. "Well if I have anything to do with it that will never change!" Resisting the urge to touch her, it turned around and walked back over to the door. Entering the room next to Marie's, Destruction smiled cunningly when it saw Danielle's sons sleeping peacefully in their beds. Gliding over to Billy, it almost felt sorry for the young man whose life was going to change dramatically.

"Billy boy, oh Billy boy, what have I got in store for you?" Looking around the room, Destruction's sinful eyes lit up when it noticed a poster displaying its name on the wall. The poster was advertising the name of a new computer game, causing Destruction's evil smile to widen.

"Destruction by name and Destruction by nature," it whispered, its heartless chest puffing up with pride. "I am going to enjoy using you as a pawn in my game of life; oops I mean game of strife." Wanting to laugh at its wicked way, Destruction managed to stay quiet. Licking its thin cracked

lips out of pure pleasure, Destruction turned its attention to Charlie.

"Little chickens for easy pickings," it said, reaching out its scrawny razor-sharp talons. "Oh. The innocence of a young child, it almost makes me wish I had a heart." It smirked. "But I don't. Oh dear, you won't be innocent for long, little boy." Unable to contain its excitement any longer, Destruction flew out of the room. Noticing a dim light coming from Danielle's room, it flew down the stairs and went out of the door.

"I am going to have so much fun," it screeched as it made its descent. "You are not going to know what hit you." Crying out in victory, Destruction disappeared into the night.

CHAPTER
TWENTY-TWO

Christmas came and went, and Danielle found herself actually looking forward to the New Year. Knowing that it couldn't possibly be worse than the last, she set her mind on what two thousand and one had in store for her, and nothing else. Mick came over as much as he could and spent most Sundays, with Danielle and her family. His drinking habits were much the same, but even Danielle had to admit that it was better having him around, even if he was drunk.

Marie had finally accepted their new home, but she was still adamant that she would never make friends with anyone. Her daughter's stubbornness made Danielle's blood boil, and many times she had to control her tongue. Convincing herself it was still early days, she held on to this fact, and carried on regardless. Charlie, however, was the complete opposite and loved telling Danielle about the new friends he had made at school. Thankfully, her son's brighter attitude lightened the load for her, and it pleased her to know that at least Charlie was happy to meet new people.

Billy, like his younger brother, welcomed the challenge of finding new friends. Being a very confident boy, it wasn't long before he found himself accepted by a group of teenagers who lived nearby. One of the boys, James, went to the same college, so they spent most of their time together. Danielle took a great liking to Billy's new friend. Having been brought up in the area, James was a tremendous help in helping her find her way around the area.

A few days after meeting James, Billy met a local girl called Jasmine. Having been blessed with a head of beautiful shiny dark brown hair, Danielle was really struck by this girl. Jasmine was a year younger than Billy, and Danielle couldn't stop herself from thinking that they would make such a lovely couple. She made her feelings known to Billy, and he took great pleasure in telling his mother that Jasmine was indeed, his girlfriend. This good news did please Danielle. Watching them interact with each other, she found it hard to believe that only a short while ago they were strangers, but now here they were, and it was as if they had known each other for years. The other thing that struck Danielle about Jasmine was her perseverance in wanting to get to know Marie. Marie stood her ground at first and constantly brushed off Jasmines effort to become friends. But Jasmine, determined not to give up, kept offering her the hand of friendship hoping that Marie would finally give in and take it.

To Danielle's relief, her powers of persuasion finally paid off when Marie began to spend more and more time with Jasmine. To Danielle this was the icing on the cake. It had taken longer than first anticipated, but now Marie was showing signs of happiness.

At last Danielle felt that life was finally getting back to normal, now that all three of her children had settled into their new way of life. Over the next couple of months, she spent time redecorating her home, and still managed to find the time to work. Christine was true to her word and helped Danielle in any way she could.

It was a beautiful crisp Sunday morning. With the turning of the season on the horizon, the wonderful sound of bird songs could be heard, and Danielle couldn't have wished for a lovelier start to her day. Spring was definitely in the air, and the sun shone so bright, it was as if it was giving a preview of what was yet to come. As per usual, Danielle spent most of the morning cleaning, and preparing the Sunday roast. Mick was due to come over at lunchtime, so she was conscious to get everything ready for when he arrived. Billy had spent the night at Jasmine's, and Danielle had made it quite clear that he had to be home for lunch.

Having done all her housework, she looked at the time. The dinner was nearly ready, and Mick was usually there by the time she dished up. Giving him another ten minutes, she asked Marie to lay the table and proceeded to get the plates out of the cupboard. Just as she put them on the worktop, the buzzer went, and she was pleased to be told by Charlie that Billy was on his way up. Thankful that at least Billy was home on time, she began to serve up the food.

"Mum, is it OK if Jasmine stays for dinner?" Billy asked as he bowled through the door. Danielle nodded her head and told Marie to set another place at the table. The ten minutes were up, and Danielle was now very concerned about Mick's whereabouts.

"Dinners ready!" she shouted. Two seconds later the kitchen became overrun by her hungry children, and she watched in amazement as they each grabbed their plates.

"It's like feeding time at the zoo," she said, trying to hide her anxieties. "I don't know it's like having a room full of monkeys." They ignored their mother's remark and took their plates out into the lounge.

Oh Mick, where are you? she thought looking at her watch again. Just as she was about to get her phone, the buzzer went. Running out of the kitchen, she picked up the intercom phone and breathed in a deep sigh of relief when she heard Mick's voice. Pressing the button, she heard the downstairs door click, and waited the few minutes it took for Mick to make his way up. Mick turned the corner just as she opened the front door.

"It's about time Mick, you had me worried," she said, instinctively looking over the balcony. "Where have you been?"

Mick was walking towards her, and as she turned to face him her jaw nearly dropped to the floor.

"What the hell happened to your face?" she shrieked, confronted with a man she barely recognised.

One side of his face was completely purple, and his eye was so swollen he could hardly open it. The other side wasn't nearly as bad, but the lump under his eye stood out like a golf ball. Reaching out her hand, she took hold of his, but he pulled it away.

"Dan, sorry babe," he muttered through his swollen lip. "That hurts." Lifting his arm up into the air, Danielle saw that his hand was just as purple as his cheek.

"Mick, what has happened? Were you attacked?" she asked leading him into the hallway.

"No Dan, I fell. I came out of the pub last night and tripped up the kerb and fell on my side. Bloody kerbs, they will be the death of me," he said, trying not to laugh. "Ouch Dan, it really hurts."

Danielle took him into the kitchen and pulled out a stool.

"There you go Mick, sit down on here."

Mick struggled to pull himself up, but with a little help from his friend, he managed to sit down. Danielle watched as he resisted the pain as he lifted a carrier bag that hung around his wrist.

"Here you are Dan; this is for you."

Taking the bag from him, she looked inside. Just as she had expected, it contained six cans of beers and a bottle of wine.

"I thought you could have a nice glass of wine to go with your dinner," he said wincing. "And, of course the beers are for me. Be a darling and open a can for me. I am gasping."

Danielle took the bottle out of the bag and put it in the fridge. Then she opened the can and gave it to him. Mick watched her every move and let out a deep sigh when the ice-cold remedy for his thirst came into his hand.

"Ah, that hit the spot," he said trying to hide the pain the beer had induced on his smarting lip. "Even a fat lip can't come between me and my friend," he said, patting the can with his unscathed hand. "Now, where's my dinner. I am starving."

Danielle laughed, and told him to go into the lounge and she would bring his dinner through. Mick obeyed Danielle's command, and after nearly falling off the stool he went into the front room. As expected, he was bombarded with questions as he walked through the door. Billy was the one who asked the most, and by the tone of his voice, Danielle could hear that he was getting very angry. The next voice was Mick's, and she couldn't quite hear what he was saying, but when the atmosphere changed to laughter, she guessed that whatever he said, it was enough to make them laugh.

The evening soon drew in, and Mick and Danielle were now alone watching the TV. Billy had gone around to Jasmine's house; Marie had gone with him and Charlie was upstairs playing on the computer. Having got through most of the bottle of wine, Danielle was now very relaxed in the company of her dear friend. Feeling quite tipsy, they shared stories of old times before they had met and reminisced back to the days when they both were happy. Mick spoke about his life before drink and took her through every detail of his wedding day. By the time he had finished, the rendition of that special day had reduced her to tears. Deciding to get her own back on him, she shared the nightmare of a marriage she had to endure, and her mission was made complete when Mick also began to cry. Looking at each other all teary eyed, they laughed.

"What a sorry pair we are," Mick said, carefully wiping the tears from his eyes.

"That we are," Danielle replied, reaching for the bottle of wine. Draining every last drop out of the bottle, she lifted the glass.

"Here is to two very sad people. Cheers."

"With two very sad stories to tell," Mick said, bringing the can to his now numb lips. "Here's to us Dan." As he took a mouthful of his beer, he suddenly realised that he was dribbling. Noticing the strange look on his face,

Danielle looked down to his shirt and saw the remnants of his can of beer all down the front of it. This caused her to shriek out with laughter. Once she had started, she just couldn't stop.

"OK Dan, it's not that funny," Mick said wiping his drink. "It comes with age you know."

Seeing her crying with laughter brought a smile to his face. "That's better Dan, you look so beautiful when you laugh." Danielle looked at him. Her laughter was brought to a halt, and she smiled.

"Oh, Mick you are so sweet, even when you look like you have gone ten rounds with Mike Tyson," she said, laughing again.

"Dan, don't laugh I am being serious…I…"

Just as he was about to finish his sentence, his phone began to ring in his pocket. Annoyed by the disturbance, Mick managed to get it out, and looked at the screen.

"It's Panos," he said, a confused expression washing over his face. "I wonder what he wants." As he lifted the phone to his ear, he suddenly remembered talking to him in the pub the previous night. His confusion soon lifted, and the reason behind his Greek friend's call became apparent to him.

"Panos me ole mate, it's good to hear your geek, oops I mean, Greek voice again my friend."

Danielle's heart somersaulted in her chest.

"Yes Panos, it would be great to see you again," Mick said a few minutes later, looking at Danielle. "I have someone here who wants to speak to you." Danielle, in sheer terror began to wave her arms in the air.

"No," she mouthed, shaking her head.

"OK, I will pass you over." With that, Mick handed her the phone. Reluctant to take it, Danielle just glared at Mick. Egging her on with his hand, she took the phone and held it up to her ear.

"H...Hello Panos," she said shakily.

"Danielle?" Panos questioned. "Is that you Danielle?" She was the last person he had expected to hear on the other end of the line.

"Y...Yes Panos, it is me." Her eyes still on Mick, she slapped him on the leg. "How are you?"

Nearly two thousand miles away, Panos was sitting at his desk stunned. When Mick had explained that he was with someone who wanted to speak to him, he thought that it was Mick's mum, who had always enjoyed taking time out to talk to him. Expecting to hear her frail voice, his heart missed a beat when it turned out to be Danielle. Suddenly, he found himself overcome with sadness, and for a split second he imagined her back by his side again. Aware that his father was in the next room, he pulled in his train of thought, and took a very deep breath.

I will not let myself be swayed by her voice he thought straightening his posture. I have come too far for that.'

"I am very well, thank you. How are you?" he asked sternly. Listening to the harshness of his tone, she was grateful that he was now a person whom she no longer recognised.

Clearing her throat, she replied. "I am also very well, thank you. So...so what reason do you have for ringing Mick?" As soon as the question left her lips she cringed.

What a thing to ask, she thought looking at Mick, who was thinking the same thing.

"Why, Michael is coming over to see me next week, and I…I wanted to go through the last-minute details with him," replied Panos his tone staying the same. "I am looking forward to seeing my crazy, English friend…H…How are your children?"

"They are fine, we are all fine." There was an awkward silence.

"OK then Panos, I'll pass you back to Michael…I mean Mick. Take care." Danielle treated the phone in her hand like it was a bomb just about to go off and thrust it onto Mick's lap. She had never been so relieved to give someone their phone back, and she found it hard to believe she had actually been madly in love with that man.

Mick finished off his conversation, and after arranging to meet Panos at Thessaloniki airport, he hung up the phone.

"Blimey Dan, what is the matter with you two. Anybody would think you were too scared to talk to each other. What happened to the love birds who couldn't take their eyes off one another? I don't know; you two need your heads banged together."

"Well, that wasn't the man I fell in love with Mick," Danielle said thoughtfully, drinking down the last drop of her wine. "And I suppose I am not the same girl he fell in love with either. It's amazing what time can do. We come from different worlds."

Mick nodded.

"Yeah, I suppose you do have to move on. Maybe one day I will where Tracey is concerned." Taking a deep breath, he sighed.

"So, you are going to see him next week?" Danielle intervened before being reduced to tears yet again.

"Yeah, yeah, the flight is booked for next Sunday," Mick replied, his thoughts going back onto Panos.

"I must admit I am looking forward to seeing my crazy Greek friend again."

"That's what Panos said. He is looking forward to seeing you too." As the words came out of her mouth, Danielle felt a twinge of jealousy. This sudden feeling took her by surprise, and she found herself wondering why he had acted so cold towards her. Retraining her thoughts back to what she had just said, the feeling disappeared.

"Well, I am sure the both of you will have a great time," she said looking at her watch. "Is that the time? I had better get Charlie to bed."

"OK Dan, I am going to go now. I've got to meet someone at nine." Mick picked up his phone and called a taxi. Danielle kissed him on the head, and then went upstairs to bath Charlie.

When Mick's taxi arrived, finding it hard to stay balanced, he shouted goodbye up the stairs and wandered out of the door. For some strange reason his head was being tormented with pain. Usually he would have blamed it on drinking too much, but this pain was unfamiliar to him. Brushing it off, he shut the door behind him, and made his way down to the car.

Danielle heard the front door close, and as soon as it did, Panos came into her mind. Finding it hard to shake off the fact that he had been so distant, she tried her utmost to push this unwanted feeling aside. Even Charlie's rendition of Mr Blobby couldn't get rid of the picture of Panos that tormented her thoughts. Marie and Billy returned home shortly afterwards, and Danielle was sure that having them to talk to would do the trick. But still, there he was, at the forefront of her mind, and she could have cried.

With Charlie now in bed, Marie in her room doing her homework, and Billy downstairs watching a film, Danielle decided to get an early night. Fighting the urge to buy a second bottle of wine, she took her own advice and went into her room to get ready for bed. Panos had still managed to dominate her mind, so after she changed out of her clothes, she opened her wardrobe and stared at the black bag that held the cuddly toy Panos had bought her. Without contemplating the consequences of what emotions, she would be stirring up, she grabbed hold of the bag and took it over to her bed. Rummaging through the contents she found what she was looking for, and for a few moments held the soft cuddly bear in her hand. Then, with no control of her tears, they began to flow. Pulling it into her chest, tiny droplets of salty water dropped down onto the bear's head, and the same sense of loneliness she had experienced many months ago gripped hold of her weakness and consumed her. Reliving her first night without Panos, every part of her body ached for his touch, so she lay down on her bed and closing her eyes, imagined him lying beside her. Remembering his gentle caress, she took her mind back to their last night. The power of the memory filled with passion felt so real, she forgot where she was.

"Oh Panos, I want you so much," she cried out into the empty darkness. The onslaught of tears kept coming, and she was certain that her newly repaired heart was near to breaking point again.

Opening her eyes, she looked out of the window and caught a glimpse of the moon. Staring through the vastness of the night sky, she suddenly realised what she was doing to herself. So, just like that, she shut her mind off to the memory of what used to be. Throwing the bear on to the floor, she wiped her eyes and pulled the covers over her head.

"You have got to be strong," she whispered, her mind going back to the awkwardness of their conversation earlier. "My Panos no longer exists."

Unable to shake off the feelings of yesterday, Panos lay in his bed thinking about Danielle. It had taken him weeks to get over losing her, and he was sure he had put her to the back of his mind. Then, just like that, the power of a voice deemed forgotten took him straight back to when his Danielle was in his arms. A freight train full of emotions crashed through the barriers of his heart, its only mission was to destroy, and Panos found himself in a place he vowed never to be in again.

The pain of watching his Danielle walk out of his life all those months ago accompanied the vision of her beautiful face, and it was as if she had only just left. Tears began to sting his eyes as he imagined his arms wrapped around her. Caught up in the memory of feeling her soft skin, his mind went back to their last night together, and he could almost smell the sweet scent of his Danielle. Remembering every moment of making love to her, he closed his eyes. Aware his tears were near to escaping, he sighed heavily.

"Oh Danielle, will I ever see you again?" he whispered into the lonely night air.

Knowing the possibility of that happening was as far away as the moon, he shut his mind off to the pain, and thought about the person he had now become. A stronger and more determined Panos had risen out of the ashes of the devastation Danielle had left behind, and all that mattered to him now were his two businesses.

That Panos no longer exists, he thought, wiping the memory of Danielle out of his mind. My life has gone on.

The following week passed by with the greatest of ease, and Danielle was pleased it had been trouble free. Sunday was upon her yet again, bringing with it the normal routine. It was lunchtime, and the tantalising smell of roast chicken filled the air, tormenting her empty stomach. Whilst washing up the dishes, she found herself thinking about Mick.

He will be on the by plane now, she thought, feeling quite envious because he was on his way to Greece. Aware that the next step of her thought process would lead her to Panos, she stopped her mind from wandering down that road, and forced herself to smile. Having pushed her resentment to one side, she focused her mind on his journey and carried on with the chore at hand. Mick had phoned her that morning on his way to the airport, and by the happy tone of his voice, he was very excited. Before saying their goodbyes, he had promised to phone her the moment he landed on Greek soil, and this eased the burden of worry that automatically came with him travelling anywhere on his own.

Thinking back to the phone call, Danielle's smile widened. Opening the cutlery drawer, she was just about to put the knives away, when the sound of her mobile phone ringing distracted her from her thoughts. Guessing the identity of the caller, she went over to the table and picked up her phone. Expecting to see her mother's name displayed on the screen, she suddenly became confused when it wasn't her.

"Mick?" she questioned, checking the time. "Is everything alright? I wasn't expecting to hear from you until later." There was a moment's silence. "Mick?" she said again, now feeling very anxious.

"They... They wouldn't let me on the plane," Mick finally said. "Dan, they wouldn't let me on the plane. Can you believe that? They wouldn't let me on the blasted plane." Detecting the disbelief in his voice, Danielle sat down and prepared herself for what was coming next. Almost too scared to ask, she took a deep breath.

"Oh Mick, what have you done now?"

"I haven't done anything!" Mick replied defensively. "They said I was too drunk, so they wouldn't let me on. What a joke! So, I fell up the stairs, I do that all the time. You know what I am like? I am not drunk; I am just clumsy. Since when has falling over been a crime? Of course, I tried to reason with them, but... but the captain refused to listen, and he said I was a liability. He actually used those words Dan. How dare he... Me, a liability? I have been called many things, but never that!"

Danielle was lost for words. Then, picturing his bruised face in her mind, she suddenly understood the captains concern.

"Then, to top that, they had me escorted off the plane. I was so embarrassed," Mick continued, becoming more and more irate.

"So, I'd had a few drinks, but I wasn't drunk. The nerve of that man! Someone's head is going to roll because of this, and I hope it is his, the self-righteous pig!"

"OK Mick calm down babe or you will give yourself a heart attack," Danielle said, trying not to laugh.

"The captain must have had his reasons. They sell alcohol on the plane. There must have been more to it than what you said babe. Were you rude to anybody? Did you come across as aggressive in any way? I know how nervous you get when you fly." Another moment of silence fell.

"Well…" Mick said, his voice almost turning to a whisper.

"Yes Mick. Well?" Danielle had a horrible feeling there was more to the story than Mick had first relayed.

"Well…They…they tried to confiscate the bottle of vodka that was in my pocket," he said childishly. "They wouldn't have known I had it if it hadn't fallen out of my pocket when I fell over those stupid bloody steps!"

"So, I am guessing you didn't hand the bottle over," Danielle remarked sarcastically.

"No, I did not!" Mick said, raising his voice. "That bottle cost me twenty quid!"

"Oh Mick, what am I going to do with you?" The reality of his problem was like a slap around the face, and Danielle realised to her regret, that Mick was no better now than before he had gone into hospital. Finding it really hard to feel sorry for him she said, "So what are you going to do now?"

"Well, what do you think I am going to do Dan? I am getting a taxi to my local pub, and I am going to get really drunk. See you later."

The phone went dead, and Danielle could feel tears burning her eyes. Fearing for her friend's health, it broke her heart and the tears began to flow. Knowing that there was nothing she could do, she took a deep breath, wiped her face and carried on with the dinner.

CHAPTER

TWENTY-THREE

*A*pril arrived. The change of season was evident by the display of pink blossom on the trees, and Danielle welcomed spring as if it were a long-lost friend. The sweet sound of bird songs filled the air, and to her this was a sure sign of greater things to come. She loved everything that spring stood for and it was her favourite season. Now that the long drawn out nights were coming to an end; she could sense the atmosphere changing around her. People seemed a lot friendlier, and everyone she saw had a huge smile on their face. At last, she wasn't made to feel like an outsider, as she was greeted with a nod of acknowledgement that went hand in hand with the smiles. Knowing that in the small village she lived in, it would probably take years to become a part of this close-knit community, this did not bother her in the least. She was just happy to feel content in her surroundings at long last.

Mick's weekly visits soon fizzled out. It had gotten to the point when the only time she saw him was when she travelled into town, and this didn't happen very often. Still wanting to stay in contact, she made the effort to phone him a few times a week, and he always seemed pleased to hear her voice. It was very rare for him to call her, so when she received a missed call from him, she was more than surprised. Predicting that something must be wrong, she called him back straight away, and waited anxiously for him to answer.

As soon as the phone started ringing, Mick's voice was on the other end of the line.

"Hey Dan, thanks for getting back to me babe," he said excitedly. "I…I am going to Skiathos at the end of the month and…and my mate was coming with me, but he has pulled out, so… so I was hoping you would come with me. The ticket has been paid for, so it wouldn't cost you anything."

Hesitating, he gasped for air, and continued. "I can help you out with spending money. Think about it, Dan, I would rather you were with me. Anyway, you can keep an eye on me then. So, what do you think?" Danielle was gobsmacked. The thought of seeing Panos again sent her heart racing ten to the dozen. Her recent sense of normality and moving on once again left in tatters.

"But Mick, I can't go back," she said trying to calm her racing heart. "You know I can't…Panos and I…"

"Dan," said Mick interrupting her. "I have spoken to Panos and he can't wait to see you," he lied. "He told me so himself."

Mick was sitting in the pub and couldn't help but smile. His friend had cancelled at the last minute that part was true, and Mick had been disappointed to say the least. Then he had thought about Danielle and through the haze of his drunkenness he had suddenly come up with a cunning plan.

"What, Panos actually said that?" asked Danielle taken aback as the picture of Panos came to the forefront of her mind. Surprised that her wall could fall so suddenly, she found herself wanting to go back.

"Yes, he did Dan, honestly," Mick replied still smiling. "Please come with me. It's not the same without you. Please."

Danielle, blinded by Mick's willingness for her to go, stayed quiet. Now her mind was racing along with her heart, and she didn't know what to do. Deep down she knew that she didn't want to miss the chance of seeing Panos, but the reality of having to walk away from him again, tried to persuade her otherwise.

Shaking those crazy thoughts out of her mind she said, "I am tempted Mick, I would be lying if I said I wasn't, but I am over Panos now, and I would be a fool to go back. We haven't got a future; we both know that. Sorry, but it's a no."

"OK Dan, I know the situation, but you are still friends, good friends, no one can take that away babe, and…and it's a holiday. I know you could do with a break. Sleep on it, and I will phone you tomorrow. Speak to you then. Bye." Without giving her anytime to reply, he put the phone down.

Mick, what are you trying to do to me, she thought as the phone went dead. You will be the death of me.

No sooner had he put the phone down on Danielle, Mick ordered himself another beer and after finding the appropriate number, pressed the call button. As his drink was placed in front of him, a familiar voice could be heard on the other end of the line.

"Ah, Panos me ole mate, Have I got a surprise for you."

Panos listened to what Mick had to say and couldn't believe his ears.

"What Danielle actually said that Michael?" he asked his heart rate increasing with Mick's very word.

"Yes, she did my friend. She told me that she couldn't wait to see you. She is really looking forward to it," Mick said grinning like a Cheshire cat. "And, before you say anything, she is fully aware that you have no future together, she just wants to be friends, honest."

Panos was dumbfounded. Somehow it pleased him to know she wanted to see him again. Reminded of what his brother had said all those months ago, a smile crept across his stern face.

I know I am strong enough to cope with her being here, he thought, setting his mind on her return. I am no fool. After all, I am a different person now.

"Well, I suppose that is great news then, Michael. Hopefully I will actually get to see you this time," said Panos laughing. "I look forward to seeing you both." Something from deep within him tried to convince him otherwise, but being a tough businessman, he chose to ignore the feeling.

Danielle's night was a restless one as she thought about Mick's invitation. She couldn't shut her mind off from the huge dilemma. She couldn't stop thinking about Panos and tried to decide whether she was strong enough to spend a week in his company. She had spoken to her mother earlier that evening, and even though Christine had expressed her reservations, she encouraged her to go, positive that a holiday was just what she needed. She still did not know what to do, however. Her mother had also reminded her of her new-found strength that the last few months had equipped her with, and she found herself being swayed in favour of going to Skiathos. By the time morning came, she had talked herself in and out of going so many times that it had made her feel dizzy. Finally, after reaching a conclusion to the dilemma that had kept her awake most of the night, she decided to go as she thought what the hell! I can cope with just being friends, I'm not an idiot. Besides, I'm a different person now, she thought trying to convince herself as she chose to ignore the alarm bells ringing in her head.

It was a bright sunny Wednesday morning and Danielle began her day in the usual way. Now with the trip to Skiathos only a week away, she had arranged to meet Mick in town to go through the final details of their holiday. The plan was to meet at a well-known bar as he had promised to treat her to lunch.

The journey took her half an hour, and all the way there her mind raced with curiosity, about how Panos would react to seeing her again. She was also curious to see how his father would react to her now that she and Panos were just friends. Every now and again her imagination would tempt her by trying to remind her of the love that they had once shared, but she quickly disarmed those thoughts and tossed them aside. It had taken a lot of willpower to overcome those feelings that had tried to win her over, but after lots of practise, she now had it down to a fine art. Pleased it had taken losing her home to build up her strength, she looked at her trip as a well-deserved break and nothing more.

Soon Danielle was walking through the bar in search of Mick. Noticing him sitting alone staring out of the window, she made her way over to the table and sat down.

"Penny for your thoughts Mick," she said patting his hand.

"Oh, hello Dan," Mick replied solemnly, still staring through the glass. "I was just thinking about how crappy my life is."

"Don't be like that Mick! This time next week we will be sunning it in Skiathos," Danielle said cheerfully attempting to lift his spirits.

"I know Dan, but I feel so useless. My life sucks."

Danielle watched as Mick took his focus off the hustle and bustle of life outside and proceeded to take a mouthful of his beer.

"Stop feeling sorry for yourself. It could be a lot worse you know. Now put a smile on your face, we are supposed to be celebrating not commiserating."

He looked at her and smiled. His face was clear of any bruises, and she was pleased to see him looking like his old self again.

"Yes, I suppose you are right Dan. I woke up in a bad mood and I just can't seem to shake it. Another one of these will help," he said raising his near empty glass. "What are you having Dan?"

"That's the spirit Mick, and seeing as we are celebrating, I will have a glass of white wine please," she replied, rubbing her hands together.

As Mick walked away, Danielle glanced out of the window. An old lady across the road caught her eye, and she watched mesmerised as the old lady went over to a rubbish bin and began rummaging through its contents. Whilst wondering what could possibly have happened in that poor old ladies' life for her to resort to going through grubby old rubbish bins, Jimmy the regular from the Kings Head, walked past the window. Banging her fists on the glass to get his attention, he looked up and saw Danielle's beaming face. Signalling for him to come in, he nodded his head and moments later was up at the bar ordering his drink.

She hadn't seen Jimmy for weeks, and she looked forward to catching up on all the gossip. To pass the time, Danielle took a menu out of its wooden box, and began searching through the many dishes it had to offer. She decided to push the boat out and chose a full English breakfast. Then Jimmy came over and sat down opposite her. Confused that he had come over alone, she asked where Mick was.

"Oh, Mick," Jimmy said rubbing his temples.

"He has just bumped into an old mate. He said he won't be long." Danielle nodded her head and couldn't help noticing that he was in pain.

"Jimmy are you OK mate?" she asked seeing the colour drain from his face. "You look awful. What's wrong?"

Taking a mouthful of his beer, Jimmy forced himself to smile.

"Dan, I have got to be honest babe, I am not feeling at all well. I have been back to the hospital and Dan its bad news."

Hesitating, he took another mouth full, but this time it wasn't followed by a smile. In fact, Danielle thought he was going to cry.

"What is it Jimmy? You are scaring me now," she said, unable to hide her concern.

Jimmy took a deep breath. "My brain tumour has started to grow again. It had shrunk, but…but it is getting bigger, only this time it's growing at a faster rate than before."

Danielle was shocked. Lost for words she looked over to the bar, wishing that Mick would hurry up.

Boy, I could do with that drink, she thought, overcome with sadness.

"Dan," Jimmy said, leaning across the table. "I'm scared babe, really scared. To top it all, I received a phone call from my youngest daughter's teacher yesterday. She was concerned because Holly kept crying in class. When they asked her what the matter was, she said that she didn't want her dad to die. I was crushed. I don't want to leave my babies behind… I am a tough man Dan, but the thought of that just breaks my heart."

Aware that her tears were desperately trying to escape, she used all her strength to keep them under control and placed her hand on his arm. Unable to find any words to help ease his pain, all she could do was hold it tight. Sighing, Jimmy looked at her hand and then looked up at her.

"Sorry Dan, I haven't even asked how you are. So, how are things with you?" Danielle was just about to answer when Mick came back over to the table and sat down.

"Blimey Dan, my life just gets worse. That bloke I was just talking to has just let me down with some work. My day just gets better and better, not!"

Danielle just glared at him. Feeling her anger rise from the pit of her stomach, she suddenly realised that Jimmy was looking at her. He was shaking his head, so calming herself down she refrained from giving Mick a piece of her mind.

"I hear you two are going back to Greece," Jimmy said, turning his attention on to Mick. "It's alright for some. You must really like that place."

"Yeah, yeah Jimmy I do," Mick replied half-heartedly, his attention on the man standing up at the bar. "I don't know. Why do people always let me down? It's a right pain in the head."

Totally oblivious to the significance of his words, Mick took a big swig of his drink. Then realising he had come in on the middle of their conversation, he sat back, huffed like a spoilt brat, and crossed his arms.

"Oh, sorry, I haven't interrupted anything, have I?" he asked sarcastically.

"Mick?" said Danielle as she could take no more. "Mick, this man is very ill, and all you think about is yourself!" she said unable to contain her anger.

"What?" Mick questioned feebly. "What have I done wrong now?"

"Mick, you are unbelievable!" Now it was Danielle's turn to lean back on her chair. "So bloody unbelievable," she huffed, crossing her arms.

"It's OK Dan," Jimmy said, shaking his head as a sign for her to keep quiet.

"I am going to go and sit and read my newspaper. See you two later and have a great time away." Jimmy got up and with his paper tucked under his arm, walked over to the quieter side of the bar.

Rubbing his hands together, and with no thought of Jimmy, Mick suddenly said, "So Dan, what are you going to have to eat? Like I said earlier, it's my treat."

Danielle's glare returned. "Oh my God Mick, you really don't care about anyone but yourself," she said accusingly putting her elbows on the table. "You selfish, good for nothing..." she forced herself to stop in mid-sentence, afraid she could say something she would later regret.

"That poor man is diagnosed with a fatal illness, yes an illness that could actually kill him, and you can't even be bothered to ask him if he is alright."

Mick could see the anger in Danielles eyes so looked down to the ground to escape her glare.

"He is not the only one that is having a bad day. I could die any minute too you know."

Now Danielle was seething with anger.

"You," she said prodding her finger into his arm. "You can choose whether you will die or not. Life and death are in your hands. If it wasn't for that poison," she pointed to his pint of beer on the table. "You have a chance of living a long life, but poor Jimmy has no choice. His life has been taken out of his hands. The chances of him living a long life are practically zero." Gritting her teeth, she just stared at him.

"Now, hold on a minute Dan, it's not easy for me you know. I can't just stop drinking. You know..."

Danielle quickly intervened. "I am not listening to any more of your excuses. I have had enough of your whingeing and whining. You are beginning to sound like a stuck record." Getting up, she put on her coat.

"W…Where are you going Dan? I…"

"I am going home." With that, she took a last mouthful of her drink and left the bar, leaving a very distressed Mick behind her.

The journey home was just as tormenting as her journey down, only this time it was Jimmy who was at the forefront of her mind. Unable to comprehend Mick's selfishness, her anger stayed with her until well into the afternoon. By four o'clock, and after many refills of coffee, Danielle began to feel guilty about leaving Mick the way she had. Having to remind herself repeatedly that Mick's problem was a tough one to overcome, her feelings towards him began to change. Many times, she had fought the urge to phone him to apologise, but she just couldn't find the courage to talk to him. Pride had gotten hold of her tongue. By half past four, she decided to bite the bullet and rang him. To her disappointment, his phone just kept ringing. She was just about to give up, when he finally answered the phone.

"Dan, Dan, is that you babe," Mick said frantically. "I am so sorry. I am selfish, I don't mean to be babe, please don't hate me."

He began to cry, and Danielle could have cried with him.

"Mick, I don't hate you sweetheart. Please don't cry."

"Oh Dan, I was so scared that I had lost you…I just couldn't bear it…I am so sorry, I will be more considerate in future, honestly I will." The distress in his voice was clear, and Danielle found it hard to contain her own tears.

"It's OK babe," Danielle said, now having lost all control of her emotions. "I know you wouldn't hurt anyone deliberately…oh, but sometimes Michael Fletcher, I could shake you." Turning this very sad moment on its head, they both laughed.

"I am with you on that one Ms Danielle Green, sometimes I wish you would." Taking a few moments to wipe away their tears, silence reined the air waves.

"So, Dan, are we OK, I mean as friends that is? You are still coming away with me, aren't you?"

"Of course, we are, you can't get rid of me that easily," she replied, the past events of the day now forgotten. "Anyway, I have got to be there. Even if it's just to make sure you will be allowed on to the plane. We can't have you missing another trip, now can we?"

"That's for sure babe. I need you more than you'll ever know."

Mick stopped and laughed.

"Thank you for being a true friend Dan, you're simply the best." Mick had never said a truer word. To him, Danielle was a Godsend.

"Now, now Mick, you will be giving me a big head," Danielle said looking at the time. "Sorry babe, but I have to go; I will speak to you tomorrow, OK?"

"Ok Dan, speak to you then…Oh before you go…" The phone went dead. "I love you."

Danielle never did phone Mick the next day. What with running a home and dealing with two stroppy teenagers, it went right out of her mind. It's a shame you only regret something when it's too late to do something about it.

Friday came, and Mick found himself spending the afternoon in the Kings Head. Feeling slightly disloyal to

Danielle, he had gone in there with the intention of only having a couple of beers and then moving on. As time passed however, he felt comfortable in familiar surroundings, and decided to stay and chat with an old friend of his by the name of Chris.

Chris's life was in much the same state as Mick's. Alcohol had also been the cause of his marriage break up, and for some strange reason, Mick felt comfortable talking to him. They both shared the common interest of beer, and even though Chris was quite a few years younger than Mick, their problem had put them on the same level of despair. Chris couldn't start his day without his friend 'Vodka' either, which helped Mick to know that at least he was not alone. Having shared the same problem, Mick was content sitting at the bar talking to his friend.

"I won't be long Mick," Chris suddenly said, getting off his stool. "I am just going to the little boy's room."

Mick nodded his head and drunk down the last drop of his beer. He was just about to order himself another, when out of the blue, Jimmy came into his mind. His tumour had been the talk of the pub circuit, and not once had Mick thought about the family he would leave behind, if the unthinkable should happen. But now, here he was, and that was exactly what he was thinking about, Jimmy's family. Shuddering at the thought of those poor little girls becoming fatherless, Mick's heart grieved.

Danielle was right, he thought looking at the empty glass in his hand. You haven't got a choice Jimmy, but I have. Finding it very hard not to compare his life to Jimmy's he suddenly felt a rush of strength rise from deep within him.

I know I can stop, but I need help, he thought, slamming the glass down onto the bar. But who is going to help a drunken fool like me? At that point, the bar door opened. Turning to face the door, he noticed two people walk in. Not recognising the couple, he thought no more of it, and turned back around. Putting his hand up to get the barmaids attention, he realised the lady was suddenly standing beside him.

"You're Chris's friend, aren't you?" The lady asked her focus on Mick. He turned to see if she was talking to someone behind him, but to his surprise, no one was there. Realising her question was aimed at him, he nodded. Then the lady put out her hand.

"Hello, I am Grace, Chris's niece, nice to meet you, and you are?" Taken aback by the gentleness of her voice, Mick found himself reaching out his hand. Aware that it was shaking, he looked down at his hand. The next thing he knew, she had hold of his hand.

"H…Hello, I'm Mick."

Quickly withdrawing his hand from hers, he suddenly realised what she had said.

His niece, but you look around the same age, he thought amazed by her looks. Knowing he had to keep his thoughts to himself, he just smiled.

"Ah yes, Mick. Chris has spoken a lot about you. This is my husband Paul. Is Chris around?"

Nodding his head at the tall broad-shouldered man, Mick explained that Chris was in the toilet.

"Oh, OK, we will wait. Paul can you get me a coke please and get one for Chris's friend. Is that a pint Mick?"

Grace smiled and looked deep into Mick's eyes. There was something about this lady, something familiar, although he was certain that he had never met her before. Even though she seemed a lovely girl, she gave off an aura that made him feel very uneasy. Nodding, he turned his head to where the toilets were.

Blimey Chris, have you fallen down the loo, he thought hurrying him up in his mind.

"So, Mick, Chris tells me you're an alcoholic too," Grace said sipping her drink, still smiling.

Blimey love, you don't hold back on the punches, thought Mick, now feeling very nervous in the presence of this woman. Again, he found himself nodding.

What am I doing? Just don't look into her eyes and you'll be OK, he thought, stupidity adding to the many emotions racing through his mind.

"Don't worry Michael; it is OK to call you Michael isn't it? We are not here to judge. I am well aware of Chris's problem and the chaos that it has caused."

Grace took another sip of her drink.

"It's funny, I feel that I already know you," she laughed. "Chris talks about you all of the time. Any friend of his is a friend of ours, isn't that right Paul?"

Mick turned to Paul and smiled.

"Oh yes, he speaks very highly of you Mick," said Paul returning the gesture.

Mick noticed that Paul was covered in tattoos and suddenly, he felt very intimidated by this man.

"Michael," Grace said softly, regaining his attention. "Michael, I don't know if Chris has spoken about us before, but we, me and Paul, are Christians." Mick's heart palpitated in his chest. He wasn't sure if he liked where this conversation was going.

"Oh, oh that's nice," he said, just wanting to be left alone.'

Come on Chris, where are you? he thought, now getting really agitated.

"And as Christians, we believe in God, and we believe that he loves you very much. Yes, you Michael." The gentle sound of her voice seemed to be like an arrow of love that pierced his heart, and he could have sworn that he actually felt it soften.

This is crazy, he thought as Grace continued.

"Do you know that he sent his son to die on the cross, so you do not have to go through what you are going through?"

Suddenly Mick's mind went into overdrive as he thought back to that day in Skiathos at the doctor's surgery. He remembered that Panos had said the exact same thing.

What is happening, he thought. This can't be real. I've got to be dreaming.

When Panos had said those words, Mick had just shrugged them off as religious clap trap, but now something had changed. To his utter amazement, this time he didn't want to shrug it off, he wanted to listen.

"Go on," he said, his voice almost a whisper.

"You do want to be well, don't you? You want to be free from this demon drink?" Grace said taking his hand. He nodded, and Grace's smile widened.

Addiction began to feel very uneasy. As soon as the couple walked into the pub, its grip on Mick suddenly weakened, but it was determined not to let go.

"OK Michael. Repeat after me, Dear father,"

"Dear father,"

Squirming, Addictions tiny scaly body began to twist to and fro. For fifteen years it had found its home around Mick's mind, and it wasn't going to leave without a fight. Digging its talons deeper into Mick's head, it clung on for dear life.

"I believe that you sent your son Jesus to the cross to die for my sins,"

Gasping for breath, Addictions bony chest tightened.

"I will not be moved," it squealed into the uncaring peace ridden air.

"I believe that you sent your son Jesus to the cross to die for my sins," Mick repeated.

Suddenly it was if hot oil had been poured over Mick's head, and Addiction found that it had no choice but to let go. Screeching like a banshee, it fell to the floor. Every word that was spoken was like a flaming sword reaching into the very centre of its soul less body. Curling over in agony, Addiction stood up, and using every last ounce of strength, it dragged its crippled body along the floor. Every inch of every bone burned with the fire of Glory. Unable to stand the pain, it managed to find enough strength to lift itself up off the ground, and it headed for the door in defeat.

"I pray that you forgive me for all the things I have done wrong. I receive Christ as my personal saviour, and I ask him to come into my heart, in Jesus name. Amen."

Death lingered around outside the Kings Head like a bad smell. It had seen Grace and Paul walk into the pub as white as snow, and it had a horrible feeling that its mission was not going to end well. Knowing that it had possessed Mick in the palm of its scrawny talon, it began to panic.

You wouldn't be stupid enough to listen to those freaks, it thought, remembering Mick's conversation with Panos so long ago. Surely you are not dumb enough to fall for that lie! Knowing that its mission was coming to an end, Death began to pace back and forth.

I don't have faith in that so-called Jesus," it cried, its hollow chest tightening at the sound of that name.

"But I do have faith in that blithering idiot Michael. He won't let me down. This selfish soul is mine!"

As Mick repeated those words, something changed within him. Unsure of what was happening to him, he felt as though he were glowing from the inside out. Whatever it was, he couldn't care less, because for the first time in his life, he felt good inside. His mind suddenly became clear, and it was as if a huge weight had been lifted from his shoulders.

"Amen," Grace said, sealing the prayer.

The energy that came from that word lifted Addiction up from the floor, and like a flaming arrow it was thrown up into the air.

"It burns, it burns," Addiction cried out, in the hope that his comrade would come to the rescue. But to his horror, he

Was on his own. Then, in a puff of ash like smoke, it disappeared.

"Amen," repeated Mick.

Carried along on a ball of fire, the word 'Amen' flew out of the Kings Head and shot straight into Deaths heartless chest. Screaming out in agony, Death, wounded by the blow fell to the floor. Every scrawny bone its lifeless body weakened; its only thought was to get out of there. Having lost its sting, Death found enough strength to pull itself up from the ground, and like an injured rabbit, fled into the safety of the dark eerie shadows. Unable to muster up enough breath to scream, all that could be heard was a pathetic whimpering which faded away as quick as its master.

Peace had won the battle of Mick's soul. He was saved.

Mick, not sure if he was in shock, looked at Grace, looked at Paul, and then looked back at Grace again.

"Is that it?" he asked, feeling bewildered and ecstatically happy at the same time. "I expected a long drawn out prayer. I have loads of things that need to be forgiven."

Grace just smiled.

"That's it, Michael. The good news is, the old you has gone, it has passed away. Now you can begin to live your life. You are now a new creation… Do you have a bible?" Mick shook his head.

"OK, that can be easily fixed. What are you doing on Sunday?" asked Grace, her gentle face radiating with a warm glow.

"I haven't got anything planned. I'm going away, but that isn't until Wednesday next week."

Mick couldn't believe it, because he felt all warm inside. Grace was right. He did feel like a new man. He wanted to dance, to sing, to praise God.

I want to praise God? He suddenly questioned, puzzled by his new way of thinking. Yes, I want to praise God! I want to tell the whole world that I am alive. Smiling at his thoughts he asked calmly, "Why, what's happening on Sunday?"

"We belong to a church not far from here. Would you like to come?" Paul intervened, shaking Mick's hand.

"I will be there! Just tell me where and when," Mick replied without any hesitation.

Paul gave him a card, and as Mick took it from his hand, he embraced him.

"See you on Sunday Michael. We look forward to seeing you," they both said in unison. With that, the couple turned around and began to walk towards the door.

"But what about your uncle Chris, I thought you wanted to see him. He will be here at any minute," shouted Mick before they left.

"No worries," Paul replied, waving his hand. "We will catch him another time." With that, they were gone.

Mick stared at the door. The sound of people talking around him filled the air. To his amazement, not one single person asked him what had just happened. It was as if time had stood still while Grace and Paul were in the room, and now they had gone, it was business as normal. He jumped when suddenly there was a hand on his shoulder.

"Alright mate, you look like you have seen a ghost," said Chris, pulling himself up onto the chair.

"I…I just met your niece Grace, and her husband Paul," explained Mick still staring at the door.

"Thank god I didn't come back sooner. Phew, I had a lucky escape there. They call themselves Christians you know," said Chris doing an inverted comma sign in the air.

"Bunch of bloody freaks is more like it…. So, are you up for another beer mate?"

"No thanks Chris," replied Mick not even having to think about his answer. "I have gone off the stuff. It's bad for my health. So, I am going home. See you later mate."

Chris looked at Mick totally gobsmacked. In all the time he had known him, not once had Mick ever refused a drink.

"Blimey mate, what's happened to you?" asked Chris his jaw nearly dropping to the floor, as he suddenly noticed that Mick's eyes were shining like precious jewels.

"I've been reborn," Mick said flippantly. "You should try it one day. You never know, it might be the making of you… See you!"

Mick grabbed his coat and walked out of the pub, leaving Chris scratching his head, wondering what the hell Grace had said to him.

Whilst walking back to his parent's house, Mick suddenly realised that for the first time in fifteen years, he wasn't craving for a drink. It was as if he had been wrapped in an electric blanket, and he had never felt so safe. He felt totally liberated.

As he neared his home, he thought about phoning Danielle to give her the wonderful news. Knowing that she was most probably busy, he thought better of it, so decided to tell her in the morning. He couldn't wait that long to tell Tracey, so he got his phone out to call her instead. The phone rang and rang, and then it went to her voicemail. Choosing not to leave a message, he made a mental note to call her later, and carried on up the garden path. He opened the front door, and as he sung a new song that was bubbling in his heart, he realised that the house was quiet. His parents were out.

Skipping into the kitchen, he put the kettle on and went in search of a teabag. Suddenly, an excruciating pain tore through his brain, and he thought he was going to be sick. Needing to get to the toilet fast, the pain ran through his head again, stopping him in his tracks. Only this time, the power of it brought him down to his knees. Unable to cry out, he held his head in his hands. But for some strange reason he felt at peace. Even though he could still feel the pain, he wasn't at all scared. Picturing Tracey's face in his mind, another wave of pain pulsated through his head. Then it went dark.

The following morning, Danielle received the call that had the potential to knock her world right off its axle. All her children were still upstairs asleep. The quietness of the beginning of the day was rudely interrupted when she cried out a scream of disbelief that echoed around the house. Mick was in a coma!

Taking sharp intakes of breath, she managed to bring the level of her shock down a notch and listened carefully to Mick's father as he gave her the rundown of what had happened. Apparently Mick had collapsed after suffering a massive stroke, and unfortunately the chances of him surviving were very slim. His life was hanging in the balance, but Mick's father reassured her that they would know more when the doctor arrived later that morning. He also told her not to worry, and as soon as he had more information, he would let her know. Although his words were clear and to the point, the fear that rose up out of Mick's situation made them seem muffled. The thought of Mick lying there helpless sent Danielle's imagination into overdrive, and all she could think about was the last time she saw him, only a few days before.

Regret sided with her fears, bringing with it the wish that she could turn back the hands of time. Now, not only frightened by the bleak outlook, she was also riddled with guilt. She was desperate to see her dear friend, so made her feelings known. She was pleased to be told that she was welcome to visit anytime that afternoon if she felt strong enough. Danielle assured him that she was, and then after writing down all the relevant information, they said goodbye.

She placed the phone down on to the table and put her head in her hands. Her head was spinning. She was at a loss as to what to do, and she had never felt so scared. Tears stung her eyes, but she was too frightened to let them go. If she did, she feared they would never stop. So, taking a deep breath, she swallowed down her anguish.

Well, he is still alive, she thought, in a desperate attempt to hold on to that tiny glimmer of hope. He's a fighter, he will pull through.

Somehow her words of comfort outweighed her fears, and this helped her to stay focused on getting through the rest of the morning.

Keeping herself busy, she spent the hours leading up to visiting Mick washing and ironing anything and everything she could lay her hands on. Her bout of energy stirred up Billy and Marie's curiosity because it was a well-known fact that she hated ironing with a passion.

"Mum are you alright?" asked Marie as she ironed a big yellow bath towel. "Those towels aren't even crinkled."

Without taking her eye off the task at hand, Danielle nodded. She couldn't even think about Mick, let alone talk about him.

Besides, I don't want to cause any unnecessary worry, after all, Mick is going to be just fine, she told herself, whilst picking up a pair of Billy's boxer shorts from the washing pile. A couple of hours later victory was won concerning the laundry basket, and all the clothes, towels, sheets, and pillowcases were neatly put away. The dreaded hour finally came, and Danielle prepared herself to face probably one of the most difficult situations of her life.

Explaining that she was going to visit a friend in need, she put Billy in charge and left for the hospital. Having successfully forced Mick to the back of her mind all that morning, she was now faced with reality. As the hospital loomed on the horizon, her fear returned like a bolt of lightning. Knowing she had to be strong, she parked the car, took a deep breath, and began to make her way over to the entrance.

Looking around the hospital grounds, she noticed there were quite a few pregnant women around her, and it broke her heart to see the many signs of new life when the life of dear friend was most probably coming to an end. Aware that her thoughts had gone down the road she had desperately attempted to block, she tried her utmost to stay positive. She could have kicked herself for letting her mind run away with her.

"No," she whispered, as she went past the shop displaying an array of pink and blue teddies. "Mick is going to be just fine."

Taking a few minutes to find the ward, Danielle stood by the main security door for a few minutes contemplating whether to press the button. Every part of her wanted to turn around and walk away, but she knew that if she did, she would regret that decision for the rest of her life. Reaching down to the very core of her being, she put her fears to one side and summoned up enough courage to continue. A few moments later, she was walking down the hygienically clean ward towards Mick's room. The door was closed and, as she reached out her hand, she imagined seeing the same Mick she had seen before on her previous visit and hoped and prayed that she wasn't going to be disappointed.

He was going to be sitting up in his bed, with a big grin on his face, she thought holding on to that image. She was sure of that.

As she pulled the handle down, her heartbeat increased, because deep down she knew she wasn't going to like what she saw. Straightening her posture, she opened the door. Her first reaction was to look around the room. Standing by the bed was Mick's mum and dad, and a lady whom Danielle did not recognise. All three people turned to look at her, and her heart stopped. Mick's mum was crying, and the other lady was holding Mick's hand.

"H…hello Danielle," said Mick's father shakily, leaving his son's side to greet her. "Have you met Tracey's sister Susan?"

Danielle, unable to talk, shook her head. Susan forced a smile, and then turned her attention back on to Mick. Mick's father took Danielle's hand, and led her over to the other side of the room.

"I am sorry Danielle," he said, looking down to the floor. "But it doesn't look good. I'm afraid to say that there has been no change. We have just been told to wait. It could happen at any time."

It, the voice in her head screamed. What is it?

Still silent, Danielle squeezed his hand, and then he walked back over to the bed. Her instincts told her to follow him, but her feet felt as though they were stuck to the floor. Fear had found its way back into her body, stopping her ability to move. Suddenly the door opened behind her and finding the strength, she turned around.

"Danielle," said Tracey half-heartedly. "It is good to see you; under the circumstances I mean." Tracey walked over to her and embraced her. "You are looking well."

Tracey's compliment took Danielle by surprise and she didn't know how to respond. Covering up her awkwardness with a smile, she cleared her throat.

"So, how are you bearing up Tracey?"

Taking a step back, Tracey quickly glanced over to Mick, and then, turning back to Danielle, looked her in the eye.

"Not so well… It's strange because I don't feel sad, all I feel is angry. It's eating away at me, and I don't know how I can get it to stop," she said looking back over to Mick. "I could hit him Danielle; actually punch him for doing this to himself. If only he had given up drinking, then…then he wouldn't be in this mess, and we…we could have a life. He knew it could kill him, but did he listen, oh no, Mick knew best. Well look where it's got you!" she screamed at him.

"Sorry Dan, but that's just how I feel."

Turning back to face Danielle, silence stole the moment. Danielle had expected to see tears in her eyes, but they were empty. Not knowing what to say, Danielle's heart grieved. The sound of the machine attached to Mick's body, beeped at regular intervals, highlighting the fact that is was solely responsible for the air in Mick's lungs.

"Is there anything you want to say to him?" asked Tracey her expression still devoid of any emotions.

Danielle nodded her head.

This is it, she thought, fighting back the tears. I said I was strong enough, and I am.

As Danielle walked over to the bed, Mick's father put his arm around his wife.

"Come on Mary, let's get some air."

The couple left the room, and as they did, Danielle began to panic.

I don't want to see him, her heart cried out. But there was no going back now, so she stood at the side of his bed, and looked down at Mick's swollen body. He looked so bloated, and his skin had turned a deep yellowy colour. She couldn't believe that the man lying in front of her was the same man she had left in the pub only a few days ago. Wires were coming out of his body, and she could have cried at the sight of her dear friend.

Aware she had to keep her tears from escaping she breathed in deeply and took hold of his hand. A few minutes passed as she stared at his lifeless body, until suddenly she could take no more. Leaning down, she kissed him on the cheek. The feel of his clammy skin on her lips took her breath away, provoking her tears to fall.

"Goodbye, my friend," she whispered into his ear. "Sweet dreams."

A single teardrop fell on to his face and she half expected him to flinch, but there was nothing. No movement, no telling her that she was being soft, no reassuring words that he was just sleeping, and he would wake up at any minute.

"Please be strong."

Stepping back, she took one last look at his face. He looked so peaceful lying there, and Danielle found it hard to believe that he could actually die. Then it happened. Her stomach tightened, her head started spinning, and she was finding it hard to breathe, knowing then that this could be goodbye. She feared that she would never see her friend again.

"I'm sorry," she said, feeling a sudden rush of nausea. Trying to catch her breath, she turned to Tracey and said, "I have to go!"

Running past her Danielle opened the door to make her escape. It felt as if a hand was around her throat choking the very life out of her, and she couldn't wait to get out into the fresh air. Suddenly her vision blurred, and she had a horrible feeling she was going to faint. Gasping for air, the feeling passed, so she carried on down the corridor, tears now streaming down her face. Everything around her seemed so distant, it was like she was caught up in a terrible nightmare, and she just wanted to wake up.

The next thing she knew, her car was in view. Quickening her pace, she ran over to the safety of her car and unlocked the door. Falling into the driver's seat, she put her head on the steering wheel. The vision of Mick lying there looking so helpless dominated her thoughts, and she tried desperately to wipe out the picture that had reduced her to tears. Now sobbing, she never imagined being in so much pain. Leaving Panos was the most difficult thing she had done, up until now.

P   a   n   o   s   !
She suddenly remembered Panos. Her holiday had completely slipped from her mind, and the realisation that she would never see him again either, added to her pain.

"Why is this happening?" she screamed, looking up into the air. "Where are you when I need you?" Suddenly something strange happened. Out of nowhere, a wave of peace flooded her body, and her tears stopped. Her head cleared, the picture of Mick fading away into a far distant place in her mind, leaving her able to think straight again. Wiping her eyes, she put the key in the ignition and started the car. All her pain had miraculously disappeared, and Danielle at last felt strong enough to drive home.

I can do this, she thought, pulling away. Mick is not dead yet. Where there is life, there is hope.

Danielle ploughed through the next day the best way she knew how. There had been no word from the hospital, so she held on to the hope that no news was good news. Grateful for having the willpower to carry on, she pushed her fears and anxieties to one side and just focused on her family. Finding it easy to ignore the sinister consequences of Mick's addiction, she soon began to realise that this defence mechanism was the product of her past experience, when disaster had first entered into her life. The aftermath of losing her home had equipped her with the strength to persevere, and even though it was beyond her understanding, she felt somehow it had prepared her for the worse. Ignorance had become her friend, her protector, and she welcomed it with open arms.

Putting on a mask painted on with the brush of denial, she pottered around the house as if she didn't have a care in the world. But all the willpower in the world couldn't hide the fact that on the inside, her heart was breaking. The evidence of this pain manifested itself through the attitude in her voice, and even though she was not aware of it, Marie knew something was not right. Unbeknown to her, Danielle's fuse was rapidly getting shorter.

"Mum, please tell me what's wrong," pleaded Marie concerned that she couldn't do anything right. "You have been shouting at me all morning."

"Marie, nothing is wrong," Danielle snapped. "Now go upstairs, you are getting in my way!"

Plugging in the vacuum cleaner, Danielle began to hoover the lounge carpet.

"Marie!" Danielle screamed, having to manoeuvre the cleaner around her feet. "I said, go away!"

Marie, stunned by the anger in her mother's voice burst into tears.

"I don't know why you are shouting at me," she cried. "I am only trying to help."

Danielle chose to ignore her daughter's distress and pointed to the doorway. Marie, understanding her mother's command, ran out of the door still in floods of tears.

Billy and Charlie were in their room, and the sound of Danielle's rage echoed around the house like a thunderous cloud. Hearing Marie's bedroom door slam, Charlie turned to his brother and said, "I don't like it when mummy is in a bad mood."

Billy put his arm around his little brother's shoulder. Considering she was going on holiday in a few days, Billy couldn't understand why his mother was so angry. It was so unlike her.

"Try not to worry. It's probably just her time of the month," he said smiling, but even he found his own words hard to believe.

All three children tried their best to stay out of Danielle's way. Inevitably, dinner time came, and they had no other choice but to go downstairs. She stayed quiet as she gave them their meals, the look on her face as hard as nails. Now Billy was concerned. His mother had on many occasions been mad at them, but not for this long, and not for no apparent reason. He was desperate to find out why his mother was behaving so unreasonably, but he didn't have the nerve to ask her. Her face said it all, 'leave me alone,' so he obeyed the sign and just hoped that her mood would soon change. But it didn't.

The next day was just as bad. As soon as Billy opened his eyes, the sound of pots banging on the work surface down in the kitchen rang around the house. This is ridiculous, he thought, putting the covers over his head.

What the hell is wrong with that woman? She has got to stop! Billy poked his head out of the quilt and suddenly realised the place had gone deadly quiet. Straining his ears, he listened out for the next fit of rage, but there was nothing. Looking over to Charlie's bed, he smiled. He looked so cute lying there cuddling his favourite teddy bear and all he felt was love for his little brother who at times, drove him mad.

Thankful that his mother's banging about had not disturbed Charlie's sleep, he decided to go downstairs to get his breakfast. Walking out of his room, he noticed Marie's door was closed, so guessed she was still asleep. Feeling quite envious of his siblings' slumber, he crept down the stairs. Not wanting to add to his mother's bad mood, he kept quiet and, in his mind, worked on a plan that would get him to the kitchen and back without Danielle jumping down his throat. An eerie silence hung in the air, and he felt as though he was walking on eggshells. Moments later he came to the kitchen door. Afraid to take the next step, his nervousness increased as he was sure his mother would find fault in something he was doing. Finding the courage to continue the conquest of pursuing his breakfast, he reached the threshold, and his heart sank. There, sitting at the table with her head in her hands crying uncontrollably, was his mother.

"Mum, what's wrong?" he asked his anxieties growing stronger by the second.

Not sure whether to go over to her, he decided to stay where he was, just in case of a back lash. He repeated the question.

Danielle lifted her head and turned to him. Streaks of mascara were visible on her cheeks, and he had never seen her look so distraught.

"Whatever it is mum, it can't be that bad," he said, walking towards her.

"Oh, but Billy it is," she said, her tears escaping down her face. "Oh Billy, I am so scared." Reaching out her hands, Billy ran over to her and fell into her arms.

"Mum, what is it… Please, you are scaring me." Tears stung his eyes, but he had no idea why.

Lifting his face up to look at her, Danielle sighed. "I, I can't cope Billy. It's been so hard," she said, turning away, afraid to look her son in the eye.

"What can't you cope with? What has been so hard?" asked Billy feeling very scared.

"Oh Billy, I…I have some bad news. Mick…Mick is…"

"Mick's dead?" Billy's heart dropped to his stomach.

"No sweetheart, he is not de…" she just couldn't bring herself to say that awful word. "No, but he is in hospital. He collapsed on Friday, and he…he is in a coma. Oh Billy, I am so sorry. I thought he was going to be alright. I convinced myself he was going to be alright, that's why I didn't say anything. But…but Billy, I don't think that he will be."

A single tear dropped on to Billy's cheek. He was unable to take it all in. Now his mother's attitude over the past two days made sense. He figured it must have been something bad, but he wasn't expecting it to be this bad. Pushing his mother's hands away, he stood up.

"Billy...Billy sweetheart are you OK?" she asked as she watched her son walk over to the window. Feeling a lump rise in his throat, he nodded.

"But surely there is something the doctors can do?" he asked quietly. "He can't die, he is Mick. He will outlive all of us," he said desperately.

Danielle got up from the chair and went over to him.

"They have done all that they can. Now it's just a matter of time," she said, putting her arm around him.

"No!" he cried, pushing her arm away. "No! I am not accepting that! The doctor's might have written him off, but...but, I refuse to. I know Mick, he is a fighter and he will pull through. He has to pull through!" he said feeling incredibly angry.

"Billy, I know it is hard. I have been telling myself the same thing." She put her arm back around him. "But we have to prepare ourselves for the worse. The possibility of him pulling through is practically next to none. He knew that if he carried on drinking it would eventually kill him!"

"Why didn't he listen to us mum, why?" asked Billy his anger rising as he fell into his mother's embrace. "I hate him!"

Sympathising with his outburst, Danielle held him tight. Five minutes passed by, and not another word was said. Suddenly Billy pulled away.

"What about Skiathos? You are supposed to be going away in a couple of days."

Seeing the concern in his eyes, she went back over to the table and sat down. His expression was like a reflection of her soul. She wasn't prepared to admit it, but after finally getting her head around the possibility of seeing Panos again, a few times she couldn't help feeling angry at Mick for spoiling things for her. Now she knew she would never see Panos again. Of course, these were only momentary lapses, because the feeling of guilt that followed made her feel like the most selfish woman on the planet. Thankfully for her this made them easy to disregard.

"It obviously wasn't meant to be," she said quietly, looking down to the ground. "Anyway, Panos is no longer in the picture," she said, a new bout of strength rising out of her guilt.

"And Mick is still alive, so we must hold on to that. You're absolutely right Billy, Mick is a fighter, and he will pull through. We have to believe that."

"But you said…"

"I know what I said sweetheart, but that's because I was upset. It got to me, bottling up my feelings I mean. Where there is life there is hope." That was the second time she had said it, but still deep down she wasn't convinced. Not wanting to cause Billy any more pain than she had to, she wiped her eyes.

Turning to him she said, "Just be strong for Mick OK. Trust me. He will be just fine, just fine. Now…what do you want for breakfast?"

The sudden change in his mother's attitude confused him and he just didn't know what to think, especially as his emotions were all over the place. One minute she was telling him that Mick was practically dead, and the next she was convincing him that he was going to be alright. He just couldn't understand how she could go from one extreme to the other in such a short space of time. Even more importantly was deciding which version he was going to believe. Weighing both her statements up in his mind, he decided to go with the latter. He knew how strong Mick could be.

Yes, he thought, he will pull through. He would never leave me. After predicting Mick's future and now feeling a whole lot better, he asked his mother to do him a cooked breakfast.

"OK sweetheart, go and wake your brother and sister, but…but please keep this to yourself. I don't want to worry them."

Billy nodded, and then went upstairs.

The rest of the day came and went, and there was still no word as to Mick's condition. Every time the phone rang, Danielle's heart jumped up into her throat. Talking to Billy had helped, but after their conversation, she fell back into the comfort of her denial. Her mood was a little bit better however, and this was a huge relief to Marie. She still felt that something wasn't quite right but seeing her mother smile again gave her reason to believe that whatever had been on her mind, it wasn't now. This was enough to convince her that things had a good chance of returning to normal.

It was early evening, and Danielle was in the lounge watching TV, when her phone rang. The number displayed was unknown, causing her heart to somersault in her chest.

Frightened to answer it, she hesitated. Taking a deep breath, she said, "This is it," and prepared herself for the worse.

"Hello."

Billy and Jasmine were sitting on the settee. As Danielle answered the phone, Billy's heart felt as if it had stopped. He watched motionless as he saw the colour drain from his mother's face.

"OK, thank you for telling me. Take care." Danielle put the phone down onto the table and stared into the air.

"Well," Billy said, panicking, fearing the worse. "Who was it?"

"It was Mick's dad; I don't believe it…" Danielle's sentence trailed off into silence.

"What mum? You don't believe what!" he asked feeling his anger rising.

"Mick…Mick is getting better," she said turning to Billy and smiling. "Mick is actually getting better. He isn't out of the woods yet, but…but Billy, he is on the mend. From what his dad was saying, he could wake up at any minute."

Billy jumped up from the settee and grabbed Danielle's arm.

"Mick's going to be alright," he sang at the top of his voice, dancing his mother around the room. "Mick's going to be alright."

Pulling Billy to her chest, Danielle gave out a cry of joy.

"See, I told you he was going to be just fine. I don't believe it. I am going to see him tomorrow, and boy, am I going to give him a piece of my mind for scaring the life out of me like that."

Twirling her body around the room, she could have cried with happiness. She had never felt so relieved.

"Hey Billy…Guess what?" she chanted. "Mick's going to be alright! He put up a fight and yes, he is going to be alright!" For the first time in days, she found herself believing that Mick would survive his ordeal.

The following morning, Danielle took Charlie to school, and on the way back she decided to go to the nearby supermarket to buy Mick a great big bunch of flowers. Pleased that she had managed to get a full night's sleep, she felt as though she was a new woman. All her worries had gone and at last, she could see a future for her and her dearest friend again. Presuming that Mick's drinking days were well and truly over, she planned all the things she would do for him to help him in his recovery. Nothing was going to get in the way of their friendship, and she vowed to be there by his side every step of the way. Knowing that it would take time, she wanted to phone Panos to ask if she could postpone their trip until later in the year. Deciding to wait until she returned home, she was convinced that this would not be a problem.

Not only did she have her lovely friend back, she also had the chance of seeing Panos again. She could have danced her way up the fruit and vegetable aisle, she was so happy.

This is going to be the turn around Mick needed, she thought, full of the joys of spring. I am glad for a happy end, for my lovely friend.

Aware that she had to keep her cool, she walked calmly over to the flower stall. Confronted by a various range of bouquets, she couldn't make up her mind on which ones to buy. Whilst choosing an appropriate bunch for her lovely friend, she felt her phone vibrating in her bag. She reached in to get it out and noticed the same unknown number from the night before displayed on the screen.

Hopefully, Mick is up and about talking, she thought, half expecting it to be him.

"Hello, Mick…," she said merrily. "Oh how silly of me. Hello Mr Fletcher… How is Mick today, I hope he isn't causing those nurses too much trouble," she said laughing.

Mick's father began talking, and as he spoke, Danielle could feel the colour drain from her face.

"No, that can't be true… He… He was getting better," she said, her mind racing as fast as her heart.

"I am so sorry Danielle, I… I am afraid that Mick died at three o'clock this morning." Danielle's head suddenly went fuzzy, and she came over all faint.

"He never did regain consciousness, but I am told that he passed away peacefully." Mick's father's words of finality echoed through her head.

Dead! Passed away! This can't be happening.

Everything and everyone around her began to flow in slow motion, and she felt as though she was going to be sick. Mick's father, unable to contain himself any longer, had no other choice but to say goodbye, and when he did, the phone slipped out of Danielle's hand, shattering into tiny pieces as it hit the white tiled floor.

"But he can't be gone," she whispered into the air. "I had so many plans… How am I going to get over this pain?"

Danielle's worse fears had now become a reality. She could almost hear the pages turning and knew then that another chapter of her life had come to a close. Just like her phone, all her hopes and dreams of a happy ending had slipped through her hands. It was an end of an era.

It can't get any worse than this; she thought tears streaming down her face. First Panos and now Mick, I can't take anymore. Just like that, the two most important men in her life had gone forever.

Smiling from across the room, Disaster could see Danielle's heart breaking right in front of its evil slanted eyes. Knowing it couldn't get too close, just seeing her so distraught was like food to its empty poisonous soul. Undeterred, Disaster had heard the news of Death's little temporary step back, and its wicked smile widened. It was confident that after licking its wounds, Death would soon be back in the game, even more determined than before.

"So, you think this is pain, little Miss Warrior... You don't know the meaning of the word... I AM PAIN!" It squealed out in victory.

"You wait until I really get going. Oh dear, I will be on my throne, and you will be as broken as your phone... Ha, Ha! This is just the beginning my girl!" Letting out a high-pitched scream, it opened its black leathery wings and turned around. Flying up into the cool spring air, it laughed at the top of its crackling voice and said, "You have seen nothing yet!"

The End

ABOUT THE AUTHOR

Lisa Labon is an author who has had her fair share of hard times. She has however allowed her life experiences to shape her into becoming an inspiration to others as her passion for writing shines through, and can be seen in this novel, *Paving The Way*, the second of a trilogy.

She is the mother of four children and lives in Kent.

Connect with Lisa on all by visiting her website lisalabon.co.uk

One last thing:

If you enjoyed this book please go to Amazon and post a short review – thank you for your support!

OTHER BOOKS BY THE AUTHOR

IN THE BLINK OF AN EYE

You never know what's around the corner! In the blink of an eye, the first of a trilogy based on a true story, tells the tale of love and chance that brings destiny and fate together, unraveling a story that will be very hard to put down!

COMING SOON

FREEDOM IN CHAINS

Tragedy brings Danielle down to her knees as she finds herself lost in the cruel, wounding web of life. Lurking in the darkness is an enemy whose only aim is to crush and strip her of everything and everyone she holds dear to her heart. Weak and alone she soon becomes an easy target and walks straight into the oncoming assault!

Has death defeated her?

How can things ever be the same again?

Find out as the finale of the trilogy 'Legacy of Love,' unfolds. You will be left wondering how on earth will she survive!

*D**ear reader/writer,*

I would like to take this opportunity to thank you for supporting one of our newest authors.

Here at Open Scroll Publications, we specialise in assisting talented writers to fulfil their dreams and aspirations. The creative process is hard enough as it is without having to worry about getting your masterpiece published once you're finally done. That's why Open Scroll Publications was formed. We demystify the process of getting published, and give a literary voice to those who would otherwise be muted in obscurity.

Our list of gifted writers is rapidly growing, and I would like to invite you to consider becoming our next distinguished author. So, whether you're working on a novel, a children's book, a poetry anthology, or an inspirational non-fiction piece, why not take a leap of faith and contact us? We would love to hear from you.

For more information, please visit us at:
www.openscroll.co.uk
info@openscroll.co.uk
Phone: 01213502422
          07506677504

Or write to us at:
Open Scroll Publications Ltd,
Kemp House,
160 City Road,
London, EC1V 2NX.